Fall of the House of Ramesses, A Novel of Ancient Egypt
Book 2: Seti

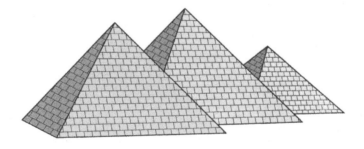

By Max Overton

http://www.writers-exchange.com

Fall of the House of Ramesses, A Novel of Ancient Egpyt: Book 2: Seti
Copyright 2015, 2016 Max Overton
Writers Exchange E-Publishing
PO Box 372
ATHERTON QLD 4883

Cover Art by: Julie Napier

Published by Writers Exchange E-Publishing
http://www.writers-exchange.com

ISBN **ebook**: 978-1-921314-22-3
Print: **978-1-925574-49-4** (WEE Assigned)

First Thoughts

A work of historical fiction comes from the mind of the writer, but it is dependent on historical facts. When I write about relatively modern times I have not only the bare bones of history to hang my story on, but also the personal writings of the characters and their contemporaries, and a host of relevant facts and opinions to flesh out the story. The further back you go in time, the less is available to draw upon, and by the time you reach Ancient Egypt, even the facts are disputed. Egyptologists have pored through the ruins of a past civilisation, examined the colourful walls of rock tombs and their contents, studied temple hieroglyphics and self-serving inscriptions of the kings, and deciphered fragments of papyrus to paint us a picture of what society was like three thousand years ago and more. It is necessarily incomplete, for much has been lost and what has not been lost is not always understood. The history of Ancient Egypt is a work in progress.

When I, as a writer of historical fiction, attempt to tell a tale from the distant past, I work with what is given me by serious researchers. But what am I to make of a character like Setnakhte, for instance? He was the first king of the Twentieth Dynasty, and features in my trilogy, but who was he really? The facts are scanty. He had a wife called Tiy-Merenese and a son who became King Ramesses III. His parents are unknown, but possibly he was a son or grandson of Ramesses II. He reigned for two to four years and stabilised Egypt after a period of strife, possibly by defeating the forces of his predecessor, Queen Tausret. And that's about it for Setnakhte.

So what do I, as a writer of historical fiction, do when faced with this paucity of factual information? I invent, but I must be careful to remain within the bounds of plausibility. I cannot make Setnakhte a favourite son of Ramesses or an older son, for the immediate succession is clear. Nor can I make him the son of a later king such as Merenptah or Seti, for their sons (or lack thereof) are known. I have to come up with a reasonable way to let him rise to prominence later in the story while remaining hidden early on.

Similarly with other characters. Messuwy may or may not be Menmire Amenmesse, depending on which school of thought you follow. I have weighed the evidence and made my decision. Tausret's parents are unknown, but some people think Merenptah was her father. She was evidently important enough to be married to Merenptah's son Seti, which makes her a royal princess. Later on, she led her army against a challenger for the throne, where did she learn her martial skills?

And so it goes on. The bones of history make the framework of my story and I must decide which opinions will clothe the bones in flesh and skin. If I choose well, my story takes on a life of its own.

I have researched this period extensively, and while I cannot claim to have read everything, I believe I have weighed up sufficient evidence to make an informed decision.

My main sources have been:

Anglim, Simon et al, 2002, *Fighting Techniques of the Ancient World*, Thomas Dunne Books

Budge, EA Wallis, 1959, *Egyptian Religion: Ideas of the Afterlife in Ancient Egypt*, University Books

Budge, EA Wallis, 1967, *The Egyptian Book of the Dead*, Dover Publications

Dodson, Aidan, 2000, *Monarchs of the Nile*, The American University in Cairo Press

Dodson, Aidan, 2010, *Poisoned Legacy: The Fall of the Nineteenth Egyptian Dynasty*, The American University in Cairo Press

Dodson, Aidan & Hilton, Dyan, 2004, *The Complete Royal Families of Ancient Egypt*, Thames & Hudson

Petrie, William Matthew Flinders, 2005, *A History of Egypt: Vol III. From the XIXth to the XXXth Dynasties*, Adamant Media Corporation

Romer, John, 1984, *Ancient Lives: The Story of the Pharaoh's Tombmakers*, Guild Publishing

Shaw, Garry J, 2012, *The Pharaoh: Life at Court and on Campaign*, Thames & Hudson

Tyldesley, Joyce, 2000, *Ramesses: Egypt's Greatest Pharaoh*, Viking

Wilkinson, Richard H, 2000, *The Complete Temples of Ancient Egypt*, Thames & Hudson

Wilkinson, Richard H, editor, 2012, *Tausret: Forgotten Queen and Pharaoh of Egypt*, Oxford University Press

I would like to acknowledge Jim Ashton, an Egyptologist, and expert on the Ramesside dynasties, who kindly read through my manuscript, pointing out any errors and inconsistencies. Similarly, Sara Waldheim, an enthusiastic and knowledgeable reader of all things Egyptian, gave my manuscript her careful attention.

Julie Napier was, as always, my 'First Reader' and I am indebted to her constant attention to my storytelling. She pulls no punches and once told me, 100,000 words into a previous manuscript, that the story lacked credibility. On re-reading it, I agreed, so I scrapped several months' worth of work and started again. Excellent reviews for the finished product have proven her right. I am truly grateful for her forthrightness and honesty.

Julie Napier also comes in for thanks as my cover artist. A skilled photographer and experienced artist, she has created all of my book covers.

I would like to thank my many readers too. Some of them wrote to me when they reached the end of my Amarnan Kings series, asking if I would write another Egyptian series. At the time, I was writing another book in a completely different genre, but I started doing some reading and eventually put my other work aside and started *Fall of the House of Ramesses*.

Some notes on Fall of the House of Ramesses

In any novel about ancient cultures and races, some of the hardest things to get used to are the names of people and places. Often these names are unfamiliar in spelling and pronunciation. It does not help that for reasons dealt with below, the spelling, and hence the pronunciation is sometimes arbitrary. To help readers keep track of the characters in this book I have included some notes on names in the ancient Egyptian language. I hope they will be useful.

In Ancient Egypt a person's name was much more than just an identifying label. A name meant something, it was descriptive, and a part of a person's being. For instance, Merenptah means 'Beloved of Ptah', and Tausret means 'Mighty Lady'. Knowledge of the true name of something gave one power over it, and in primitive societies a person's real name is not revealed to any save the chief or immediate family. A myth tells of the creator god Atum speaking the name of a thing and it would spring fully formed into existence. Another myth says the god Re had a secret name and went to extraordinary lengths to keep it secret.

The Egyptian language, like written Arabic and Hebrew, was without vowels. This produces some confusion when ancient Egyptian words are transliterated. The god of Waset in Egyptian reads *mn*, but in English this can be represented as Amen, Amon, Ammon or Amun. The form one chooses for proper names is largely arbitrary, but I have tried to keep to accepted forms where possible. King Amenmesse's birth name was possibly Messuwy, though this royal name can have various spellings depending on the author's choice. It is also sometimes seen as Amenmesses, Amenmose, Amunmesse and Amunmose. I have used the first of these spellings (Amenmesse) in *Fall of the House of Ramesses*, and most names that include that of the same god is spelled Amen-. The god himself I have chosen to call Amun.

Similarly, the king known in *Fall of the House of Ramesses* as Merenptah is often known as Merneptah. Either spelling is acceptable.

The names of the kings have been simplified. Egyptian pharaohs had five names, known as the Horus name, the Nebti name, the Golden Falcon name, the Prenomen and the Nomen. Only the Nomen was given at birth, the other names being coronation names. The Horus name dates from predynastic times and was given to a king upon his coronation. All kings had a Horus name, but by the eighteenth dynasty it was seldom used. The Nebti name dates from the time of the unification of Egypt and shows the special relationship the king had to the vulture-goddess Nekhbet of Upper Egypt and the cobra-goddess Wadjet of Lower Egypt. The Golden Falcon name conveys the idea of eternity, as gold neither rusts nor tarnishes, and dates from the Old Kingdom. It perhaps symbolises the reconciliation of Horus and Set, rather than the victory of Horus over Set as the titles are usually non-aggressive in nature.

By the time of the eighteenth dynasty, the prenomen, or throne name, had become the most important coronation name, replacing the Horus name in many inscriptions. Since the eleventh dynasty, the prenomen has always contained the name of Re or Ra.

The nomen was the birth name, and this is the name by which the kings in this book are commonly known. The birth names most common in the nineteenth and twentieth dynasty were Ramesses and Seti. Successive kings with the same birth name did not use the method we use to distinguish between them, namely numbers (Ramesses I and Ramesses II). In fact, the birth name often ceased to be used once they became king and the coronation prenomen distinguished them. Ramesses I became Menpehtyre, and Ramesses II became Usermaatre, while Merenptah became Baenre, and Seti II became Userkheperure.

Another simplification has occurred with place names and titles. In the thirteenth century B.C.E., Egypt as a name for the country did not exist. The land around the Nile Valley and Delta was called Kemet or The Black Land by its inhabitants, and the desert Deshret or The Red Land. Much later, Greeks called it Aigyptos from which we get Egypt. Other common terms for the country were The Two Lands (Upper and Lower Kemet), and the Land of Nine Bows (the nine traditional enemies). I have opted for Kemet. Likewise Lower Egypt (to the north) was known as Ta Mehu, and Upper Egypt (to the south) was known as Ta Shemau. The name 'Nile' is also from the Greek, so I have used the usual designation of the time, Great River, or Iteru.

Similarly, the king of Egypt or Kemet was later known as 'pharaoh', but this term derives from the phrase Per-aa which originally meant the Great House or royal palace. Over the years the meaning changed to encompass the idea of the central government, and later the person of the king himself. The Greeks changed Per-Aa to Pharaoh. I have decided to remain with the ubiquitous title of 'king'.

During the eighteenth dynasty, the kings ruled from a city known variously as Apet, No-Amun or Waset in the Fourth province or sepat of

Ta Shemau, which itself was also called Waset; or just 'niwt' which meant 'city'. This capital city the Greeks called Thebes. The worship of Amun was centred here and the city was sometimes referred to as the City of Amun. I have called this great city by its old name of Waset.

Ramesses II built a new capital city in the eastern delta and called it Per-Ramesses, meaning literally 'House of Ramesses'. Merenptah moved the capital to the ancient city of Men-nefer, known to the Greeks as Memphis, as this city belonged to the god Ptah and Merenptah was literally 'Beloved of Ptah'.

The gods of Egypt are largely known to modern readers by their Greek names; for instance, Osiris, Thoth and Horus. I have decided to keep the names as they were originally known to the inhabitants of Kemet, Asar, Djehuti and Heru. The Greek names for unfamiliar gods can be found in the section Places, People, Gods & Things in the *Fall of the House of Ramesses* at the end of this book.

Mention should be made of the incidence of writing amongst the characters in this book. It is generally accepted that no more than 1% of ancient Egyptians were literate and that knowledge of the complex hieroglyphic writing was the purview of the scribes and priests. Hieroglyphics are commonly seen in the formal inscriptions on temple and tomb walls. However, there was also another form of writing in ancient Egypt. This is called hieratic writing and is a form of cursive script used for writing administrative documents, accounts, legal texts, and letters, as well as medical, literary, and religious texts. This form of writing is commonly found on papyrus scraps, painted on wood or stone, or scratched onto pottery ostraca (shards). Thousands of these have been found, often closely associated with the lower strata of society, and it is believed that many more people were at least marginally literate than is commonly accepted. There is every reason to believe that people for whom some form of notation was essential to their everyday lives were capable of some level of writing.

When I refer to a person writing in *Fall of the House of Ramesses,* it should not be assumed that the person is fully literate, but instead has knowledge of writing consistent with their place in Egyptian society.

Simplified Family Tree of
Fall of the House of Ramesses (II)

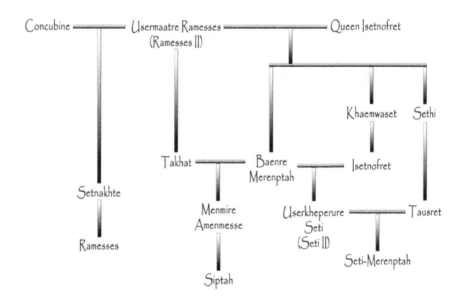

Per-Wadjet Djanet
Per-Ramesses
Perire Zarw
Per-Bast

Iunu
Men-nefer Per-Asar

TA-MEHU Timna Valley

Hetwaret
Henen-nesut

Khmun Amarna (Akhet-aten)
Zawty

Khent-Min
Abdju

Iunet
Ta-sekhet-ma'at Waset

TA-SHEMAU Ta-Senet
Nekhen

Behdet

KEMET Nubt

Abu
Aniba

Chapter 1
Year 9 of Baenre Merenptah
Year 1 of Userkheperure Seti

The Royal Barge 'Wisdom of Ptah' sailed slowly upriver from Mennefer, its great painted sail bellied out from the fresh northerly wind, its bow wave white against the deep green of the Great River. The current reduced its progress to no faster than a man could walk along the riverbank, but that did not matter as Prince Seti had given orders that the oarsmen be rested. Now, they lay back on their benches or sat looking out at the passing reed beds, without a care in the world. The captain of the barge, together with a small crew of experienced sailors, managed the course of the vessel, manoeuvring as needed to avoid other craft on the wide river, a herd of pehe-mau blowing and snorting in the shallows, or wind-ruffled water where contrary winds might impede their progress. Sun-dazzles sparkled on the waters and birds called from the reed beds, mingling with the sounds of lowing cattle in the green fields and the murmur of men's voices from the rowing benches.

Prince Seti Meryenptah, heir to the throne of Kemet and favoured son of Baenre Merenptah, king of Ta Mehu and Ta Shemau, Son of Re, Contented with Ma'at, lounged on cushions beneath a wide awning on the foredeck next to his sister wife Lady Tausret Setepenmut, and contemplated the Great River that spread out before and around them. He yawned and stretched in the shade offered by the awning, and pointed to the great stone edifices on the plateau beyond the western shore, now slipping slowly past.

"I shall build something as magnificent when I am king," Seti said.

"Those ben-ben?" Tausret asked, shading her eyes. "What is magnificent about them? They look neither ornate nor grand. You will build far greater monuments to celebrate your reign. Long may that day be delayed, of course, for I would not wish ill on the king your father," she added.

1

"Of course. My father is old but my grandfather was older still when he died. I am sure he will be king for many years yet. But have you never been up close to them, to the pyramids of stone?"

Tausret shook her head, making the delicate golden lotus blossoms in her wig tinkle like cool waters on a hot day.

"I stood beneath 'Khufu's Horizon' once and craned my neck to see to the top. The sun reflected off the polished casing stone as if it was beaten silver or gold, a flare of glory as if I looked into the face of Re. When I turned away, my eyes aching, it was several minutes before I could see clearly. They are truly huge, you know. I paced along the base for over two hundred steps and still did not reach the corner. Such are the works of our ancestors, and I would bring those days back."

"You would build a pyramid?"

"Why not?"

"If they are as big as you say, it would be a lot of work. Very expensive too."

Seti shrugged. "Perhaps, but it would be a magnificent achievement, wouldn't it? How long has 'Khufu's Horizon' been standing? A thousand years? Remember what grandfather Usermaatre used to say? The House of Ramesses will last a thousand years. I would like to build something that lasted that long, so men could look on it and say, 'How glorious were the days of King Seti that he could leave that as a monument to the gods and the Land of Kemet'."

"Then you must build it, dear husband, when you take your place on Kemet's throne," Tausret said. "But first things must come first. We must see what is amiss with your tomb in the Great Field, and correct it."

Seti nodded, dragging his gaze away from the now diminishing pyramids of stone that were disappearing into the haze behind them. "It will be a good opportunity to reacquaint myself with Waset and the palace there."

"Are you thinking of making Waset your capital?"

"I don't know. Per-Ramesses is too far north, it's more suited as a military base to guard the northern borders. Men-nefer is beautiful, but Waset is ancient and has a certain grandeur."

"There are some in the south who are less than friendly, husband," Tausret said. "Amun has favoured your brother Messuwy."

"All the more reason to stamp my authority on the city then. Messuwy won't give me any trouble if I cut off his support in the city."

"What will you do with him?"

"Nothing for now. If he behaves himself I might reward him with a governorship of one of the northern sepats."

"I will feel better with him in the north, husband. Especially as he has a living son. Being a brother of the next king and already with an heir makes him dangerous."

Seti reached over and squeezed Tausret's hand. "Siptah is not much of an heir, and we will have a fine son yet, Queen of my Heart."

Tausret nodded and smiled. "Our next child will be a healthy boy. I feel it in my waters."

"A king must have an heir," Seti mused.

"And I will give you one." Tausret looked askance at her young prince. "Do not think I will let you sow your royal seed in another woman's field."

"Hush, my love. You will always be my Queen, my principal wife."

Tausret withdrew her hand from Seti's. "Your *only* wife, husband. If you pleasure yourself with slaves when I am indisposed, that is one thing, but I forbid you to marry anyone else."

Seti stared at his wife. "*You* forbid *me*? Must I remind you that I will be king when my father, may he live a million years, joins Re? No one forbids the king."

"I will be queen..."

"If I allow it..."

"...and you will not so dishonour me as to put me aside for some palace slut."

"Enough, woman," Seti snapped. "Your chatter draws the pleasure from the day. I will be king and my word will be law."

Tausret scowled, but held her tongue, not wanting either of them to take up positions from which neither of them could reasonably withdraw. "Let it be as you say, husband...for now," she added under her breath.

A hail from the watchman at the stern interrupted their thoughts and the captain hurried forward. He bowed and held his hands out at knee level.

"A boat closes with us, Prince Seti. It flies the palace colours."

"A messenger?" Seti got to his feet and stared past the captain. "For us, or does he carry some news elsewhere?"

"Who can say, Prince Seti?"

"Let him catch up then."

The captain ran off, shouting orders to his sailors, who hauled on ropes, spilling wind from the sail. The barge settled lower as it slowed, and Seti walked to the stern to watch the smaller vessel overhaul it. As it came within hailing range, a man stood up and shouted across the water.

"Message for Prince Seti."

The captain looked at Seti, who nodded. "Come alongside," the captain shouted.

The boat scudded closer and then at the last minute dropped its sail, easing in close alongside the barge. A man threw a rope up and a sailor tied it off, another lowering a knotted rope for the kilted messenger who swarmed up on deck.

"Prince Seti," the messenger said, bowing low and extending his hands. "A letter for you."

"From the king?"

The messenger removed a flat package from a pouch at his waist. "From Tjaty Merysekhmet, my lord."

Seti took the folded papyrus, examined the seal and then broke it, scanning the few lines of writing, his lips moving silently. He took a step back and breathed hard, turning to look downriver.

"What is it, husband?" Tausret asked. "Bad news?"

Seti handed his wife the letter and stared at the messenger. "Did you come for me alone or do you carry letters to other people?"

"I have letters for the governors of every southern sepat, my lord."

"Do you know the contents of this letter? Of the others?"

The messenger licked his lips. "No, my lord, not exactly, but... there are rumours."

"You will keep those to yourself." Seti thought for a few moments. "You know who I am?"

"My lord?"

"Who am I?"

"Y...you are Prince Seti, Crown Prince and...and Heir."

"So in light of my position and the rumours you have heard, you will obey my commands instantly?"

"Y...yes, my lord."

"Then you will forget the rest of your mission and return immediately to Men-nefer. On the way there, you will intercept any other boat heading upriver and order them back, on pain of death. You will tell them it is on the orders of the king. Do you understand?" Seti beckoned the barge captain closer. "Have the barge turned and exercise your oarsmen. We return to Men-nefer and I want to be there by nightfall."

The messenger saluted and scrambled back into his boat while shouted commands from the captain resulted in the sail coming down with a clatter and the oarsmen rushing to their places. The barge heeled over as the current caught it, and a few unsecured objects splashed unheeded into the river.

Tausret came to stand by her husband and took his hand in hers. "Can it be true?" she asked.

"Merysekhmet would not say it unless it was."

"Our father the king is dead." Her voice trembled and she wiped away a tear. "Oh, husband, I grieve for us both, for he was as a father to me..."

"Enough, Tausret. Control yourself. We will grieve later but for now, we are the only people on board who know the truth. I would keep it that way."

"But why?"

"Was the letter not plain enough? The king has died suddenly and possibly at the hand of another."

"That cannot be. Who would dare?"

"I can think of one."

Tausret considered for a few moments, and as the oarsmen picked up the beat of the oars, sending the craft surging downriver, she nodded. "Messuwy."

Men-nefer was in an uproar by the time the 'Wisdom of Ptah' docked at the royal wharf and Seti disembarked. Within minutes of his arrival, Tjaty Merysekhmet and a squad of soldiers trotted up and worriedly greeted the heir to the throne.

"Thanks be to the gods the messenger found you so quickly, my lord."

"What is the news? Has my father the king truly died?"

"Yes, my lord, and I fear his death was not natural."

"You have evidence of this?"

The Tjaty shuffled his feet and looked away. "The physicians are not in agreement, but it is possible the neru pehut administered something a little while after you left."

"Has the man been questioned?"

"He was sent for but is missing. I have soldiers scouring the city for him."

Seti thought for a few moments. "What measures have you taken to contain the news, Merysekhmet?"

"Contain, my lord? I... I have already sent out messengers to all the cities and towns of Ta Mehu and Ta Shemau as is the custom."

"Well, it's too late to call them back, but close the city gates at once and put a guard on the docks. No word must leak out until I have everything in hand."

Merysekhmet bowed and immediately issued orders to the officer of the guard. Men ran off to carry out the heir's commands. "What is your will, my lord?"

"Convey Lady Tausret to the women's quarters and see that she is guarded. Then bring the physicians to me in the throne room, together with..."

"Husband, I am coming with you," Tausret said quietly.

"It would be better if you did not," Seti said, frowning. "I mean to find out who or what killed my father, and it may be that I must put men to the question."

"He was my father too, and as for blood, I have seen it before, husband, and will not faint at the sight of it, nor quail at the necessity of spilling it."

Seti nodded. "Come then, if it please you."

Merysekhmet and the remainder of the guard escorted Seti and Tausret to the palace and thence to Merenptah's inner chamber where tapers had been lit against the twilight creeping over the city. The embalmers were present, gathered about the bed, waiting impatiently to convey the king's body to the Place of Purification. They grovelled when Seti strode in and pushed them away from the bed.

He looked down at the waxen body of his father and took one cold hand in his. Tausret stood beside him with tears in her eyes. "What is that stink?" Seti asked. He rounded on the embalmers. "Have you started your work without permission?"

"No, my lord," said the head embalmer. "We have not touched the Son of Re."

Merysekhmet waved the embalmers aside and said in a low voice, "The smell is from the ointment applied by the neru pehut, my lord. Mentmose, the chief physician has taken a sample from the king's nether regions, and has his opinion as to what it is."

"I will be interested to hear it."

The Tjaty had sent word ahead, and the palace physicians awaited the heir's pleasure with varying degrees of trepidation in the throne room. When Seti and Tausret walked in, they all bowed and extended their hands at knee level.

Seti stared coldly at the assembled physicians for a while, making them all feel thoroughly uncomfortable, as evidenced by sidelong looks and shuffling of feet.

"Where is Ahmes, the neru pehut of my father?" Seti asked at last.

"He is still unaccounted for, Son of Re," Merysekhmet said. "The soldiers are searching."

Seti opened his mouth to correct the Tjaty's form of address, and then realised that he was, in truth, now the King and Son of Re. He nodded to Merysekhmet.

"Mentmose, you are chief of all the palace physicians, and was familiar with the health of my father the king. Was his death natural?"

Taking his cue from the Tjaty, Mentmose bowed low again before addressing his king. "Son of Re, Baenre Merenptah was an old man and displayed many of the attributes of age. He suffered from toothache, from distensions of the anus, and from many aches and pains of the joints..."

"Yes, I know all this," Seti snapped. "Answer my question."

"Any number of ailments could have proved fatal, Son of Re..." He saw the look of anger settling on Seti's face and hurried on. "...but it is my considered opinion that he was poisoned."

Tausret gasped. "Poisoned? How?"

"A cream had recently been applied to the...the swollen parts of the king's anus, my lady. This cream had a sharp, unfamiliar smell, so I took some to examine it more closely."

"And what did you find?" Seti asked.

Mentmose drew himself up and unconsciously posed as if lecturing to his students in the House of Life. "I compared the small amount of odiferous cream to every sample of medicinal plant that we have in the House of Life, and though it did not match any exactly, it was closest to some used by the priesthood in the mysteries of the god Min. I then took some of the cream from the king's anus and applied it to the soft skin of the inner cheek lining of a slave, watching him closely for symptoms..."

The chief physician broke off as Tausret made a moue of distaste. "My lady, I could not risk anyone of importance. As it was, no lasting harm came to the slave."

Tausret shook her head. "That was not what concerned me. You took the cream from the king's anus and..." she grimaced. "Never mind. Please go on, Mentmose."

"My lady." Mentmose bowed again to Seti before continuing. "Son of Re, after a short time, the slave said his cheeks felt numb, his throat dried out and his eyes became sensitive to light. He cried out and fell down, shaking and talking nonsense, but then slowly recovered. My lord, my lady, it is my considered opinion that his sickness arose from the cream. He survived because he was young and healthy, but your father the king was already in ill health. Whatever was in the cream was enough to kill him."

"And the cream had to have come from the neru pehut," Merysekhmet said.

"What say the rest of you?" Seti asked of the other physicians. "Is this how the king died?"

Several physicians nodded or murmured agreement. Two or three muttered under their breath and one complained, "I would like to have tested the cream myself. It is possible there was some other cause."

Seti recognised the complaint as little more than professional jealousy and ignored it. "Find Ahmes and I shall put him to the question," he ordered.

Nothing more could be resolved in the absence of the neru pehut, so Seti dismissed the physicians and retired with his wife to his inner chambers and ate a light meal. After his repast, Seti called Merysekhmet to him again.

"This cream, this preparation that Ahmes used," Seti said. "Where did it come from? Did Ahmes make it himself, or did someone send it to him?"

"I don't know, Son of Re. I will make enquiries."

"Have any letters or packages arrived from the south recently?" Tausret asked.

"The south, my lady? Er...it has been several days since...that was when the letter came for you from the Overseer of the Great Field, Son of Re. It was brought to you by the Royal Butler Bay."

"He may know if anything else arrived. Send for Bay."

Bay arrived, decked in the finery of his exalted position within the palace household and bowed low before Seti, hands held extended at knee level.

"Bay, you brought me a letter a few days ago from the Overseer of the Great Field. Do you remember?"

"Yes, Great One."

"How did it come to be in your hands? Royal messengers deliver letters direct to the king, the Heir, or the Tjaty."

"You have said it, my lord. Royal messengers have immediate access to the king, the Heir, or the Tjaty, but lesser ones often come to me, knowing I have been granted much status in the royal household. This letter from the Overseer of the Great Field came with others to diverse members of the household, and as soon as I recognised what it was, I delivered it to your hands."

"Was anything else delivered? A pot of ointment perhaps? For Physician Ahmes, the neru pehut?"

Bay lowered his gaze, hesitating just a fraction before answering. "My lord, no delivery came for Physician Ahmes."

"You are certain of this?"

"Yes, my lord."

Seti pondered the Royal Butler's response for a few moments, then said, "Ask around, Butler Bay. This pot of ointment that fell into the hands of Ahmes must have come from somewhere. I would know where it came from and who sent it."

"I shall ask of the palace servants, my lord."

Bay bowed again in preparation of leaving the royal presence but a clamour outside Seti's chambers interrupted him. He stood and stepped back at the attention of the royal couple and the Tjaty turned toward the entrance. The guards, upon a signal from Tjaty Merysekhmet, rushed to open the doors and hauled Ament, the Captain of the Palace Guard inside.

Ament bowed low and addressed Seti. "Son of Re, we have discovered Physician Ahmes, neru pehut to your father, King Baenre."

"Then why have you not brought him into my presence, Ament? Send for him at once. He has much to answer for."

"Alas, Son of Re, I could not, for when I found him he was already dead."

"Dead? Who, knowing I desired words with him, dared to kill him?"

"He...he seems to have taken his own life, Son of Re. He lay on the floor in a storage room with his throat cut and a blood-covered knife in his hand."

"An admission of guilt, I think," Merysekhmet murmured.

"And convenient," Tausret added.

"Convenient? How so?"

"Convenient for the guilty ones, my lord. It is hard to imagine that Ahmes contrived to kill the king because of some slight done him, but is more likely some other person persuaded him to this course of action. We cannot now question the neru pehut and determine who his conspirators were."

"No, curse the man," Seti said. "I want this investigated fully. Who spoke to Ahmes in the last month? Where did the ointment come from? Who sent it? How did it get into the palace? Someone must have seen something, so..." Seti broke off and looked at Bay. "Are you still here, Bay? You have your instructions already, go now."

Bay bowed again and hurriedly left the inner chamber while Seti and Tausret started an earnest conversation with Tjaty Merysekhmet.

Chapter 2

Royal Butler Bay speaks:

I left the royal chambers with the sweat of my terror cold upon my limbs and could scarcely believe that others had not seen my guilt written upon my features. Although I had denied it to his face, I felt sure the Heir had detected something amiss with my answer. I knew, of course, whence the pot of poisoned ointment that had slain King Baenre came, it must have been the pot that came from the southern city of Khent-Min, wherein the king's son Messuwy, my brother-in-law, lives. The pot that I passed on to the neru pehut. If once Prince Seti makes that connection, my life is lost.

I hurried to my room and sat on my pallet, thinking what I should do. My inclination was to flee the palace at once and somehow make my way upriver to Messuwy, and plead with him for protection. If I left now, it might be dawn tomorrow before my absence was noted, but then the obvious connection would be made and soldiers would be dispatched to hunt me down. Besides, I have no guarantee that Messuwy would protect me. Living within the royal palace at Men-nefer, I am of use to him as a source of information, but as a refugee, I am useless. I can ask on the basis of my relationship, brother of his dead wife Suterere and uncle of his son Ramesses-Siptah, but that is all. It is not as if Messuwy has gained anything by this assassination, Seti is Heir and he will soon be King, unless he plans more killing.

What must I do to survive? The answer is plain, I must ensure that the connection is never made. The chain linking the courier that brought the poison to court, me, and Physician Ahmes, must be sundered completely. Ahmes is dead, slain by his own hand...and for a moment his action beckons enticingly. I have no doubt that if the king, the new king, puts me to the question to find out what exactly was my complicity, I will beg for the mercy of a swift death. Better to end it myself with only a little pain.

Well, perhaps, if no other route can be found. Think, Bay, think, while you still have time.

The courier that brought letters from the south and the fatal ointment has left Men-nefer, and by the time he returns he may have forgotten the particulars of what he brought. Even if he remembers he brought a pot for Ahmes, who is to say it was the fatal pot? It could conceivably have been any concoction brewed by anyone. At least, it could be any concoction until I am put to the question, then they will force a confession from my lips. So, how do I avoid that?

There is also the servant who carried the pot from me to Ahmes, what was his name? His could be an inconvenient memory, and one that will be hard to hide. Moreover, I cannot rely solely on obliterating the trail that leads to my door. I must create a false trail that points in another direction...but how? I can invent another courier, another person from whom the poison came, but all it takes is a cursory investigation, a few pointed questions, and my duplicity is laid bare.

The evening grew old and I was running out of time. What was I to do? Perhaps the answer lay in the task the heir had given me, ask the palace servants if they know anything about the pot of ointment. I knew where it came from and how, but they did not. Could I muddy the waters sufficiently to obscure my part in it?

I changed into fresh tunic and kilt, for my others are sweat-stained and stinking. I donned my finery and the badges of my office, for I must command respect and fear among the servants, thereby deflecting any suspicion. After settling my nerves with a cup of wine, I made my way first to the wing of the palace where Ahmes had his room, where I found the servants who clean and fetch and carry for the physicians. I adopted my most daunting demeanour and addressed them.

"Who is responsible for the rooms of Physician Ahmes, neru pehut to King Baenre Merenptah?" I ask.

They looked at one another nervously and then pushed one of their number forward. He looked panic-stricken and tried to step back among his fellows, but they closed ranks against him.

"Rem is the man you seek, sir," muttered one of them.

"Only one?" I asked. "Do no others clean or fetch and carry for him?"

"Dede helps sometimes, sir," Rem said, plucking at the arm of another young man.

"Very well. Rem and Dede, you will stay behind. The rest of you can go."

The other servants fled, leaving their two hapless fellows behind to face my wrath. I stood and stared at them for what must have seemed a long while. I have found that a studied silence can often achieve more than harsh questions.

"So," I said softly after a time. "Which of you was it who delivered the pot of poisoned ointment to Physician Ahmes?"

Both men blanched. Rem fell to his knees, arms outstretched imploringly, while Dede stuttered and stammered, protesting his innocence.

"Come, do you take me for a fool?" I asked. "I have never met a servant who is completely innocent. I can see it in your faces that you are guilty of something. What is it? You had better tell me or I will have you whipped and thrown out of the city."

"My lord, I...I am guilty of nothing more than...than taking a little medicine for my sick daughter," Dede assured me. "Perhaps a little cloth to use as a bandage, my lord, but soiled cloth that was being discarded."

"And I a little food, my lord, but only scraps," Rem declared. "The dregs of the beer pot too, but everyone does that."

"I do not," I said coldly.

"No, of course not," Rem said hastily. "I only meant that...that..." He trailed off, looking miserable.

"Forget such paltry crimes," I said. "I am interested in greater things. A pot of poisoned ointment was delivered to Ahmes within the last few days. What do you know of that?"

"N...nothing, my lord," Rem said.

Dede also shook his head, but then opened his mouth, hesitated and closed it again.

I dismissed Rem to his duties and turned once more to Dede.

"Yes?" I asked. "You were going to say something?"

"Forgive me, sir, but I was only going to say that Semut brought a small sealed pot to Ahmes three days ago. I took it from his hands myself. He said you gave it to him, sir."

I frowned, as if thinking hard. "This is the Semut who works under Overseer Mentu? You are sure of this?"

"No, sir," Dede said. "It was Semut on Chamberlain Ptahmut's staff."

"This is strange," I said, "for I have never employed either Semut as a courier. One must ask why he would say I had given him the pot for Ahmes when I plainly did not."

"I don't know, sir."

"Well, of course you don't. I wouldn't expect you to." I stroked my chin as if in thought. "It is plain that this Semut seeks to lay the blame elsewhere, covering up the guilt of one of his associates." I stood in silence a while longer and then I smiled. "You have done well, Dede, and I shall not forget you. Where are you from, that I might praise you in the proper quarters?"

"From the village of Seb-ammit, my lord. It is in the west."

"And your name, Dede, that sounds almost like a Ribu name?"

The man essayed a tentative smile, soothed by the pleasant tones in my voice. "I was named for my grandfather, sir. He was once a trader from the western desert and rich, by Seb-ammit standards anyway."

"Well, perhaps you will soon be as rich as him, Dede. I may need to summon you soon. Be ready to come at once. Oh, and say nothing to anybody of what we have discussed."

I dismissed him and Dede left with his chest puffed up with pride. The seeds of a plan were sprouting in my mind and I thought I could construct another trail that would bypass me.

I am a great believer in getting others to do unpleasant tasks for me, but sometimes it is best to keep things close to the chest. Semut and Dede were the living links in the chain that bound me to Ahmes, and I would have to sever these links, for Semut might well remember that I handed him the poisoned pot. Some men become fat when they have good food and are required to do little physical labour, but I have always tried to keep my body lean and muscular. That would serve me now.

I summoned the Semut I knew and when he arrived, gave him some innocuous duty, and told him to meet me behind the palace stables at midnight, intimating that I needed his assistance in apprehending a spy.

"Would the guards not be more suitable, Butler Bay?" he asked.

"Why should they get all the glory...and all the gold? I have heard they are offering ten deben of gold for his capture, and I am willing to split it with you. Of course, if you don't want to..."

Semut assured me he would be there, and hurried off about his duties. I sent for Dede and gave him similar instructions. They were both young men, but even youth cannot stand against a blade in the silent shadows. I waited for them, hidden by the night, and first one, and then the other, died on my blade and severed the link. I put a bloodied knife in each dead hand, then cleaned myself thoroughly and hurried to the Tjaty, spinning a tale that would make me look good.

"I made enquiries amongst the palace servants, my lord, and I think I might have found the culprit. One of the servants of Physician Ahmes is a Ribu by the name of Dede. In light of Baenre Merenptah's defeat of his people, maybe he sought revenge."

"But why would Ahmes get involved in his revenge?"

"I do not know, my lord, but maybe we can ask this Dede."

"Indeed. Where is this Ribu now?"

"I saw him leaving the palace in the direction of the stables, my lord, and bade Semut of Chamberlain Ptahmut's staff keep an eye on him."

Tjaty Merysekhmet sent for the guard and ordered them to search for Dede, starting with the stables. They were back after only a short time, with the news that both Dede and Semut were dead, apparently having killed each other.

"So he was guilty after all," I said to Merysekhmet. "He must have seen Semut following him, thought he had been found out and attacked him. Oh, it is my fault that worthy young man Semut is dead."

"Nonsense," Merysekhmet said. "You were not to know. However, I don't suppose we shall ever know the full truth of it now that he is dead. I shall have the other servants in the Physicians quarters questioned."

"I doubt you will find out more than I did, my lord."

The Tjaty nodded. "You have done well in rooting this plot out, Butler Bay. Be assured that I will mention you favourably to Prince Seti. No doubt there will be a reward."

"I seek only to do my duty, my lord," I said. "That is reward enough." I bowed deeply and withdrew, satisfied with my night's work. I had protected Messuwy and been of service to Prince Seti. Whichever man won out and claimed the throne of Kemet, my future looked good.

Chapter 3
Year 1 of Userkheperure Seti

essuwy's servants shivered and hid themselves when their master's temper flared. Even little Ramesses-Siptah cried and hid his face in the folds of his nurse's robe when his father stalked about the house in Khent-Min in agitation and shouted at anyone who got in his way or spoke to him. The eldest son of Baenre Merenptah succumbed more to the cold sweat of fear with every passing day, and wished that he had Sethi by his side to bolster his courage. It was fifteen days since Messuwy had given the little pot of poisoned cream into the hands of the messenger, a pot addressed to his late wife's brother Bay, and as soon as he had handed it over, his fears began. His imagination conjured visions of Bay betraying him, of the plot discovered, and the king's guards arriving to arrest him and drag him off to an ignominious and degrading death. As the days passed without discovery, his fear changed to excitement that his plan really was going to work, and with the passage of yet more days, to anxiety that something had gone wrong.

By the tenth day, he knew to look for the passing of the royal barge bearing Prince Seti on his way to his tomb in the Great Field, and for the news of the king's death to arrive from Men-nefer. It was now the fifteenth day, and ominously, there was no news whatsoever from the northern capital. He had sent trusted men downriver to spy on the city but they reported it shut up tighter than a sheep byre with wolves about.

"Nobody comes and goes, sir, but something's going on." The spy hesitated. "The Royal Barge returned sudden-like, sir, with Prince Seti aboard, a day after he sailed. I have that from a farmer what seen it. Don't know what it signify though, sir."

Messuwy dismissed the man with silver and went off alone to think about it. Part of his plan had already failed in that Seti had not taken the bait and gone south to the Great Field where Sethi was waiting to kill him.

What of the king though? Is he dead, or has that plan failed too? It could be that the whole plot had been discovered, that Bay and Ahmes were being put to the question and that soon they would discover Messuwy's part in the conspiracy. *How long can they last? Should I flee before the king sends soldiers after me?*

The thought of capture, disgrace and public execution filled Messuwy with horror, and he at once decided that he would not wait meekly in Khent-Min for the king's soldiers. He would flee to Waset, consult with Sethi and the Hem-netjer of Amun, Roma-Rui, and together they would determine what must be done. Messuwy felt the claws of terror gripping his bowels relax at the thought. Sethi would know what to do, and so would the High Priest. The protection of Amun would fold over him, and even the king would hesitate to act precipitately.

Messuwy issued his orders. A man was sent to ready a boat for the trip south to Waset, another to gather such wealth as his estates could muster at short notice and yet another by swift boat to warn Sethi of his imminent arrival. He debated whether to take his son Siptah with him, but decided against it. If he decided to make a stand in Waset, to claim the throne for his own, he did not want to be encumbered with a small child. Better to leave him with his nurse in familiar surroundings in Khent-Min. *But what of Seti if it should come to war? Will he punish Siptah for my actions?* The thought gave Messuwy pause, but he dismissed it as unlikely. *No man wages war against children, and if I succeed, he will not dare.*

Messuwy slipped away as soon as everything was ready, taking his gold and silver, a dozen members of his household as a guard, and his hopes. The boatmen cast off from the docks of Khent-Min, attracting as little attention as possible, and quickly hoisted the sail, catching the north-easterly breeze. Fishing boats plied the green waters, but there were few other boats and certainly no messenger craft carrying letters between the two kingdoms. Messuwy urged the boat captain to greater efforts, handing over extra silver to have the oars used whenever the wind died away, and by the third day came in sight of the great walled city of Waset.

Sethi met him on the docks with a large squad of soldiers and escorted him toward the Great Temple of Amun, where Hem-netjer Roma-Rui awaited them. Messuwy could not wait until they arrived at the temple however, being consumed by fear and trepidation.

"What news? Did we succeed? I have heard only that Seti turned back to Men-nefer."

"I know little more," Sethi replied. "My spies believe the king is dead, and Seti alive, but nobody knows what else is happening."

"So what do we do?"

"That is what we must discuss... Guards, alert!"

A number of soldiers of the Amun legion trotted into view and blocked the street ahead of them. The men and women crowding the streets of the capital melted away down alleys and drew back from the armed men. Sethi signalled his men to halt and strode forward to confront the line of soldiers.

"By what authority do you block our way?" he demanded. "Who is your captain?"

A tall Kushite soldier with a gold armband and faience pectoral pushed through to stand in front of his men. "I am Captain Tarqa of the Amun legion, and I act under the authority of Tjaty of the South, Neferronpet. I have orders to take you into custody, Lord Sethi."

"On what charge?"

"That you did conspire with the enemy Ribu for the overthrow of the king."

Sethi stared and then laughed. "That is nonsense. Now get out of our way."

Tarqa rapped out an order and the soldiers behind him lifted their spears. "You will come with me, Lord Sethi."

Messuwy strode forward to stand beside Sethi. "You recognise me, Captain Tarqa?" he demanded.

"I do, sir."

"This man..." Messuwy indicated Sethi, "...is a member of my household and as such is under my authority."

"I am sorry, sir, but I have my orders."

"From Tjaty Neferronpet, yes, you said. I am the king's eldest son though, will you disobey me?"

Tarqa looked uncomfortable. "I have my orders, sir," he repeated.

"And you are to be commended for loyally attempting to follow them, but blind adherence to duty will get you killed, Captain Tarqa, you and many of these fine fellows behind you. Must we shed blood to resolve this issue?"

Tarqa looked down and scuffed the dust in the street with one sandaled foot. His hesitation encouraged Messuwy.

"My man Sethi will remain by my side, Captain Tarqa," Messuwy went on. "But you alone are welcome to accompany us to our destination. If the

Tjaty convenes a legal court to charge my servant and can produce evidence, I will turn him over to you. Agreed?"

"My lord..." Sethi muttered. "You must not..."

"Are we agreed, Captain Tarqa?" Messuwy demanded.

"What is your destination, sir?"

"I go to the Temple of Amun to offer thanks after my voyage to his holy city. There I will converse with the Hem-netjer of the god."

"And then you will turn him over to me?"

"When a proper court is convened and the evidence of his guilt is produced."

"I... I must send word to the Tjaty," Tarqa said.

"Do so, by all means," Messuwy replied, "but in the meantime, stand your men aside for I mean to worship at Amun's feet and it would not be wise to interfere with his worship in his own city."

Messuwy started forward, striding toward the levelled spears of the soldiers of the Amun legion. At a quick order from their captain, they raised their lances and moved aside. Sethi and the members of Messuwy's escort followed the king's son toward the temple. Tarqa quickly gave a message to a runner and sent him off toward the Tjaty's palace, and then trotted after Messuwy.

They entered the temple precinct by the side gate, past the small temple of Ptah, and were met by a senior priest of Amun. The priest bowed and led them across the open forecourt and into the maze of corridors and rooms inside the Great Temple. Sethi instructed the guard to wait outside while he, Messuwy and Tarqa followed the priest inside. The priest handed lit torches to the others and bade them follow. Their footsteps reverberated in the narrow stone corridors and in darkened chambers and through dimly lit halls they glimpsed other priests engaged in temple duties or taking their ease. Odours of incense wafted over them, and sounds of low rhythmic chanting washed over them like a wave surge. Walls decorated by representations of the god flickered in the lamplight, making the images of Amun move. Tarqa's breath came faster and he made the sign of protection as they wound their way deeper into the temple complex. Finally, mounting a long curving staircase, they found themselves in an airy room atop the tallest part of the temple.

"Wait here," Messuwy instructed the Kushite captain.

"Where Sethi goes, I go," Tarqa declared.

"These men have been summoned by the Hem-netjer of Amun," the priest said to Tarqa. "You have not."

"Nevertheless, I will accompany Sethi, for I am charged with his custody."

The priest sighed. "Captain, you are not invited into his holy presence, so you will wait here or suffer the consequences."

Tarqa looked uncertain. "Consequences?"

"Nobody enters the Hem-netjer's presence unbidden. If you persist, I will summon priests to send you quickly to the ground." The priest smiled and indicated the window that looked out on the temple pylons and hypostyle hall, and further away, the river and western cliffs. "Come, you are a loyal soldier of Amun and I know you do not want to cause offence. Let me send for food and drink and you may take your ease while these gentlemen are with the Hem-netjer."

Tarqa gave in and watched as Messuwy and Sethi passed beyond the heavy curtains into the presence of the Hem-netjer.

"Welcome, Lord Messuwy." Roma-Rui smiled and added, "Or should I perhaps say 'Son of Re'?"

"What have you heard?" Messuwy asked sharply. "You have news?"

Roma-Rui nodded.

"I have heard little, despite my network of spies," Sethi said. "It is possible the king is dead, but that is all."

"The king is dead," Roma-Rui stated. "Of that you can be sure. As to the rest, there is a measure of uncertainty. Prince Seti remains in the palace and is thought to be investigating the manner of his father's death. I imagine he hopes to lay the blame at your door, Lord Messuwy."

Sethi shrugged. "It is of no concern. No matter how hard they dig, they will find it hard to provide proof of our involvement in the king's death, and without it Messuwy son of Merenptah has an excellent claim to the throne of the Double Kingdom."

"Not as good as if Prince Seti had died too," Roma-Rui said. "If that had occurred as planned, then none could deny him his rights."

"There is no good weeping over what might have been," Sethi said. "We must decide what to do now, before any support for the young prince can arise."

"None will support him over me," Messuwy declared. "I am the eldest son of the king."

"But not the Heir," Sethi pointed out. "In fact, you have no official position within the kingdoms. Make no mistake, my lord, the north will declare for Seti. Our only real hope is to declare for the rightful king here in the south and be prepared to fight for what is ours."

"That is a bold plan," Roma-Rui declared, "but can you back it up with soldiers? You will need an army."

"Who would dare march against their rightful king?" Messuwy asked.

"Many would," the Hem-netjer replied. "So where is your army?"

"There is the Amun legion..."

"Which is under the control of Tjaty Neferronpet and Commander Merenkhons."

"Merenkhons? Who is he loyal to?" Sethi asked.

"Difficult to say. He works closely with Neferronpet though."

"Then we must do away with them both."

"There are junior officers loyal to Amun, but even if you should claim their loyalty you will need more than one legion to counter Seti's army."

"There is the Kushite legion. It is at full strength and more men could probably be raised at short notice," Sethi said.

"They are under the command of King's Son of Kush, Khaemter. Can you be certain of his support?" Roma-Rui asked.

"Of course," Messuwy said at once.

"Perhaps," Sethi corrected. "Openly, he is loyal to the king, but in private he has indicated he will favour my lord Messuwy."

"We must make certain of him," Roma-Rui said. "To move against Prince Seti with only one legion would be suicidal."

"You were happy enough to do it before," Messuwy grumbled. "What has changed? Or are you losing heart?"

The Hem-netjer of Amun scowled. "I am guided in all things by the will of Amun. He has made it plain that he will support you as king, but he requires us to make you king in the first place. Our original plan called for the death of the king and the Heir, leaving only you as candidate for the throne. The king is most likely dead, but the Heir is not. This puts a completely different complexion on things. With the Heir dead, men would flock to your standard, with him alive, the north with follow him and, I think, the south too. All you have to support you is the goodwill of the god, the Amun legion, and possibly the Kushite legion. I'm just saying it might not be enough."

"I have a natural claim to the throne," Messuwy said. "My father was Baenre Merenptah and I am his eldest son. On top of that, I have the support of Amun. The people must accept that."

"Fornicate the people," Sethi said. "They are cattle and unimportant. They will do as they are told or suffer the consequences. It is the nobles we must convince."

"How do we do that?"

"Gold. You must be prepared to be generous."

"I am not a wealthy man," Messuwy complained.

"What? Despite all the gold you have skimmed off the king's mines in Kush?" Sethi laughed. "You are wealthier than you know, but you don't have to part with much gold if it distresses you. Promises will turn many heads, promises of land and position once you are king."

"Well, that's all right then. Get to it, Sethi. Deliver me the nobles and perhaps I'll make you my Tjaty."

"You are most generous, my lord," Sethi said. He sketched a bow to disguise the anger he felt. "I would rather remain by your side though."

Messuwy laughed. "Too much opportunity to enrich yourself, eh? You'd prefer to let another man busy himself with the affairs of government while you plunder the king's mines. Well, just remember that I will be king, and that those mines will be delivering the gold to my treasury. I don't want my servants stealing from me."

A muscle jumped in Sethi's jaw as he lowered his eyes. "I merely wish to serve you, my lord. Your good will is reward enough."

Roma-Rui coughed, wishing to spare Sethi the embarrassment being heaped upon him by Messuwy. "So we must delay announcing your succession it seems, but for how long? If we move too soon we risk not having support, but if we wait too long, Seti will crown himself king and we become mere rebels."

"I cannot risk claiming the throne if nobody supports me," Messuwy declared. "I need an army." He glared at Sethi. "If I have so much gold, I should be able to buy one."

"It is easy enough to buy men," Sethi said, "but they will be of dubious quality. If a man once sells himself for gold, more gold might buy him again. Such men cannot be relied upon."

"So buy me soldiers. Round up a few thousand Kushite tribesmen and arm them, promising them gold and cattle once they have conquered Kemet for me."

"As my lord commands."

"And how long will that take?" Roma-Rui asked.

"A few months," Sethi replied.

"That long?" The disappointment was heavy in Messuwy's voice.

"Such things cannot be hurried."

"So we must delay after all?" Roma-Rui asked. "And become rebels?"

A smile tugged at Sethi's lips as he regarded the Hem-netjer. "They will call us rebels until we succeed, and then none will dare."

A priest coughed gently from beyond the curtains and slipped into the room, bowing toward the Hem-netjer. "A messenger comes from the north, Hem-netjer. The vessel flies the royal banner."

"What does that mean?" Messuwy demanded.

"Official news from Men-nefer," Roma-Rui said. "I would hazard it carries news of the king's death and Seti's accession."

"What do we do?"

"There is nothing you can do, Lord Messuwy," Roma-Rui said. "Bow to the inevitable, for now. Greet the messenger, attend upon Tjaty Neferronpet and pretend joy at your brother's imminent enthronement. As for you, Sethi, I advise you to flee ahead of the news, else you will be arrested. This priest will show you a way out that avoids the soldiers waiting for you."

Chapter 4
Year 1 of Userkheperure Seti

Tjaty Neferronpet was in an ill humour, having spent much of the previous night suffering from a burning sensation in the pit of his stomach. Every time he lay down, burning fluid would rise into his throat, forcing him upright again. He nibbled on a little dry bread, hoping it would soak up the fluid, but the respite it provided was only temporary. From past experience, Neferronpet knew there was a more lasting remedy, but it inevitably ruined his digestion the next day, so he resisted the temptation to call the physician. As the moon set he was able to put it off no longer and gagged on the clay-based slurry the physician offered him. It calmed the burning sensation but sat like a stone in his belly, and he knew he would find it hard to digest his food the next day. Rest was more important though, so the Tjaty snatched a little sleep before dawn.

His spies brought him interesting news mid-morning, and he broke off the court case he had been adjudicating with relief. It was all he could do to remain awake during the long speeches by plaintiff and defendant, so he hurriedly adjourned to consider the news. Lord Messuwy, eldest son of Baenre, would be docking at Waset sometime after noon, and his servant Sethi had been seen in the city. He could not help but think the two facts were connected.

"Send for Commander Merenkhons," he instructed a servant.

When the commander of the Amun legion arrived with his adjutant, he told them of the news he had received. "I want Sethi arrested. He is still wanted for questioning concerning possible traitorous actions."

"Lord Messuwy too?" Merenkhons asked.

Neferronpet considered carefully and shook his head. "Not without evidence of wrongdoing. He may hold no official position but he is still the king's eldest son. Just arrest Sethi on those old charges of aiding the Ribu and put him in the dungeons."

"Those charges were never proved," Merenkhons said. "if they could be, the king would have moved against him long ago."

"It doesn't matter, it'll be enough to arrest him. Then I'll notify the king and see what he wants done."

Merenkhons sent the adjutant off with his instructions, and joined the Tjaty in a light meal of beef, bread and beer. They sat out on a veranda where cool river breezes eased the heat of the day.

"No news from court?" Merenkhons asked.

Neferronpet looked up sharply, his eyebrows coming together. "A strange question coming from you. Why do you ask?"

"Forgive me, Tjaty, I did not mean to pry into official business, but everyone knows Men-nefer has been shut up tighter than a roach's arse for days. Something's going on and I wondered if you'd heard anything."

"I dare say we'll know when we're meant to know."

"Of course." Merenkhons stared into his cup and swirled the creamy beer for a few moments. "It's just that there's a rumour the king's dead."

Neferronpet stared at the Amun legion commander. "I wouldn't go voicing that around."

"You must have heard the rumours though."

A twinge of pain stabbed in his gut, and the Tjaty turned away, massaging his belly. "Rumours," he muttered. "Dangerous rumours."

"Even more so if he really is. Perhaps that's why Messuwy has come to Waset."

"He'd be better off going to Men-nefer if his father's dead. Why come to...gods preserve us...he wouldn't..."

"What?"

"The bastard's going to bid for the throne."

Merenkhons smiled. "A bastard he is not. He's the eldest son of Baenre..."

"But not the Heir, and that fact has rankled ever since he was passed over. This is his chance, while there's no word from the capital."

"You worry too much, Neferronpet. He cannot claim the throne without the army at his back and the Amun legion is loyal."

"You are certain of this?"

"Of course. I am the Commander and I am loyal to the king and the Heir."

"And are you equally certain of all your officers? Your men?"

"They will do as they're told."

"Need I point out that the leadership of the legion could change between one breath and the next? I'd hate to see you lose your life because of another man's ambition."

Merenkhons grimaced. "Sethi is being arrested as we speak. Do you want me to have Messuwy arrested too? I could do it, you know."

Neferronpet shook his head, stifling a belch. "Too dangerous. He has supporters within the city. No, I must send word of the situation to Mennefer and wait for orders."

"Well, there are a few things we can do in the meantime," Commander Merenkhons said. "I'll confine the legion to barracks and have the officers whose loyalty is in any doubt relieved of duties. I can lock the city up tight until we hear what's happening."

Merenkhons left the palace to set about securing the city, and Neferronpet sought out his physician. The physician listened intently to the list of symptoms the Tjaty described and mixed up a further series of potions to alleviate the feeling of sickness that had resulted from the clay slurry imbibed earlier. A servant held a bowl while Neferronpet vomited, and then the physician examined the vomitus, stirring the thin liquid with his forefinger. He sniffed the fluid and wiped it on his robe before signalling the servant to take it away.

"Your stomach contents are excessively sour, my lord. I will prepare you some clay pills you can take if you suffer again from the burning affliction, but you must watch your diet. Avoid meat and fish, partake of no bread, nor beer and wine."

"You mean to starve me?" Neferronpet grumbled.

"Drink only plain river water," the physician went on. "You may eat most vegetables, but make sure you take plenty of lettuce and onions, garlic, melons, cucumber, and dried dates and figs."

The Tjaty felt hungry after emptying his stomach, and the thought of a meatless diet made him irritable, to say nothing of having to do without good strong wine from his own vineyards. He sent orders to the kitchens for a variety of vegetables and fruit, but also for a roasted goose and some fatty beef. Servants brought him wine and cool river water, and he took his lunch on a secluded veranda, reading through various letters from the governors and mayors of the southern cities. Despite his irritation and hunger, he took some heed of the physician's words and only ate meat moderately and watered his wine.

A discreet knock on the doorpost took his attention away from the troubles of the mayor of Ta-Senet, who complained of depredations on outlying farms by desert dwellers. He made a quick note to follow up on this complaint, and looked up to see who disturbed him.

"Forgive me, Excellency," a servant said. "A vessel is approaching the royal wharf, a messenger boat, flying the royal banner."

Neferronpet put aside his scrolls and the remnants of his lunch and got to his feet, feeling excitement building inside him. "Call out the guard," he instructed. "I will go to the docks to meet the messenger."

A short time later, Neferronpet emerged onto the royal wharf, slightly out of breath, just in time to see the messenger leap from the boat and be greeted by Messuwy. He pushed forward in alarm, telling his guard to follow close behind.

"Lord Messuwy, what are you doing here?"

Messuwy turned and stared at the slightly dishevelled Tjaty. "I came to see if there is news of my royal father. What is that to you?"

Neferronpet looked past Messuwy to the messenger. "You have letters for me? Tjaty of the South, Neferronpet?"

"Yes, Excellency," the messenger said, bowing deeply with hands extended.

"And for anyone else?" Messuwy asked.

The messenger looked sidelong at Messuwy and hesitated, looking back at the Tjaty. Neferronpet nodded and the man said, "No, my lord."

"Then come up to the palace and you can deliver your letters," Neferronpet said. He turned and ushered the messenger toward his guards. Messuwy followed, and the Tjaty turned back to him.

"Forgive me, my lord," he said. "There are messages I must attend to..."

"Which might be from my father the king."

"Indeed. And you may be sure that if they concern you, I will send for you to make his wishes known."

Messuwy bristled at the idea that he would be sent for like any lowly servant, but could think of no retaliatory argument. Instead, he scowled and watched the Tjaty hurry off to the palace with the royal messenger.

Neferronpet took the messenger back out onto the veranda, accepted the written message from the sealed pouch, and indicated the food and drink from his meal. "Please eat and drink as you will while I read this letter." He broke the seal on the papyrus scroll and carried it to the steps down into the palace garden before opening it and reading.

He read silently, though his lips moved as he sounded out each syllable. As the import of the words sunk into his understanding, he put his hand to his head, his mouth dropping open in shock. He looked over at the messenger gainfully working his way through a platter of roast goose, and asked, "Do you know what's in this letter?"

The messenger looked up, swallowed and wiped his chin with one hand as he stood up. "Begging your pardon, Excellency, but...er, sort of. I mean, I don't know what's in the letter, exactly like, but I can guess."

"It's true then? The king is dead? Poisoned?"

"He's dead, Excellency, yes. As to how, well, nobody's said for sure. The court's as busy as a kicked anthill though, so something's up."

"All right," Neferronpet said. "Go back to your meal." He called for a servant and told him to find Merenkhons immediately.

The servant bowed low. "Excellency, Lord Messuwy awaits your pleasure."

Neferronpet considered for a few moments and then told the servant to show Lord Messuwy into the audience chamber. "Then go and find Commander Merenkhons. Tell him to attend on me urgently."

Leaving instructions for the messenger to be allowed to finish his meal and then be shown to a private room, the Tjaty walked through the palace to the audience chamber where he often heard disputes in his capacity as the king's deputy in Ta Shemau. There was a raised throne in the chamber to seat the king should he ever visit Waset, and a slightly smaller one the Tjaty occupied during formal occasions. Neferronpet's jaw tightened as he entered the chamber and found Messuwy waiting for him, seated on the royal throne.

"That is hardly fitting, Lord Messuwy," he said. "Even I who represent the king in Ta Shemau do not sit on the king's throne."

Messuwy shrugged, but did not get up, forcing Neferronpet to cross to the lower throne. "I am the son of the king. What news have you?"

"You are no longer son of the king, for the king your father is dead."

Messuwy leapt to his feet. "I knew it!" The animation in his face slipped away and was replaced by a look of avarice. "What else?"

"There was nothing else," Neferronpet said. "I grieve for you, my lord. King Baenre will be sorely missed."

Messuwy waved a hand nonchalantly. "Yes, yes. Did the letter say nothing about..." he hesitated. "Anything else? The succession, perhaps?"

"Prince Seti has already been named Heir. I cannot think the king would change that on his deathbed."

"You would tell me if there was anything else?"

"Of course." Neferronpet kept his face impassive as he sketched a shallow bow. Messuwy did not return the courtesy, nor offer the deeper obeisance due the position of Tjaty, but instead stalked out of the audience chamber as Merenkhons hurried in.

"Much good it will do you, Merenkhons," Messuwy snarled as he left.

"My lord?" Messuwy did not reply, so Merenkhons watched him go and then bowed to Neferronpet. "You have news?" he asked.

"Indeed I have. Come and sit beside me." Neferronpet pointed to the dais steps and seated himself as Merenkhons approached.

"The messenger was from Men-nefer? It's official?" Merenkhons sat on the steps and looked eagerly at Neferronpet.

"King Baenre Merenptah ascended to Re seventeen days ago. His son and heir, Prince Seti Meryenptah will mount the Double Throne."

Merenkhons whistled. "Someone's going to be upset."

The Tjaty nodded, his expression thoughtful. "I cannot see him accepting his younger brother's elevation quietly, but there's more. Baenre was poisoned. His neru pehut introduced a poisoned cream to the king's body."

The legion commander gaped. "Assassinated? Has the neru pehut admitted why he did it?"

"He died by his own hand before he could be arrested. It seems a palace servant plotted with him. The servant was of Ribu descent, so we must assume it was revenge, perhaps for a family member killed in the invasion four years ago. The servant is also dead."

"Thank the gods for that, then," Merenkhons said. "Better a simple plot by disgruntled servants than a palace plot involving the nobility or..." He broke off and looked toward the servants at the door before shrugging. "It would mean civil war."

"It may yet," Neferronpet murmured. "You should have seen Messuwy's reaction when I told him his father was dead. There was no grief or even sober reflection, but rather joy and calculation. I don't think the news came as a surprise."

"The king was an old man."

"True, but though I cannot say exactly what was amiss, I thought there was more to it."

"You think he knew the king was about to die? Gods, you don't think he actually had a hand in it? You said a Ribu servant was responsible."

"That is what the letter from Men-nefer said. Royal Butler Bay says there is no doubt." Neferronpet frowned and watched the servants cleaning the walls of the chamber.

"How did Messuwy react to the news of the poisoning and the Ribu involvement?"

"I didn't tell him." The Tjaty saw Merenkhons' look of surprise and offered a wry smile. "I'd like to choose who hears about that and when. It's not that I suspect him...not really...but if I thought that the news might precipitate a response from him...I don't want complications."

"He's bound to hear soon. Better from your mouth than garbled gossip."

Neferronpet nodded. "I'd like to decide what I'm going to do first."

"What do you mean?"

"There's one other thing the letter mentioned, Prince Seti is on his way up to Waset. He's probably half way here already."

"That's no surprise, I suppose. Like his father Baenre, he'll be making a progress to the principal cities. Waset is a logical stop."

"Baenre came with just an honour guard. Seti is bringing the Ptah legion. The Royal Barge and five transports in all. You don't bring that many troops unless you're expecting trouble."

Merenkhons shifted uneasily. "The Amun legion is loyal."

"I don't doubt it, but Waset has ever had an uneasy relationship with the House of Ramesses, something that Messuwy, Sethi and Roma-Rui have fostered."

"Traitors all, my lord Tjaty. Let me act against them and deliver a peaceful city to the king when he arrives."

"A thought that had crossed my mind."

"Give me the word and it is accomplished."

"You have already sent men to arrest Sethi. Has that happened?"

"He seems to have eluded the fool I put in charge. My men are scouring the city, though. We'll find him."

"You can't arrest the Hem-netjer of Amun; you don't have the authority. Neither do I, for that matter, so that must wait on Seti's arrival. I believe it would be useful to deliver Messuwy to him, though. Do you think you can detain him without fuss?"

"I'll throw him in a dungeon so fast his feet won't touch the ground."

"No. There must be no arrest. He is still the next king's brother and has been charged with no crime, let alone been proven guilty. Detain him, politely but firmly, and let him be held alone and in comfort until Seti arrives. Can you do it?"

Neferronpet stared at the commander's face as he wrestled with the difficult task he had been given. Neither man saw one of the servants slip out of the audience chamber.

"What if he resists?"

"Then subdue him, but let no lasting harm come to him."

"All right. If that's what you want, I can do it," Merenkhons said.

Chapter 5
Year 1 of Userkheperure Seti

T he royal barge 'Wisdom of Ptah' arrived at Waset, but remained in mid-river, the oars stroking slowly to keep the barge stationary while the troop-carriers disgorged the Ptah legion onto the docks. Commander Besenmut was under orders to make his disposition of the men under his command look like nothing more than an honour guard, but he also had to make absolutely certain of the safety of Prince Seti, so he drove the populace back, ringing the area with armed men.

As the royal barge hove into view, the Amun legion also turned out, with Commander Merenkhons leading them, but was prevented from getting too close by the Ptah legionaries. Merenkhons made a formal complaint to a Ptah Troop Commander and was escorted into the presence of Commander Besenmut, who had set up a command post in a granary near the docks.

"I must protest, Besenmut. You are treating my men like criminals," Merenkhons said. "It is my duty to provide an escort for royalty in Amun's city."

"Ah, Merenkhons, I was wondering how long it would take you to show up. You are welcome to join me as I greet the Son of Re."

The Amun legion commander's eyebrows rose. "He is king already?"

"As good as, and you'll offer him full kingly honours if you're wise."

Merenkhons scratched his chin. "Why is he here in Waset?"

"You think I am privy to every decision made by my betters? I follow orders, Merenkhons. See that you do too."

"Of course." Merenkhons looked through the open door of the granary to the river and the royal barge with its oars beating time on the green waters. "How long before he comes ashore?"

"There you go again, asking questions instead of simply obeying orders. How did you ever rise to the rank of legion commander?"

"I rose through the ranks, if you must know," Merenkhons growled. "Doing some real soldiering in Kush."

"Didn't see you at Perire though," Besenmut said. "You heard about that did you? When we smashed the Ribu and Sea Peoples? Where were you and the Amun legion then?"

Merenkhons caught sight of two of the guards on the door grinning and scowled. "It was not my decision. I was only a Troop Commander then. Now, are you going to let my men do their duty by the Heir?"

Besenmut considered. "What exactly do you see as your duty?"

"Waset is Amun's city, and therefore the Amun legion controls everything. If the king or the Heir is visiting, it is my duty to turn out the legion to protect and honour him, and keep the peace."

"Very commendable, I'm sure. A pity the king cannot rely on the loyalty of Waset...and by extension, the Amun legion."

Merenkhons stared at the other Commander, his face suffusing with blood. "What do you mean by that? Are you implying I am disloyal to the king?"

"Be easy, Merenkhons," Besenmut said. "Reports have reached us from Neferronpet that assure us of your personal loyalty. Regrettably, not everyone in Waset is of like mind. The Hem-netjer of Amun...I forget his name..."

"Roma-Rui."

"Yes, that's it. He's a centre for disaffection in the city and he is a known associate of the new king's brother Messuwy."

"Is Lord Messuwy guilty of something?"

"Let us just say that the Son of Re greatly desires to have him brought before him. You have knowledge of his whereabouts?"

"He has rooms in the temple, I believe. By chance, I have dispatched men to bring him to the Tjaty's palace. I hoped to have his adjutant Sethi in custody too, but he slipped the net."

"Sethi, by the gods. You know he was implicated in the Ribu invasion, though nothing could be proved? In the circumstances, his presence would be much desired. You say he has gone, though?"

"I have men searching for him," Merenkhons assured Besenmut.

"Then let us hope these men are loyal to the king and not his brother."

Merenkhons looked uneasy. "You believe Messuwy to be guilty alongside Sethi?"

"I dare say that is what the new king seeks to determine. Please make sure Lord Messuwy is waiting in the Tjaty's palace by the time the Son of Re disembarks."

"But what of the Amun legion's duty? We should provide the honour guard of greeting."

Besenmut regarded Merenkhons coolly. "As I said, you are welcome to join me as I greet the Son of Re. However, your men would better serve finding Sethi and Messuwy and keeping the populace quiet. I have no desire to have bloodshed mar the king's visit to the Southern Capital, but if there is any trouble, I won't hesitate to guard the king's person by any means available."

Before Merenkhons could respond, a Leader of One Hundred of the Ptah legion entered the granary and saluted his Commander. "The docks are secure, sir, and all is in readiness."

Besenmut raised an eyebrow. "Well, Merenkhons? Your answer?"

Merenkhons capitulated. "I would be honoured to accompany you."

Besenmut nodded. "Good. Lead on Panhesy."

The Leader of One Hundred trotted off with the two legion commanders strolling after him. As soon as they were out in the open, Merenkhons beckoned to one of his officers and issued instructions that the men were to police the street corners in pairs, ready to quell any disturbance. Besenmut smiled to hear the instructions and issued his own commands to a waiting Troop Commander.

"Signal the Royal Barge that we are ready for them."

The Troop Commander saluted and ran off, shouting orders of his own, and soon the rhythm of the oars on the Royal Barge changed, the craft angling in toward the docks.

Merenkhons stood beside Besenmut, watching the approaching barge. "What's he like?" he asked. "I only saw him once, when he was a young lad. He came to Waset in a fishing boat with his sister. It was quite a scandal."

"I wouldn't remind him of it," Besenmut cautioned. "He was a boy then, but a king now, and an able warrior." He broke off and strode a few paces to the same Troop Commander who had signalled the barge. "Sound the horns of greeting."

Rams' horns blared out, the sound rising and falling as the oars swept once more the paused aloft, river water sluicing off the blades as the barge lost momentum, nosing in toward the dock. Sailors leapt and scrambled, hurling heavy flax ropes ashore and securing them to timber posts, the ropes creaking and groaning as the weight of the vessel tugged on them, easing to a stop. A gangplank clattered into place, and soldiers of the Ptah legion raced to their places on either side. Their kilts were white, their

34

sandals new, and the tips of their bronze spears gleamed in the bright sunshine as they stood to attention, their eyes fixed and raised.

Besenmut and Merenkhons advanced to the end of the double line of soldiers and, as Prince Seti walked across the gangplank onto the Waset dock, bowed deeply, their hands outstretched at knee level.

"Greetings, Son of Re," Besenmut said. "The docks are secure."

"Welcome to Waset, Son of Re," Merenkhons added.

"Who is this?" Seti asked.

"Merenkhons, Commander of the Amun legion, Son of Re," Besenmut said. "His men are keeping the peace within the city."

"Where are the priests? They should be here to greet me."

"They seem to be taking their lead from Amun, Son of Re, and Amun is absent."

"Have the Hem-netjer brought to me."

"It shall be done, Son of Re."

"And what of my brother Messuwy?"

"Son of Re," Merenkhons said. "My men have gone to bring him to the Tjaty's palace."

Seti nodded and walked on, the two legion commanders stumbling out of his way. He continued walking toward the cordon of Ptah soldiers, and signalling frantically, Besenmut conveyed his orders to his men, who fell in around their king. They walked through the streets of Waset, the population pouring out of houses and running from side alleys, eager to catch a glimpse of their royal visitor. A cheer went up from the crowd and fed on itself, conveying the hopes of a people and the promise of a new king.

Soldiers of Amun were visible at each street corner, busy trying to keep the crowds under control, but without much success. Men and women jostled one another, calling out and making comments, chattering amongst themselves, while children ducked and darted through the throng and raced across the street ahead of the procession. Dogs, half-starved and mangy, yapped and barked, and fights erupted over scraps of food littering the dusty streets. The stink of the city was almost tangible, thousands of people crammed together, the stench of ordure pervading the hot air, and mingled with scents of sweat, of cooking food, of spices, and the wet scents of the river mud. Over everything hung the sun, the visible manifestation of the god and father of the young man who now walked the streets amidst his subjects.

Tjaty Neferronpet stood on the steps of the palace and bowed low as Seti arrived and, on being allowed to stand and greet the young man, welcomed him officially to Waset. A number of other officials and dignitaries were also present and Neferronpet introduced them all as they came forward and bowed. Seti muttered a few pleasantries, and then insisted on moving inside.

"Where is Messuwy?" he demanded, as soon as they reached the audience chamber.

"He is not here, my lord," Neferronpet said.

"I sent for him," Merenkhons said. "I am sure he will be here soon."

"Perhaps my lord would like some refreshment after his voyage? I have ordered food and drink."

Seti sat down to a light meal of fatty beef, fine bread, crisp vegetables and rich wine, watched by the Tjaty, the legion commanders, and several servants. When he had finished, the servants cleared away the remains of the meal and, at a word from Neferronpet, bowed and withdrew from the chamber, closing the doors behind them.

"Well, where is he? He should be here by now."

"I... I will go and find out, Son of Re," Merenkhons said. He bowed and hurried away, calling for his officers as he went.

"Is that man competent?" Seti asked.

Neferronpet shrugged. "He has given me no reason for dissatisfaction. He is loyal, at least," he added. The Tjaty hesitated a moment and then pressed on. "Do you suspect Lord Messuwy of...of having a hand in the death of your father?"

Seti sighed and picked at a fragment of food caught in his teeth. He waved his other hand toward chairs near the wall and said, "Sit, both of you. I think we can dispense with formality in private." The prince looked around and nodded toward the throne on its raised dais. "Too grand for me today. Just bring me an ordinary chair, Besenmut. Today I am as other men."

"Never, Son of Re," Besenmut protested.

"Not yet. Until I am crowned, just call me Seti..." he saw the look of horror on the legion commander's face and grinned. "...or 'my lord', if you must."

"Yes, Son of...my lord." He brought the best of the chairs over for Seti, and then went back for another for himself. Obviously feeling ill at ease, he sat down, but could not relax in the presence of his king.

"That's better," Seti said. "By the gods, you have no idea how good it is to be able to relax instead of having to keep up the facade of the godhood day after day. I'm not even crowned yet, and I can already feel the weight of the Two Kingdoms on my shoulders. No wonder my father aged so rapidly in the last few years."

"That will not happen to you, my lord," Neferronpet said. "You have an advantage few of your predecessors had, namely youth. Your father Baenre was an old man when he came to the throne, and even Menpehtyre Ramesses and Menmaatre Seti were mature men. Only Usermaatre Ramesses was a young man and look what a long and illustrious reign he had."

Seti beamed. "If I can achieve even part of what my grandfather did, I will be well pleased. My father should have been able to build on his achievements, but he was struck down before his time. We of the House of Ramesses are long-lived and my father could have continued alive another ten years at least." The complacent smile on Seti's face slipped and was replaced by a frown. "I will have the truth of it."

"My lord?" Besenmut ventured.

"The death of my father the king, Besenmut. He was poisoned, you know."

Besenmut looked down at the floor, not knowing how to respond.

"So said the official letter I received," Neferronpet murmured. "It intimated the Ribu were responsible."

"Butler Bay investigated and found evidence that pointed at a Ribu servant and the neru pehut. Unfortunately, the physician killed himself and the Ribu was not taken alive, so I cannot find out how deep the plot goes."

"The Ribu connection is interesting," Neferronpet said. "Particularly when you take into account the fact that a certain man called Sethi was involved with the Ribu when they invaded a few years ago."

"Ah, you made the connection too? None of my advisors seems willing to point out that this Sethi was military advisor to my brother Messuwy."

"My lord. You cannot think Lord Messuwy would..." Besenmut's voice trailed off. "My apologies, my lord. I am a simple man. My mind is suited to the battlefield, rather than looking for traitors."

"And I have need of such simple men, Besenmut," Seti said. "But also of devious minds such as that of my loyal Tjaty Neferronpet. It does not surprise you that Messuwy might be involved in the death of my father?"

"It grieves me to say it, my lord, but no," Neferronpet said.

"Explain."

"Messuwy was sent south as a young man to become Deputy King's Son of Kush, whence he rose to become King's Son of Kush when the old viceroy died. He chose as his military adviser Sethi, son of Horire, and it is from this time that we can detect discontent in Messuwy's communications. It is my belief that this Sethi has fostered a desire for the throne in his master's mind, and seeks to bring that about through various ways." Neferronpet paused to collect his thoughts. "If you remember, my lord, Messuwy first sought to be named heir in your place, and when that did not work, it is believed his man Sethi entered into a traitorous alliance with the Ribu, hoping to remove the king and Heir together. Only your father and your mighty deeds saved Kemet then, but now we see another plot which again points at Sethi."

"But not Messuwy?" Seti asked. "I can believe the most evil things of this Sethi, but my brother is more misguided than evil, isn't he? He merely took bad advice?"

"It is possible, my lord," Neferronpet conceded, "but Messuwy should be questioned on this."

"I fully intend that he should give a full accounting of his actions and those of his adviser Sethi."

Footsteps sounded in the hallway outside the audience chamber, together with raised voices, and a few moments later, Commander Merenkhons re-entered and bowed low.

"Majesty, Lord Messuwy is nowhere to be found, and neither is the man Sethi."

"They have fled?"

"Proof of their guilt, my lord," Neferronpet said.

"I will not judge him unheard," Seti replied. "Scour the city for them."

"Majesty, I regret... that is to say... er, Troop Commander Amenhotep and some five hundred men have deserted their posts. It is thought they have sworn allegiance to...to Lord Messuwy."

"The rest are loyal?"

"Yes, Majesty."

"Besenmut, you will flood the city with your men. You will find Messuwy and Sethi and bring them before me. If any man of the Amun legion challenges you and does not swear instant allegiance to me, you will kill them. Is that understood?"

The Ptah Commander sprang to attention. "Yes, Son of Re, but..."

"But what?"

"You should go back on board the barge, Son of Re, and stay in the current. If there is treachery, you would be safer..."

"Safer? I will not run from Messuwy, even if he had a hundred legions behind him." Seti glared at Besenmut, and then softened his expression. "How would it look if the king fled at the first sign of trouble? Now, you have your orders, Commander Besenmut. Carry them out."

Seti waited until Besenmut had left and then turned to Merenkhons. "There is one rotten fruit left in Waset if the others have fled. Go to the Great Temple of Amun and arrest the Hem-netjer, Roma-Rui, and ask the Second Prophet Bakenkhons to attend on me at once."

"What do you intend, my lord?" Neferronpet asked as Merenkhons left, calling for his men.

"Roma-Rui all but openly opposed my father, and his loyalty is to this city and Messuwy. I intend to depose him and elevate Bakenkhons to his place."

"A dangerous course, my lord. Amun is powerful."

"More powerful than the King of Kemet?"

"Of course not, my lord, but what will you do with him? You cannot have him killed without risking the whole of Ta Shemau rising in rebellion."

Seti stared at his Tjaty. "They would not dare."

"Maybe, maybe not, but the Amun priesthood is powerful in the south. It would be a risk and, well...maybe it is one that should be carefully considered...my lord."

Seti's stare turned to a glare. "What would you have me do then?"

"Remove him by all means, my lord, for in Waset he will always be a focus of disaffection, but be circumspect. Invite him north to visit and report on the conditions of the Amun temples in Ta Mehu. Say that you wish to repair and rebuild the Houses of Amun and would value his assistance. I believe his sense of his own importance will encourage him to accept. Bakenkhons, who is Second Prophet anyway, can look after things in Waset in his absence."

"I will consider your words, Neferronpet."

A little later, Merenkhons returned with a squad of soldiers and Roma-Rui bound with ropes in their midst. Bakenkhons walked unhindered, but he looked troubled by the situation. The Amun Commander saluted and indicated his prisoner. "There was a bit of trouble, Son of Re, and a crowd threatened us on the way here. We had to break a few heads, but I don't think anyone died." A distant swelling roar intruded on the quietness of the audience chamber.

"You hear that?" Roma-Rui asked. "That is the sound of the people coming to free me. You have listened to bad advice, son of Baenre, if you think to remove the Chosen One of Amun."

Seti shook his head. "This is not what I wanted, Hem-netjer. I instructed you be invited here, not arrested. Merenkhons, you have made a grievous mistake. Release the Hem-netjer at once."

Merenkhons looked unhappy, but hurried to obey his king. When the ropes had fallen to the floor, and Roma-Rui had brushed down his robes, he turned to Seti with a look of disdain.

"I accept your apology, son of Baenre, for you are but a youth and have not yet had time to surround yourself with able counsellors."

"You forget yourself, Roma-Rui," Neferronpet said. "You are addressing not just a son of Baenre, but the Heir, and indeed, Son of Re."

"Not Son of Re," Roma-Rui snapped. "Seti is not king until I have placed the crowns on his head at the behest of Amun-Re. That will take place when the god decides."

"That is treason," Neferronpet exclaimed. "Seti is king by will of his father and the gods and does not need your permission."

"Peace!" Seti roared. In a calmer voice, he added. "All things will be done according to custom, Hem-netjer, and you may be sure that Amun-Re will take his rightful place in the kingdoms. In fact, Roma-Rui, that is what I wanted to talk to you about."

He approached the priest and put his arms about the older man, before leading him out onto the balcony. The seething crowd below roared at their appearance, the anger turning to joy as they saw the Heir's arm around their beloved Hem-netjer of Amun.

"Smile, Roma-Rui," Seti said quietly. "Wave to them. Let them see you support the House of Ramesses."

"The House of Ramesses is greater than any one man."

"So show your support for the whole if not the part. Or would you rather see the city, the kingdoms even, descend into strife and bloodshed?"

Roma-Rui hesitated a few moments longer, and then nodded, lifting his hand and waving to the crowd.

"I want you to do something more for me," Seti said, turning away from the balcony and drawing the older man inside once more. "And again, it will benefit everyone rather than just me. I need to know the state of the Amun temples. Are they being looked after? Do they need more gold to make them fitting abodes for the god?"

The priest looked at Seti, his forehead wrinkling in a frown. "The temples of Waset glorify the god most suitably, as do most of the lesser temples and shrines in Ta Shemau. We can always use gold though, if it is being offered."

"It is, Roma-Rui, it is. But you only mention the temples of the south. What of the north? Are they in good repair? Do they need gold also? Are there enough temples? Where should I build more?"

"I am not as conversant with the temples in the north," Roma-Rui admitted. "I get reports from the priests, of course, but in no great detail."

"That must be remedied. I need someone to tour the north, to visit every city and town and village in Ta Mehu, and determine the state of every temple to Amun. I need to know how much gold is needed to glorify Amun to the extent he deserves, and how many new temples must be built. Know that I intend Amun to be strong once more throughout the Two Kingdoms."

"That is most gratifying...Prince Seti. May I suggest Bakenkhons here? As Second Prophet of Amun he is qualified to make these investigations."

Bakenkhons bowed low at mention of his name.

Seti laughed, though not unkindly. "You would send a sheep where I need a lion. Bakenkhons is an able priest, I am sure, but he is in too much awe of me. He will tell me exactly what I want to hear rather than what I need to hear. He will fear my wrath and tell me I need spend only a little gold, and as a result, the god Amun will live in temples unworthy of his position. No, I need a fiercer man, one who is not afraid of me, who will stand up to me and demand the god's due."

"Amenhotep, perhaps. As Third Prophet of Amun..."

"Another sheep. There is only one man fierce enough to stand up to me, Roma-Rui, and that is you. I want you to tell me what must be done in the north."

"I? I cannot leave Waset..."

"You have a Second and a Third, even a Fourth. They are able priests and I am sure you can leave Waset in their care for a little while, particularly if it means so much more wealth flowing to the temple coffers of Amun. Come, Roma-Rui, can you not see that Amun and all of Kemet will benefit?"

"I... I suppose I could..."

"Excellent. I will issue the orders immediately. We sail for Men-nefer in the morning."

Chapter 6

Messuwy speaks:

My brother has shown himself for the tyrant he is. Hard on the heels of the king's death, he came south with the Ptah legion and took the city of Waset, filling it with armed men. At once, he ordered my arrest, and that of my faithful lieutenant Sethi, and even dared to send men for the Hem-netjer of Amun, Roma-Rui. The god protected me then, for I was in the privy when the soldiers arrived, and when I emerged, found that the priest had been taken. I take this as a sign of the god's favour.

Sethi had already fled to a friend's estate outside Ta-senet, and there I joined him a day later. I was not without friends in Waset, having always been attracted to this ancient City of Amun and had taken pains to show myself supportive. Commoners hid me from the soldiers and fed me, fishermen smuggled me out on a small vessel and conveyed me upriver to the private estate where I could plan my future. I shall not name my friends, for there are spies everywhere and I would not have them suffer for their loyalty. Suffice it to say that I know who they are and they will be rewarded as soon as I achieve the throne.

Yes, that is my aim, for I am the eldest son of Baenre Merenptah and was once King's Son of Kush. That position must surely have been another sign from the gods, because a member of the royal family is paradoxically never given that eminent post. The King's Son of Kush, a position second only to that of the king, is non-hereditary and is always given to a commoner. Perhaps it is felt that a commoner will not be ambitious, or that a member of the royal family having such power within his grasp will reach out for the throne. Whatever the reason, and I can find no scholar or scribe who knows the truth of it, I was both King's Son of Kush and Eldest son of the King.

I mean to be king in my brother's place, though how I will achieve that is not known to me at present. I acted to remove the king, but because my planning was imperfect, did not gain the ultimate prize. I will not fail again.

Sethi met me at the gates of the estate outside Ta-senet and bowed low before me, hands outstretched, as befits a man of low status greeting his future king. The Lord of the estate was with him, I will give him the name of Mose for now, and he too greeted me, though with less ceremony.

"Welcome, Lord Messuwy," he said. "My home is your home, for as long as you need it."

"Thank you, Mose. How many know I am here?"

"Not many. My wife and children, of course, my overseers, and possibly some of the servants. Be assured they won't talk."

"Everyone talks," Sethi said. "Moreover, there are five hundred members of the Amun legion an hour upriver who will soon know of your presence. They followed me out of the city, deciding to follow you, my lord, rather than the pretender to the throne."

"Wonderful," I exclaimed. "They will form the nucleus of the new 'Loyal Amun' legion."

"Indeed, my lord. However, they are no match for the Ptah legion, and we are too close to Waset. If the pretender finds out you are here, he will send the legion after you."

"What to do then, Sethi? Can we defend this estate with five hundred men or would Ta-senet be safer? It has walls, after all."

"Neither, my lord," Sethi said. I thought Mose looked relieved. "You will only truly be safe in Kush. There we can build up your army until it is strong enough to retake the land of Kemet and place you on the Double Throne where you belong."

"What of Khaemter?" I asked. "He was once my friend, but Baenre raised him to become King's Son of Kush after me."

"He is still your friend, and while he may not support you openly yet, he knows you are the rightful king and will not move against you."

"Then Kush it will be." I sighed and looked around me at the estate buildings, at the orchards and gardens, green pastures with lowing cattle and fields of lettuce, onions and melons. "I will miss Kemet though."

"It will not be for long, my lord. Six months...a year...two at the most."

And so we set out for Kush after taking refreshment and rest at the estate of Mose. Sethi and I moved quietly and discreetly to where the 'Loyal Amuns' were camped and spent a day there organising the men. I elevated Troop Commander Amenhotep to the rank of Legion Commander and he raised men he could trust from the rank and file to be officers under him. Sethi sent out spies to keep an eye on Waset and the movements of the Ptah legion, but they returned almost at once with the news that Seti and the legion had sailed for Men-nefer with Roma-Rui.

"As a hostage?" I asked.

"No, Great One. It seemed as if he went willingly."

I dismissed the spy and turned to Sethi. "Has he deserted my cause?"

"I think not. He has ever hated the House of Ramesses for spurning Amun and Amun's City..."

"Not something I will do when I am king."

"Quite. As I was saying, I don't know why he has gone north with the pretender, but I will lay odds it is to his, and our, advantage. What it does mean though, in the short term, is that we cannot look to Waset as a place of safety. With Roma-Rui gone, Neferronpet rules, assisted by Second Prophet Bakenkhons and Legion Commander Merenkhons."

"Will they come after us?"

"I doubt it."

With that, we marched south for Kush. Or at least, my legion marched while I sailed upriver, keeping pace with their slow progress along the western shore. It has been many years since I lived in the north, in the flat and fertile lands where the Great River splits into branches leading down to the Salt Sea. It is a pleasant land, I admit, but my home is in the south now. The river narrows and the cliffs loom closer. Fields and orchards crowd in upon the life-giving waters and the heat and light from the god Re are fiercer. I think the harsher climate produces a hardier people, and I will need an army of such hardy people if I am ever to wrest the kingdoms from the hand of my younger brother.

And so we came to the island of Abu on the northern border of Kush. Its rounded grey rocks so reminiscent of the great beast Abu that bears great tusks of ivory, greeted me as if a traveller returning home. There is a fort on Abu, though, and a garrison of Kushite soldiers under a Kemetu governor, and I was unsure of my welcome here. My five hundred men would probably prevail if it came to a fight, but I would rather not test the issue.

Governor Tarkahe sent out a boat when mine appeared, bearing an envoy and an order to land on the island and present myself. Sethi confronted the envoy on my behalf, though the envoy looked uncertainly at Sethi and me standing side by side.

"My lord Messuwy is King's Son of Kush," Sethi said. "Your commander insults him by ordering him into his presence as if he was a common man."

The envoy stared at Sethi with a half-smile on his face. "I understood Khaemter was now King's Son of Kush."

"Lord Messuwy is Son of the King's Body and rightful ruler of the Two Kingdoms."

"King Baenre has ascended to Re? We had not heard anything more than rumours."

"He has, this month past."

"Prince Seti is Heir, is he not?"

"That is a matter of dispute. By right of birth, Messuwy is true heir and will shortly take up his throne."

"Yet here he is fleeing to Kush from Kemet."

"We flee from no man," Sethi said hotly. "We come south only to gather an army with which to defeat the usurper. Governor Tarkahe would do well to remember who the rightful king in these southern lands is."

The envoy opened the pouch at his belt and took out two sealed letters. He look at first one then the other, and put one back in his pouch. "Governor Tarkahe bade me give you one of these letters depending on your response to his summons. This is now the one I must deliver into your hands." He held out the letter to me, and when I made no move to take it, to Sethi.

Sethi took it, broke the seal and read it.

"What does it say?" I asked.

"Governor Tarkahe to Lord Messuwy," Sethi read. "I cannot prevent your passage south, nor would I desire to. I will await your return and place the garrison of Abu, two hundred men, at your disposal when you do. May the gods speed you on your path, one that will surely lead you to your rightful place on the Double Throne of Kemet."

"What does the other letter say?" I asked the envoy.

The envoy bowed low to me, and then turned and climbed back down to his small vessel. Soon, it was scudding back to the island of Abu, and Sethi gave the signal for us to resume our voyage.

The first cataract is not far above Abu, where the river is squeezed between rocky walls and the sound of the cascading waters sounds like the roaring of lions. It was impossible to navigate up the cataract, but Sethi deployed our men and, hauling on stout ropes, brought the boat to the calmer waters of the river within northern Kush.

Here we found Khaemter, King's Son of Kush, blocking the road south, the Kushite legion standing resolute at his back. It was pointless to sail past him, for that would mean leaving my men behind, so we disembarked and advanced on the Kushite legion in battle array, prepared for anything. In theory, Khaemter was my friend, but he was also a royal appointee, and may have decided to uphold my brother's claim. If that was the case, my struggle was over before it even began, for we were outnumbered three to one.

We halted a hundred paces from the Kushite legion, and Khaemter advanced to meet us. Ten paces away he halted and stared piercingly at me before dropping to his knees and holding his arms out in supplication.

"Welcome, Messuwy, Lord of the Two Lands. Kush waits to do your bidding."

I smiled and, advancing, raised him to his feet and embraced him. The two legions, Loyal Amun and Kushite, cheered, and beat the hafts of their spears on their leather shields. I had come home to Kush, and soon I would hurl my army northward to conquer my brother.

Chapter 7
Year 1 of Userkheperure Seti

Baenre Merenptah lay dreaming in the House of Purification in Men-nefer, his body stripped of every vestige of moisture by the natron bath and packed with costly aromatic spices and resins. His vital organs had been taken from his body and stored in four jars which would accompany him to the tomb, though his heart remained in its place within his chest and his brains, recognised as the source of the mucus that had drained from his nostrils during life, had been drawn out and discarded. The king would have no need of mucus in the afterlife.

The body wrappers of the Place of Beauty had taken the king's body and reverently wrapped it in long lengths of pure white linen cloth while priests of all the gods intoned prayers or gave the embalmers scraps of papyrus on which were written protective prayers. These prayers were inserted into the folds of cloth, along with amulets that also offered protection. Resins were daubed on the cloth to stick them together and hold them in place, and when all had been accomplished, the wrapped body was placed in a series of gilded coffins, each fitting snugly inside the next largest, every coffin a work of great beauty and wealth.

At last the old king was ready to face eternity and was loaded, with great ceremony, aboard the Royal Barge 'Wisdom of Ptah' for the king's last earthly voyage upriver to the dry valley known as Ta-sekhet-ma'at, the Great Field, where his tomb lay ready for him. Many people accompanied the old king, for there were many ceremonies yet to be conducted. Prince Seti, as Heir, remained beside his father, and made offerings to Re at the dawn of each day on his behalf, while priests of Re and Ptah offered up many prayers, dinning the ears of gods continually. Nobles, and lesser members of the royal family, followed in other boats, while the common folk gathered on the banks of the Great River to watch the flotilla of boats cruise slowly upriver, their sails outspread and catching the prevailing northerly winds.

The ornate coffin enclosing the dead king was offloaded on the western funerary docks opposite the city of Waset. The city walls were bare, all the banners that normally adorned them or flew from above the gates of from the tall pylons of the temples, having been removed. A great gilded sledge, drawn by teams of oxen, hauled the body up into the dry valleys where soldiers guarded the Great Field wherein the kings of Kemet slept. Teams of masons waited by the tomb prepared for Baenre, the wooden door jambs of the tomb's many chambers and sloping corridors having been removed so the huge stone sarcophagi, four in number, could be hauled into place within the burial chamber. The masons put the finishing touches to blocks of stone that were crafted to dove-tail with each other and could be rapidly installed in place of the missing door jambs.

The coffin was offloaded and eased down the first flight of stairs and into the first descending corridor. Every trace of dust and rubble had been removed, soot from the ceilings where years of smoking torches and oil lamps had left their marks scrubbed off, and the painted and carved inscriptions and pictures touched up so the colours gleamed brightly in the light of the torches brought into the tomb for the last time.

Deep into the tomb the procession passed. Servants scurried to finish the last little touches, adding small items, dusting the funeral furniture, rearranging fresh food and drink on the offering tables. Rich wines, roasted meats, freshly baked bread, fruit and vegetables in abundance were prepared and placed within the tomb so the dead king would not hunger or thirst, nor lack for any of the worldly goods he had enjoyed during life.

The gilded coffin was raised high and then lowered into the nested stone sarcophagi, the lid of each being raised and slid into place, offering the dead king layers of security so none could possibly disturb his slumber. Seti moved back to the chamber where the Ka statue stood, a representation of his dead father, and watched as the priests of the main gods, Amun, Re, Ptah, Asar and Anapa, washed the statue with pure river water. Lustrations of sacred oil followed, while prayers were chanted and incense burned.

Then Bakenkhons, acting Hem-netjer of Amun, handed Seti a forked instrument of rose quartz. Seti took the Pesheskef and held it to the lips of the Ka statue, uttering the ancient prayers for the opening of the mouth. An adze made of the blue sky metal followed, the Seb Ur sceptre, held to the lips of the statue, and lastly the Ur Hekau sceptre.

Now that the dead king's mouth had been opened, the Ka of Baenre could return from the underworld and partake of the spirit of the physical food and drink offerings left in the tomb. The burial party withdrew from the tomb, leaving the torches behind to gutter and die in the silent chambers. The masons fitted the new stone door jambs, the doors were closed, bricked up and layered with mortar and sealed one by one, the mourners slowly ascending back to the world of life that lay above. The final doors were sealed and the descending shaft filled with rubble.

The funeral party made its way back to the green and growing world of life from the dry barren valleys of the Great Field, hurrying back to take care of the necessities of life, officials and soldiers to their duties, priests to their temples and sacrifices, and the masons to their village at the entrance of Ta-sekhet-ma'at, where they would prepare themselves for their next tomb.

Seti drew Neferronpet and Bakenkhons to one side, ignoring the soldiers of his personal guard who stood nearby.

"Any word of Messuwy?" he asked.

"Fled to Kush, it seems," Neferronpet replied. "I send word to Khaemter, but he says he has not seen your brother or the men who accompanied him." The Tjaty snorted. "How he can fail to find five hundred men using the King's Road into Kush baffles me."

"Perhaps Khaemter is not as loyal as he claims to be."

"Will you recall him? Or dismiss him?"

"I haven't decided. If he really is loyal to Messuwy, then removing him from office might precipitate open rebellion. I don't want that."

"You can't afford to ignore it."

"And I won't," Seti said sharply. "I have other things to concern me right now, like my coronation. I am king already but I must be seen to be accepted by the gods. Is all in readiness, Bakenkhons?"

"Yes, Son of Re, but... would it not be better to wait for Roma-Rui to return to Waset? He is much more experienced..."

"And a lot less loyal," Seti finished. "I want you, Bakenkhons, so just do it."

"As you command, Son of Re."

The three men started walking back down to the road where chariots awaited them, the soldiers tramping along beside them.

"Have you decided on your throne names?" Neferronpet asked.

Seti nodded. "I intend to honour Re and Ptah."

"Not Amun?" Bakenkhons asked.

"Not if I'm ruling from Men-nefer." Seti grimaced. "I have no great quarrel with Amun or Waset, but my heart is in the north and my royal names will reflect that. Userkheperure Setepenre Seti Meryenptah."

"Powerful are the manifestations of Re, the chosen one of Re, Seti, beloved of Ptah," Neferronpet murmured. "That will gnaw at the liver of the priests of Amun. No offence, Bakenkhons."

The acting Hem-netjer of Amun kept his tongue silent and his face impassive, bowing his head to the inevitability of the king's decision.

"Day after tomorrow then?" Seti asked.

"That is the most auspicious day, Son of Re."

"Then open up the granaries and slaughter cattle, Neferronpet, brew beer and open up the wine jars. Let us give the people of Waset something to remember."

"May I remind you that Waset is but one city? If you are this generous everywhere, you will soon strip the royal treasury."

"Hmm, a good point. Tell the nobles then that I expect them to give of their wealth in celebration of my coronation. Note down the names of any that are slow to give or stingy."

"It shall be done, Son of Re," Neferronpet said with a smile.

The ceremonies of the coronation were designed to lower the king to the level of a commoner before raising him to the level of a god on earth. Seti stood outside the Great Temple of Amun in Waset, clad only in a simple linen kilt, his feet bare in the dust still cool from the night, and the shadow of the pylon chilling his body. He had fasted since the previous night and would eat nothing until the feast that night, but he thrust the pangs of hunger and thirst to one side and concentrated on the gateway ahead of him where he saw movement in its shadowed depths.

Horns sounded deep within the temple complex and Seti strode forward, his bare feet kicking up the dust as he passed through the gateway of the pylon into the courtyard beyond. The early morning light had not yet turned the courtyard into the furnace it would later become, but the sun's rays struck his shaved head with pleasant warmth. Priests awaited him in the courtyard, crowds of them of every god of the multitudes that guided the land of Kemet. Priests of Amun predominated within this precinct of Amun, but Seti could see those of Ptah and Geb, Set and Re, and the sight warmed his heart. The nobility of Kemet stood to one side, men and women, to watch the cleansing and elevation of this son of Baenre. Later, the common people would be let in to acclaim and celebrate the presence of the god-on-earth.

Bakenkhons stepped out from amongst the priests of Amun and led Seti to the Lake of Cleansing, a large shallow pool of water off to one side. Standing knee-deep in the cool water, Seti allowed his kilt to be stripped from him and he stood naked before the mass of people. Now four gods drew near, men dressed as gods, but in the context of the holy place it was as if the gods themselves walked the land.

Djehuti, face masked with an ibis beak, stepped down into the water, his robes clinging to his legs, dipped a golden vessel into the clear water of the sacred pool and straightened, facing the young king at the southern end of the pool. The god-priest Set was next, his masked face drawn out into a curved muzzle with erect ears. He dipped his golden vessel and faced the king from the northern end. He was followed by falcon-beaked Heru Behutet who took up his position in the east, and Heru Dunawy, also hawk-headed, who faced the king from the west.

"The water of divine life transforms man to god," Djehuti said, his voice muffled by the mask. "Enter into the presence of the gods and be welcome." He lifted the golden vessel and poured a stream of pure water over Seti's head. One by one, the other god-priests drew close, uttered the same words and likewise poured the water of cleansing over the young king.

Priests waded into the pool and guided Seti out, drying him with clean linen and dressing him in linen that had never yet touched the body of man. Two other priests, representing the gods Atum and Heru of the Horizon took him by the hands and guided him forward, into the Hall of Jubilation. The light from many torches shone in the darkness of the hall, reflecting off the beaten electrum sides of two tall obelisks, dazzling his eyes. Seti looked away into the dim recesses where rows of papyrus ribbed columns marched into the shadows. Released by the two god-priests, Seti walked alone to a great pavilion of stone in the northern part of the Hall, the Per-neser or House of the Flame. Here other gods in the guise of men greeted him, raising aloft hymns of joy as the newest god, the divine king of Kemet, was welcomed into their midst.

Exiting from the northern pavilion, Seti crossed the floor of the great Hall of Jubilation to the southern side where another stone pavilion loomed. The inside was dark with only a single torch to dispel the gloom. Shadows leapt and danced and scales rasped against the stone floor as Wadjet, the cobra protector of the kings of Kemet emerged from her shrine. The snake approached, its glittering eyes black and expressionless, its tongue flickering as it tasted the air, seeking any fear the figure of the man might exhibit.

Seti stared at the snake, knowing its bite was death. *Is this how it will be done?* he thought. *Will the priests of Amun encompass my death here within the god's holy place?* He stood still as the cobra reared up, its head swaying at waist height, its neck expanded in a great hood. It hissed, and before he could move, it struck. He felt the open mouth of the cobra strike his right thigh, felt needle-sharp teeth prick his skin, and fought back the cry of anguish that rose in his throat. *If I am to die, I will do so with dignity, not weeping like a child.*

The cobra withdrew a pace and reared again, but this time a figure of a man, a priest, detached itself from the shadows and slipped forward to stand beside the snake. Bending, the priest picked up the hissing serpent and draped its coils around him. He stared at Seti and smiled.

"Wadjet, daughter of Amun, accepts you."

Seti stared back wordlessly. His hand slid down to where the cobra had struck him, his fingers trembling slightly as they sought the puncture marks of the fangs.

"She struck without her fangs," the priest said. "If she had not accepted you, you would be dead already. Go now and take up your throne, divine one."

I... I have not heard of any king killed during the ceremony. Does Wadjet never use her fangs...does she even have fangs?

Seti turned and left the pavilion and was met by the Iunmutef, or Pillar, representing the god Heru. He welcomed the young man with a smile, comparing him to Asar, reborn from the dead, while an assembly of lesser priests watched in solemn awe.

"Welcome, Divine One, for you have died to your former life as a man and have been reborn as god-on-earth."

The Iunmutef took the white conical Hedjet crown of Ta Shemau and placed it on Seti's head, the assembled priests crying out in exultation, praising him as King of Ta Shemau. Iunmutef removed the white crown and replaced it with the red Deshret crown of Ta Mehu. Again the priests cried out, praising Seti as King of Ta Mehu.

Other crowns followed, the Double or Padsekhemty crown, the Atef crown of Re, the Seshed headband used on informal occasions, the Ibes crown, and several headdresses that represented the king's power and majesty in any foreseeable circumstance. Each time, the assembled priests cried out, praising their king. Finally, the Iunmutef lowered the blue leather war crown or Khepresh onto Seti's head, and left it there. He fastened a giraffe's tail to Seti's belt and attendants brought new sandals with figures of the Nine Bows, the nine traditional foes of Kemet, engraved on their soles. With every step he took, Seti would be symbolically treading his enemies underfoot.

Atum and Heru of the Horizon now guided the king deeper into the temple, to the innermost shrine of Amun, where the god's holy light glowed. The walls of the shrine were carved of rose quartz so thin the light shone through, bathing everything in a dim red light. Amun, ram-headed, and bearing the solar disk on his head, stood within the shrine and Seti gasped when he saw the god, his heart suddenly hammering in his chest. Then he noticed the god's fingers twitching and realised this was just a man posing as the god. He calmed down, and knelt at the god's feet. Amun leaned down and removed the Khepresh crown, lifting it and then replacing it on Seti's head.

"Accept this crown from your father Amun."

Seti backed out of the shrine and turned to find a hundred smiling faces. Priests of every god awaited him, and even the senior priests who had played the part of the gods had divested themselves of their masks and greeted him as men. They led him to a low throne on a raised dais in the open courtyard of the temple where thousands of people crowded in to view their new king. Five priests now moved to the front and addressed the young man sitting on the throne.

"Let Heru empower you," cried the first priest. "Your name in Heru shall be Kanakht Werpehti, Strong Bull, Great of Strength."

"Nekhabet and Wadjet name you also," the second priest said. "Your name of Nebty shall be Nakhtkhepesh-der-pedjut, He who strikes victoriously the Nine Bows."

"The gods recognise you as their son on earth," said the third. "Heru Nebu names you Aaneruemtawnebu, He whose victories are great in all the lands."

"Nesut-byt, King of Ta Mehu and Ta Shemau, North and South," cried the fourth priest. "Userkheperure Setepenre, Powerful are the manifestations of Re, the chosen one of Re."

"Sa-Re, Son of Re," the fifth priest said. "Seti Meryenptah, Seti, beloved of Ptah."

Complete silence hung over the forecourt of the Great temple of Amun for the space of three breaths, and then a swelling murmur broke forth as the listeners, the witnesses to the new king's naming realised that he had excluded the god Amun from his titles. Re, Set, and Ptah were named, but Waset and Amun would have no hold on this new king. His father Baenre had stepped away from Amun, and now his son had continued his action. The forecourt buzzed with conjecture as the people of Waset viewed their fresh-faced young king and the unhappy looks on the faces of the priests of Amun.

Userkheperure Seti arose and made his way to the processional chariot, leading the troops of the Ptah and Amun legions through the streets of Waset under the silent gaze of the populace. Once back in the old palace, Seti tossed his Khepresh crown to a servant and demanded wine. While he refreshed himself, Besenmut, Merenkhons and Neferronpet entered and stood close by, waiting until their king deigned to notice them.

"Was it worth it?" Neferronpet asked quietly. "I'd say you've managed to alienate the whole city by not taking Amun into your titles."

"I refuse to be bullied by those cursed priests of Amun," Seti growled. "I will rule by the light of Re and the wisdom of Ptah rather than the darkness of Amun."

"So you will head north now? Coronations in Iunu for Re and Men-nefer for Ptah, I suppose."

"And Hut-waret to honour Set. My place is in the north. I will rule from there."

"What of Waset, Son of Re?" Merenkhons asked. "Are we to be abandoned?"

"Never. I am king of both kingdoms, and I will return to Waset when I am able, or if I am needed. Build up your legion, Merenkhons, and keep a watchful eye on Kush, Tjaty Neferronpet. I have a feeling my brother will cause trouble before long. We must be ready for him."

Chapter 8
Year 1 of Userkheperure Seti

The coronation ceremonies that took place in the cities of Ta Mehu were an altogether different affair from the sombre and dark rituals in the ancient temple of Amun. White-walled Men-nefer was decked out in gaily coloured banners; incense burned in all the temples, and the voices of the common folk was raised in joy at the accession of their young king. No man living could recall the last time Kemet had rejoiced in a young king, not since the days of Usermaatre Ramesses, and everyone foretold a time of prosperity and glory.

The granaries were opened, and herds of cattle slaughtered, meat and bread and beer being made available to all on every street corner. The coronation of Userkheperure Seti was a reason to celebrate, and not just in Men-nefer. Similar ceremonies were enacted in the city of Iunu, the Place of Pillars, with its many temples. The gods Re and Atum presided over the rituals, and though the form of the ceremonies was similar to the southern ones, the tenor was different. Re as the principal god of the sun brought light and warmth in place of darkness, and Atum the creator promised new things in place of the old. Priests and commoners alike lifted their voices in songs of praise and joy, and not a few heads were sore the next day after celebrating heartily with the donated meat and beer.

The north-eastern city of Hut-waret, now hardly more than a suburb of Per-Ramesses, contained the main temple dedicated to the god Set, lord of the desert, of storms and disorder, of violence and the unknown foreigners. Dreaded by many people, he was not a god to ignore or avoid, as even the god Re employed Set as a counter to the serpent of chaos on his daily voyage across the heavens. Kemetu society was ever a balance of dualities, of the black soil of Kemet and the red deserts of Deshret, of the continual battle between Set and Heru. Moreover, the king himself had honoured Set by taking the god's name, and for that reason alone the people of Kemet would celebrate at Set's red sandstone temple. The drinking and rejoicing were slightly more restrained at Hut-waret for fear of disturbing the Ma'at of the Kingdoms by lending strength to the god of disorder, but people enjoyed themselves nonetheless.

But all this happened later, after Seti returned from Waset.

Tausret had not been happy to be left behind when her husband journeyed south. Seti said the reason had been her pregnancy. She had been quite happy to go with him as a voyage would not tax her strength and she was early in her pregnancy, but her husband would have none of it.

"I'm taking the full strength of the Ptah legion with me. Doesn't that tell you something?"

Tausret grimaced. "I'm no stranger to battle, remember. I should be at your side."

"Not while you are with child. I will not risk it."

"It is my risk and..."

"Enough, Tausret. In this you will obey me."

Tausret remained behind and governed Men-nefer, assisted by Tjaty Merysekhmet in the king's absence. Seti was gone a month and then returned, grim-faced, before setting out once more with the body of his father. Tausret had protested anew.

"He was my father too. I should be there for his burial, not to mention your coronation afterward."

Seti laid his hand gently on his wife's belly, where their child was just starting to show. "Now, more than ever, should you remain at home. Say your farewells to our father in the Place of Beauty and wave goodbye as we sail. Your duty is to carry my son safely for the next few months."

"And your coronation? Am I to miss that? Did you not once say I was to be your Queen? I feel more like one of the cows in your herd."

"You will be Queen, my love, but you will be crowned here in Men-nefer where people love you, when I return."

And so Tausret stayed behind again, grinding her teeth at the enforced inaction, and desiring more than anything to be with her husband in the south. Another month passed, and Seti returned, now officially as King Userkheperure Seti, and though a youth had left Men-nefer, a confident man returned, radiating kingship and positively glowing as god-on-earth.

Officials and the nobles were delighted to bow down before him, for Ma'at had been restored to Kemet, and the gods smiled once more.

Seti's coronation took place in Men-nefer, and on this occasion Tausret was invested as Queen, taking her place on a throne beside her husband, though of course on a lower level, and being guided through various rituals by priests of the gods and priestesses of Auset, Mut, Nut, Sekhmet and Wadjet. She was now addressed as Tausret Setepenmut, and bore the titles of Great Royal Wife, Chief King's Wife, Great Lady and God's Wife.

Her face was creased in a smile when she entered the royal bedchamber later that day and greeted her husband. She bowed and then burst into laughter. "Ah, husband, it feels good to be Queen and wife of the god."

Seti laughed too, and tossed the ceremonial Khepresh crown aside, taking Tausret in his arms and kissing her. He pressed up against her, but Tausret, feeling his urgency, drew back, her hand cupping her belly protectively.

"We must not, husband. You have already sown a son inside me. Start another and they will fight within me, for it is in the nature of boys to contend with each other."

"I have need of you, Tausret."

"And I of you, husband, but we must restrain ourselves until after the birth."

"That is months away."

"It will pass quickly," Tausret said with a smile. "You will be so busy making your royal progress in the north, and going through more interminable coronation ceremonies, that you will hardly notice the days passing."

"That does not help me today," Seti muttered.

Tausret hesitated, frowning. Then, with an effort, she spoke calmly. "Take a slave or a young girl from among the maidservants then, my husband. Take her to your couch and plough her field until you are weary and your lust is spent."

Seti's eyebrows rose in surprise. "You would not mind?"

"I am Queen," Tausret said slowly. "Nothing can alter that. What does it matter if a man, or even a king, scatters his seed among lesser women? It does not lessen me."

"Nothing could lessen you, my love. You are truly a Queen among other women and one of great beauty as well. You have a nobleness of spirit and..."

"Enough, husband. I know well the love you have for me, for we have shared it since we were children. Go now and take your pleasure with a pretty young girl, but do not forget our love."

"I will not be able to find a girl to match your beauty, my Mighty Lady. Every girl in the palace is ugly and hunch-backed compared to you. I will spend my lust on some hag while I think of you."

"Now you are talking nonsense, husband. The palace is full of beautiful women with the bloom of youth upon their cheeks, their bodies firm and inviting. Choose one of them and take pleasure in her, for you are the king and all things in Kemet belong to you. Just do not forget me when you lie with her."

"Never, my love." Seti kissed Tausret once more and hurried off, scarcely able to disguise his eagerness.

Tausret grimaced as she watched her husband go, knowing that ultimately she had no hold over his actions. As god-on-earth, he could do whatever he liked, within law, and every custom of the land allowed him to take as many wives and concubines as he liked. So far, he had limited himself to one wife, and possibly a handful of bed warmers over the years, but Tausret knew that situation could not continue forever.

"As long as I am always foremost in his mind," she murmured. "As long as he takes no other wife, I am content."

Seti left Men-nefer a few days later, travelling north to Iunu and the next round of rituals, leaving Tausret behind as usual. At the wharf, when she bade farewell to her husband, she noticed a young woman, a girl really, weeping as she stared after the Royal Barge. Calling one of her maidservants to her, she pointed out the weeping girl and asked, "What is her name?"

Her maidservant hesitated and lowered her eyes. "That is Tiaa, Great Wife."

"And who is she?"

"The daughter of Panare, the Overseer of the Palace Granary, Great Wife."

Back in the palace, Tausret sent for the girl and received her in the small audience room off the main hall. She had seated herself on the throne there, arrayed in her finest clothes and most resplendent jewellery, and when the girl was shown in, said nothing, just delivering a hard stare.

Tiaa entered and offered the correct bow due to their respective stations, but then stood and looked back at the queen as if she was, if not an equal, at least in possession of something shared. Her initial expression had been one of smug complacency, but the presence of the silent queen unnerved her, and she again bowed, waiting for the queen to speak.

"Your name is Tiaa, daughter of Panare, the Overseer of the Palace Granary?"

"Yes, Majesty," Tiaa whispered.

"Speak up, girl...and the title is Great Wife." Tausret stressed the latter part of the title and saw Tiaa blush and look down. "What did you think would happen?"

"A...about what, Maj...Great Wife?"

"About the king. He ploughed your field did he not?"

"Y...yes, Great Wife."

"You did not think to refuse?"

"No...How could I, Great Wife? He is the king."

"And my husband. I am Queen and Great Wife." Tausret stared at the young girl a little more. "What do you hope to get from the king's act of lust? Do you think he will marry you? You are only a servant."

The comments stung and Tiaa's head came up. "I am not a mere servant, but the daughter of an Overseer, and the king was pleased with me."

"Of course he was, you silly girl. He lusted after a woman, any woman, and you just happened to be there. Now that he has satisfied his desire, he will not look at you again."

Anger flickered across the young girl's face. "Unless I am with child."

"What?"

"The king was most generous with his seed, and sowed my field most diligently. The women of my household are fertile and bear many sons. It may be that I will bear his son. A king must have a son to live on after him."

Tausret paled. "You dare to say that to me? Even as I carry the king's son and heir within me? Get out. Go!"

Tiaa stared for a moment, and then fled. Tausret scowled and called for her maidservant. "Send for Tjaty Merysekhmet."

"Great Wife, I cannot...send for him. He would have me beaten for impertinence, and rightly so."

Tausret sighed. "Then tell him that the Queen desires him to attend upon her as soon as possible in the Small Audience Chamber."

The maidservant hurried off and Tausret sat back on the throne to await the arrival of the Tjaty. She thought about the words of the girl and steadily worked herself up into a rage, one that was not confined to the girl but also encompassed the king. Unable to sit still any longer, she leapt to her feet and started pacing, prowling the room like a lioness. Merysekhmet found her like this a little later and bowed to his Queen.

"You are upset, my lady," he said. "How may I help?"

"The king has insulted me and...and I will not stand for it."

"May I enquire the nature of this insult, my lady? In my experience the king is not one to insult those he loves."

"He has taken another woman to lie with and may have got her with child. If he has, and it is a son, he will marry her and supplant me."

Merysekhmet frowned. "The king told me a few days ago to find him a suitable young girl. He said that you suggested it because you were indisposed."

"Does the whole palace have to know? And even if I did, he did not have to do it," Tausret muttered.

"My lady, with respect, the king is the Bull of Heru and a young man besides. If he desires to lie with a woman, it is his right. Rather than being consumed by anger, you should be thankful that he lay with a common woman."

"Of course you would say that, Merysekhmet. You are a man too, and you found this...this slut for him."

"Yes, I did, my lady, and I made sure she was not just a common servant girl, but a decent girl from a lower grade family. Not a slut, nor yet a virgin, but rather a girl who would give the king some pleasure and make no demands upon him. And, my lady, even if she birthed a son he would not marry her or acknowledge the boy. She is too far beneath him and her belly has been visited by other men, he could never be sure whose child it was. Nor would he ever forget himself so much as to put you away, Tausret Setepenmut. You are daughter and granddaughter of kings and

Great Wife of King Userkheperure. Your son, when he is born, will be king too. Such jealousy of a common girl is beneath you, my lady."

Tausret scowled and turned away, but after a few moments her shoulders slumped. "I am duly chastised, Merysekhmet. How could I so forget my dignity?"

Merysekhmet recognised that the question did not require an answer, so remained silent.

"I do not want to see her again," Tausret said after a short while. "She may be nothing to me, but every time I see her I will be reminded of this."

"Leave it to me, my lady."

"What will you do?"

Merysekhmet thought for a few moments. "I will find her a husband in another city. Someone who will soon make her forget her place in the bed of the king."

"Find her a good man. I would not want her to suffer on my account."

"As you command, my lady."

Chapter 9

Tausret speaks:

I am so angry I could stamp my feet and scream, but that would accomplish nothing and damage my dignity. What is it about men that they understand nothing of what passes between a man and woman? It signifies little that the man is a king and the woman a queen. A king is used to getting everything he wants, when he wants, but a woman, even a queen, must bow to the needs and desires of her lord. I blame it all on the gods. Atum is the creator and for all he is a god, he is still a male. Existing alone, he became lonely, but instead of simply creating other beings by an act of will, he pleasured himself as a man does and shed semen, from which Shu and Tefnut sprang. A little later he cried and mankind was born from his tears. I think this is why no matter what we do; sorrow is at the end of it. If a woman had been creator, things would have been managed much more reasonably.

But I blaspheme, and digress. I am angry because I love a man and he repays my love by dallying with other women. Oh, I know, he has every right to do so. He is King, Bull of Heru, and it is expected that he will plough many fields and beget many children by many women, but why must he throw it in my face? Tjaty Merysekhmet is a man and delighted in pointing out to me that I had suggested the king find another woman when I declared myself indisposed, but that is not the point. What was I supposed to do? I have already lost a child, and I do not intend to lose this one. Of course I had to refuse the king, but I could not leave him aroused, for men do stupid things when they are aroused. He had to relieve his lust so I told him to find a girl, plough her field and spend his seed. A suggestion from a queen, a queen who loves him. But he did not have to seek out a beautiful woman.

My grandfather Usermaatre had two queens whom he loved equally, many lesser wives, and very many concubines. Some people say that half of Kemet is descended from his loins, so widely did he sow his seed. I think that is exaggerated, but I know many officials in the palace and in other cities who are sons or grandsons or great-grandsons of that king. My real father Sethi had a single wife and loved her dearly and my adoptive father Baenre had two wives. My Seti, when he married me, swore I would be the only one.

Oh, I know enough not to be taken in by the promises of men, or even by the promises of kings. Seti has sown his seed elsewhere from time to time, it is useless to expect a prince or a king to be utterly faithful, but it is reasonable to expect him to be discreet. As long as he took a lowly servant or comely slave to his couch, I could ignore it, and when I made my suggestion, that is more or less what I expected. Instead, he, or Merysekhmet perhaps, chose a girl from a good, if low-ranked family, and took her to his couch. A servant or slave one can ignore, but the daughter of an Overseer has a measure of standing. Heirs have been born to such women.

Take the case of Tiye, daughter of Yuya. He was a landowner and Superintendent of the King's Oxen, yet King Nebmaatre took her to be Great Wife and Queen, and she bore the-king-who-must-not-be-mentioned, the heretic. There was a lesson to be learned there, but I could not expect my Seti to learn it while his mind was clouded by lust. Therefore I had to act.

I called the girl Tiaa to me and confronted her, meaning to shame her. One night with the king, though, had filled her head with all manner of foolish thoughts, as well as her belly with other things. She even suggested that she might bear the king an heir, thereby hinting that she might supplant me. For a few moments I thought I might strike her down, so great was my rage, but I realised it was beneath my dignity to lay hands on her. I sent her away and called Merysekhmet to me. He told me what had transpired between him and the king, and again I felt rage that here was another person seeking to influence the king to my detriment. I ordered the girl be sent away, and I knew that Merysekhmet would not dare to disobey me. If the king had been in Men-nefer, he might have dared, but he was away and she was just a girl.

A few months later, I sent for Merysekhmet again, and asked him what had become of the girl Tiaa. He bowed to me and looked at me with compassion in his eyes. Instead of comforting me though, his pity tore my wounds open once more.

"I arranged a marriage between her and the heir of a vineyard near Iunu," he said. "You will be glad to hear she is already with child, and will never return to court."

"Is she happy?"

Merysekhmet looked at me strangely.

"I do not wish her ill," I explained. "Just gone from here."

"She is as happy as any other woman, I suppose. She has a husband, a little wealth, and a child on the way."

"Then she is happier than me."

I turned away, feeling my grief overwhelm me once more. Only a month ago, I lost my son. Three times now I have tried to bear my lord and husband a child, and three times I have failed, a boy, a girl, and now this last time another boy. I was assailed with doubts. Perhaps Seti would be better off with another wife, even that Tiaa. It was an agony in my breast as if a bronze spear plunged into my heart, but I may have to encourage him to marry another woman. A king must have an heir and I have not been able to give him one. I thought about it, and I saw I was mistaken to insist on being the only one. I can still be Great Wife, but I must allow my Bull of Heru to rut with other cows and perhaps bear him a bull calf. I wept, for the days of our youth were over and the world was a harsh place, even for a queen.

Chapter 10
Year 1 of Userkheperure Seti

Userkheperure Seti settled into his reign and started mapping out the things he wanted to accomplish in the years ahead. He was a young man and he had no reason to think the gods did not mean him to have a long and illustrious career like his grandfather Usermaatre. Almost everywhere he looked in Kemet reminded him of the great future that awaited him, though some things were less than perfect.

Not least of these was the continued coolness of his Great Wife Tausret. He had returned eagerly from the round of coronations and display of the king's person to the northern cities and towns, only to find her little changed. She still refused to lie with him, despite assurances from some physicians that ploughing the Queen's field while the crop was maturing would not harm it. Seti looked for the girl he had enjoyed before he went away, but she was gone and Merysekhmet was unaccountably vague about what had happened to her. He sampled a few other girls whose looks or inviting bodies aroused him, but none pleased him after his body's urgency had been satisfied. Putting his desires aside, he sought out the Tjaty once more to discuss the nature of his coming reign.

"There are many things that will attract your attention, Son of Re," Merysekhmet said. "You must beware of spreading your energies too widely."

Seti looked at his Tjaty through narrowed eyes, wondering if this was some reference to the several girls he had recently spent pleasant times with. "What things?"

"I'm sure you know them as well as I, Son of Re."

"No doubt, but enumerate them anyway."

"Your role as High Priest and Lawgiver is paramount."

"That goes without saying, Merysekhmet. Tell me of the other things by which my reign should be known."

"First you must honour the gods," Merysekhmet said. "I have drawn up a list of the temples and shrines that need repair, together with an approximation of the gold it will cost. It is somewhat more than is held in your treasury."

Seti grunted. "There are always ways to find gold. Go on."

"Hem-netjer Roma-Rui has added a number of cities and towns that he feels should be consecrated to Amun. That will involve extensive building."

"Perhaps Amun can be persuaded to contribute from his own overflowing coffers. I had better talk to Roma-Rui, I suppose."

"He has returned to Waset, Son of Re."

"Good, I will be spared the trouble then. He is a humourless man who cannot think beyond the furthering of his god. What else is there?"

"Pertaining to the temples, there is the priesthood and priestly rituals. There are a number of priests who do nothing but suck off the teat of the kingdoms. We should have capable, hardworking men in the priesthood. You, Son of Re, as chief priest of every god, should set an example by cleansing the local temples."

"Yes, approaching the gods in praise is the greatest honour a man can have. The priests must be worthy. Have a scribe draw up a memorandum. What else is there?"

"The Law is also important, Great One. You are often in the law courts and when you are not, your Tjaty shoulders the burden. However, most laws have been in place since the time of Nebmaatre Amenhotep or longer, and need revision."

Seti sighed. "That will be a tiresome occupation."

"I can draw up a list of the ones most in need of rewriting. I can have scribes trained in each facet of the law draw up suitable changes for you to look over."

"Do so, Merysekhmet. What else?"

"War. The Nine Bows are restive, the Hatti, the men of Retenu, the Ribu, the Sea Peoples. Possibly even the Kushites."

"Khaemter will look after the south. As for the north, well, I need to exercise the legions. Have my generals report to me, Merysekhmet."

"There is the ongoing problem of your brother Messuwy. It is unthinkable that he should be allowed to get away with ignoring you, Son of Re. He should be forced to kneel before you and beg your mercy."

"You'll have to find him first."

"I am certain Khaemter knows where he is. My spies have intercepted letters that could be construed as a dialogue between them."

"That is disturbing. Keep a close watch on Khaemter and see if you can find out where Messuwy is."

"Of course, Son of Re, but perhaps you should send out a royal command for Khaemter to appear before you and to bring Messuwy with him. Have them swear allegiance or throw them into prison."

Seti thought about it for a few moments and then shook his head. "Messuwy is my brother. I do not wish to openly show my distrust of him."

"Khaemter then? You have a right to the absolute loyalty of all your officials."

"He is openly loyal, but if I summon him, he may decide he has nothing to lose by rebellion. I'd rather just leave them both alone for now."

"As you wish, Son of Re. On a related note, the production from the Kushite gold mines is down again."

Seti looked at his Tjaty. "Why is that related?"

"Production was low when Messuwy was King's Son of Kush because bandits plundered the donkey trains coming from the mines. There was talk that the bandits were in the pay of a certain Sethi, military adviser to Messuwy. Whether or not that was true, the depredations eased when Messuwy was relieved of command, but have now fallen again."

"That is serious. We need that gold for my building program."

"More serious if Messuwy is stealing it again. Gold will buy many men for his cause."

"There is no proof of that, is there? That Messuwy would steal the king's gold?"

"Not as yet, Son of Re, but my spies are ever vigilant."

"Send word to Khaemter that I desire gold production to be increased and that it is his responsibility to guard both the mines and the gold caravans. If he thinks I am watching, he may be more reluctant to let others steal my gold. All right, what else?"

"Your tomb in the Great Field, Son of Re."

Seti frowned. "What of it? I had that message when my father died that there was a problem, but a mistake must have been made. When I was in the south, I found out there had been no problem after all."

"You have some good masons and artists in the Workmen's Village, and they accomplish much with the gold you have allocated to them, but now you are king you should be spending more. Have the size and grandeur of your final resting place increased. It is one thing to be Crown Prince, quite another to be Lord of the Two Lands."

"I will discuss it with the treasurer, and the Scribe of the Great Field, what's his name?"

"Kenhirkhopeshef, but he's an old man now."

"There is nothing wrong with an old man being scribe. I think he was scribe under my father and grandfather, and if it is the same man, he will be experienced."

"That is true, Son of Re, but the men under him, the Foremen of the teams are at odds, I understand. One of them, Neferhotep, has an adopted son Paneb who often drinks and gets in fights with Hay, the Foreman of the other team."

"Is it affecting their work?"

"Not yet, but it is not a situation that can continue."

"I will look into it when I am next in Waset."

Tjaty Merysekhmet raised his eyebrows in surprise. "You are thinking of going south again?"

"Sooner or later. I am king of Ta Shemau as well as of Ta Mehu. I cannot appear to favour one kingdom over the other."

"Go in strength when you do, Son of Re. Trust no one."

"And what sort of comment is that on the love the people of Kemet have for their king?"

"The people love and respect their king. So do most of the nobility and priests. It is only a handful of the royal family members and high priests who bear you animosity. You know of whom I speak, so let me send the legions to arrest these men and restore Ma'at to the land. I don't mean just Messuwy and Khaemter, but the priests of Amun too."

"No. Those men must be given the opportunity to remain loyal."

Merysekhmet could plainly see that he was not going to sway the king, so he left the subject alone, turning it back to the northern borders and the more appealing subject of warfare. "You will have to settle with the Ribu and Sea Peoples soon, Son of Re, but the Kanaanites are of more immediate concern."

"Oh? What have you heard?"

"Rebellion, as in your father's time."

"Therefore I shall deal with it in like manner," Seti said grimly. "Though it pains me to kill men in such a dreadful way, it seems the

Kanaanites have not learned their lesson. What legions have we at our disposal?"

"Ptah, of course, near Men-nefer, Re and Set on the northern borders, Heru at Per-Ramesses."

"More than enough. I'll take Set on a punitive expedition into Retenu, impale a few chiefs, lop a few heads, burn a few villages, capture a few slaves. A month should do it."

"Very good, Majesty. I'll send a messenger to alert Commander Iurudef that you are on your way."

Userkheperure Seti set off a few days later with a squadron of chariots for Per-Ramesses and beyond to the legions on the northern borders. Before he left, he called on Tausret to bid her farewell. He was hesitant, for she still grieved over the loss of their son, and was inclined to snap back at any injudicious remark. It was useless him assuring her that he felt the loss too, because the truth was he had formed no attachment to the dead child and had difficulty accepting it as a real person. 'Unformed clay on the potter's wheel,' he had been overheard to say, and the phrase, carried back to the queen, had provoked a burst of anger and renewed coolness.

"I am leaving, Tausret. I should be no more than a month, maybe two if the rebels put up a fight."

"I wish you joy of them, husband. Take no risks though, for Kemet needs its king."

"As the queen needs her king?"

"Of course, my lord."

"Yet you still do not allow me to bed you, although you are no longer..." Seti shrugged. "I am sorry. I know you do not believe I...I do love you, you know."

"I am, of course, yours to command, my lord. If you wish to bed me you have only to say so."

"A plague on it, Tausret. That is not what I want and you know it," Seti snapped. "You took joy in our coupling once, and it was my delight to plough your field all night long, but you have turned our bed into a dry and barren dustbowl where none can find pleasure."

"That is just it, Son of Re. I am effectively a barren field for I cannot give you a living heir. Though you have promised to keep me as Great Wife, a promise I will hold you to, you must look elsewhere for the mother of your son and heir. I should not be angry with you for seeking your pleasure in another woman's bed, but rather than bedding common women, you should marry again. It would not be seemly for you to have a son by a common woman."

Seti stared, his heart swelling in his throat and tears pricking his eyes. "I do not want to marry again, Tausret. I have you, and my Great Wife is all the wife I want. Relent and be again the wife of my youth, for I want you to be the mother of my heir."

"I thought perhaps Takhat. She is family and Kemet would accept her."

"Takhat? You want me to marry the mother of Messuwy? She is far too old to bear children anyway, even if I did desire her, which I don't."

Tausret laughed, a sharp bark devoid of amusement. "Not that Takhat. Her daughter, and your half-sister."

Seti frowned. "That's right, there is a daughter, but I do not know her, for I have not seen her since she was a child."

"She is in Per-Ramesses and is sixteen, ripe for marriage. See her when you pass by the city and if she finds favour in your eyes, marry her and beget an heir on her. Then your son will be born of royalty on both sides."

"I don't want her."

"I am told she is beautiful and probably fertile."

"Tausret, we can have other children. Some couples lose far more than we have and eventually bear strong healthy children."

"Perhaps, but you must have a son and heir. It is essential for the well-being of Kemet. Marry this girl, have a son by her and maybe we can try again if you still want to."

Seti gave his grudging promise to see Takhat when he passed through Per-Ramesses and departed Men-nefer, he and his chariot squadron being ferried over the Great River so they could take the East Road. They raced along the road, churning up clouds of dust and scattering farmers bringing their goods to market, flocks of sheep and goats and herds of wide-horned lowing cattle. Any yells of displeasure were quickly stilled when the people saw who drove the lead chariot and they fell to their knees in the dust and waited for the squadron to pass. Then they set off to gather their scattered animals and pick up vegetables and fruit spilled on the ground.

The squadron came into the outskirts of Iunu toward dusk, and while the squadron camped near a well, and feasted on roasted goats bought from farmers, Seti set off into the city to pay his respects to the gods in their temples and to attend a dinner with Wenefer, the governor of the city. Wenefer spared no expense, entertaining his king with the best foods, the finest wines and the most talented musicians and beautiful dancers. The noble women of the city, both married and unmarried, vied for their handsome young king's attention but Seti's heart was elsewhere and his thoughts concerned only Tausret, so they went home disappointed. Wenefer had prepared a comfortable bed for his king, but Seti preferred the company of his charioteers that night, and the hard sand and desert chill of the campsite.

They drove on the next day and arrived in Per-Ramesses two days later, having camped near small villages along the way. Though Seti was eager to wage a war of retribution against the men of Retenu, he was curious about his half-sister Takhat and ordered her into his presence in the Throne Room of the palace.

She was slim and of medium height, with features that spoke of their father Merenptah, rather than of her mother, but she had taken care in her dressing and cosmetics to show off her assets. Entering the Throne Room in the company of an elder aunt, Nebsitre, she advanced toward the king and prostrated herself before the throne. Seti had not been expecting such behaviour and quickly signed to the older woman to raise the girl up.

"Do you remember me, Takhat? From when we were children together, here in the palace of Per-Ramesses?"

"Yes, Great One," the girl murmured.

"Tausret Setepenmut, Great Wife and Lady of the Two Kingdoms recommends you. What do you say to that?"

"I...I don't...in what regard, Great One?"

"She believes I should take another wife. Not a Great Wife, you understand, for my beloved Tausret is that, but a secondary wife. Would you like to marry me, Takhat? Live with me in Men-nefer and bear my children?"

Takhat bowed low. "As...as my lord commands."

"You do not want this honour?"

Takhat flushed and bit her lip, looking at Nebsitre beside her.

The older woman sighed. "Forgive the girl, Son of Re. She has been immured far from the court for too long and has developed an infatuation for one of the many grandsons of Usermaatre. It is a girlish thing and something that would have been nipped in the bud if we had known of your Majesty's interest."

"She is still a virgin, though? Untouched?"

"Of course, Son of Re. It is only an infatuation. She has seen him from afar and been attracted to his good looks, nothing more."

Seti nodded. "So there is no objection to the marriage?"

"None whatsoever, Son of Re," Nebsitre said firmly. "You do the girl much honour."

"And that is what you want, Takhat? To be my wife and bear my children?"

"As my lord commands," Takhat whispered.

"Good, then that is settled. I am heading north into Retenu to dispense justice to some ungrateful tribesmen, but when I return, in a month or two, I will take you as my second wife. I will leave her in your care, Nebsitre. Make all the arrangements, and we'll have it on the first favourable day after my return."

The Set legion was in a state of readiness for the king's arrival and Commander Iurudef immediately ordered camp to be struck when the dust cloud from the chariot squadron was first sighted. Accepting a flask of water to wash the dust from his throat, Seti rode with Iurudef while the Commander told him of the latest intelligence gathered by his spies.

"Five hundred tribesmen, maybe a few more, gathered in the foothills three days away."

"You have a plan, Iurudef?" Seti asked.

Iurudef grinned. "I do, Userkheperure, and one that I think will meet with your approval." He quickly outlined his idea and his king nodded his agreement.

Three days later, at dawn, the men of the Ptah legion swarmed out of the rocky hills and fell upon the rebel camp, yelling and screaming and beating on their hide shields with the hafts of their spears. There was some fighting, but as the Kemetu soldiers had unaccountably omitted to close the circle before attacking, the bulk of Retenu tribesmen streamed away to the west, away from the hills and toward the broad flat plains.

The sun was climbing toward noon as the enemy, having lost any semblance of order in their hurried retreat, gained the level ground, and the Retenu chieftains, emboldened by the legion's reluctance to close the gap between pursuers and pursued, turned their men to face the Kemetu. They milled around, regaining their breath and drinking such flasks of water they had snatched up before fleeing, while the men of the Set legion stood in a great semicircle to the east and just watched.

A cheer arose suddenly, and the drubbing of spears on shields sounded like thunder. The Retenu men grasped their spears and swords and stared at the legion, expecting an attack, and so were taken entirely by surprise as the king's chariot squadron, forty strong, swept in from the rear, slicing their way through the crowd of Retenu men. They fell in droves, men fleeing in every direction, cut down by archers, by the hooves of the horses and sharp-bladed chariot wheels, by the spears and axes of the men of the Set legion as they joined in the slaughter.

The dust cleared, drifting away to the south, and revealed the devastation of the Retenu hopes. Of the five hundred or more men who had camped the previous night, scarcely fifty remained. They threw down their weapons and begged mercy of the king. As his father had before him, Seti granted the ordinary tribesmen the mercy of a clean death, but he impaled the leaders, coldly watching them scream their lives out on the blood-soaked stakes set upright in the hot sun.

When the last of the agonised voices had fallen silent, Seti accepted a cup of wine and rested his men for half a day before they set out to burn the rebel villages and capture slaves.

The villages had been stripped of fighting men and when the first Kemetu soldiers appeared, the women and children fled, leaving behind the elderly and sick. Those who fled were hunted down and captured, while those who stayed were slaughtered and the villages burnt around their corpses. Before a month had passed, the Retenu rebels had ceased to exist as a free people, and their remnants became slaves within Ta Mehu.

Chapter 11
Year 1 of Userkheperure Seti

Userkheperure Seti returned to Per-Ramesses in triumph, parading his victorious army before the city walls and enjoying the adulation of his people. Hundreds of dishevelled Retenu women and younger children became slaves, given out as spoils to soldiers who had earned the king's praise, while older male children were earmarked for a variety of building projects in and around Per-Ramesses.

True to his word, Seti took his sister Takhat as wife. The ceremonies were simple as they simply involved transferring the young woman from her room in the palace of Per-Ramesses to the Women's Quarters in the palace of Men-nefer. Her maidservants would accompany her and would provide some continuity in her existence, but her status had changed. No longer would she be known as King's Daughter and Sister of the King, but instead as God's Wife. She would not be Queen, but her children by the king would be legitimate and could inherit. Seti lost no time in implanting his seed in his sister-wife's belly.

The governor of the Khent-abt sepat sought an audience with the king, and was welcomed by Seti in the Audience room of his grandfather's palace. Governor Piankhe was elderly, and straightened up from his formal bow with a stifled groan, wincing as a stab of pain lanced his lower back. Seti beckoned to a servant to bring over a stool for Piankhe, and bade the old man sit.

"You are welcome, Governor Piankhe. You have managed the sepat of Khent-abt most ably since the days of Usermaatre and Baenre."

"Thank you, Son of Re."

"Why have you come before me today, Governor Piankhe? Do you have something to report?"

"As you will know, Son of Re, your blessed father Baenre put the copper mines of Timna in my care. Since then, I have managed them well, each year increasing the amount of copper ore extracted."

"If that is so, then you are to be praised, Piankhe, for Kemet has much need of copper and bronze. Do you seek a reward for your efforts?"

"I am amply rewarded by the knowledge of doing my duty, Son of Re, but I do have a request."

"Name it."

"Recently, disease carried off over a hundred slaves in the Timna mines. Production will certainly fall unless I can replace them. I have found twenty able-bodied men from among the denizens of the dungeons, but I need more. I ask for slaves from your punitive expedition into Retenu, great One."

"The only slaves I brought back from Retenu were boys. All the able-bodied men were killed as rebels."

"Then give me boys, Son of Re, so that I might bring production up to the levels you require."

Seti pondered the request. "The boys are young and not very strong, Piankhe."

"Then they will eat less, Majesty."

"And no doubt die sooner. Still, they are only Kanaanites and sons of rebels. I will give you two hundred boys for your mines, and a squad of soldiers to escort them there. Where is Timna, anyway?"

"Thank you, Majesty. Timna is a valley on the far side of the Land of Sin, about a month east of here. It is a dry place, Son of Re, a wilderness where the only precious things lie beneath the earth, and water is worth more than gold." Governor Piankhe allowed a small smile to crease his face. "I have used the Timna mines as a punishment detail for my guards. It is not an assignment they enjoy."

Seti nodded. "And no doubt it is worse for the slaves who must toil within the mines. Well, no matter, there are always more slaves. Was there anything else, Governor Piankhe?"

"One small matter, Son of Re. The temple of Hut-hor at Timna has fallen into disrepair. Five years ago, the ground shook and stones fell from the temple roof and walls. I lack skilled masons to repair it."

"Why did you not report this before now?"

"I did, Majesty, to Baenre."

"I desire to have my works known throughout Kemet and even beyond the borders into the lands we control. You shall have skilled masons to repair your temple. I will send them across the desert with the slave boys."

"Thank you, Son of Re. May the gods bless you with a reign lasting a thousand years."

Ten days later, a caravan set off into the Land of Sin. Two hundred young Retenu boys were shipped off to the copper mines in the Valley of Timna, along with a dozen skilled masons, a donkey train carrying supplies, and a squad of twenty soldiers to guard them on their journey. Seti thought about which officer to put in charge of the detail and remembered one who had been relegated to palace duties in Men-nefer following the near loss of his sister to the enemy in his father's day. Perhaps it was time to forgive him and bring him back into active service. He sent for the officer, and when the caravan left for the valley of Timna, Ament was the officer in charge.

Ament cursed the day he had been born, and also the day his younger sister Ti-ament had come into his life. He had been quite comfortable as a common soldier in Men-nefer during the days when the old king Usermaatre had still lived, and even the first month of king Baenre's reign. He had been rising slowly but steadily up the ranks and could reasonably have looked forward to becoming a Leader of One Hundred in time, or even possibly a Troop Commander. Then the young lord Seti and the young lady Tausret had appeared and knocked him off the ladder of advancement.

True, he had advanced speedily for a while under the patronage of the prince and lady, but then Tausret had developed an interest in warfare and Ament found himself putting her in the charge of his sister so she could follow the army as it went to war. For perhaps the hundredth time he cursed his decision. Far better to have taken the Lady Tausret's demands to the king and let him sort it out. Instead, because he had been slightly infatuated with the young girl, he had given in to her nagging. She had been captured by the enemy but thankfully escaped, else his own punishment would have been death instead of just disgrace. Relegated to palace duty, Ament had worked hard to better himself once more and had risen to the rank of Captain of the Guard, but it was work that ate away at his spirit. He longed for the life of even a common soldier, rather than living comfortably within a palace.

Then the king had sent for him and for a few days, as he journeyed to Per-Ramesses, he had dared to think his punishment was over, that he would once more join a legion and serve the king on active duty.

"I am sending slaves and masons to Timna," the king had said. "You are in charge of the guard detail."

All Ament could do was bow low, arms outstretched to his king, and accept the assignment. He was twelve days out now, with perhaps another thirty to go, and he hated every moment. The road was hot, dusty and monotonous; and the men under him were either slaves, the dregs of the legions or skilled craftsmen who thought themselves too good to associate with soldiers. Every member of the caravan had to walk across the huge wasteland that was the Land of Sin with the exception of himself. Ament could ride a donkey if he so chose, but he preferred walking. The bony back of the beast dug into his rear and had caused him much pain the first two days. Thereafter he had walked with his men, though at least he only had to carry a skin water bottle and a curved copper sword. The other soldiers were also weighed down with spears and a leather bag containing two days' rations of dried meat, hard bread and a handful of onions.

Dust billowed into the sky as they passed, kicked up by hundreds of human feet and almost as many hooves of small, wiry donkeys. These beasts of burden carried mostly food, and water skins that were replenished at the infrequent wells that dotted the east road. The dust kicked up by their passage caught in the throat, irritated the eyes and chafed the skin where it lodged in the folds of their clothing.

The soldiers stood up well to the hardships of the journey, being used to the heat and dust while on campaign, and the masons, too, remained in good humour, having all the food and drink they required and a pace that was not too taxing. It was the boys from Retenu who suffered most, despite being used to a life of deprivation in the poor villages of their homeland. Coming hard on the heels of seeing their fathers and elder brothers killed and their mothers and sisters raped and sold into servitude, they stumbled through the desert toward an unknown fate. None of the boys were over the age of twelve, and some were as young as seven years and many cried themselves into an exhausted sleep at the end of each day's march.

The boys had started out bound together with flax ropes, but five days out Ament had ordered their bonds removed. Escape was unlikely in the wilderness of Sin, and anyone who tried it without water would die quickly. The only sources of water were the infrequent wells along the road and these were guarded. On the first night after they were unbound, ten boys slipped away. Ament ordered a pursuit, recapturing six within a few hours. Another two returned of their own volition, but the other two were presumed dead. Ament did not punish the returned fugitives, preferring that they mingle with the other captives and relate just how hostile the land was out there. There were no other attempts to escape.

Boys started to die on the twentieth day, just collapsing beside the road and refusing to get up, even when beaten by the soldiers. Ament had the weakest and youngest boys slung over the backs of donkeys and probably saved some lives that way, but they continued to fall aside. Exhaustion claimed some, while others just gave up rather than survive as orphans. Ament and the soldiers left the bodies beside the road, unwilling to spend the time and effort to bury them. On hearing about Retenu customs though, Ament allowed a little earth to be scattered on each tiny corpse, and sometimes another boy would mutter a prayer to one of their gods as well.

Despite the desolation of the Land of Sin, numerous tribes inhabited the wasteland, though some were little more than bands of robbers. One such was the Rephidim. They were three days out from the coastal town of Eilah when the Rephidim struck without warning. The first Ament knew of the presence of the tribesmen was when a shower of badly aimed arrows cascaded down on his soldiers. One dropped dead on the spot and three others cursed as they were wounded, while the rest struggled to haul small hide shields from off their backs and free up their spears. Two soldiers roared in anger and charged the Rephidim position but Ament cursed them.

"Get back here, you sons of whores. The rest of you, close up, shields to the front, spears ready."

The boys had scattered, screaming, when the bandits struck, and the masons cowered behind the braying donkeys. Rephidim men emerged, about fifty of them, about five or six with ill-made bows, the rest bearing a variety of hand weapons that bore more of a resemblance to farming implements than to weapons of warfare. Ament grinned when he saw them.

"See them, men? These are mangy bandits used to fighting farmers and women. We'll go through them like shit through a goose."

The two soldiers who had charged the enemy returned to the ranks shamefaced, while their fellows laughed at them for their lack of discipline. Ament held his men back, drawing the Rephidim out of the rocks and onto the road. The bandits seemed to gain in confidence as the Kemetu soldiers stood fast, and some of them started toward the donkey train, obviously meaning to grab what they could.

"Wait for it," Ament muttered. "Wait."

The bandits lost what little cohesiveness they had displayed and moved around Ament's small force, stringing out in a haphazard fashion. One or two of the archers shot off an arrow that bounced off the hide shields without effect. Others jeered at the soldiers, encouraged by their inaction and believing they were afraid.

"Now," Ament yelled. He led the charge, racing across the rocky ground, swinging his bronze sword. Behind him, his men lowered their spears and charged the enemy, impaling several and trampling others. The shock of the sudden assault sent the bandits reeling in disarray. Many fell beneath the bronze-tipped spears of the soldiers or their sharp blades, and those that tried to resist with copper axes or wooden farming implements were rapidly cut down. The rest fled, leaving behind twenty dead and another ten wounded.

Ament ordered the wounded Rephidim slaughtered on the spot, and set his men to rounding up the scattered slaves. The physician bound up the wounds of the soldiers and administered a few foul-tasting potions. A few boys could not be found, and Ament left them to their fate, not wanting to split his force by searching for them. He hurried the caravan onward, fearing that the Rephidim might regroup and renew their assault, but they had disappeared back into the wilderness.

Three days later they reached Eilah and the coast. A body of water larger than a river was a foreign concept to most of the soldiers and all of the boys, most of whom had, until their capture, never gone further from their homes than the next village. Grinning, Ament led them down to the shore and watched as they hesitantly entered the water and started to wash the dust of their journey off them.

"It's salt," yelled one, spluttering and choking after dunking his face in the sun-warmed water. Others tried drinking it, and added their chorus of startled cries.

Small streams debouched into the sea, flowing down from rocky hills, and though they were no more than trickles, everyone managed to slake their thirst and provide draughts of fresh water for the donkeys. When everyone had rested, Ament turned the caravan north along the coast to the town of Eilah. He had the boys bound again, not because they might escape (there was nowhere to escape to) but because the commander of the local garrison might think it strange that prisoners wandered freely.

Leaving the caravan to set up camp outside the town, Ament went looking for the garrison commander. He found him near the waterfront, bargaining with a fisherman for the supply of fish for his men. Ament waited until he had finished his transaction before approaching him and saluting.

"Commander, I am Ament, Captain of the Guard, transferring prisoners to the mines at Timna." He handed across the folded papyrus containing his orders.

The Commander perused the document. "You are a captain of the palace guard in Men-nefer. What are you doing transporting prisoners? Some sort of punishment, is it?"

"Probably, sir. Long story. I need to reprovision the caravan, but lack gold or silver to pay for it. The letter mentions credit..."

The Commander read the letter again and nodded. "I can supply dried fish, bread, some vegetables. Will that do?"

"Thank you, sir. Fodder too, if you have it."

"How many of you are there?"

"One hundred and sixty-three prisoners, young boys, twenty soldiers and eleven masons. And thirty donkeys."

"I'll have someone look after it. You'll join me for dinner tonight. I'd enjoy hearing about what's happening back home." The Commander waved a hand around at the town and the barren hills. "A three-year duty and only one year gone," he said with a laugh. "I swear I'm no better off than one of your prisoners."

Ament dined with Commander Meres and feasted on roasted goat, fresh fish, a passable bread, thin wine and a selection of local fruits and vegetables, while his men and the prisoners ate dried fish, coarse bread and onions, and though the soldiers drank barley beer, the boys had only water.

Meres pressed Ament for all the news and listened attentively as he recounted the death of Baenre and accession of the new king Userkheperure.

"You actually did duty within the palace," Meres said enviously. "I suppose you've even seen the king." Ament nodded. "And now you carry orders from him...given to you by his scribe, of course, but still to be so close...almost intimate...with the king."

"Actually, the king himself gave the orders. The scribe wrote them, of course, but Userkheperure ordered me into his presence and told me."

"He spoke to you himself? Not through an intermediary?"

"Face to face." Ament smiled wryly. "I think he enjoyed giving me the task. He's never really forgiven me for slipping him an egg with a half-formed chick inside when he was a boy."

Meres almost choked on his wine.

Ament related the story of when he had taken two small children from Men-nefer to Waset, all unaware that they had been Prince Seti and Princess Tausret.

"Spoilt kids are what they were, though of course, he's king now and she's Great Wife."

"And you knew them when they were just..." Meres laughed. "They were never 'just' though, were they? Fancy talking to kings and queens as if they were actual people. I wonder, though, that you're not a general or something by now if you mix with royalty." The Commander looked suspiciously at Ament. "Are you telling the truth, or is this just some entertaining tale?"

Ament raised a hand solemnly. "The truth, I swear it. As to why I'm not a general, that's another story."

"Go on, man. You can't leave it there."

Ament smiled. "For a while, Baenre looked on me with favour as I had looked after his children. Then he went to war against the Sea Peoples and Lady Tausret asked me to smuggle her into the camp so she might see what war was like."

"And of course you refused."

"I should have, but I left her in charge of my sister who was a washerwoman among the camp followers. The two girls left the camp and were captured by the enemy. Luckily they escaped, but of course I was punished for letting them be there in the first place."

Meres shook his head disbelievingly. "Why did you do it?"

"Lady Tausret...Queen Tausret...is very persuasive. She continues to look upon me with favour, but her brother the king..." Ament shook his head. "Leaving me on palace duty was punishment enough, but now it seems he is finding unpleasant tasks for me."

"Well, it's not too unpleasant in Eilah," Commander Meres said. "When you've delivered your charges to the Timna mines, return here and I'll see if I can find something to entertain you."

Chapter 12
Year 1 of Userkheperure Seti

The king returned to Men-nefer, bringing his new wife Takhat, who was already known to be with child, having missed her monthly courses. The news of her ready fertility had stabbed Tausret to the heart, despite having pushed her husband toward taking his sister as wife. Queen Tausret knew her duty, however, and was on the docks to greet her husband, standing under the shade of a linen parasol. She was at the height of her beauty and was aware of the many admiring looks sent her way by the nobility waiting with her. It would have been foolish to pay any heed to her admirers however, so she kept her eyes demurely downcast as the Royal Barge eased into the dock and a cheer arose from the waiting crowd.

A plank was laid down and Userkheperure strode down it to the stone dock, glancing back at the slim figure of Takhat as she was helped ashore. He then strode toward the Queen and accepted her obeisance before embracing her to renewed cheers from the crowd.

"You are well, Tausret?" Seti asked.

"Better for being in your presence, my lord."

Seti caught the coolness in the Queen's voice and frowned, though he did not pursue it further. Instead, he half-turned and beckoned to the slim girl walking up behind him. "You know Takhat, of course, though I believe it has been some years since you have seen each other. Takhat, this is Queen Tausret."

Takhat blushed and bowed awkwardly. "My...my lady, you do me much honour."

"You are welcome, Lady Takhat. You were no more than a little girl running naked in Usermaatre's palace when I last saw you, yet here you are wife to the king."

Takhat glanced up at Tausret's face, evidently hearing the sharp edge to her voice. Seti shook his head slowly, knowing the young girl must be feeling a slight thrill of fear as she realised she would now be completely under the control of the Queen in the Women's Quarters of the Men-nefer palace.

"My lord Seti has honoured me greatly by taking me as wife," Takhat replied. She hesitated, and looked directly at the Queen. "The king is truly the Bull of Heru, for I am already with child."

"I am glad for you, but do not raise your hopes too high that you will bear him an heir. The king has weak seed."

The courtiers within earshot gasped at the insult and turned fearful eyes toward the king. Seti gave no overt sign that he had heard the Queen's remark, but a muscle in his jaw clenched and his nostrils flared. He turned away and, after calling for a chair for his wife, strode off toward the palace with a few soldiers, leaving the women to make their own way up.

Seti called for Tjaty Merysekhmet as soon as he reached the palace and took him to an inner room where they could speak in relative privacy. Servants hurried to bring fresh linens, clean sandals, perfumes and wine for the king, ministering to his needs as he spoke.

"What is it with women, Merysekhmet?" he asked. "First they refuse you, and then suggest an alternative, only to be upset when you follow their advice."

Merysekhmet knew the king was talking about Tausret, but guarded his tongue, falling back on platitudes. "It is said there are three indecipherable things, Son of Re, the way of a fish in the sea, the way of a bird in the sky, and the workings of a woman's heart."

"I don't remember my father having these problems."

"Baenre was an older man, past caring what women thought. Put it from your mind, Son of Re, and no doubt their hearts will warm toward you soon enough."

"What do you do when your wife is upset with you, Merysekhmet?"

"I, Great One?" Merysekhmet smiled. "When Nefer frowns on me, or repels my advances, I buy her a piece of jewellery."

"And that works?"

"Not always," the Tjaty admitted. "A woman's concerns are for different things. A man has his work, the gods, and making a name for himself, whereas a woman has the home and children to occupy her time. Our own children have households of their own to run, and our grandchildren do not visit as often as we would like, consequently, Nefer is bored and seeks out argument as a finger seeks out a scab, picking away at it until it bleeds. Then a man's house is no longer peaceful, and he seeks to placate his wife with gifts to restore ma'at."

Seti frowned. "Tausret has no children, and Takhat's field has only just been sown."

"A royal woman has even less to occupy her time, Son of Re, for servants cater to her every whim. She needs something to take her mind off her troubles." Merysekhmet cleared his throat before continuing. "Perhaps you could take both wives to Waset when you go."

"I am going to Waset? Why?"

"Two reasons, Son of Re, actually, three. You planned on adding to the Great Temple of Amun, you need to inspect your tomb in Ta-sekhet-ma'at, and you... ah... need to make your presence felt in the South."

"I don't like Waset," Seti grumbled. "I always feel ill at ease there."

"All the more reason for you to go, Great One. Let them see you add to the splendour of the temple and be seen by the population and they will warm to you."

"Perhaps you are right." Seti sighed and thought about it, sipping at a cup of wine a servant had placed in his hand. "There's no sign of Messuwy, I suppose?"

"It is as if he has vanished from the Kingdoms, Son of Re."

"Well, that makes me happier, at least."

Seti worried that his two wives would be at odds on the long voyage upriver, and ordered that three cabins be built out of rushes and linen cloth on the rear deck, one for each of his wives and the middle one for himself. He was certain Takhat would welcome his presence in her bed, but he did not want to display any preference so he slept alone. The days were spent on deck, under the shade of an awning, with the sailors and soldiers busying themselves as if the barge carried no passengers. Seti dreaded the prospect of the two women together on deck, but in fact they seemed to have called a truce and spent their days in conversation, almost ignoring their husband.

The king, thrown on his own resources, engaged first the officers and then the captain of the barge in conversation, broaching a jar of beer to share with them. At first, they were reticent in the royal presence, standing stiffly to attention or sitting uncomfortably in silence as the king spoke. As Seti's informality and the strong beer took hold, their limbs and tongues loosened and they started telling the king about their families, their hopes and dreams for the future. Their tales fascinated the king who had little knowledge of the lives of common people.

On other occasions, Seti organised archery contests, loosing arrows at floating debris or wildfowl disturbed from the reed beds by the passing barge. The king quickly lost interest however; when it became evident the soldiers were deliberately losing the contests.

Seti ordered the barge to moor whenever they came across a town or village with a dock, and went ashore with a small company to meet the local mayor or elders. They were generally overawed by the king's presence, but warmed quickly to the presence of the two women. Seti was surprised at the high regard the common people had for Tausret and often stood back to allow them to talk to her. Takhat was a person of interest too, and when they learned that she was with child, Tausret told them, not Seti, they fussed over her and sang her praises. Seti started to see the common people in a different light.

He also started to see the land of Kemet differently. Where before he had seen river and farms only in terms of their worth, the towns and villages as sources of men for the army, and the deserts and reed beds as his hunting grounds, he now saw them for the things of beauty they had always been. Day after day he sat in the prow of the barge, the bow wave hissing and curling beneath him as they forged through the calm green water, driven by the northerly wind in the sail. Smaller craft, fishing boats for the most part, dotted the surface near the towns, sails spread as they crossed the Great River, or furled as men stood to hurl nets wide. A splash, a wait, and then the strands were drawn in, the catch pulled aboard, the meshes filled with silvery-scaled fish.

At other times, the barge ran alone past reed beds where wildfowl erupted into the air, wings flashing with bright colours, or white-plumed egrets stalked in the shallows searching out fish and frogs. In other stretches of the river, the pehe-mau wallowed, blowing hard as the barge came close and disappearing in swirls of green water. Crocodiles could be seen sunning themselves on muddy banks, slipping silently into the water as they drew close.

Sometimes, one or both of his wives would come and sit with him, and he would point out the wonders of the natural world that surrounded them. Takhat tended to chatter and found it hard to sit still, but Tausret would remain quiet or utter soft murmurs of appreciation. Seti found his heart softening toward his Queen and hoped that a similar process was happening in her breast. He did not test it though; content to sit in companionable silence with her beside him.

With all the stops along the way, the voyage to Waset took eighteen days, but Seti was in no hurry. He sent word ahead of him to Tjaty Neferronpet, and when the Royal Barge hove into view of the docks soon after dawn, there was a large official deputation waiting for the king and his wives. The women were whisked off to the Women's Quarters, while the king spent the day in a round of the largest temples and in meetings with merchants and local nobility. As a result he was exhausted by evening and ate only a little light supper with his wives before retiring for the night, sleeping alone once more to avoid offending either wife.

The next day, Neferronpet brought the Royal Architect Kadjedja with him, to discuss the additions the king wanted to make to the Great Temple of Amun.

After making obeisance to the royal person, Kadjedja asked, "Have you thought about what you want to do, Son of Re?"

Seti nodded. "My father once told me there is ample room in front of the main entrance of the temple for many structures. I agree with him."

The architect's eyes lit up. "A pylon perhaps, your Majesty. A towering edifice that speaks to all of your grandeur and the power of the god."

"That would be very expensive," Neferronpet said.

"Not necessarily," Kadjedja countered. "Mud brick with a facing of stone would reduce the cost considerably..."

"I am reluctant to spend a lot on the temple of Amun when so many other shrines and temples are in need of repair."

"Of course, your Majesty," Kadjedja said, "but..." He hesitated, biting off his words.

"But what, Architect Kadjedja?"

"Forgive me, Great One, but though repairs are necessary, not much glory rebounds on the repairer unless inscriptions are effaced and written over. Your Majesty should have new building, new walls, on which to record your deeds."

Seti pondered the architect's words. "And you, Neferronpet, what do you think?"

"Undoubtedly there is much repair work necessary, but I agree that you should also have something new so that the gods may see your piety."

"In Amun's temple?"

Neferronpet grimaced. "We are in Waset, Son of Re, and this is Amun's city. It would be politic to make some sacrifice to the god."

"I suppose so, but it rankles. Roma-Rui made no secret of the fact that he thought me an upstart and my brother the real king."

"Roma-Rui is no longer Hem-netjer of Amun, Son of Re, and Bakenkhons is loyal. Your building work is for the god, not his priests."

"Something new then, but not too expensive. What do you suggest, Architect Kadjedja?"

The architect thought for a few moments. "A shrine, perhaps, your Majesty. Close to the temple but not of it."

"Go on."

"There are many shrines to other gods within and around Amun's temple, your Majesty. Another shrine, or even two, would be seen as an act of piety, but need not show overt support for the priests of Amun."

Seti nodded. "I like it. Which gods?"

The architect pursed his lips. "You are named for Set, your Majesty, and for Ptah..."

"Ptah has a temple there and Set is carrying it a bit far. For some reason, people think a shrine to Set would bring ill luck. He is favoured in the north, but I do not wish to cause unrest by dedicating a shrine to him here. Think again, Architect."

"There are many gods..." Kadjedja started.

"How about the local triad," Neferronpet interrupted. "Amun-Re, his consort Mut, and their son Khonsu."

"That might work," Seti mused, "but they have shrines already."

"Then chapels to hold their barques," Neferronpet went on. "A threefold structure outside the temple, holding the barques of each god. The barques are currently housed within the main temple but a building to specifically house them would be well received."

Seti clapped his hands in delight. "I like it. So, a triple chapel in front of the temple, to the left of the avenue of rams, I think. What do we make it out of? Kadjedja?"

"I can lay my hands on some beautiful quartzite, your Majesty."

"All right, draw up some plans and calculate the costs. I will have a look at them in a few days' time."

"As you command, Great One." Kadjedja bowed low again and walked backward out of the king's presence.

"I want to visit my tomb," Seti told Neferronpet. "Tomorrow I will take Tausret to the Great Field. Make the arrangements."

"As you command, Son of Re."

The next day, Seti rose early and conducted the main prayers in the temple of Amun-Re before partaking of a light meal and setting out across the river to the western shore. Tausret accompanied her husband. Takhat had wanted to come too, but Seti told her to rest.

"The Great Field is a dry and forbidding place, and would tax your strength. Remain here and rest, for I will not endanger our child."

"It is a son, my lord. I feel certain."

"All the more reason to stay behind then."

The ferry sailed with Seti and Tausret, accompanied by Scribe Kenhirkhopeshef, a doddery old man who could only walk with the aid of a stick, but whose mind was still sharp and active. Kenhirkhopeshef was aided by a younger scribe, a grandson of his called Remaktef, who carried a basket containing papyrus, inks and pens, as well as a record of everything associated with the Great Field. Tjaty Neferronpet did not accompany them as he had duties within the city, but Commander of the Amun legion, Merenkhons and a guard of twenty men went along as a security escort.

Chariots awaited the royal party at the docks on the western shore, and these carried the king and queen in one, and the scribes in the other, while the soldiers ran behind. The road lay through farmland and fields before opening out onto a plain in front of the western cliffs where the mortuary temples of the kings presided. Priests turned out from the temples as the king passed by, bowing and offering up hymns of praise, but Seti did not stop, nor even deign to notice.

They came to a road paralleling the line of the cliffs and turned right, winding their way up an increasingly dusty road to a workmen's village surrounded by a low stone wall. The road passed by the village, but Seti ordered the charioteer to halt and he jumped to the ground, helping Tausret down as well. Kenhirkhopeshef took a few moments to climb down, and then hobbled toward a small group of villagers who had gathered.

As Seti and Tausret advanced, the villagers bent low, their outstretched hands almost touching the dusty ground as they made their obeisance. Seti signalled for them to rise and the Scribe of the Great Field issued the command through his grandson.

"Son of Re," Kenhirkhopeshef said. "This is the village of Sek-ma'at and these are the Servants of the Place of Truth, dedicated from generation to generation with excavating and decorating the tombs of kings and exalted persons within Ta-sekhet-ma'at. This..." he indicated a frail old man almost as bent and bowed as himself, "is Neferhotep, Foreman of the First Team and overseer of the excavation of the tombs. With him are his wife Wabkhet, his adopted son and acting foreman Paneb son of Nefersenet, and his adopted son Hesysenebef son of Anupenheb."

The villagers so identified bowed low again and offered up mumbled phrases of praise for their king. Seti nodded pleasantly, eyeing the workers with interest.

Kenhirkhopeshef turned to another group of workers. "This is Hay, son of Anhirkawi, Foreman of the Second Team, senior sculptor and fashioner of the images of all the gods in the House of Gold. With him is his wife Hatia."

Hay and Hatia bowed low and uttered their prayers for the king in clear voices.

Seti looked over the group of workers and beyond to the mud brick village where other men and women peered from the doorways and corners of the buildings. "Why are they not at work?" he asked.

"Son of Re, when they heard you were visiting the Place of Truth, they asked to be allowed to greet you." For the first time, Kenhirkhopeshef looked uncertain. "I gave my permission."

Seti nodded. "See that they make up the time they have had off. My tomb is behind schedule as it is."

"There is a reason for that, Son of Re," explained the Scribe. "Acting Foreman Paneb can explain better than I."

"Stand forward, Paneb."

The young man shuffled forward, his truculent expression fading as he confronted his king. "It were better I show you, Great One," he muttered. "It be hard to put inta words what make sense."

"Let this man and the other foreman accompany us up to the tomb then. Commander Merenkhons, I put these men in your charge."

The royal party continued past the workers' village and into the dry valleys that housed the tombs of the kings and queens of Kemet. The sun rose higher, reflecting off the sheer sandstone cliffs and piles of rubble that littered the dry valley beds, dazzling the eyes and causing waves of heated air to wash over them. They turned off the main valley into a smaller side valley that ran in a southwest direction. Dust that had previously blown away in the light river breezes now hung about them in a choking cloud as they travelled deeper into the Great Field, but fell away when the chariots at last stopped.

"This is it?" Tausret asked. "I do not see a tomb, just piles of rubble and a few holes in the ground."

"A tomb should not appear to be a tomb, your Majesty," Kenhirkhopeshef explained. He wiped the dust-caked sweat from his brow. "There are men who do not fear the righteous anger of the gods and would rob tombs if they could." He pointed up at the surrounding cliffs. "There are guards up there who watch day and night, but they are not always successful."

"So where is my tomb?" Seti asked.

"There, Son of Re," Kenhirkhopeshef said, pointing at a hole at the base of the cliffs.

"And what is wrong with it?"

"Please allow Foreman Paneb to explain, Son of Re. See, he approaches now."

The soldiers trotted up, sweating and dusty, with Paneb and Hay among them. The Scribe beckoned Paneb forward and instructed him to tell the king what was holding up the excavation of the tomb. Paneb nodded and started toward the hole in the cliff face. Seti and Tausret followed and Merenkhons barked out orders to his men. Some formed a cordon round the site while two ran ahead. These two picked up oil lamps from a niche beside the tomb entrance and, striking a spark, coaxed one of the wicks alight. By the time the king was ready to enter, several oil lamps were lit and casting a pale glow in the harsh sunlight.

"Follow me, your Majesty," Paneb said. He stooped and walked ahead of the king into the vestibule of the tomb.

"You might like to stay out here," Seti said to Tausret.

"Where you go, I go, husband," she murmured in reply.

"I fear I must stay up here, majesties," Kenhirkhopeshef said. "My infirmities will only allow me one more descent into a tomb."

Seti nodded. "May that day be long delayed. Send Remaktef instead."

One after the other, they stooped and entered the passageway, each holding a lamp. Hay followed, the junior scribe and two of the soldiers, all with lamps of their own. The sputtering wicks released thin curls of smoke, but cast a small pool of golden light over the rough walls and floor. Soot smeared the ceilings where men had worked with oil lamps in the past, and the atmosphere was close and oppressive, though the heat of the valley floor had been left behind in the bright sunlit world above.

"Why is the passage so cramped?" Seti demanded, his voice echoing off the stone walls. "This is not the tomb of a king."

"Early days, Majesty," Paneb said. "We carve out the form of the main corridors and rooms first, then go back and enlarge and then tidy up. By the time we finish, everything will be smooth and spacious. Then Foreman Hay's team take over, decorating the walls."

"How long will that take?" Tausret asked.

"A few years, Majesty. The plans are fairly simple, a northeast-southwest axis, gradually descending to a well, a pillared room and burial chamber. Side rooms will hold the furnishings and treasury." Paneb stopped his stooped descent and turned to face his king. "We knows our business, Majesty. We'll get it done for you."

"Show respect for the king," Remaktef snapped from the rear. "You can be replaced easily enough."

"Go on, Paneb," Seti said. "Show us the rest of the tomb and where the problems lie."

Paneb turned away and started back down the gently sloping corridor carved through the solid rock. "Behind us lies the first corridor; we are now in the second and soon...yes, here is where the third corridor starts. Doorways will divide the corridors, and of course there will be niches for funerary objects, statues, and other things." He stopped and delineated an area just beyond the third corridor. "Here is where the well will be dug, and beyond, Majesty, you can see where we have started the pillared room. Between the pillars, still only roughed out, we will start the steep corridor down to the burial chamber itself."

"All very good, Foreman Paneb, but where is the difficulty that is threatening to hold up work?" Seti asked.

"Here, Majesty, in the pillared room." Paneb crossed to the right-hand wall and held his lamp up to shed golden light on the rough sandstone. "You see this slight crosswise stain or discolouration? I believe it is a thin fissure, a crack in the otherwise solid rock."

"And why is that of importance?"

Paneb grimaced. "If we excavate further in this direction and it indeed turns out to be a fissure, it could wreck the whole tomb. We would have to start again elsewhere."

"Why?" Tausret asked. "It is a tiny crack, hardly visible."

"Indeed, Majesty, but a crack can channel water and water is the enemy of the tomb builder. Say we excavate in this direction and enlarge the crack, the next rains could bring a flood of water into this room and thence down into the burial chamber. If that was to happen while we were making the tomb, we could repair it, but what if it happened after his Majesty was buried here? Long may that day be delayed, of course."

"Of course," Seti said, "but I fail to see the problem. If excavating this side could cause a problem, then don't do it."

Paneb looked at Remaktef. "They are your grandfather's plans."

Remaktef cleared his throat. "Er, yes, Great One. My grandfather drew up the plans on the recommendations of the priests. Well, er, Great One, the pillared chamber is in the heart of the mountain of Asar, and the chamber itself represents the stomach of Hut-hor, from whence regeneration takes place. The priests insist that a chamber, an annexe, must be carved on the right-hand side."

"Why?"

"Why, Great One? Er, because the priests say so."

"Why must it be on the right-hand side, Remaktef? Is there some significance to that side? Does some god or goddess require it?"

"I don't know, Son of Re. The priests told my grandfather to put it in the plans. He did so, and the Servants of the Place of Truth carried out the work, but now..." Remaktef's voice trailed off and he pointed at the wall.

Seti sighed and shook his head. "For this all work has stopped? The solution is simple. Put the annexe on the other side." The king pointed at the left-hand side of what would become the pillared chamber.

"But...but the priests, Son of Re...and the plans."

"Alter the plans. I am the High Priest of every god in Kemet. I think that if the gods forbade it, they would have told me. Plaster over the crack and start work on the other side."

Remaktef looked at Paneb and Hay. Both foremen shrugged their shoulders, so the junior scribe nodded and said, "It will be done, your Majesty."

They emerged squinting into the bright sunshine of the valley floor, taking lungfuls of fresh air after the stale air of the tomb passages. Seti looked around at the stark landscape and the crumbling cliff face above and around his own tomb. He called his Queen to his side and pointed to an area of smooth rock a little to one side, where the cliff faced almost due east.

"I am minded to build a tomb of your own for you there, my love, so we can be as close in death as we are in life."

Tausret gasped. "My lord and husband, that...that is a great honour. I thought that I might have a small tomb in the valley where the queens reside, or at most a small niche within your own tomb, but to be close to you in a tomb of my own...thank you."

"Kenhirkhopeshef, you heard? Good. See to it. I want plans drawn up immediately and work is to start as soon as possible. And...are you listening? You will not skimp on it. I want this to be a grand tomb, one that will reflect the love I bear for my Queen."

"As you command, Son of Re." Kenhirkhopeshef and his grandson Remaktef walked to one side to discuss the matter with foremen Paneb and Hay, while the royal couple crossed to their chariot and the soldiers of the guard formed up around them to escort them away from Ta-sekhet-ma'at.

Chapter 13
Year 1 of Userkheperure Seti

Unseen by Seti or the ones accompanying him across the river to the Great Field was a man of non-descript appearance who lounged near the docks in apparent conversation with a woman whose dress and heavily applied make up declared her profession. He watched the royal party attentively while she talked, and whenever a person passed nearby, spoke as if he was engaging in a business transaction with her.

"I would want to spend the afternoon with you. I am virile."

"That would be a pleasant change from my usual customers, but I've already told you I cannot. I have an appointment in an hour."

"You make appointments? I took you for a street whore."

The woman bridled. "I am better than you've ever had." She started to walk away.

The man grabbed her arm and drew her back. "I can pay in silver." His eyes strayed to where Queen Tausret was boarding the barge. "Silver is worth an afternoon, isn't it?"

Avarice gleamed in the woman's eyes. "Let me see it."

The king now followed his wife aboard the barge and the two moved off toward the prow of the vessel. "What?" the man asked, his attention fixed on one of the sailors near the rear of the barge.

"Prove to me you have silver."

"I show you my wealth and you'll snap your fingers to summon a pair of ruffians to beat me up and rob me. You'll get if afterward, if you please me." The Scribe of the Great Field and his junior boarded the barge and the soldiers started up the gangplank.

The woman laughed scornfully and waved her arms about. "Can you see these men? Would I try a trick like that with so many people around? Show me the silver. How do I even know you have it?"

"I have it, and you shall have it too after you satisfy me." A splash distracted the man and he glanced toward the dock but saw that it was only one of the mooring ropes that had fallen in the water. The barge itself was easing away from the dock as the slow current pulled it out into the river.

The woman grimaced and shrugged. "How much silver? It would have to be enough to compensate me for my missed appointment."

The man checked the progress of the barge and saw that it was well out into the stream and showed no signs of returning to the dock. The sailor in the stern of the vessel raised first one hand and then the other in his direction and the man nodded in satisfaction.

"Well? How much silver?"

The man grunted. "I've changed my mind. I don't want you after all." He started to walk away, into one of the streets that led toward the markets.

"Son of a diseased donkey!" screamed the woman. "How dare you proposition me and then walk away? I'll have the Medjay onto you."

The man grinned but did not turn or give any sign that he had heard, and soon lost himself in the crowds that filled the streets. He turned down a street that lay parallel to the Street of the Weavers, and paused to watch a group of youths battling it out with staves over some slight, moving on as the first Medjay arrived on the scene. Pushing through the crowd, he slipped into a narrow alley which opened out into a courtyard, and knocked on a door.

A man opened it after a few moments and stared through slitted eyes before nodding. "What news, Montu?" he asked.

"He's gone across the river, together with the Queen, the Scribe and Merenkhons. My contact on the Royal Barge confirmed their presence."

"What about the Tjaty?"

"No sign of him."

The second man nodded again. "Go back and watch. Let me know if they return unexpectedly." He started to close the door.

"What about my pay, Mose? I have expenses."

Mose stared, his lip curling into a sneer. "What possible expenses could you have? You stand on a street corner and watch."

"It's hot out there, Mose, thirsty work. And besides, I had to promise silver to a whore to maintain my cover."

"What you do with a woman is your own affair, Montu, and you pay her yourself. That's nothing to do with me." He hesitated a moment and then said, "Go to the Fighting Dog tavern and have a beer. Put it on my tab, but only one, you hear? If I find you've cost me more I'll fillet you."

Mose slammed the door and turned back into the darkened house. He wrote a few symbols on a piece of paper, then summoned a servant and gave him the paper and some instructions. "Go to the house of Ahhotep the goldsmith and give him this paper. Into his hands, mind, no others."

The servant bowed and left the house, hurrying through the streets in the direction of the goldsmiths and jewellers. He looked at the writing on the paper from curiosity but could make no sense of the lines, so tucked it into his wallet and concentrated on his mission.

The House of Ahhotep was a grand affair with many servants. Mose's servant was stopped by the major-domo who demanded to know his business.

"My business is none of yours," the servant retorted. "I have a letter to deliver to Ahhotep from my master Mose, so announce me."

The major-domo held out his hand. "Give it to me and I will take it to the master. He is too busy and too important for the likes of you."

The servant shrugged. "Then he will not get his letter and will be angry. I would not be in your sandals when he finds out."

"Wait here." The major-domo turned on his heel and stalked away into the house, returned after a little while with a scowl on his face. "Follow me." He led Mose's servant to a chamber where a portly man in rich clothing sat with a lean man over a jug of wine and some honey cakes.

"I am Ahhotep," the portly man said. "Give me the letter."

The servant bowed and handed over the piece of paper. Ahhotep looked at it and said, "You may go."

The servant and the major-domo departed and Ahhotep handed the lean man the scrap of paper. "They are out of the way. Merenkhons too, which is a bonus."

"Good, though it's a pity Neferronpet is still in the city. He'll be able to mobilise elements of the Medjay and Amun legion."

"Not enough to matter, Lord Sethi," Ahhotep said.

Sethi got up and straightened his kilt. "I'll set things in motion then."

"Er, you will make sure my property is protected, won't you? Mobs have a habit of getting out of control."

"No doubt you will be compensated for anything you or the other loyal traders lose," Sethi sneered. "It is a small loss anyway, a temporary inconvenience at most, but enormous profits once the true king is installed."

"Yes, yes, I understand," Ahhotep said hastily. "I am loyal, never fear, Lord Sethi."

"Oh, I am not afraid that you will be disloyal, Ahhotep. You have much more to fear in that regard."

Sethi slipped out the back of the goldsmith's house and made his way quickly along the streets to the Brothel of a Thousand Flowers. A brothel was a place where men could come and go without a second glance, and Sethi had already organised a meeting with the leaders of various gangs of toughs. All they needed was the signal to loose havoc on the city, and Sethi was about to give them that signal.

Several heavyset men fanned out from the Brothel of a Thousand Flowers shortly after Sethi arrived. They sped to different areas of the city and, at a pre-arranged time, set their gangs into motion. One gang converged on the docks and set about throwing goods into the river, smashing holes in fishing boats and administering beatings to anyone who protested. Another gang targeted the markets, overturning stalls and smashing the crates containing wildfowl, opening the goat and cattle pens, driving the frightened beasts into the streets. Citizens were set upon in the streets, men being beaten and women molested, the perpetrators vanishing into alleys whenever the Medjay responded to cries for help. Fires were set, and soon the Medjay were kept busy fighting the conflagrations that sprang up all over the city.

The Amun legion was called out, but in the absence of its commander, achieved little. The Troop Commanders, lacking a central authority, could not decide on a course of action and limited itself to patrolling the streets in small groups but avoiding fights. Finally, Troop Commander Djau took it upon himself to report to the Tjaty.

"Rioting in the streets, sir. Commander Merenkhons went with the king, so there's nobody to issue commands."

"Who is responsible for the rioting?"

"Gangs, far as I can tell, sir. Setting fires and assaulting people. What should we do?"

"Why aren't the other Troop Commanders exerting their authority?"

"They only takes orders from Merenkhons, sir. In his absence, nobody wants the responsibility."

"So you came to me?"

"Yes sir. You is above Merenkhons."

"Very well." Neferronpet scribbled on a piece of paper, then inked and stamped his seal on it. "This is your authority. I'm naming you Acting Commander. Restore order to the city, without bloodshed if possible, but if you have to crack a few skulls then so be it."

There was some disagreement back at the Amun legion barracks, especially from Troop Commander Menkauhor, who argued that they should wait for the return of the king. It was well known, he said, that Merenkhons was in favour with Userkheperure and they should be cautious about doing anything without his express permission.

"I'm ordering my men not to take any action until the king returns and issues his commands," Menkauhor declared.

Acting Commander Djau promptly arrested Menkauhor and ordered the other Troop Commanders into the streets with orders to quell any violence by any means necessary. They obeyed, if somewhat reluctantly, and the presence of the troops allowed the Medjay to control the fires, gradually restoring order in a large part of the city.

The gangs turned to other targets, breaking into and looting shops and homes. Soldiers rushed to stop them and pitch battles ensued in several streets. Djau directed the battle, utilising the discipline of his soldiers, and showed that trained men could defeat a mob many times their number. Several gang members died, clubbed to death on the dusty streets, and several more were captured, being hauled off groaning to the prison cells. Time and again the gangs were thrown back and dispersed, but by the time peace was restored on the streets of Waset, scores of its citizens lay dead or wounded, dozens of shops and homes had been looted, and entire city blocks were burnt out ruins.

As the gangs withdrew, Sethi sent out other men to drip poison into the ears of any that would listen, hinting that the rioters were in the employ of the king, and that he sought to punish the city and its inhabitants because they were loyal to Amun. Many listened, and by the time Seti returned from the Great Field, unrest of a different sort was bubbling beneath the surface.

The royal party had seen the smoke rising from the city long before they landed at the Royal Dock, and Commander Merenkhons readied his twenty men to protect the king and queen. He also conscripted the forty sailors on board, pressing them into temporary guard duty armed with whatever they could find on board or on the dock. Forming the soldiers and sailors up in a protective cordon, Merenkhons hurried the king and queen through the streets toward the palace, very mindful that he was vastly outnumbered by the silent and sullen crowds that started to gather. He was very glad to see other Amun soldiers patrolling the streets and ordered them to follow.

Tjaty Neferronpet, having been alerted to the approach of the king, hurried to meet him and escorted him deep inside the palace, while Merenkhons set up successive rings of defences.

"What is going on?" Seti demanded.

"Rioting, it was serious for a time, but it's under control now."

"Why were they rioting? Who is responsible?"

Neferronpet shook his head. "I can't be sure, but it started with various gangs like the beggars, the watersiders, the street cleaners. Others joined in and started setting fires."

"The legion should have stamped them flat immediately," Seti said. "Why didn't they?"

The Tjaty looked across at Commander Merenkhons. "It seems not all is well within the legion. Not every officer wanted to act. I made Troop Commander Djau the Acting Commander and he got things moving."

"Make an example of these recalcitrant officers, Merenkhons," Seti ordered. "Remove any disloyal ones and if any acted in concert with the rioters, execute them." He turned back to Neferronpet. "I want to know who was behind these riots. You have prisoners?"

Neferronpet nodded. "I have put some to the question already. It is possible Sethi is at the bottom of it all. There have been some sightings of him in the city recently."

"See if you can find out any more. If they die during questioning, it will save us the trouble of executing them afterward."

"Husband," Tausret murmured. "Simple rioting is not a capital offence."

Seti scowled. "They rebelled against my authority, and that is."

"My lady," Neferronpet said. "The rioters burned and looted shops and homes and several people died as a result. Those are capital offences."

"But surely they must be tried in a court of law, first?" Tausret asked. "There may be extenuating circumstances. If they were incited to riot, then..."

"You are too soft," Seti snapped. "These rebels must be made an example of."

"Many were caught in the act, my lady," Neferronpet added. "They have no defence."

"Yet I worry that a harsh judgement may alienate the ordinary citizens," Tausret said. "They may have legitimate grievances, and that is why they rioted."

Seti opened his mouth to reply in a similar vein to his previous utterance, but drew his wife aside and spoke quietly. "Go to your quarters, Tausret, and leave these matters to be sorted by men. Your feminine soft-heartedness has no place here."

Now Tausret opened her mouth for a sharp retort, but controlled herself, lowering her gaze. "As you wish, husband... but remember the people of Waset are your people too." She bowed to her husband as king, and left the room.

Seti turned back to his Tjaty. "If Sethi is involved, then so is my brother Messuwy. Find out for me."

"As you command, Son of Re," Neferronpet said, bowing. "Majesty, while you are here, there is one other thing I would like to bring to your notice though I hesitate to mention it. It has no immediate bearing on the rioting, but I feel it is all related."

"Yes?"

"Royal Butler Bay. He has strong ties to Messuwy, being brother to Messuwy's dead wife Suterere. I fear that his sympathies lie with your brother rather than you. He is well placed to spy on you."

Seti regarded his Tjaty thoughtfully. "He has never given me reason to doubt him."

"And yet, if his loyalty lies with family, he could do great harm to you."

"As I said, I have seen no evidence that he is disloyal. In fact, he aided me in determining who had a hand in the death of my father Baenre."

Neferronpet nodded. "His finger pointed away from the South, and involved enemies of Kemet who were conveniently dead and so could not be questioned."

"It was a plausible story."

"Indeed, Son of Re, but you could get at the truth of it. Put him to the question."

"Not without cause."

"Messuwy has designs on your throne; Bay is his brother by marriage."

"Enough, Neferronpet," Seti said sharply. "I trust Bay. Now do as I asked here in Waset and leave the court at Men-nefer to me."

Chapter 14
Year 1 of Userkheperure Seti

A ment led his captives north from Eilah to the Timna Valley and took the road that led through the valley to the slave camp a few thousands of paces from the valley entrance. Here he handed them over to the Mine Overseer, a heavyset, hairy-bodied man by the name of Mentopher. The Overseer grinned and licked his lips when he saw the boys and ordered his guards to take them to the slave barracks and feed them. Ament evidently looked surprised at the humane treatment of the young slaves, for Mentopher leered and explained.

"There are some good-looking boys in that lot and they'll be much in demand. No sense in spoiling their looks by use of the whip. They need a bit of feeding up too."

"I thought they were destined for the mines."

"Some will be, but that is hard and dangerous work and frankly they don't look strong enough. The processing camps will take many of them, that's where we smelt the ore and turn out copper ingots. The better looking ones will work in the kitchens and such, looking after the needs of the guards."

Ament grunted. He did not like the gleam in the Overseer's eyes when he talked about the boys. Mentopher was obviously not a Kemetu, and he knew foreigners had some strange customs. He hoped that the boys would not be worked too hard, but when all was said, they were slaves and as such, had no choice in their fate. The gods had ruled that he remained a free man while these others became slaves, how could he go against the will of the gods? He nodded to Mentopher and marched his men off to the military barracks, where he reported to the commander there, Nebamen.

"Captain of the Palace Guard in Men-nefer, eh?" Nebamen queried. "Nominally you outrank me, but don't get any funny ideas, Ament. I rule here, and we do things my way."

"Yes sir. My orders were to bring the slaves to Timna, but having done that, I suppose my orders are at an end. It was my understanding that I was to return to Men-nefer, but my orders don't specifically say that. With your permission, I'll remain until I and my men have recovered from the crossing of Sin."

Nebamen nodded. "See the barracks quartermaster. He'll provide beds and food." A smile creased the Commander's lips but did not touch his eyes. "I can have a young boy attend upon you if you like."

Ament shook his head. "That won't be necessary, thank you sir."

"Maybe when you are rested."

Ament got his men settled, and after a light meal decided to have a look around the mine site. He asked for and was granted a guide so that he could make sense of what he saw. The guide was a local tribesman whose duties included the transport of water from the ephemeral stream that sometimes ran down the valley floor and the numerous wells that dotted the low-lying land.

"I am Zephan, honoured lord," the tribesman said. "Please to tell me what your heart desires and I will do it."

"Just show me round the mines and...what else is here? Copper smelting, is it?"

"Yes, honoured lord."

"I'm not a lord, Zephan, so either call me Ament or... or 'sir' if you must."

"As sir wishes. Will sir please follow me?"

Zephan led Ament away from the barracks and through the small settlement that had sprung up around the mine and its large slave camp. The camp was largely deserted as the slaves were hard at work during daylight hours, so there was little of any interest to see. A road led from the camp toward some low hummocks near the valley side, where many people milled around. Ament pointed and asked what was happening.

"The mines, sir."

"All right, let's start there."

They set off down the road that crossed the valley floor and passed through areas of rock, or scattered rubble and drifts of sand. Scraggly plants grew in the depressions, but the overall impression Ament gained was of a dry wasteland. Closer to the valley sides, outcroppings of sandstone had evidently been blasted by winds into strange shapes and tall columns. He stood on a slight rise and looked about him. Although the predominant colour of the sand was red, there were streaks and patches that were closer to orange, yellow, brown and black. An area off to one side caught his eye and he set off across the sand with Zephan trailing after him. He reached the patch and stared down at it in bemusement, for the sand held hints of light green and blue.

"I've never seen blue or green sand before."

"It is more common near the mines, sir. I am told it is because copper ore is close by; though copper is a red metal and why it should make sand or rocks green, only the gods know. You will see them bring out green rock from the mine, and then see how the green rock burns to give red metal. It is all very mysterious, sir."

"It sounds like it," Ament commented.

"Some rock is brought up with beautiful patterns of green and blue in it, and this is saved, being shipped off to make jewellery or if the blocks are large enough, to be carved into statues."

They resumed their walk toward the mines and soon came across streams of slaves, weather-beaten and burnt black by the sun, trudging endlessly from the mines with baskets of rock and returning empty handed. Ament and his guide earned a few tired looks, but apart from a scattering of guards who spared them a glance, they were otherwise ignored.

"There are only a few guards," Ament commented. "Aren't they worried they'll escape?"

Zephan grinned. "Ah, sir, where would they go? Except for the road to Eilah, there is only desert around us. Without water, they would die very quickly and with much misery. They know this and prefer to work until they collapse, at which point they earn a swift death by a spear thrust. You see? Everybody benefits."

Ament made no comment, but stepped through the lines of slaves toward the mine entrance itself. It was no more than a narrow portal in the solid rock, the edges worn smooth by countless feet and myriad baskets of ore. A wooden ladder descended into the depths and a tripod had been rigged over it with a rope by which slaves hauled rock to the surface. He edged close to the pit and looked into the dusty darkness lit only by a flickering oil lamp in the depths.

"You wish to descend, honoured sir?" Zephan asked.

Ament shook his head. "I can imagine what it must be like."

"I have been down there, sir. It is hot and cramped, with barely enough room to stand up. The sweat pours from you and you are assailed by cramps. You must chip off rock with copper tools, fill up the baskets and pass them back, your mouth and throat dry from the ever-present dust, coughs racking your chest, and every muscle aching. If you do not fill enough baskets in your allotted time, you are whipped; if you fill your quota you are fed just enough to enable you to go down again the next day. In a month or two, you die; but there is always someone else to take their place. Why, you brought many replacements with you, honoured sir."

"I brought boys, not mine workers."

"It is all the same, sir. A small boy is less cramped, or can move into smaller spaces. He might not have the strength to chip the rock, but he can still fill baskets and push them to the bottom of the shaft. If fate smiles on him, he might be assigned a task on the surface, fetching and carrying, or... other occupations."

Ament looked around at the slaves and the blank looks on their faces. Their vision could encompass the whole of their short lives at a glance, so where was there room for hope? Survival would be their only concern, and even then it was only for a short time. Zephan's words registered in his mind and he looked at the tribesman.

"What other occupations?"

"Ah, sir, you will have noticed there are very few women at Timna. The slaves have no desires left, of course, but the guards have the needs of any man. Your consignment of boys was very welcome to certain men."

Ament stared at Zephan with growing horror. "It... it happens, I know, there are always stories...but only between men. I mean, the gods Set and Heru also, in the temple tales, but... the boys do not agree to it, do they?"

"They have no say in the matter, sir. If they please a guard they draw extra rations, or are exempt from the mines and live a little longer..." Zephan shrugged. "It is not something I would ever do, but I do not face the choices they do."

Ament remembered the look on Overseer Mentopher's face and his remarks. A vague possibility of abuse had just grown into sickening certainty. "I... I spoke with Mentopher. No Kemetu man would force a child," he stated, hoping that was true.

"Mentopher is not Kemetu," Zephan said. "Nor are many of the guards, though some are. Guard duty out here is almost a punishment so anything that makes life more pleasurable is grasped with both hands."

"But you don't."

Zephan smiled. "My tribe is two days away..." he gestured vaguely to the north. "...and besides, I have a wife and children of my own. I could never abuse children like this."

"It is a horrifying thought. I... I must protest this. I should confront Mentopher..."

"It would do no good, sir. He has been placed in his position by the Tjaty himself and he has sole power within the slave camp."

"Commander Nebamen then. He can enforce..."

"Your concerns do you credit, sir, but Commander Nebamen keeps the peace and will not contradict Mentopher. Besides, he enjoys the company of boys himself. A slave's lot is an unhappy one, but we can do nothing."

"I could go to the king," Ament said.

"Perhaps you could, sir," Zephan replied.

Ament glanced at him and saw a pitying look in the tribesman's eyes. He was humouring him, not believing anything could be done. "You seem to know a lot about this situation."

Zephan nodded. "When I first arrived in Timna, I protested some of the practices being visited upon the slaves, for they were contrary to the laws of my people, but I was ignored, and when I persisted, threatened. I have no power here, sir, no means to alleviate their suffering. I think you have very little power too, and may meet with harm if you protest too loudly."

"I will take this matter before the king when I return to Men-nefer. I know him. He will act, I am certain."

Zephan nodded. "If I may offer some advice, sir? Do not say anything of this to anyone else here. If others believe you could influence the king you would never live to talk to him." Ament looked shaken. "Would you like to see the smelting works while you are here, sir?" Zephan went on.

Ament could not trust himself to speak, so just nodded.

The road from the mine was dusty in the baking sun, and the heated air shimmered and seemed to create black pools ahead of them that evaporated and reformed as they walked slowly up the valley. Close at hand, snaking queues of prisoners carried baskets of ore, or hauled bundles of wood up from the camp. The wood, Zephan told him, was shipped into the port of Eilah and transported up to Timna on the backs of donkeys. From there, prisoners took up the burden. Off to one side, Ament saw great domed structures made of clay, and it was to these structures that the bundles of wood made their way.

"Charcoal kilns, sir. The best fuel to extract the copper is charcoal."

Further up the valley were the copper kilns. Zephan explained that the kilns fouled the air, so they built them up here, far away from the camp.

Clay was dug out from the often dry riverbed to make the kilns, but these were very different from the ones that made the charcoal. While air was excluded from the charcoal furnaces so the wood did not burn, the copper furnaces required a steady stream of air to fan the flames, generating sufficient heat to crack and melt the pulverised ore. Giant bellows made of leather pumped air into these pit furnaces, the interior fires flaring a white heat with every exhalation of these huge artificial lungs. The men working the bellows were naked, sweat pouring off them as they heaved and pushed. Overseers kept a close eye on them, ready to encourage them with a tickle of the whip or replace them as heat and exhaustion drained their limbs. Small boys ran around with hide buckets and wooden dippers, providing the workers with water or splashing the charring leather and wood bellows where the heat of the furnace threatened to set them alight. Over this whole vision of torment hung a choking pall of fumes that caught at the lungs; a stink made up of burning rock, smoke, sulphur and charred hair.

"How do they stand it?" Ament wondered.

"Dreadful though it is, such tasks are better than being in the mines, sir."

"How do those things work?" Ament asked. "How is rock turned into metal?"

Zephan looked around and then approached one of the guards, explaining who Ament was, and the question he had posed. The guard called over one of the men working on a nearby kiln.

"This be Rabi," the guard said. "He be like the foreman for this kiln. Rabi, tell this man..." he gestured at Ament, "...what you does."

Rabi grimaced. "Youse knows about ores, lord?"

"Nothing," Ament said.

"Well, inna old days we usta dig a pit, line it with stone an' then make layers of charcoal an' ore an' top it with stone to keep th' heat in an' light it. Next day, after it cools like, we dig it up an' find a lump of copper with something we calls slag on it. We knocks the slag off, melts the copper an' pours it into moulds."

"Amazing," Ament commented. "Who would think these ordinary rocks..." he picked up and hefted a green-tinged rock "...contained red metal? You said 'in the old days', what do you do now?"

Rabi grinned. Despite his slave status, he obviously took a certain pride in his work. "Some sorta thing, lord, but now we don't dig a pit. We makes a big clay bowl on toppa the ground an' add layers as before, then tops it off as before an' keeps the fire nice an' hot until the copper melts outa the rock an' runs down inta the bowl what we made."

"How is that different?" Ament asked, trying to visualise the whole process. "It sounds the same except the molten copper is above ground instead of in a pit. You'd have just as much work making a dome as digging a pit and no real benefit."

"Ah, that's where youse wrong, lord, beggin' your pardon. Come an' have a look round here." With the guard's permission, he led them round the nearest dome and pointed to a clay protrusion low down, near the ground. "We calls it a nipple, 'cause it looks like..."

"Yes, I can see that. What does it do?"

"Th' pool of molten copper is behind it, lord. When we knocks off the end of th' nipple, the copper comes pouring out an' inta these moulds, leavin' th' slag behind."

"Most ingenious."

"Youse wants to see it happen?" Rabi asked. "This one's about ready like." He looked at the guard, who nodded. "Youse might wanta step back a bit, lord. It gets plenty hot like when we cracks it."

As Ament, Zephan and the guard moved back some twenty paces, Rabi flexed his muscles, spat on his hands, and grasped a long wooden pole with a copper blade on one end. He swung the blade, and the heavy metal smashed into the brittle clay of the nipple, shattering it. White hot metal sprayed out. Rabi screamed and stumbled back, dropping the pole, while molten copper that resembled a bright bar of the sun god's very substance splashed into a groove and ran down it into the moulds. Dense clouds of smoke and noxious fumes swept over the spectators, making them cough and step back, while the glowing copper ingots slowly dimmed.

"By all the gods," Ament muttered. "That was some sight. It was as if the god Re had stepped down from his solar barque and walked upon the earth."

"I think Rabi is hurt," Zephan said.

Other men were running over to where the foreman Rabi was rolling in agony on the far side of the kiln. One of them snatched a bucket of water from a boy and threw it over the injured man, drawing forth a shuddering cry. The guard pushed through to the fallen man and examined his cursorily, nudging him with his coiled whip.

"Stupid man," the guard snarled. "Your action will no doubt cause a delay in production. You and you..." he pointed his whip at two men. "Carry him back to camp and then return. Move!" He turned back to Ament. "A few scorch marks, but a bad burn on one arm. He might live, but if not, I'll have to train up another man." The guard yelled at the men still standing around and unfurled his whip. "Back to work, you sons of whores."

Zephan and Ament turned away, and a youth detached himself from a group of slaves, running across and throwing himself at Ament's feet, throwing his arms about the soldier's legs.

"Help me, lord, I beg."

"What? Get off." Ament shook his leg, and Zephan dragged the boy off. "What do you want?"

"You brought me here, lord. Please help me and my brother Jerem."

Ament drew the boy to his feet and looked round in case the guard was showing an interest, but he was busy getting the other slaves back to work. "I can't help you," he said. "I don't have the authority to free slaves."

"I unnerstan', lord, but please help me little brother. He's been taken off to be... to be used by the guards. I heard what happens to these boys from others here. It... it isn't right what happens."

"No, it's not," Ament agreed. "But I don't think I can do anything."

"Please, lord. What would it matter if Jerem was put out here with me? He could carry water and...and at least he'd be safe from those men."

The young boy looked like he was about to burst into tears, so Ament said, more to comfort him than in the hope of being able to achieve anything. "I'll see what I can do. Your brother is Jerem, you said? What's your name?"

"Ephrim, lord. From the village of Tanah. Thank you, lord; I'll pray to all our gods to bless you."

"Pray to them for your own sake, Ephrim. I can't promise anything."

"Here, what's going on? Back to work, you, and don't be bothering your betters." A whip cracked near Ament and he looked across to see the guard striding toward them.

Ephrim started to back away, fear on his young face. "You'll remember, lord? Jerem's his name. Please?"

Ament stepped into the guard's path and held up a hand. "Stop. This boy is coming with me."

Zephan frowned and plucked at Ament's arm. "Not a good idea, sir," he muttered.

Ament shook off the tribesman's hand and faced the guard. "This boy has information for me. I'm taking him back to camp."

The guard scowled. "I can't allow that. He's one of the smelter workers."

"You dispute my authority? I was given it by the king himself. Take it up with your commander if you wish, but he's coming with me now."

"Ahh, what's it to me?" The guard shrugged and started coiling his whip again. "Send him back when you've finished with him." He turned away and started shouting at the other slaves.

Ament, Zephan and Ephrim made their way back to the camp, Ament in silence, Zephan muttering darkly about 'sir making a big mistake', and the boy babbling on about how his gods would smile upon the lord for his kind act.

"Cease your babble," Ament growled at last. "Why would I want foreign gods smiling on me? I may not be able to do anything anyway."

Arriving back at the camp, Ament left the boy with Zephan and went in to see Commander Nebamen. When he was shown in to the commander's room, he saluted despite being of superior rank.

"Commander Nebamen, I have discovered that one of the slave boys that I brought out has information I need. I have brought him back from the smelters and I also need to question his brother who is held in the guards' camp. I ask that you release them both into my care."

"What information?"

Ament hesitated, as he had not really thought this through. "Information relevant to...to the...to the campaign into Retenu that the king conducted recently. He was looking for...for a rebel leader...but nobody knew where he was. I think these boys might."

"After all this time?" Nebamen asked, his voice betraying scepticism. "Are you sure you do not have some other motive? I said you could have a boy if you desired it. There is no need for an excuse."

"It is no excuse sir. I need them for the information they carry, nothing else."

"Well, question them then for all I care. How long will you need them for?"

"I must take them back to Men-nefer with me."

"Out of the question. The boys are slaves and stay here. You can have them for a day, a day and night even, but no more. If you need help extracting the information, let me know. We have some skilled interrogators here, a bit crude, perhaps, but they get results."

"Thank you sir. You will release Ephrim and Jerem to me then?"

"Do I care what their names are? Just take them, extract the information and send them back to their duties."

Ament led Zephan and Ephrim into the guards' camp, and reunited the brothers. Mentopher objected to the younger boy being taken, but gave way when Ament showed him the signed order from Commander Nebamen.

"I've taken a fancy to him myself," the Overseer said. "Start with his interrogation, so you can have him back by tonight. Preferably uninjured." Mentopher grinned and winked. "Any injuries the boy takes, I'll inflict on him myself."

Ament kept a straight face and marched the two boys away.

"What are you going to do, sir?" Zephan asked. "You won't get far in a day, and the commander will send men after you. Stealing slaves is not looked upon kindly."

"I don't know," Ament admitted. "I hadn't thought that far ahead. I suppose I'll have to cut across the desert rather than take the road to Eilah."

"You really haven't thought it through, have you, sir? You can't carry enough water with you to reach the nearest well, even if you knew where it was, and without water you'll be dead in a day."

"We'll have to try. I'm not leaving them behind."

"What about all the other boys?"

"I can't help them, but I can help these two."

"You can't even help yourself, sir."

"So you help me, Zephan. You know the desert; you hate what's happening to these boys."

Zephan looked away over the valley for a while and then sighed. "If they catch us, you'll probably just be reprimanded. The boys will be flogged and returned to their duties, but I'll likely be executed."

"You're right. Forgive me, Zephan, I had no right to ask you. We'll manage on our own somehow."

Chapter 15

Userkheperure Seti speaks:

To be King of Kemet, Lord of the Two Lands, Son of Re, Divine Father, Lord of Appearances, High Priest of Every Temple, Mighty Bull, is an exalted position, far above every other king that reigns under the solar disc. It is only because I am a god that I have the strength to lead my people, to guide them and protect them from our traditional enemies. A mere man could not do it and the fact that I am still here accepting the fervent obeisance of my subjects nearly a year after my accession is proof of my divine status. Why then do men seek to displace me from the throne and put another in my place? The gods of Kemet do not allow such a thing, are they perhaps following some foreign god?

It is not as if I neglect my sacred duties. I arise each day before dawn; wash and dress in simple attire and make my way to an open space to greet the sun as he rises above the horizon, uttering up such praise as any dutiful son must give to his father. Khepri, the Reborn Light, sun of the dawn that drives away the shadows of night and bathes the Land of the Gods in its gentle morning heat, this is the aspect of Re that I love the most, though all aspects are worthy of worship and receive my sacrifices.

After my dawn service, I break my fast and then make the rounds of the main temples to all the gods, offering up sacrifices as is proper for the High Priest. This takes time, but it is a necessary task, for the Ma'at of the Two Kingdoms depends on the good will of the gods. I am a god myself, so I know that without food and drink, without clean clothes, perfume and jewellery, I too would not be so inclined to look on my subjects with a glad eye. I oversee the cleansing of the statues of the gods in their precincts, the fresh clothing in which they are clad each day, and the food and drink laid out before them so they may partake of the spirit essences and nourish themselves.

After my priestly duties I bathe and don the garments proper for my duties to the kingdoms. I sit in the Hall of Audiences and hear legal cases which any of my subjects, be they commoner or noble, can ask to be heard by the highest in the land. In point of fact, my Tjaty will hear most cases, as do judges and governors of every sepat and city, and it is usually only the more serious ones that come to my attention.

For instance, just the other day, the Commander of the Guards of the Great Field brought before me three miscreants apprehended in the act of looting one of the minor tombs in their care. If I had not been in Waset, then Tjaty Neferronpet would likely have heard the case, but as I was here, I had them brought before me.

The guards brought them in, a man, a youth and a boy, and hurled them to the stone floor, their copper chains clashing as they grovelled and begged for mercy. Commander Pamont read out the charges, and outlined the evidence against the thieves. There was no point in asking for a defence because of course they would say they had not done it. The evidence was clear, so I asked them if they had anything to say before I passed sentence.

One of them, the man, struggled to his knees and held his hands out beseechingly. "Great One," he quavered. "Have mercy I beg. These are my sons and I led them to this. The fault is mine alone."

"Yet they took part in the robbery," I replied. "They are equally guilty, and this is not just a crime of theft of property, but theft of a man's eternal life."

And of course that is what it was. A tomb is built to be a secure haven for the dead person, and is stocked with his worldly goods, with food and drink and gold, all the good things he enjoyed in life and has a reasonable hope of enjoying through eternity. A rich man has a lot of grave goods and a poor man little, but each has according to his station in life. Where is the justice in a rich man being robbed in death and having to spend the rest of eternity as a poor man?

"Hunger drove me to it, Great One. I was a sandal maker but my house and shop burned down in...in the rioting, and I could not feed my family. I led my sons into this course of action, so the fault is mine. Great One, I have a wife and three daughters. What is to become of them if you...if you...?" The man broke down, weeping.

"How old are your sons?"

"S...Sem is fif...fifteen floods, Great One, and Bak is...is only ten. They are good boys and do as they are told."

"So it seems. And have your wife and daughters benefitted from your thievery?"

"No, Great One. This was...this was my first time."

I looked questioningly at the guard commander.

"We searched their house, Son of Re, and found nothing."

I considered the evidence and the plea for mercy, but I knew there was little I could do, even if I had been minded to. Robbing a tomb is a serious offence and merits death, often a particularly painful death, but I saw no good reason to visit this man's crime on his family. Still, justice had to be seen to have been done or other tomb robbers would take advantage of my perceived leniency.

"The penalty is death by disembowelling..."

My words were interrupted by a great cry of anguish and a stink of faeces as the man's bowels released and he fell prostrate on the stone floor. A guard stepped forward and silenced him with a blow from his spear haft, while a servant hurried over with cloths to clean up the worst of the mess.

"As I was saying, death by disembowelling or such form of death as may be decided upon given the particular circumstances. You and your sons are condemned to death for the crime of grave robbing, but I am aware of the situation your family will find itself in. Without a man, your wife and daughters will suffer, and that is not justice."

A gleam of hope appeared in the condemned man's eyes.

"I will execute you and one of your sons for the crime. The other will return to his family and support it by the sweat of his brow."

My words sunk in and the man shuddered, before struggling back into a kneeling position. "Bless you, Great One, for your mercy, but...but which son will you spare?"

"That is your choice."

The man stared at the youth and the boy, both now sobbing and shaking with fear. He held out his hands to them both. "How can I choose, Great One? I love them both."

"Choose, and I will grant you both a merciful death. Make me choose and suffer disembowelling."

The man cried out again and shuffled across the floor on his knees to embrace his sons. He kissed them both and turned back to me.

"Which of your sons will live?" I demanded.

The man shut his eyes and said, "Sem." The young boy screamed and collapsed, sobbing.

"The older one?" I asked, thinking perhaps he had made a mistake. "You send the young boy to his death?"

"I...I love them both equally, Great One, but m...my wife and daughters whom I love as well, will n...need a man to look after them. Sem is almost a man."

I nodded, and contemplated the scene before me. "A good answer," I said. "Let it be recorded that I commute the boy Bak's sentence to a life of servitude as a brick maker. Commander Pamont, release the elder son, convey the younger to the brickworks and take the man out and execute him by beheading."

The man and his sons cried out their farewells as they were led off to their fates, but the man also called on the gods to bless my name for my act of mercy. Then servants hurried to clean up the last of the mess on the floor and sprinkle perfume before the next case was called.

You might think that a king who ruled with justice tempered by mercy would be beloved by his people, yet this is not so in Waset. I have been in Amun's City for a few months now, ever-conscious that my brother Messuwy and his cohorts have poisoned men's minds against me. I would much rather be in the north where men love me, but I am determined that the men of Waset shall see me as a true king, so I stay.

I am glad that my wives are with me, and now that Takhat is far along in her pregnancy, I have an excuse to visit Tausret's bed once more. I know, I am the king, and I can take any woman to bed if I choose, but with all my other troubles, I want a peaceful life within the palace, so if either wife would rather sleep alone, I am content. In truth, these days spent in an unfriendly city have been good for me and my Queen. We have spent more time together, talking and playing games of Senet (she is much better at it than me), taking our ease in the royal gardens or laughing at the antics of the apes in the menagerie. It is almost as if we had never quarrelled and we are as we were in our youth.

Tausret recounted with a laugh our trip from Men-nefer to Waset when we were children and spoke fondly of Ament, saying that we both owed him our lives and that she was glad to be able to offer him a secure position as captain of the palace guard in Men-nefer. She must have seen my expression, for she stopped her reminiscences and asked me why I looked out of sorts. Was it something to do with Ament?

"I gave him a task that removed him from the palace. He is taking slaves to the mines in the Timna Valley in the Land of Sin."

She frowned and thought for a moment. "Well, I suppose it will do him good to get out of the palace for a while. How long will he be gone?"

"Er, well, there was no instruction for him to return."

"So he's out in this wilderness, under the impression you have banished him? How could you? You know we are in his debt."

I drew myself up and looked down my nose at my wife. "You may be in his debt, and a young boy many years ago might have been, but the King of Kemet owes nobody."

"You gave him to me, husband."

"Nonsense, I just assigned him to your service."

"Then bring him back. Send word immediately for his recall."

I shrugged, pretending nonchalance, but knowing myself in the wrong. Ament had made me feel small when I was a boy, though perhaps not deliberately. Even so I had, I admit, borne him a grudge. That hurt had motivated me to omit his recall from my instructions, but now I saw that such spitefulness was beneath me. A king should rise above such slights, whether real or imagined.

"I will send the recall when we return to Men-nefer in a month or two. Ament will resume his place in your service and I will have nothing to do with him in future."

I have to admit it made me feel good to please my wife, especially as it cost me nothing. While she was in a good mood, I decided to ask her opinion on how I could make myself more loved by the people of Waset.

She considered this for a while, staring out of the window at the dusk falling over the city. The noise of the day was on the wane, and the cooking fires in a thousand houses raised thin curls of blue smoke, while the scent of frying fish and herbs overcame the usual stink of the streets.

"It seems to me; husband," she said at last, "that you cannot compel people to love you. You can order them to obey you, to offer up taxes and to bow before you, to fear you even, but not to love you. That must be freely given."

"So there is nothing I can do?"

"I did not say that. You must give them what they need."

"What people want is a bottomless well," I grumbled. "I could drain the treasury and still not satisfy people."

"I did not say to give them what they want but what they need. Any man or woman, rich or poor, needs food, shelter and to feel secure. Increase the grain ration, lower the cost of mud bricks, and honour the gods so they smile upon us all."

I thought about Tausret's words. They made sense, and would cost little to implement, or at least the grain and bricks would. Building temples was a costly business, but I was already committed to that.

"There is one other matter, husband, though I hesitate to tell you."

"Speak without fear, Tausret."

"You excluded Waset and Amun in your coronation names. I feel that might have been a mistake."

"How can it have been a mistake to glorify Re? I am Userkheperure Setepenre, Powerful are the manifestations of Re, the Chosen One of Re. I will not insult Re by dropping his name from mine."

"I do not suggest that," Tausret said, "but you honour three gods in your name, Re twice, and Set and Ptah once each. You could easily make it four by including Amun."

"Changing one of the names of Re?" I asked, feeling slightly disturbed at the thought.

"It is just a thought, husband. Change Setepenre to Meryamen, beloved of Amun. I believe the people of Amun's City would be delighted."

"I will think on it," I said.

I did, and also consulted with Neferronpet, the Hem-netjers of Re and Amun, and in the end, made the announcement that henceforth I would be known as Userkheperure Meryamen. I was heartened by the enthusiastic response of the people. Perhaps my troubles in Waset are at an end and support for my brother will now fade and die.

Chapter 16
Year 1 of Userkheperure Seti

On Zephan's advice, Ament and the two slave boys had left the camp and journeyed east then north, finding a place of temporary refuge among the sandstone pillars and jumbled rock of a spur of the valley's north wall. They were challenged as they left camp, encumbered by water skins and some food, but Ament merely hinted that he wanted a quiet place in which to interrogate his prisoners.

"I would not want to disturb the camp with their screams for mercy," he said with a laugh.

The guards had joined in the laughter, and Ament made a show of pushing and shoving the boys until they were out of sight. Then he cut the ropes binding them and they made haste to reach the designated spot where they could shelter from the fierce heat of the sun and rest up before their journey. Zephan had told them he would meet them shortly after moonrise and that they must be prepared to travel until sunrise. By then, they must be under cover and far enough away that patrols sent to look for them would find no trace.

Ament spent most of the day in a state of anxiety, certain that men were on their trail already. He sheltered under an overhang part way up one of the sandstone pillars, shading his eyes as he scanned the rough terrain for any sign of pursuit. The two boys huddled together a few paces away, whispering to each other until they fell asleep in each other's arms. Ament woke them as the sun touched the hills at the head of the valley and encouraged them to eat some bread and a few dates, to drink sparingly from the water skins.

The sun set swiftly in a blaze of orange that deepened to red and purple light before leaching from the sky as the body of Nut spread over the landscape. The stars blazed in a clear sky and the temperature dropped, leaving them shivering in their thin clothing. Ament descended from the pillar and the three of them huddled together for warmth, not daring to try lighting a fire.

"H...how long d...do we stay h...here, master?" Ephrim asked, his teeth chattering.

"Until moonrise. Zephan said he would meet us here."

"When's th...that, master?"

"I don't know," Ament admitted. He got up and paced about, swinging his arms to generate a bit of body warmth, looking toward the east for any sign of the rising moon. The north took his attention too, for that was the direction they would likely take, and was perhaps the direction from which Zephan would come.

After a long time the moon rose, silver and cold, casting shadows over the desert. Where everything had been uniform shadow, now the very light that spread over sand and rock created deeper shadows, black pools where anything could hide. Ament stared out into the night, but there was no sign of Zephan, and he felt his spirits sink. If he failed them, Ament would have to chance the road to Eilah.

Something cried in the night, a high-pitched quavering call, and Jerem whimpered. Ephrim murmured soothing words, but the tremor in his voice betrayed his own fear. Ament felt uneasy too, but knew he could not show it. He fingered the sword at his belt, knowing it would be almost useless if some demon or savage beast attacked. The call came again, farther off, and Ament breathed a sigh of relief. The only sounds now were the quick scurry of tiny feet on the sand, and the chirp and buzz of insects.

The moon had risen well above the eastern horizon before they heard sounds moving toward them. Ament signed to the two boys to keep quiet and they hunkered down in the shadows, their eyes wide, holding their breath. A shadow moved, then another one, and a third.

"Hsst. Honoured sir, are you here?" a low voice called.

"Zephan?"

"I am here, sir, with two donkeys. We must hurry."

Ament stood and moved out of the shadows. "I was expecting you at moonrise."

"My apologies. I ran into a patrol and had to wait until they had moved on." Zephan grinned, his teeth glimmering faintly in the moonlight. "Are the boys here too?"

"We are here," Ephrim said softly. "May the gods bless you, master."

"Well, they might," Zephan conceded, "but not before we have got you to safety. Come. We have a long way to go before daybreak."

Zephan loaded a boy onto each of the donkeys, distributing the weight of water and food in panniers about their unprotesting bodies.

"We can walk," Ephrim said.

"Later," Zephan replied. "You are weak still, and can ride while my donkeys are fresh."

They set off to the northeast, Zephan leading the two donkeys tied in single file, with Ament bringing up the rear. Their path led between a maze of eroded sandstone pillars before they emerged into a broad expanse of open sand and jumbled heaps of rock. Zephan led the party into a shallow dry streambed that wound its way toward the valley sides, visible only as a slash of blackness unsullied by the pinpricks of stars. When the streambed vanished, they crossed a slight ridge and found another one leading in more or less the same direction.

The night passed, the moon reaching its zenith and slipping down the western sky as if fearful of the sun that paced behind it, though still below the horizon. Zephan stopped and looked back the way they had come, and then off to the east. Ament looked too, wondering if the tribesman had caught sight of pursuing soldiers.

"The dawn comes fast," Zephan said, "and we are too exposed here. We must hurry. Boys, get down. You must run now so the donkeys can match your pace."

Zephan set off again, now with Ephrim and Jerem each holding the halter rope of a donkey, and Ament encouraging the pace by flicking the rumps of the donkeys with a branch snapped off a low shrub whenever their pace faltered. The escarpment at the side of the valley drew closer, but the sun came faster, lighting up the eastern horizon in shades of pink and yellow.

Ament slowed abruptly and looked up, startled, realising that they were now ascending scree slopes where rock, assaulted by wind and freezing temperatures, had been fractured from the sandstone cliffs and dropped toward the valley floor. His eyes rose higher, following the slope to the towering cliffs.

"There's no way forward," he cried out. "We can't climb those cliffs."

"Trust me," Zephan called back. He started moving across the loose rock and just as the sun burst over the horizon, stabbing the tops of the cliffs with a golden light that slid rapidly down to meet them, Ament saw a slash in the rock, a gap where torrent waters had once burst through. Into the gap they slipped, stumbling over boulders and clambering up a steep slope, suddenly in shadow once more.

Zephan called a halt, and the weary boys sank to the ground, their chests heaving with the effort. "We can rest here," the tribesman said. "We have shade and no one will see us."

They rested, eating a light meal and drinking the tepid goatskin-flavoured water from the water flasks. Zephan fed the donkeys some hay from one of the panniers and doled out some water. Then the boys curled up and slept, and the men dozed in turns, the other sitting in a shaded place where they could scan the valley floor spread out before them. The sun rose higher, bringing heat with it, and flies attracted to the pungent odour of donkey droppings buzzed and settled on lips and eyes of men and beasts. They woke, ate and drank again, though sparingly, and lay down again, a draping of thin cloth keeping the flies off their faces.

When Ament woke to take his turn on watch in the early afternoon, Zephan pointed out a thin cloud of dust to the south.

"Soldiers?" Ament asked. "Are they after us?"

"Very likely," Zephan replied.

"Coming this way?"

"I first saw them around noon, travelling east toward the Eilah road. Now they are coming toward us, and at the rate they are moving, will be here by sunset."

"Then we must go," Ament said, rising to his feet.

"Soon," Zephan agreed. When Ament remained standing, he added, "They have been running through the heat of the day and will be tired by the time they reach here. By that time we will be at the top of the cliffs, refreshed and ready for a night march. They will not catch us, sir."

"Enough of the 'sir'," Ament grumbled. "Call me Ament."

Zephan grinned. "As you wish, Ament."

The pursuing soldiers were appreciably closer by the time Zephan was prepared to move. The tribesman carefully scooped up all the donkey dung and put it in a small cloth bag, adding it to one of the panniers.

Ament nodded approvingly. "I should have thought of that. Remove the traces of our presence and they might look elsewhere."

"Other men know of this cleft," Zephan said, "and we have left enough footprints to guide even a blind man to us. However, we now have too great a start for them to catch us providing we keep moving. I picked up the dung because when it dries out it can be used as fuel."

The dry bed of the torrent stream became steeper and narrower, but there was still room to scramble up and haul the donkeys after them. In places, Ament thought it looked as though a path had been gouged out of the sandstone, and he realised that this was a well-used trail connecting the valley floor with the desert beyond. Toward sunset, they emerged onto the top of the cliffs and stood doubled up, gasping for breath for a short time. Zephan and Ament moved cautiously to the cliff edge and peered over, quickly spotting the pursuing soldiers as they started up the loose scree toward the cleft.

"They have moved faster than I thought," Zephan said with a frown. "They will be at the cleft before sunset and may try to scale it before dark. We must leave immediately."

The two men hurried back to where the boys and donkeys waited, and Zephan urged them west and north, angling away from the cliffs. The terrain was undulating, mostly sand and low rocky outcrops, and Zephan kept them to low-lying areas as much as possible. Dusk came on, swiftly plunging the desert into darkness before they saw any sign of pursuit. Zephan called a halt and they ate and drank something while they waited for full darkness. He oriented himself by the stars and moved off once more.

Their pace was necessarily slow, but Zephan had been this way before and guided them easily between boulders and eroded sandstone bluffs, across expanses of sand and loose rock. Later, when the moon rose, they were able to move faster, and by the time the sun rose, they were far from the cleft, surrounded by red desert as far as the eye could see. Zephan found them a shallow shaded patch under the overhang of a large frost-split boulder.

"Sleep through to late afternoon," Zephan said. "We have to make a push to reach the next water source."

"Will the soldiers come after us?" Ament asked.

"Not if they're sensible. The next well is three days away."

Ament looked at their own depleted water skins. "Have we got enough water?"

"About a day's worth." He saw the expression on Ament's face and smiled. "Don't worry; I know something the soldiers don't." He would not say any more, just wrapping himself in a cloak from one of the panniers and falling asleep.

"Master," Ephrim whispered a little later, while Jerem watched wide-eyed. "I heard what Zephan said about the water. Are we gonna die of thirst out here? I mean, I sorta would rather die out here of thirst than beaten to death as a slave in the camp, but I'd rather not die at all, if you know what I mean."

"We're in Zephan's hands," Ament said. "He knows a lot more about the desert than I do. If he says not to worry, then I won't."

Ephrim thought about this and then said. "I think I might pray to my gods anyway."

"Couldn't hurt," Ament murmured. "Now get some sleep."

The sun was sinking fast in the west when Zephan woke them, and the heat was already dissipating into the cloudless sky. The tribesman doled out some food and allowed them each a mouthful of water before they resumed their journey. In the last of the light, they reached a great expanse of sand with a low range of hills just visible on the other side.

"That is where we must be before the sun rises," Zephan said, pointing.

The sand dragged at their feet as they walked, sapping their strength. Zephan led them onto a ridge of sand and along its length, counselling them not to walk too close to the unstable face of the dune. Jerem did not listen and with a despairing wail fell over the edge and tumbled down the slip face, ending up buried to his waist in the loose sand. They dug him out and struggled back up to the ridge again and after that they were all careful where they put their feet.

"We have lost too much time," Zephan said. "Now we race the sun, and if we lose that race, we face death." He urged them on and set a fast pace.

Despite the urgency, Zephan stopped frequently to give them a moment to catch their breath and also to realign their march, orienting himself first by the stars and later by the rising moon. They slogged on through the sand, and consumed the last of their water just as the eastern horizon turned gray. Ahead of them, the range of hills loomed high, and Zephan nodded in satisfaction.

"I think we might make it. Come."

The sun was burning down on them by the time they reached the hills, and Zephan led them along the rock face where it rose precipitately out of the sand. Their strength was fading, and their mouths were parched before Zephan pointed to a shimmering green hue at the base of the rock ahead of them. As they approached, the donkeys lifted their heads and sniffed before ambling faster. The light wind shifted, and now Ament and the boys could detect a cool and delicious smell on the breeze.

"Water?" Ament croaked. "I thought you said there weren't any wells out here."

"There aren't," Zephan replied, "but in a good year there are sometimes soaks."

The green resolved itself into a grove of thorn trees, scrawny shrubs and lank grass clustered around a tiny pool of greenish water. By the time Zephan and Ament arrived, the boys were vainly trying to pull the donkeys out of the pool to stop them churning it into a muddy mess.

Zephan laughed and told them to leave the donkeys and follow him. "The water comes from the rock, and it is purer at its source."

A crack in the rock leaked a thin rivulet of water into a small rocky basin at the base of the cliff, from whence it oozed over the lip and ran down toward the muddy pool where the donkeys were drinking thirstily. The boys eyed the water avidly, but Ephrim held his brother back until Ament reached them.

"Go ahead," Ament said. "Just don't drink it all."

When they had all drunk their fill and refilled the water skins, they lay in the dappled shade of the thorn trees and idly watched the donkeys grazing on the grass. Ephrim and Jerem, their spirits restored by water and rest, wandered off amongst the vegetation, exploring their surroundings, and presently Ament smiled as he heard their laughter.

"How quickly they forget their troubles," Ament said.

"I doubt they have forgotten them," Zephan replied. "They are young though, and resilient, and will seek a scrap of pleasure where they can find it. At the moment, it seems as though catching grasshoppers is enough for them."

Ament shaded his eyes and looked up at the hills and crack in the rock, stained dark by the trickle of water. "Where does it come from?" he asked. "How can water come from a rock?"

"I have heard it said that a holy man, or maybe it was a holy woman, for the stories vary, struck the rock here with his staff and ordered water to gush forth for his followers. Others say there has always been water trickling from this place, sometimes more than this, sometimes less, but I have only been here once when there was no water at all." Zephan frowned, remembering. "Two old men died that time, though we shared what water we had."

"Yes, but where does it come from?" Ament waved in the direction of the peaks. "Is there a river up there? Or a lake?"

"Who can say except the gods? Rain falls sometimes, but this cannot be sky water for it has not fallen for some months now." Zephan yawned and closed his eyes. "Just thank the gods and leave it at that, Ament. Then get some sleep. We leave at dusk once more."

"Where to?"

"West. Two days to a well, then another two to my tribe. Then we will see."

Ament had to be content with this for Zephan refused to say any more, just turning over and falling asleep. He lay awake a while longer but drifted into sleep himself to the muted sounds of the two boys at play.

Chapter 17
Year 1 of Userkheperure Seti

The annual viceregal report came in from Khaemter, King's Son of Kush, and it made for dismal reading. Tribal incursions from the west and south had tied up the Kushite legion in a series of indecisive encounters, and in the absence of a military presence, bandits had increased their hold on the countryside. In particular, the king's gold mines which had been struggling back to their former efficiency, slid to new lows of production.

"This is preposterous," Seti exclaimed, crumpling the report in his hands. "Gold production was higher when even my brother Messuwy was in charge. Now that his thieving adviser Sethi is gone, there should be more gold coming into the treasury, not less."

"The province is experiencing unrest," Neferronpet observed. "Perhaps Khaemter is right when he says he has insufficient men to guard the province and guard the mines."

"The Kushite legion is at full strength and he has native levies he can call on. This never happened before, so why now? Advise me, Neferronpet."

"Khaemter will eventually triumph; the tribes are not well organised. You could just wait it out..."

Seti shook his head. "No, something must be done now."

"Then you must send soldiers into Kush."

"To bolster the Kushite legion? It should be strong enough already."

"I was thinking more in terms of taking the burden of guarding the mines off his shoulders, your majesty. Leave him free to pursue the tribes while your appointee tackles the problem of the bandits."

"Who do you suggest?"

"Troop Commander Djau."

"Do I know him?"

"He took charge of the Amun legion during the recent troubles when Merenkhons was with you in the Great Field. None of the other commanders was prepared to act."

"Yes, I remember. Good. How many men will he need?"

"His troop should be enough, your majesty. Three hundred men."

"Draw up the orders," Seti commanded.

Djau set off within days of receiving his orders, loading the three hundred men of his Troop aboard barges for the long voyage upriver to Abu and the first cataract. They would not need to travel further than that by water for the gold mines of Kush lay in the hills far to the east of the river, and the best way there was to follow the Royal Road through the dusty sun-seared wilderness.

Seti sent word of their coming to Khaemter, stressing that as the burden of protecting the king's gold was lifted from him, he had no excuse in bringing the province under control once more. Unbeknownst to the king, another messenger left Waset within half a day of his signing the order for Djau. This messenger slipped away under cover of night and carried a verbal message to Sethi, recently returned to the land of Kush. Travelling much faster than the heavily laden barges, the messenger was admitted to Sethi's presence in the hinterland of Kush before Djau and his men reached Abu.

"My lord Sethi, Hem-netjer Roma-Rui sends his greetings..."

"Roma-Rui has been made Hem-netjer again?" Sethi asked. His question was spiced with malice for he knew very well that Roma-Rui was still deposed.

"No, my lord," admitted the messenger. "Forgive me, I misspoke. Former Hem-netjer Roma-Rui sends his greetings and bids me tell you that Troop Commander Djau of the Amun legion is on his way to Kush with three hundred men. He is tasked with protecting the gold mines and the gold caravans."

Sethi dismissed the man and paced about his tent while he considered the news. Since Khaemter had been made King's Son of Kush, his master Messuwy had been steadily gaining control of the province and amassing troops for his eventual assault on the Two Kingdoms. Reports of unrest that filtered back to the king were actually disguised reports of troop movements as Khaemter and Messuwy crisscrossed the province bringing men under his banner. Such efforts required the expenditure of much gold, however, for the loyalty of most men had to be bought. Ironically, the king's own gold mines were funding Messuwy's bid for his father's throne, but only as long as Sethi could continue to capture the gold caravans. The mines themselves were well-nigh impregnable, but the caravans were vulnerable, especially if spies kept one well informed of the route taken and the number of guards.

Sethi made his decision and called for one of his men, bidding him carry a summons to a local bandit chief. A day later, when the bandit arrived with a small but well-armed band of his men, Sethi met him under the shade of a tamarisk tree, pouring him thin wine in a stone cup.

"Greetings, Bennu. Wine?"

Bennu, short and stocky with black hair and swarthy beneath the layered dirt on his skin, grinned, displaying broken and discoloured teeth. "Won't say no." He took the cup and drank, screwing up his face in an expression of disgust. "You don't believe in bringing out the good stuff, do you?"

"I'll be happy to drink better wine with you if you're successful."

Bennu shrugged. "So what do you want me to do?"

"Three hundred men of the Amun legion are coming south to guard the gold caravans. I want you to take your men and attack them, draw them out and test their strength."

A bray of laughter greeted Sethi. "You don't want much, do you? I'm not attacking three hundred soldiers."

"I'm not asking you to. Taunt them, draw off a small force and attack those. I need to know their skill at arms before I commit my own men."

Bennu considered, and then gathered his saliva and spat in the dirt. "You're happy enough to risk my men though."

"Your men are scum and you can find more in any cesspit in Kush. You won't be risking your own life, I'm sure."

"They're still my men. I'd expect recompense, for their families if nothing else."

"A kite of copper for each man who falls."

"Five," Bennu replied.

"Two each," Sethi countered, "and a deben of silver just for you."

"Done." Bennu spat on his palm and held it out.

Sethi hid his distaste and touched palms with the bandit chief. He knew Bennu thought he had made a good deal, but Sethi would have paid ten times that and still counted himself fortunate to have got off so lightly. Little if any of that copper would find itself to the families of the fallen, but that was not his concern.

"How are they coming?" Bennu asked. "The river, I suppose. And when?" he added.

"The Royal Road from Abu. The latest news I have indicates they'll be in Abu in a few days."

"I'll send my own spies out then. As for an ambush point..." Bennu thought for a moment. "The well at Nak-pilu perhaps. Three hundred men will crowd the well surrounds, so they'll have to spread out."

"I'll leave the details up to you," Sethi said. "Just make sure you engage them fiercely enough so I can gauge their ability."

"You just make sure you have my copper and silver ready."

Sethi sent one of his own men, a native of Kush, along with Bennu to observe the fighting and report back. The bandits moved fast, taking up positions near the well of Nak-pilu while others of their band scouted out the slow advance of Djau's troop up from the cataract above Abu and into the hilly uplands of Kush. By the time the Amun soldiers reached the well, the scouts had formed their opinions of the fighting worth of the men.

"Soft men," one said scornfully. "City men."

"Men playing at being soldiers," said another.

"Ill-disciplined," said a third.

Bennu grinned, although if the soldiers were as poorly trained as his scouts suggested, his casualties would be light and he would collect little copper from the lord Sethi. Still, there were always the spoils of war. Weapons taken from the fallen would be useful, and who knew what else might be plundered.

"Ready the men," he instructed. "You," he said, pointing at Sethi's man, "Come with me."

From the hillocks, rubble piles and thorn thickets surrounding the well, Bennu and his men looked down on the Amun camp. The soldiers had formed into groups of five, erected a tent and were now engaged in preparing a meal on several small campfires. As far as Bennu could see, there were no guards, no sentries posted with the exception of a few men standing around near the well.

Bennu grunted and pointed out how the attack should take place, whispering to his most trusted men. "You see how some twenty tents are separated from the others by the bend in the road and those thorn trees? We will attack them from two sides and sweep back, away from the main camp."

He waited for them to get into position and then led the charge down into the encampment, yelling and screaming along with his men. Tents collapsed as men trampled them, fires were kicked apart and scattered, and soldiers died from spear thrust and axe blow as the bandits poured over one end of the Amun camp. The din of battle rose as the surviving soldiers grabbed any weapon to hand and fought back.

A ram's horn sounded, and the rest of the Amun camp leapt to their feet. Commander Djau yelled his commands and the Amun soldiers formed up in rough columns and started toward the camp under attack. Bennu heard them coming and signalled for his men to retreat. The supporting soldiers were barely in sight before the bandits melted away into the scrub and the rocks, leaving a scene of devastation behind them.

The bandits regrouped further down the road and Bennu listened to reports from his men. He nodded in satisfaction and beckoned to Sethi's man. "You heard? Six of my men dead, another eleven wounded, but at least twenty of the enemy dead, maybe more."

"You'll get your copper," Sethi's man said, "for my master is an honourable man, but may I make a suggestion? The Amun camp is like a kicked anthill. If you were to hit them again, you could inflict more casualties with minimum loss."

"I should get a bonus for the men I kill."

"Put it to him. Lord Sethi is a generous man and will surely reward you."

Bennu grinned and beckoned to his men, leading them back toward the Amun soldiers milling around the overrun camp site. Djau and his men were more concerned with putting the camp to rights rather than putting out sentries to guard against a vanished enemy, so were taken by surprise once more as the bandits swarmed out of the thorn scrub and fell upon the enemy. The bandits were outnumbered but had surprise on their side as well as an intimate knowledge of the terrain, so by the time Djau had managed to regroup his men in a defensive position, dead and wounded soldiers littered the open ground. Bennu withdrew and, well satisfied with his men's efforts, left the Amun soldiers to lick their wounds and returned to Sethi's camp.

"Thirteen of my men dead, another twenty wounded."

Sethi nodded. "As I promised, two deben and six kite of copper, plus one deben of silver," he said.

"My wounded need some recompense," Bennu pressed.

"Another deben of copper shared between them."

Bennu nodded, knowing that none of his men or their families would see the copper he had negotiated on their behalf. "There is also the matter of the dead Amun soldiers."

"We did not agree on any price for them. Your job was to test their resolve, not to kill them."

"Nevertheless," Bennu said, "every man I killed is one less for you to worry about later. Your man said you would be generous."

"Did he, indeed?" Sethi glowered at the man he had sent. "How many of the enemy were killed?"

The man shrugged. "Hard to say exactly. Maybe as many as twenty..."

"At least forty," Bennu interrupted. "Twenty alone in the foray, more when we attacked again."

"I suppose you did not think to bring me proof, like cutting off their hands?"

"We had other things on our minds."

"So, you say forty, my man says twenty...how can I know the truth of it? Shall we say thirty, and I will give you another deben of silver in payment?"

Bennu accepted and Sethi arranged payment before dismissing the bandit chief. When they were alone, Sethi's man prostrated himself before his master.

"Forgive me, lord. Bennu pressed me for payment for the enemy dead and I had to say you might pay him."

Sethi nodded. "A deben of silver is a small price to pay for a tenth of the enemy dead without risking a single one of my own soldiers. But next time, do not make promises on my behalf or I will take the price out of your hide. Understand?"

"Yes, my lord."

"Now, what is the quality of these Amun soldiers invading Kush? Are they good soldiers?"

"My impression is that Djau is a good commander but the soldiers are unused to warfare. Bennu's men described them as undisciplined and soft. City men rather than battle-hardened warriors."

Sethi smiled and dismissed the man. He thought about the lay of land around the gold mines and the road leading there, and then called his officers to him.

"We are going hunting," he said. "Two hundred and seventy rabbits are challenging our right to harvest gold for the rightful king."

A month passed and a patrol sent out by the governor of Abu found a wounded man, emaciated and sick, stumbling out of the hinterland of Kush. He mumbled incoherently and held up the stumps of his arms where both hands had been removed. The soldiers cleaned him up, fed him, and took him to Governor Tarkahe.

The man knelt and held out the stumps to the seated governor. "Hear me, noble one. I have a vital message for Userkheperure. Find me passage on a boat that I might travel to Waset and deliver my message to the king."

"Who did this to you?"

"A lord called Sethi, noble one. He is the leader of a band of soldiers marching under the insignia of the Kushite legion. They fell upon us and slaughtered us, leaving only me alive to bear witness to our humiliation. I escaped, though bearing this mutilation, and have been many days on the road."

"Us?" asked Tarkahe. "Who is 'us'?"

"I...I am Troop Commander Djau, noble one. I passed through your city two months ago with three hundred men of the Amun legion to protect the king's gold mines. I have failed in my duty and lost my men, and I must now throw myself on the king's mercy. Have pity on me, noble one, and send me into the king's presence that I might tell him what he most needs to know, the whereabouts of his traitor brother Messuwy."

Governor Tarkahe considered Djau's words and then called soldiers of his personal guard to him. "Take this man out and execute him. He has betrayed his king and does not deserve to live a moment longer."

"No, noble one," Djau screamed as the guard hauled him to his feet. "I must tell the king what I have seen. He needs to know that his brother Messuwy..."

"Silence him!"

A guard smashed the base of his spear into Djau's face, and the man's cries broke down into a bubbling scream as blood sprayed out. He was hauled away and his screams ceased abruptly outside the governor's chamber.

Tarkahe called a scribe to him. "Take a letter." He waited while the scribe sat cross-legged on the floor and assembled his papyrus, his pots of paint and thin-tipped brush. "Governor Tarkahe of Abu, to His Majesty Prince Messuwy, rightful Lord of the Two Lands, greetings..."

Chapter 18
Year 1 of Userkheperure Seti

Zephan, it turned out, was a younger son of Jochim, chief of the Shechite tribe. To call him 'chief' was perhaps to elevate him to a higher status than he deserved, for the Shechite were made up of many widely-scattered families and Jochim was but the head of this particular family. His word was law, however, and the forty or fifty men, women and children encamped at the Well of Beeran obeyed him in everything.

Zephan was greeted warmly when he arrived at the encampment, dusty and tired and leading three strangers. The two Retenu boys were accepted without comment but Ament, as a Kemetu, was viewed with suspicion. The men of the tribe gathered round, staring and fingering their daggers, and Zephan had to loudly proclaim that he had granted them safe passage. They drew back slightly at that, but sent them to the patriarch of the family.

Jochim stood outside his tent and, when Zephan knelt before him in the sand, put his hand on his son's head. A woman and two small children stood off to one side, eagerly watching, and Jochim beckoned them over.

"Greet your wife and children, boy, and then bring these strangers into my tent." He turned on his heel and strode back into the shadowed interior.

Zephan embraced his wife Sarai and hugged his children. Ament remembered Zephan telling him he had children but could not recall if he had said anything about their gender. He could not be sure if these two children were boys or girls as they were equally swaddled in voluminous clothing. Zephan squatted and allowed the children to climb all over him, chattering all the while in their own language, while his wife stroked his head. After a little while, Zephan told his wife and children to leave, and ushered Ament, Ephrim and Jerem into his father's tent.

They trooped in and sat in the places pointed out to them, and then Jochim studied them intently while Zephan explained the circumstances that brought these strangers into his father's tent.

"You are a Kemetu army officer?" Jochim asked Ament, with his son translating.

"Yes, my lord."

"There is no need to call me 'lord'; I am simply the father to my family."

Zephan translated again and added that a more suitable honorific would be 'Sa'ner' which meant 'father' in the Shechite tongue, though not simply the head of one's own family but rather a man of renown.

Ament bowed from the waist and said, "I am honoured to be received into your tent, Sa'ner."

"What is a man of Kemet doing stealing two young boys from the camp in the Timna Valley?" Jochim asked. Zephan started to say that he had already told his father of the reason, but Jochim held up a hand. "I would hear it from his own lips."

"Sa'ner, I was...I was horrified to see the treatment of the boys at the camp and determined to release them."

"But they are slaves, aren't they? Is this not how slaves are treated?"

Ament grimaced. "Slaves are worked hard, it is true, but they...they should not be beaten or starved."

"Slaves in Kemet are not beaten?"

"Yes, Sa'ner, but...but not boys."

"Truly?" Jochim looked surprised. "I have heard otherwise."

Ament struggled with his conscience and then said, "It is true boys are beaten, Sa'ner, but no boy should suffer abuse at the hands of grown men. This older boy..." he pointed at Ephrim, "...asked me if I could rescue his younger brother who was to be made use of by the guards. I could not allow that so I took them."

"And having taken them, made my son Zephan help you. You realise he can now never go back to Timna?"

"I am sorry for that, Sa'ner. I was going to try for the Eilah road but Zephan dissuaded me. I did not mean to involve him, get him into trouble, but he saved our lives."

Jochim ruminated for a while and then turned to the young boys, lapsing into a rough trading language that could be understood by Kanaanites.

"This man speak truth? You boys abuse by Kemetu soldier?"

"We was going to be, noble lord," Ephrim said, kneeling in front of the chief. "Least ways, me bruvver Jerem was 'cos he's young an'...an' he heard the guards talking 'bout him. I was in the copper smelter camp an' just got beaten."

"What do you want? That this man takes you Kemet? You serve him?"

"He be a good man, noble lord. Jerem and me, we talk it over 'cos we thought first we escape an' try go home, but our village burnt, family killed an' he good to us, so we stay his slaves." Ephrim shrugged. "He won't do nuthink to Jerem, an' I don't think he beat us too often."

"Ament, what do you intend for these boys? Will you take them back to Kemet as slaves?"

"I've got no use for slaves, Sa'ner. I'm a soldier, plain and simple."

"So you will sell them when you get home?"

"I, er, hadn't really thought that far ahead..."

"They might be worse off under another master than if they stayed here."

"Here?" Ament asked. "In the Shechite camp?"

"I would allow that if they wanted it. You would have to agree, as their master."

"I'm not their master...not really...but if that's what they want, I agree."

Jochim addressed Ephrim again. "This man Ament say he no use for slaves in Kemet. He maybe sells you other master. Or you stay here with Shechites, no slave but work hard as servant. What say?"

The two boys discussed it in low voices, and Jerem burst into tears. Ephrim shrugged and turned to the chief. "We thanks you, noble lord, but, well...Jerem wants to stay with him. I ain't going where he ain't."

Jochim smiled and nodded. "Ament of Kemet, you will take the boys back with you to your home and you will care for them or else you will not return to your home at all."

Ament had Zephan explain that last bit to him at length, and then grimaced. "It seems I have no choice," he grumbled. "Well, I can take them with me, but exactly what I'm going to do with them when I have to go off to war, I don't..." He paused as a thought occurred to him. "My sister Ti-ament and her husband own a small vineyard in Ta Mehu. They could live there, with them."

"If the boys agree."

"All right," Ament agreed.

"Swear it, on your gods," Jochim said.

Ament swore an oath, binding himself to looking after the boys when they were back in Kemet, or letting them stay with his sister, but insisted on adding a proviso. "I am only Captain of the Palace Guard, a mere soldier. If the king or Tjaty, or a superior officer orders me to do otherwise, I must obey."

"Even then you will do your utmost to ensure their safety," Jochim countered.

Ament sighed and nodded. "Agreed." This whole exercise was proving to be a lot more trouble than he had anticipated when he first thought about removing the children from their enforced captivity. He could not see any way around it, so he swore to protect them as Jochim wanted. It surprised him that he felt so good about his decision after he had given his oath.

Jochim next made arrangements for his youngest son Zephan to take a companion and guide Ament and the two boys across the trackless waste of the Land of Sin. After three days of fattening up and securing sufficient supplies, they loaded up four donkeys and set out, travelling slightly north of west toward the nearest well. Zephan explained that without a guide, someone who knew where the wells and soaks lay, a man would quickly die of thirst. They carried food for a month, though the fare would be rather monotonous.

"I can arrange for you to replenish your stocks of food for the return journey," Ament said. "Once we reach the rich farmlands of Ta Mehu, there will be an abundance of food."

"I thank you, Ament," Zephan said, "but I shall not be accompanying you into Ta Mehu. Once we reach the Black Land I shall bid you farewell."

"But you must let me offer you the hospitality of my land, just as you and your father have offered it to me."

"Alas, my friend, not all in your lands would welcome Shechite men." Zephan would not explain further, so Ament had to let the matter rest there.

The boys spent the trip being boys, a pastime interrupted by the Kemetu army's descent on their village and their months of captivity. They roamed widely, investigating anything within sight of the donkey caravan, chattering non-stop, or throwing stones at anything they saw. During the rest periods and after the evening meal, they would hunt lizards or scorpions among the rocks or listen attentively to stories the men told, wrapped in cloaks around the camp fire. Afterward, they would fall into an exhausted sleep and not even the eerie calls of jackals and owls could disturb them.

The Land of Sin, stony, sandy and dusty passed slowly beneath their feet, the sun baking them by day and the clear skies sucking the heat from their surroundings at night, leaving them shivering and huddled together around a camp fire. Days passed, stretching out to a month, and toward the end of their journey, as they neared the Black Lands, they happened upon military roads and patrols of Kemetu soldiers. Here Zephan led them away into the wilderness, taking the long route around where they would encounter no one. Ament said nothing, though he believed he could have used his rank to secure them fresh provisions and comfortable beds at night. He knew that the Shechite tribesman must have his reasons for avoiding other Kemetu, so did not object to the thousands of extra paces added to their journey.

At last, stony desert passed by degrees into scrubland, and then into pasture. When they encountered the first cultivated fields and villages, Zephan stopped.

"We must part here, Ament my friend. I can go no further."

"It pains me that we must say goodbye," Ament said, "for I would like to offer you my own hospitality, but I know you have your reasons."

Zephan embraced Ament, and then each of the two boys who cried as they parted. The other Shechite tribesman, Orran, who had kept to himself the whole way, nodded and cracked a small smile as he turned the donkey's heads and started back toward their desert home. Zephan gave Ament a last embrace and lifted his hand in farewell.

"May your gods smile upon you, man of Kemet."

"And yours upon you, man of Shechem," Ament said. He put his arms around the shoulders of the two boys and turned them away, facing the west whence came a breeze laden with moisture and the odours of livestock and growing things. When at last he turned his head to look back, Zephan had disappeared from sight, lost in the scrubland that bordered on the Land of Sin.

Ament found a small village nearby and, using his name and rank, secured some fresh food for the boys. I was nothing fancy, bread and a few vegetables, but it was a lot tastier than the meagre fare that had been theirs since leaving the Shechem camp. They continued on and a day later reached the bank of one of the branches of the Great River. Ephrim and

Jerem were amazed that this amount of potable water could even exist and happily splashed in the shallows while Ament kept an eye out for crocodiles.

A copper armband, Ament's last article of any value, enabled them to hire a fisherman to take them upriver toward Men-nefer. An added benefit was fresh river-caught fish fried over a small fire every night with wild herbs and the remnants eaten cold the next day. Every turn of the river, every reed bed or patch of weed, every swirl of the water, the herds of lowing cattle in the pastures and farms where ploughed fields burst with growing plants, wheat, barley and millet as well as onions, lettuce, radishes and melons, amazed the Retenu boys and they continually exclaimed in wonderment. This truly was the land of the gods, they said.

Two days later they caught sight of the city of Men-nefer with its high walls blazing white in the morning sun, the river lapping at its feet crowded with small boats, and people, small in the distance, thronging its wharves and docks. Ament grinned, looking forward to a soft bed and some decent food, perhaps even some wine.

"What will become of us, master?" Ephrim asked, staring wide-eyed as they drew close to the burgeoning city.

"Eh? Oh, you'll be all right. I'll have you looked after by one of the palace overseers while I inform Tjaty Merysekhmet of the abuses taking place in his name. Once that's all sorted out, I'll see about getting you up to my sister's vineyard."

The boat docked at one of the lesser wharves as, unnoticed, a swift messenger boat drew out into the current and raised its large sails to catch the northerly breeze. Ament kept the boys close as he led them through the crowded streets to the palace, trying not to let them get distracted by the sights and sounds and smells that bombarded them on every side. Aromas of spices and fresh-baked bread, roasting meats and freshly brewed barley beer made their mouths water and stomachs grumble, and Ament smiled once more in anticipation.

"We'll get a good meal inside us first," he told the boys.

They arrived at the palace and Ament spoke to one of the guards on duty, telling him to send for an overseer. The guard stared at him and then frowned.

"Captain...er, Ament? The...the Tjaty is...he is to be informed of your arrival."

"Well, do so then, but by the gods send for an overseer at the same time. My stomach hasn't seen decent food in over a month...and I'd kill for a draught of rich wine."

The guard sent messages via servants and indicated a small room that Ament and his companions could wait in. Ament looked thoughtful as he waited and tried to engage the guard in conversation, but without success. A little time passed and Ament was trying to decide whether to wait or just head through to the kitchens when the tramp of footsteps outside the chamber announced the arrival of one or both of the parties the guard had sent word to.

A squad of soldiers entered the chamber, an officer bearing the insignia of Captain of the Palace Guard, Ament's own position, entered. The soldiers ringed Ament and the boys, hands on their swords.

"Ex-Captain Ament, you are charged with desertion and..."

"Neferhotep? It is you, by the gods. Did they make you Acting Captain?" Ament smiled and raised his hand to clasp the other officer's arm, but Neferhotep stepped back, his face impassive.

"Ex-Captain Ament, you are charged with desertion and theft of His Majesty's property. Tjaty Merysekhmet orders you to be incarcerated pending his pleasure. Come with me now."

"But I haven't...this can't be right...wait, please."

"I am merely following orders, Ament," Neferhotep said. "You know how it goes. Either come willingly or by force. Your choice."

"I demand to see the Tjaty."

"You will, when he's ready for you. Now, are you coming or must I order my men to take you by force?"

Ament went, if not willingly, at least without resistance, and the boys went with him.

Chapter 19
Year 2 of Userkheperure Seti

The messenger boat that had left the docks of Men-nefer as Ament arrived sped south, the captain of the small craft cramming on every bit of sail he could. The usual voyage to Waset took ten days, even with a fair wind, but Tjaty Merysekhmet had promised the captain and owner a whole deben of gold in addition to his normal fee if he could reach Waset within eight days and the captain meant to collect that extra fee.

The landscape slipped steadily by, while the captain kept his eyes open for the smallest vagary of the wind as evidenced by ruffled water, making adjustments to the set of the sails. Cliffs on both the east and west banks influenced the direction of the winds and the captain often tacked back and forth across the wide expanse of water, trading extra distance for a stiffer breeze. When night fell, he did not put into shore until well after dark, and was always on his way again before first light. If the northerly wind fell, he took out his sculling oar and made slow progress along the shore where the current often eddied and helped him on his way.

Waset came in sight near sunset on the seventh day, and the captain grinned in delight, thinking of the fine tomb furnishings he could buy with his extra gold. He tied up at the city docks by the light of flickering torches and the official messenger, grasping his message pouch, importuned two Medjay, paying them to escort him to the palace. Once there he dismissed his escort and bade a servant carry news of his arrival to the king, saying he carried urgent dispatches.

He waited while the king ate his evening meal and then was shown into the small audience chamber where Seti, his wives Tausret and Takhat, and Tjaty Neferronpet awaited him. One of the soldiers escorting him through the palace was Commander Merenkhons and he stayed after dismissing the other guards. The messenger advanced on the throne, deeply bowing with his arms outstretched in supplication.

"I bear messages from Tjaty of the North, Merysekhmet, O Son of Re. He greets you as Lord of the Two Lands, Divine Father, Great One, and Priest of Every Temple, and asks that you read his humble words. Son of Re, your servant has carried this message on the wings of the wind so that Your Divine Majesty might..."

Seti hardly listened to the long and involved phrases uttered by the official messenger. He had heard them innumerable times and knew better than to interrupt the flow. The common people needed to express these sentiments if only to remind themselves that the king, God on Earth, was set high above them and could intercede for them with the gods. Seti's attention was still on the fine supper he had just eaten, and the shred of goose flesh that was caught in his teeth. Sticking a finger in his mouth to prise loose the offending morsel was beneath his dignity, so for the time being he had to content himself with ineffectual probing with his tongue.

He became aware that the messenger had stopped talking and was holding out a sealed letter. Tjaty, Commander and wives were looking at him expectantly. Clearing his throat and trying to recall if the messenger had said anything of importance, Seti signed to Neferronpet to take the sealed letter proffered by the bowing man. As the Tjaty's fingers lifted the letter, the messenger straightened, stifling a sigh of pain, and stepped back before bowing again and exiting the chamber.

Neferronpet broke the seal on the letter, unfolded it and scanned the writing, his lips moving as he formed the words. His face tightened as he read, and when he finished, he read it again and frowned.

"Well? What does it say?" Seti asked, finally sneaking a finger into his mouth and snaring the piece of goose flesh with a fingernail.

"The men of Retenu have rebelled again and joined with some of the Sea Peoples. An army has marched on Ghazzat, looting temples and killing officials. The Governor of Ghazzat asks for your help."

Seti swore, suggesting things that the Retenu rebels should do to each other. Takhat looked shocked, but Tausret merely raised an eyebrow and allowed herself a small smile.

"What will you do, Son of Re?" Neferronpet asked.

"Do? What do you think I'll do? I have to answer this act of rebellion and smartly, before other tribes think they can rid themselves of our presence."

"It is not a good time to be leaving Waset, Majesty. Changing your throne name to Meryamen has increased your popularity, but there is still unrest in the city."

"Nothing that you can't handle, Neferronpet, together with the loyal Amun legion. Stamp on the troublemakers if you must, do anything necessary to preserve the peace, but I need to go north."

"Let it be as you say, Son of Re," Neferronpet said. "When will you depart?"

"In a day or two."

"My lord," Tausret murmured, "Lady Takhat is near her time and should not travel."

Seti looked at his wives solicitously and asked, "Lady, how are you feeling?"

"I am well, my lord," Takhat replied. "Though I do not relish the thought of being on board a barge for so many days."

"Perhaps I should leave you in Waset until after the birth. Lady Tausret can stay with you and keep you company. I should be back in two or three months."

"My lord, I thank you for your consideration, but it is not necessary that Lady Tausret stay with me. It is better that she accompany you for you should not be deprived of the ministrations of both your wives."

Seti smiled, looking fondly on both women. "I will be going to war, and that is no place for a woman."

"My lord, forgive my presumption," Takhat continued, "but Lady Tausret has experience of war. Her knowledge may be of use to you, if not in the face of the enemy then at least in support. I will be all right here in Waset; I have my women and it will only be for a few months. When you return, I will be able to present you with a fine son...or daughter."

Tausret frowned at this but said nothing, and Seti laughed. "Did any king ever have such wives?" he asked. Wisely, nobody refuted the king's statement.

Two days later, just after the dawn services to Khepri the Reborn Light, which Seti conducted on the wharves of Waset, the Royal Barge pushed free of its moorings and eased out into the river. With its oars threshing the water into foam, the vessel, aided by the strong current, surged forward. Seti stood in the prow, staring forward, eager to reach Men-nefer and put into motion his plans to punish the rebels and their allies. Tausret stood with him, revelling in the breeze that tugged at her dress and keenly anticipating a return to her duties in the northern capital.

The captain of the barge knew the river intimately and made full use of the currents, allowing his sailors adequate rest periods without unduly sacrificing speed. He even drove the barge on through the night, with watchmen on either side to shout warnings if shallows or either shore loomed in the darkness. They made it through the long stretches of the river without incident, only having to come ashore three times to replenish stores, and on the seventh day after leaving Waset, saw the high white walls of Men-nefer in the distance.

The city was in an uproar, for Tjaty Merysekhmet had not been idle while the king was en route. Every able-bodied man had been pressed into service, either by bolstering the strength of the legions or in producing materials to further the war effort. Armourers worked from dawn to dusk, moulding and forging copper ingots into arrow heads and bright spear points, peasants cut straight reeds for arrows, fletching them with brightly dyed goose feathers, fine hide strips for strings, and workers in wood mended chariots or fashioned shields out of timber and stretched bull's hide. Horses were exercised and groomed, and soldiers marched and practiced with axe and spear. Farms around the capital and throughout Ta Mehu were scoured for foodstuffs and the produce packed into wicker baskets and sent northeast to Per-Ramesses to await the king's army.

Despite the multitude of things happening in and around the city, both the Tjaty and the king found time for the usual round of business in the law courts and hearing petitions. Merysekhmet had had Ament brought before him on the charges of desertion and theft a few days before the king arrived back, but Ament had appealed to the king, saying he had news that only the king could hear.

"You realise if this is just a ploy to gain you more time, it will go badly for you?" the Tjaty asked.

"I do, my lord. Nevertheless, I must see the king."

"Very well." Merysekhmet had Ament returned to the cells to await the king's pleasure. In the hubbub that followed the king's arrival though, it was the last day before Seti departed for the north before Ament's case came before him.

"Ament?" Seti asked. "Not the same Ament who was Captain of the Palace Guard before I sent him to the east? What's the charge?"

"Desertion, Son of Re, and theft of the king's property."

"Those are serious charges. Naturally he denies them?"

"No, Son of Re. He can scarcely do that, having the effrontery to come to Men-nefer without orders and to bring with him the two slaves he stole from Timna, I have the official complaint from the overseer of the Timna Mines."

"Well...you can deal with it, Merysekhmet. You don't need me. A pity though, he was a good man once. Grant him a clean death, at least."

"He appeals to the king, Son of Re. He says he has news that only you can hear. He won't tell me what it is."

Seti scowled. "How inconvenient. Doesn't he know there's a rebellion I have to put down?" He thought for a moment, and then smiled. "Tausret can hear his case."

"He did ask to speak to you."

"Well I'm busy. Tell him he can either speak to the Queen or wait until I get back. Or he can just accept his fate," he added.

Seti and the conscripts, together with the Ptah legion and a massive train of supplies left the next day, and a day later Tausret sent for Ament, having him brought to a small private audience chamber instead of the formal law court. Merysekhmet accompanied him, along with a small squad of soldiers.

The Queen gasped when Ament was brought in with chains clinking and the filth of the prison cell clinging to him. She immediately ordered the chains struck off and the prisoner be given the opportunity to wash and don fresh clothes.

"He is a prisoner, Majesty," Merysekhmet murmured. "He is charged with a very serious crime."

"Do you imagine he will flee, surrounded as he is by guards? Do as I say."

Merysekhmet bowed and went to do the Queen's bidding. A little later, he escorted a washed and perfumed Ament back to the chamber and presented him. Tausret beckoned to him to come closer.

Ament bowed low and extended his arms. "Lady Tausret, Great Wife, I must see the king on a matter of some import."

"Seti is with the army," Tausret replied. "He bade me listen to your case and judge it. Ament, what has happened? These are very serious charges."

"I know, Majesty, but I am innocent of these charges."

"How can you be?" Merysekhmet demanded. "Your very presence here with the two slaves you stole shouts your guilt for the very gods to hear."

"Is this true?" Tausret asked.

"Yes...and no."

"I think you need to explain that."

Ament paused to collect his thoughts. "Lady Tausret, the king himself gave me my orders, which were to take in hand a squad of soldiers and escort two hundred men and boys, slaves all, to the mines of the Timna Valley in the Land of Sin. The boys came from Retenu after Userkheperure put down the rebellion there."

"Those were your orders," Tausret confirmed. "What happened then?"

"I delivered my charges, aside from a few who had succumbed along the way, but while in Timna I saw the horrors that were visited upon the children. They were beaten, given little food and worked harder than their bodies could stand. Some were even forced underground to work in heat and foul air, always with the threat of the lash if they did not move fast enough."

"They are slaves, Ament," Merysekhmet said. "That is how you treat slaves, or at least those consigned to the mines and quarries."

"They are also innocent children..."

"Not so innocent. Their fathers rebelled against Kemet, taking up arms against the king. Would you excuse that?"

"Of course not, but that was the fathers, not the sons."

"Spare the sons and they will grow up to seek revenge for their fathers," Tjaty Merysekhmet pointed out.

"Anyway, that is not the worst of it," Ament said. "The younger boys...the better looking ones...were kept in the camp to serve the guards..."

"The fortunate ones," Merysekhmet opined. "Freed from drudgery with nothing more onerous than cooking and cleaning..."

"And being abused by the guards at night."

"Abused how?" Tausret asked.

Ament coughed and looked down. "Er, well, Lady Tausret...some men like to er, use other men...as they would a woman."

Tausret frowned. "How? I mean...er, how?"

"Majesty," Merysekhmet said, "it is not unknown for men to use their wives in such a way as to not allow conception to take place, spilling their seed in an unclean place, her pehut. Well, sometimes men will perform this act with other men."

Tausret considered this for a little while. "It is not something I would countenance," she said at last, "for the whole point of conjugal relations is to produce children. And for men to do it together would never result in children, so why would they?"

"Yet they do, Majesty. Not often, and they are usually discreet, but it does happen."

"If they choose to do it..."

"Forgive me, Lady Tausret," Ament interrupted, "but that is the whole point, consent. A man can consent to another man using him in this manner, but a child cannot. A child is completely within the power of a man. The guard compels a child slave to commit this act and thereby surely commits a crime."

"Actually no," the Tjaty said. "No crime has been committed. We may not favour such an act, but there is no actual law against it."

"Then there should be," Ament declared. "Or at least against using children in such a way."

"And if the child consents?" Merysekhmet asked. "What then?"

"A child is not capable of making such a choice. He would not know what was being demanded of him."

"I'm inclined to agree," Tausret said. "I cannot remake the law, that is for the king, but it should be discouraged. Ament, you were saying that slave boys were abused in this way at Timna, does this have a bearing on your subsequent actions?"

"Yes, Lady Tausret. A boy asked me to intervene to save his younger brother from this fate and so I took them both from the camp and, with the help of a local tribesman also outraged at the practice, brought them back to Kemet."

"Thereby deserting your post at Timna," Merysekhmet said, "and stealing the two young boys, property of the king." He turned to Tausret. "My lady, we have an admission from his own mouth."

"I do not think the king will miss two small boys," Tausret said with a smile. "I will dismiss that charge for his heart was acting in a kindly fashion."

"There is still the charge of desertion," the Tjaty said.

"Why did you leave Timna without permission, Ament?" Tausret asked.

"There was no way I could stay there and still protect the boys, my lady. I...my orders were...well, ambiguous, you could say. I was to bring the prisoners to Timna and hand them over. They did not actually say I could leave and come home, but they also did not say I could not. I chose to come back with the boys so I could rescue them and also to plead with the king to change the fate of the captured boys still at Timna."

"That seems like a reasonable excuse," Tausret said. "I am of a mind to forgive Ament that charge too. What do you think, Merysekhmet?"

"I suppose the lack of specific orders to the contrary could be so interpreted."

"Then I shall talk to my husband the king immediately upon his return. He will change the law so that children cannot be used in this way."

Ament glanced at the Tjaty and took a deep breath, exhaling it raggedly. "Forgive my presumption, lady, but they need help a lot faster than that. Children are being abused even as we stand here and talk about it. The practice is rife in Timna..."

"If one or two men take it upon themselves..."

"Commander Nebamen and Overseer Mentopher are the ones encouraging this practice." Ament glanced at Merysekhmet again. "And their orders come from the Tjaty himself."

"Preposterous," Merysekhmet said. "A blatant lie, and without any shred of evidence."

"That is a very serious accusation, Ament. Do you have proof?"

"No, my lady, but it is common knowledge in Timna."

"I repudiate that utterly," Merysekhmet said, "and I ask that you act against this vicious slander immediately."

Tausret nodded. "I cannot allow lies to be spread, Ament, so if you have no proof..."

"The scribes will know," Ament exclaimed. "Any order to the Commander or Overseer will have had to be written down and copies made. The Chief Scribe will know where that order is to be found."

"*If* that order is to be found," Merysekhmet corrected. "Which it won't. It never existed. I'd remember something like that."

The Chief Scribe was called for (still old Anapepy) and the problem put to him. Anapepy stood in thought, idly scratching his bare belly, and eventually nodded. "I remember something that might apply."

"What? How can you?" Merysekhmet demanded. "I have never issued an order allowing the sexual use of boy slaves."

"With respect, Tjaty, your mind is filled with so many things you might have forgotten."

"My lady, this is preposterous," Merysekhmet said. "I do not favour the sexual exploitation of children so why would I issue a document ordering it?"

"Perhaps it was an order that could be misinterpreted," Ament observed. "Could you have given permission for something that..."

"I don't believe it," Merysekhmet interrupted. "Can you produce this document?"

"Possibly," Anapepy said. "There are a lot of scrolls to search through."

"It is necessary we find it if it exists," Tausret said. "Look for it, Anapepy."

"I shall do my best, Lady Tausret." The old scribe excused himself and went off to search through the baskets and shelves full of scrolls that made up his library in which, he claimed, resided a copy of every order and pronouncement made at the royal court since the latter days of the great Usermaatre himself.

"Whether he finds it or not," Tausret said, "I want you to draw up a document to be sent out to all mines and quarries, in fact, anywhere slaves are kept, forbidding the use of slaves for sex." She saw Merysekhmet's expression and frowned. "I mean it, Tjaty."

"It will have to be passed as law by the king."

"I will see to that. You just draw up the document."

"As you wish, Majesty."

"While we wait for Anapepy to return," Tausret said, "I am prepared to rule on Ament's actions, for his removal of the two slaves is not contingent on finding an order allowing abuse of boy slaves."

Merysekhmet shrugged. "The king has given you the power to so rule, Lady Tausret. Your decision in this matter is final, subject only to the king."

Tausret nodded. "Then I find that Ament has not deserted his post as the command to take the slaves to Timna did not include instructions as to what to do afterward. Lacking specific instructions it was a reasonable decision to return to the palace here in Men-nefer to resume his duties as Captain of the Palace Guard. Comments, Merysekhmet? Ament?"

"Let it be as you say, God's Wife," Merysekhmet said formally.

"Thank you, Lady Tausret," Ament murmured.

"Next we turn to the matter of the supposed theft of two slaves," Tausret continued. "If the boys were being ill-treated, then it was Ament's duty to report it. They are the king's property, after all. If he felt that further hurt would be visited upon them while he was in the process of reporting the acts, then he was justified in removing them."

"It was still theft, Majesty," Merysekhmet said. "No permission was sought to remove them from Timna."

"Timna belongs to the king?"

Merysekhmet frowned at this statement of the obvious, but nodded.

"As does this palace, this city, the Two Kingdoms themselves?" Tausret went on. "All of this is the king's land?"

"Of course, Majesty."

"Then where is the theft? Ament was merely moving the king's property around within his lands. In fact, you could commend him for protecting the king's property. I find Ament innocent of these charges and worthy of reinstatement to his former position."

Merysekhmet looked as if he had taken an unexpected draught of vinegar instead of rich wine, but he bowed to the inevitable. "Let it be as you say, God's Wife."

"Then that's settled. Welcome back, Ament."

"Thank you, my lady. Er, what about the slave boys?"

"I will have them returned to Timna," Merysekhmet said. He raised a hand to forestall any protest from Ament. "I will send an order back with them prohibiting any unnatural acts to be performed on any boy."

"I er, sort of promised them I wouldn't send them back," Ament said.

"That was not a promise you could make," the Tjaty said. "They are the king's slaves."

"No more," Tausret said with a smile. "I will gift them to Ament. As his slaves he can keep them here in Ta Mehu."

"I don't want slaves, Lady Tausret."

"Then free them and keep them as servants."

"I'm a soldier, lady Tausret. What would I do with servants? I am not a lord to have servants in my service."

"Other people have servants," Tausret observed.

"People who are well-off, not common soldiers."

"If that is what it takes."

Ament frowned. "Eh? Forgive me, lady, but I don't understand you."

"If only the well-off can afford servants, then that is what you must become. Where do your sister and brother-in-law have their vineyard?"

"Er, just outside of Per-Bast, Majesty, but what did you mean...?"

"Then I shall make you Overseer of Vineyards in Per-Bast, with enough land adjoining your sister's vineyard to enable you to live in comfort and afford servants. You will reside there and your two servants shall minister to your needs."

Ament gaped, and Merysekhmet muttered about the foolishness of rewarding crime, but when the Queen lifted an eyebrow in his direction, he bowed in acquiescence.

"Let it be as you say, God's Wife."

Chapter 20

Royal Butler Bay speaks:

I find myself in a quandary. I am brother-in-law to Messuwy, eldest son of the late king Baenre Merenptah, but also Royal Butler to the present king Userkheperure Seti. I ask myself to whom I owe allegiance, and the answer eludes me. If my sister was still alive, there would be no doubt, I would side with her husband and see him crowned king. Then her son Ramesses-Siptah would be heir to the throne and one day I would claim the title of God's Father like that old man a hundred years ago. And like that old man, Kheperkheperure Irimaat Ay, I might even find myself ascending the throne and becoming Lord of the Two Lands. Would that not be a wonder to behold? An Amorite servant seated on the throne of Kemet?

But my sister Suterere is dead and I cannot be certain that Messuwy, my erstwhile brother-in-law will honour my position. I could render him a signal service, help him to the throne, and still be cast aside. My nephew Siptah would ever be his eldest son, but he is sickly and who knows when the gods may call him to the afterlife. Messuwy is sure to marry again and have other sons and they would inherit if their mother was of higher status than my sister Suterere, so where is my advantage in choosing him?

On the other hand, why should I choose to stay loyal to the present king of Kemet, Userkheperure Seti? Royal Butler is an exalted position, but how much higher can I reasonably hope to climb? If I was from one of the old noble families of Kemet, or even from a decent Kemetu family among the commoners, I might rise to become Chancellor or Tjaty, but that is unlikely. Too many people look down on my origins, despising any Amorite who attains position within Kemetu society. No, Royal Butler is as far as I am likely to rise. So then, do I remain loyal? What is in it for me?

The king has gone north, pursuing Retenu rebels and their allied Sea Peoples, hoping to bring them to battle and crush them into the stony ground. He will likely do it too, but for a month or more he will be as far from the southern city of Waset as he is ever likely to get. The news of the king's preoccupation will filter down to Waset, of course, there are plenty of people prepared to share what is common knowledge up here in Ta Mehu in the hope of reward, but few know how to get a message to Messuwy swiftly. I can, for gold from his lieutenant Sethi reaches me at irregular intervals and I send word of inconsequential things south from time to time. By reason of my contacts, the information of the king's whereabouts would fly like an arrow to Messuwy's ears.

Imagine for a moment that I decide on this course of action. Userkheperure is a month from here even if he could disentangle himself from the enemy at once. Say I send word by the fastest boat to Waset, and beyond, into Kush. Twenty days after leaving here, the message is in Messuwy's hands. He reacts immediately, gathering his forces and marching on Waset, another twenty days, whereupon he takes the city and is crowned king. From here the news flies north by a hundred ways and reaches the king in far-off Retenu in another twenty days. He marches south at once and meets Messuwy's army which is, by now, nearing Mennefer. Userkheperure's army outnumbers Messuwy's but Messuwy's is fresher, not having just fought a war. The outcome is in the balance, and therein lies part of my problem, the south favours Messuwy and the north favours Userkheperure. The north is richer and stronger, but the south is more fiercely loyal. Which would win? Alas, only the gods know and they are not telling me.

If Messuwy wins, he is aware of my help and rewards me. If Userkheperure wins, I fear that someone will tell him of my part in the rebellion and I would have to flee for my life. Of course, a single battle may not decide the outcome. If Messuwy wins that first battle indecisively, Userkheperure retreats north to Per-Ramesses and gathers the northern legions to him. If Messuwy loses, he retreats south to Waset and prepares for a siege. The war could drag on for years, but if I could make my way down to Waset, Messuwy would surely grant me a place in his court. But is a possible position at Messuwy's court worth more than my present position here as Royal Butler?

I must decide, but how?

I think my decision must rest on my nephew Ramesses-Siptah. The boy is descended from Usermaatre and Baenre, and if Messuwy succeeds in his righteous rebellion, then Siptah's father will also be king. For the sake of the boy, I must hand him his birthright. He is descended from kings and I have it in my power to...well, if not make him a king, at least give him the opportunity to become one.

There, I have made my decision. I will send word to Messuwy that the time is ripe for him to seize power, to march on Waset and have himself crowned king of all Kemet. Userkheperure is heading north, if I send word now, then Messuwy can start his march by the time Userkheperure first engages the enemy, and he will be king in Waset before Userkheperure knows he has made his claim. Then we shall see what we shall see.

Chapter 21
Year 2 of Userkheperure Seti

C ommander Iurudef and the Set legion awaited the king just north of Per-Ramesses and escorted the king to the frontier along the coastal road, relegating the Ptah legion and its auxiliaries to a rear-guard position. Besenmut was visibly upset with his relegation, but could say nothing. Iurudef made the most of it, often riding in the king's own war chariot and discussing the forthcoming punitive expedition. He outlined the latest information he had on rebel movements and the more important dispositions of the Sea Peoples.

"Commander Emsaf is up near Ghazzat with the Heru legion, harassing the army investing the city. They will have had word that you are on the way and will be in a hurry to take the city."

"And where is Re?" Seti asked.

"Disebek is pursuing the rebels, preventing them from joining up with the Sea Peoples. They are like water, Son of Re, dissolving and disappearing into the desert sand as soon as we get close to them. We can drive them though, so the Re legion with a troop or two of the Sets are keeping them busy."

"What is the strength of the Sea Peoples' army?"

"Two, three thousand, Son of Re."

"So Heru, Set and Ptah together will outnumber them."

"Yes, Divine One. Er, what of the Ptah auxiliaries? Are they trained?"

"They are learning and will learn faster or die when we attack. It would be wise not to rely on them though."

"I'm sure we can find a use for them."

The army advanced up the coast road, past the string of forts that marked the ancient borders of Kemet, and into the occupied territories loosely held by the legions of a succession of kings since the days of Menkheperre Thutmose. The red desert lands, Deshret, already dry and inhospitable far from the life-giving waters of the Great River became more barren and dust, whipped up by strong winds, filled their mouths and nostrils, causing man and beast to choke.

Iurudef pointed toward the east where what looked like a long low cloud, yellow-brown in colour, slowly advanced toward them. He coughed and spat, turning his back to the stinging sand so he could talk. "We must stop our march, Son of Re, and take shelter. A storm of sand and dust is almost upon us and no army can keep going in that."

Seti called a halt and ordered a camp to be set up, having his men erect tents and stretch linen cloth between poles to offer some shelter from the wind. Food and water were distributed to the men and the horses were herded into the middle of the camp and surrounded by temporary stables to protect them. The king retired to his tent with his two commanders, Iurudef and Besenmut, and ordered wine to be brought.

Seti rinsed his mouth with wine and spat onto the dirt floor, wiping his lips to rid them of the gritty residue. "Why do we even bother with lands like these?" he asked. "There can be little of any value in them."

The two commanders sipped and swallowed, exchanging glances. Seti saw them and waved a hand impatiently. "No, go on, tell me. Except for my brief foray against the rebels last year, this is the first time I've been up here since my father punished them. He never explained why we bothered with Retenu. Can either of you do so?"

"Well, er, we've always held this territory, Son of Re," Besenmut said. "It's part of Kemet."

"Then why did we conquer it in the first place? It's dry and useless. The only thing they grow around here is poor quality barley and scrawny goats. Don't tell me we coveted those things when we have such rich farmland by the Great River."

"Because the Hatti owned it," Iurudef said quietly. "One of their kings with an unpronounceable name enlarged their empire right up to the borders of Kemet and threatened us. We had to take it over or else suffer a hostile army within striking distance of the cities of Ta Mehu."

"Now that I can understand," Seti said, holding out his cup for more wine. Besenmut poured. "My grandfather Usermaatre even carried the fight to the Hatti as far as Kadesh or even further. He won a great battle there when he was a young man, you know."

Iurudef hesitated and then decided it would serve no purpose to debate the truth of that claim with the king. "Indeed, Son of Re," he said instead. "And a victory that you will eclipse when you meet the Sea Peoples."

Seti looked pleased. "I shall relieve the city of Ghazzat and drive the Sea Peoples back into the Sea they came from. How far are we from Ghazzat?"

"Eight or nine days once this dust storm subsides."

"Then let us pray to the gods it does so soon, for I thirst for the battle."

"Sometimes they last two or three days, Son of Re."

The dry storm showed no signs of abating by sunset, not that the sun was in sight as it descended the western heavens. Instead, the dim light grew dimmer, the gloominess intensifying by slow degrees until full dark fell. Flames were rapidly extinguished by the choking dust and sand, so no camp fires could be lit, though oil lamps could be coaxed into fitful use if sufficiently shielded within a tent. The men ate cold rations, a little dried fish, a handful of dates and a hunk of barley bread, washed down with gritty water. Afterward, most of the men curled up with cloths covering their heads and shoulders and tried to sleep. The Commanders set out guards, though it was unlikely the enemy would be abroad in the night. Visibility was limited to an arm's length in any case, and many of the guards just covered their heads and waited for the storm to ease.

The sandstorm lasted two days and there was nothing the Kemetu army could do except wait it out in enforced inactivity. Seti grew increasingly fractious and snapped at his commanders whenever they offered any comment. Finally, he was persuaded into a series of games of Senet, though such was his lack of attention, it was all the commanders could do to lose their games.

On the third day, the winds died down and by midday the army was able to pick itself out of the sand, shake loose the accumulated dust and dirt and form itself into ranks to resume its weary march north and east.

Seti scratched and pulled at his clothing continually, the sand grains having inserted themselves into every orifice and his skin felt dry and abraded. Iurudef noticed his king's discomfort and offered a suggestion.

"The men will fight better if they can rid themselves of the sand and dust, Son of Re. The sea is close by; perhaps we could bathe and refresh ourselves."

The king weighed his options, wanting to relieve the city of Ghazzat without delay, but also recognising his own discomfort and knowing his men were probably worse off. He gave the order to turn aside, and by mid-afternoon the army arrived at a sandy beach in a broad bay. A cool breeze blew off the sea, carrying with it a dampness and salt smell that was, in itself, refreshing.

The commanders gave the orders, and troop by troop the legions cast aside weapons and clothing and ran into the waves. There were many yells of surprise as some men, reared alongside Kemet's Great River, encountered salt water for the first time. Once the initial shock had worn off, they gambolled and splashed in the shallows, laughing like children. Others were waiting for their turn, so after a few minutes, a troop would be ordered out and another would strip off and plunge into the water. Clothing was rinsed and laid out on the sand to dry, and naked men stood guard in the dunes behind the beach with weapons drawn, eyes cast wistfully at their fellow soldiers enjoying themselves in the sea.

Seti swam off to one side, accompanied by his legion commanders. Although he could swim quite well, having often disported himself in the river as a child, the huge expanse of salt water unnerved him and he stayed close to the shore. Besenmut swam further out, having spent his youth in the north of Ta Mehu, and had often swum in the sea. Iurudef ventured in no further than waist deep though, fearing what he could not see or understand. Waves surged around his legs, threatening to unbalance him, and he looked around wildly when this happened, crying out that something under the water had grasped him.

It was too late to move on by the time the legions had washed and dried themselves and their clothing, so they set up camp on the beach, using the water's edge as one boundary and setting up guards on the landward side. Driftwood became crackling, spitting fires, and the army enjoyed a cooked meal for the first time in days. Some of the more enterprising men speared fish in the shallows and enjoyed fresh food. One soldier brought the king a particularly fine fish he had caught and was rewarded with a gold armband worth far more than the fish.

The crash and suck of the small waves on the sandy beach lulled them to sleep that night, and they woke refreshed and eager the next day. Seti offered up thanks to the Ascending Light, standing atop a sand dune where all the men could see him, and then ordered the rams' horns be blown. The army sorted itself back into ranks, and to the sound of horns and drums, and the cheerful voices of the men lifted up in song, marched away from the shore and back onto the road to Ghazzat.

The legions had barely started along the road before a small fast-travelling cloud of dust appeared behind them. A messenger chariot raced through the ranks of men who parted to let him through, and up to the king's chariot. The messenger jumped off before it had stopped, stumbling and almost falling in his haste. He bowed, breathing hard, and proffered the sealed letter he carried.

"Son of Re, an urgent dispatch from Tjaty Merysekhmet."

Seti had an officer hand him the letter which he opened and scanned. A frown settled on his features and he crumpled the letter in his hand, jumping down from his chariot and walking a few paces away. The commanders hurried from their positions at the head of their legions.

"Bad news, Son of Re?" Iurudef asked.

"I will have his liver for this," Seti muttered.

"Whose, Majesty?" Besenmut asked.

Seti turned back to face his commanders. "My brother Messuwy. He has come out of Kush at the head of an army and advances on Waset. He means to make himself king."

"How many men can he possibly have? A hundred? Two?" Iurudef asked. "The King's Son of Kush Khaemter will move to stop him, and the Amun legion will crush him."

"Khaemter and the Kushite legion have already joined him. Commander Tarkahe of the Abu garrison has done likewise, declaring for him publicly. The Amun legion has deserted. In fact, the whole of Ta Shemau has risen in support of Messuwy."

The commanders stood silent, digesting the news, then, "Your orders, Son of Re?"

"I must answer this threat, yet I am loath to turn back from Ghazzat and my enemies there."

"Even if Ghazzat falls the Sea Peoples will not threaten the borders of Kemet," Iurudef said. "Not yet, anyway. Take your legions and defeat your traitorous brother, Divine One."

Seti paced back and forth, muttering under his breath. "Who is your second in command, Iurudef?"

"Ahmes, Son of Re."

"He now leads the Set legion. They, and the Ptah legion will turn south to meet the new foe. We must hurry."

Iurudef looked pale. "Son of Re, why have you replaced me? How have I displeased you?"

Seti stopped his pacing and stared at his commander. "Eh? You have not. I did not explain myself, I need someone senior that I can trust. I want you to pull together the Heru and Re legions left on the borders into a coherent fighting force. Judge whether you can defeat the Sea Peoples and relieve Ghazzat. If you can without endangering your army, do so. If not, then pull back to the line of forts and prevent any from entering Kemet." Seti called for a scribe and dictated a short document making Iurudef General of the North.

Iurudef bowed low and uttered thanks and prayed to the gods to grant the king a swift and complete victory over his enemies.

"I'll be back before you know it, General Iurudef," Seti said. "So make sure you leave some foreigners for me."

The king sprang into his chariot while Iurudef hurried to inform Ahmes of his promotion and Besenmut ordered the Ptah legion to turn their faces toward Kemet once more. Iurudef claimed a single chariot and driver and watched and waited as the army lurched into motion. Before the sun had climbed half way to the zenith, the legions were out of sight of Iurudef. He sighed and told the charioteer to drive east and north to find the Heru legion.

Chapter 22
Year 2 of Userkheperure Seti
Year 1 of Menmire Amenmesse

Messuwy's army poured out of Kush two legions strong with over a thousand Kushite tribesmen who refused to discipline themselves by forming military units. They fought as individuals or as small tribal groups and sought mostly plunder. Tribesmen washed over the southern farms, burning, pillaging, killing and stealing as if this was some foreign land they conquered rather than the land of Kemet claimed by their commander. Messuwy was disturbed by their excesses and ordered Sethi to stop them.

"Can't be done, my lord, unless we want a pitched battle on our hands. Besides, these are farmers technically under the control of the false king Seti. The example we set with them will serve as an object lesson for any of his other supporters."

"But they are my lands now."

"So you are giving them as a reward to your faithful followers."

"I don't like it. I want the support of the people, not their resentment."

"And you shall have it, my lord, as soon as you are crowned king in Waset."

Commander Tarkahe opened his garrison at Abu to the invader and knelt before Messuwy, hailing him as king. Two hundred of his men joined the march northward and every town and village they passed through swelled their numbers. By the time Messuwy's army reached the gates of Waset, it was five thousand strong.

Reports had reached Tjaty Neferronpet and Merenkhons, the Commander of the Amun legion long before the rebel army appeared, and urgent messages and pleas for support had been sent to the king. Nothing had happened, no support had been sent, and now the rulers of Waset had a difficult choice to make. They conferred together, and then Merenkhons, with half a hundred loyal men, fled the city and made his way north, while Neferronpet elected to remain at his post. A small detachment of men loyal to the Tjaty stood guard over the rooms where Takhat, wife of the king, resided.

As soon as the soldiers loyal to Seti had gone, the Amun legion threw open the gates and arrested Neferronpet, throwing him into a cell to await the pleasure of Messuwy. The Kushite troops marched in and took possession of the city. Messuwy, arriving later, learnt that his sister Takhat was in the palace, and ordered his own men to replace those of the Tjaty, making it clear that no harm was to come to her, or disrespect be shown.

"She was my sister before she was his wife," Messuwy declared.

The townspeople lined the streets of Waset as Messuwy entered in a chariot, escorted by a strong force of loyal soldiers, but they were there more from curiosity than support. They watched in almost-silence as Messuwy drove his chariot to the palace steps and alighted, at which point Sethi almost pushed Messuwy aside and harangued the crowd.

"This is Lord Messuwy, eldest son of Baenre Merenptah, and rightful king of Kemet. His half-brother Seti stole the throne from him by whispering lies in his father's ears, but Lord Messuwy is back now, at the head of a large army to claim what is rightfully his. Any man who supports him will be well rewarded, while any who oppose him will meet with death and confiscation of all his wealth." Sethi stared out at the mass of humanity gathered around the palace and stretched out his hand toward Messuwy.

"Know this, men of Amun's city, Lord Messuwy has always supported Amun and Amun's city against those who would denigrate the supreme god and shift power away from its rightful place here in Waset to the lesser cities of Per-Ramesses and Men-nefer. Lord Messuwy will be crowned here in Waset, by all the rites and rituals of Amun, and will take as his Name Amenmesse Heqawaset, fashioned by Amun, ruler of Waset, signifying that he reigns by the will of Amun, in Amun's City. Once more, Waset will achieve its rightful place as Kemet's first city, and great will be the wealth that flows into this city. Acclaim him, people of Waset. Support your rightful king and throw down the usurper."

The murmuring of the crowd, which had been growing as Sethi spoke, now erupted into cheering, and many people threw their support wholeheartedly behind Messuwy, or Amenmesse as he soon would be, yelling and cursing.

"Amenmesse for king!"

"Down with Seti. Kill him."

"A curse on Seti. May he and his family disappear from the land forever."

"Amun and Messuwy, Amun and Amenmesse."

Sethi turned to Messuwy with a look of triumph. "Behold, my lord, for I have delivered your people to you."

Messuwy frowned at Sethi's words, but merely nodded, turning and walking into the palace where servants, little caring who ruled them, hurried to make him welcome. He strode through the palace to the throne room and, with a look of triumph, sat down on it, savouring the sensation.

"Send for Neferronpet, Merenkhons, Khaemter and Roma-Rui," he ordered.

Sethi issued the commands to soldiers and servants and presently Commander Khaemter turned up, followed a little later by Roma-Rui, and then by Tjaty Neferronpet, bound in copper chains that scraped and dragged on the floor as he shuffled along under the weight of them.

Messuwy ignored Neferronpet and held out his hand to Roma-Rui. "Hem-netjer of Amun, you are welcome."

Roma-Rui bowed low. "I am no longer Hem-netjer," he said. "Bakenkhons replaced me by order of the one who calls himself King Userkheperure."

"That order is rescinded," Messuwy said. "As is every order of that man. You are again Hem-netjer, Roma-Rui. Do with Bakenkhons as you see fit."

"Thank you, Son of Re, Son of Amun. May the gods bless you in all your endeavours."

"What will you do with him?" Sethi asked.

Roma-Rui thought for a few moments. "I have some onerous tasks the Fourth Prophet would normally be required to do. I think Bakenkhons will benefit from a time of humility."

"I thought you'd be killing him, or throwing him into a dungeon at the very least."

"He is still a servant of the god, no matter what any king asks of him."

"Where is Merenkhons?" Messuwy asked. "I ordered the Commander of the Amun legion be here."

"I have sent for him," Sethi said. "He should be here by now...ah, this will be him." A tap sounded on the door and an army officer entered and saluted. "Well, where is he?"

"My lord, Commander Merenkhons has fled the city. I...I am senior officer now, I suppose."

"And you are?"

"Troop Commander Menkauhor, Lord Sethi."

"Then on your knees before your king, Menkauhor." Sethi stood back and indicated the presence of Messuwy on the throne.

The Troop Commander bowed before Messuwy, hands outstretched, and then fell to his knees. "Forgive me, Lord Messuwy...Majesty. I swear to you my allegiance. I will serve you faithfully."

Messuwy nodded and gestured. "Stand, Commander Menkauhor. You are now Commander of the Amun legion."

Menkauhor gaped and then beamed with pleasure, bowing again before backing away.

"Neferronpet, once called Tjaty by the pretender," Messuwy said. "Step forward."

"Not just named Tjaty by King Userkheperure," Neferronpet said as he shuffled across to stand before Messuwy. "I was named Tjaty of the South by your own father, Baenre Merenptah, Lord of the Two Kingdoms. Userkheperure Seti is also Lord of the Two Kingdoms, crowned and elevated to the godhead by Amun himself in this city. Nothing you say or do can alter that."

"Bow to the rightful king," Sethi snarled, giving the older man a push.

Neferronpet staggered and almost fell. "I bend my knee only to Userkheperure Seti, not to this pretender."

"I am my father's eldest son," Messuwy said. "You cannot deny it. I should by rights be king. Seti stole that from me and..."

"You were never Heir," Neferronpet interrupted. "Baenre made his son Seti the Crown Prince, partly because of a promise made to Usermaatre, and partly because he simply did not trust you. He could see what you were, Messuwy..."

"Silence!" Sethi roared. "You speak treason against King Amenmesse."

"Is that what you are calling yourself? Fashioned by Amun? More likely fashioned by this jumped-up noble and a priest of Amun..."

Sethi stepped forward and hit Neferronpet in the side of the face, and as the older man staggered back under the constraint of his copper chains, dealt him another blow that felled him. "You will die for your traitorous remarks."

"I haven't decided his fate," Messuwy said.

"You cannot do anything else," Sethi replied. "Anything less will be interpreted as a sign of weakness. You agree, don't you Roma-Rui?"

The Hem-netjer grimaced but nodded. "He maligned Amun and your Majesty. He cannot be allowed to get away with that."

"You cannot sentence me to death, Messuwy," Neferronpet groaned, struggling into a sitting position. "Only the king can sit in judgement over me."

"I am the king, you fool."

"You will never be the king. Do you imagine Userkheperure will do nothing? He will descend on you with his legions..."

"Messuwy will be King Menmire Amenmesse tomorrow," Sethi said. "Roma-Rui will take great pleasure in crowning him in Amun's holy name, and then we shall see. The southern legions are more than a match for the northern ones and the whole of the south will rise and take arms for the rightful king. You heard them earlier today, acclaiming Lord Messuwy."

"And as for you, Neferronpet," Messuwy added. "You will be dead for the day after I am crowned I will sit in judgement over you and pass sentence of death. All will be done in accordance with law."

Neferronpet managed to shrug, his chains clinking as he moved. "You will not succeed, Messuwy. Userkheperure will defeat you."

"But you will not be here to see whether he does or not. Take him away, and bring him before me when I am king so that I may sentence him to a traitor's death."

Commander Menkauhor ordered the soldiers to haul Neferronpet to his feet and escorted the older man out. When they had gone, Messuwy instructed Sethi to organise the soldiers of Kush and the Amun legion into a cohesive fighting force.

"That is Khaemter's duty," Sethi said. "I have more important things to do. I must grasp the reins that Neferronpet has relinquished."

"No, Khaemter will be Tjaty of the South," Messuwy said.

"What? Messuwy, you promised me..."

Messuwy raised an eyebrow at Sethi's outburst. "Khaemter is Tjaty. I have other duties for you." He saw the anger in Sethi's face and though he hid it, felt unease. "More important duties, General Sethi. The army is yours; mould it into an efficient fighting force for me."

"General? But Khaemter, surely..."

"Khaemter was King's Son of Kush, an able military commander but a better administrator. He is more suited to running Ta Shemau on a daily basis."

Khaemter bowed low. "Son of Re, I am honoured. I will serve you ably."

"I know you will. General Sethi here has overall command of the Southern Army. Appoint whom you will within the legions and raise more men. We must hold the south and prepare to invade the north."

"I have the freedom to do what needs doing?" Sethi asked.

"Have I not said it? Do what you need to do as long as you build me an army."

"But first we must crown you king, Great One," Roma-Rui said. "With your permission, I will set things in motion." He bowed and left the throne room.

The next day, the coronation ceremony that had played out a few short months before when Userkheperure Seti was accepted by Amun, repeated itself as Messuwy shed his former life and became god-on-earth. If any among the crowds watching the public parts of the ritual thought there was something odd about a king being crowned while his predecessor still lived, they kept it to themselves.

As his younger brother had done, Messuwy stood outside the Great Temple of Amun in the early morning light. He was similarly bereft of regalia and jewellery, his stomach was empty, and his heart beat fast from excitement. As Seti had done, he strode forward into the temple, passing through the entrance pylon, through the hypostyle hall, the next two pylons and toward the inner temple. He turned aside to the Lake of Cleansing where he was stripped naked and the four men dressed as gods symbolically cleansed him, transforming him from man into incipient god.

Cleansed and dressed in fresh clothing that had never been worn, Messuwy was escorted into the inner temple by Atum and Heru of the Horizon. Gods in the guise of men sang their songs of joy in the House of Flame, and the toothless cobra of Wadjet bestowed its harmless bite of acceptance. Messuwy had been told of this ritual beforehand, so felt no fear, just a mild contempt for the games the priests played.

The ceremony of crowns followed, with Iunmutef the Pillar placing crown after crown on Messuwy's head, to the acclamation of the assembled priests. Into the shrine of Amun he was guided, where Amun himself crowned him once more with the Khepresh crown. Seated once more on the throne in the open courtyard of the temple, and viewed by thousands crowding in to witness, the five priests stepped forward for the naming ceremonies. As they had done with Seti not long before, the priests called on their gods and bestowed the names of power by which this new King of Kemet would be known.

"Let Heru empower you," said the first priest. "Your name in Heru shall be Kanakht Merymaat Shementawy, Strong Bull, Beloved of Maat, He who strengthens the Two Lands."

"Nekhabet and Wadjet name you also," the second priest exclaimed. "Your name of Nebty shall be Werbiayt-em-ipet-sut, He who is Great of Miracles in Ipet-sut, the most Secret of Places."

"The gods recognise you as their son on earth," said the third. "Heru Nebu names you Aa-ipet-sut, Great One of the most Secret of Places."

"Nesut-byt, King of Ta Mehu and Ta Shemau, North and South," cried the fourth priest. "Menmire Setepenre, Eternal like Re, the chosen one of Re."

"Sa-Re, Son of Re," the fifth priest said. "Amenmesse Heqawaset, Fashioned by Amun, ruler of Waset."

Complete silence hung over the forecourt of the Great temple of Amun for the time it took to count to twenty, so long that the king stirred on his throne at the ill-omened pause. Then, after the priests of Amun encouraged the crowd, cheering broke forth as the witnesses to the new king's naming stamped and called, throwing their arms up and praising the king.

Menmire Amenmesse arose and made his way to the processional chariot, leading the troops of the Kushite and Amun legions through the streets of Waset while the cheers of the crowds washed over him. Arriving back at the palace, he was greeted by his new Tjaty, Khaemter, and General of the Southern Army, Lord Sethi.

"That went well," Amenmesse said. "The people love me."

"That is good, Son of Re," Khaemter said. "We have need of their support."

Amenmesse caught the stress in his Tjaty's voice and stared at him. "What has happened?"

"Userkheperure..." Khaemter started.

"Don't use that name. I have supplanted my brother as king and he holds no legitimate throne names. He is just plain Seti now."

"Then Seti is marching to throw you out of Waset," Sethi said dryly. "King or not, he controls the northern legions."

"The Kushite is a match for any of them."

"Perhaps, though they are all battle hardened against the Ribu and Sea Peoples. Besides, he has several legions to call on, whereas we have one half decent one and the Amun."

"I thought I told you to build up an army," Amenmesse complained.

"There are limits to what I can do in a day...Son of Re."

"So what do we do?" Amenmesse demanded. "You are my Tjaty and my General. Advise me."

"You have two choices," Sethi said. "Fight and risk all on a single battle, or flee and try again."

"I am King of Kemet. I do not run."

"Then you must win that first battle or die."

"We could seal ourselves up in Waset," Khaemter suggested. "The walls are strong."

"They would starve us out," Sethi said. "The city has limited supplies and many useless mouths whereas they can plunder the surrounding farms for food."

"Then we fight," Amenmesse decided. "We fight and we win."

"So we march to meet them?" Khaemter asked.

"Let them come to us," Amenmesse replied. "We will have the advantages of being well-rested and fed, and can choose the place of battle."

Chapter 23
Year 2 of Userkheperure Seti
Year 1 of Menmire Amenmesse

Seti drove the Set and Ptah legions south as fast as the men could march. When they were safely inside the borders of Ta Mehu, he left the men to continue south under the command of their officers and raced ahead with his chariot squadrons to Men-nefer. There, he conferred with Tjaty Merysekhmet, listening to the latest information to emerge from the southern kingdom, ordering men, equipment and stores to be readied, and only then did he visit his wife.

"You have heard?" Seti asked Tausret. "The South has risen against me."

"How could I not, husband? Will you be in Men-nefer long?"

"Only as long as it takes my legions to get here. Set and Ptah, both at full strength."

"And your chariots?" Tausret asked. "They could well be decisive."

"A hundred, or thereabouts. My two legions will be more than enough to crush my brother. I will hang him in chains from the walls of Waset."

"Don't underestimate him, husband. He has the Amun and Kushite legions and by all accounts, the support of most of Ta Shemau."

"No match for my battle-hardened warriors. Besides, he has few chariots and his men know they face the king."

"They have made their own king."

"You heard that too?"

"Menmire Amenmesse," Tausret said.

"Don't call him that. Messuwy is good enough for him. Anyway, where did you hear that? Merysekhmet has been most careful to keep that secret. He doesn't want people up here getting the notion he's been legitimately crowned."

"Nothing happens in Kemet that I don't hear about sooner or later, husband. Your Royal Butler Bay has proved invaluable. It seems he has a wide network of informants in both kingdoms."

"Indeed? I thought that he might throw in his lot with Messuwy, seeing as how he is uncle to Messuwy's young boy."

"He came and abased himself before me when the news arrived. Swore his loyalty to you and asked me to use him as I saw fit. He says he will trust to your divine mercy and justice to deal fairly with the boy, Ramesses-Siptah, after you've defeated his father the traitor."

"He said that?" Seti asked. "You may tell him I will reward loyalty, and...well, I don't wage war on innocent children. How old is he now?"

"Five years old or thereabouts. And speaking of small children, what of Takhat? She must have had her baby by now."

Seti lifted his eyebrows in mock surprise. "Your informants have not told you? Well, neither has mine. I believe she is still in Waset and must trust that my enemies do not make her suffer for my sake."

"Messuwy will not harm her, for she is his sister. And if he does I shall rip his heart from his chest," Tausret declared.

"So fierce? I thought you didn't like her."

"What gave you that idea, husband? Because I am no longer sole wife but must share you with her? Because she is with child by you? Or because she is young and attractive while I grow old?" Tausret smiled. "She loves you, and anyone who loves you is good in my eyes."

"I do not deserve you, Tausret," Seti said, shaking his head.

Tausret grinned. "No, you don't. In fact, you can tell me how much you need me and love me every night on our journey down to Waset."

Seti stared. "You are not coming. Do you think I'd take you into danger?"

"What danger?" Tausret asked with laughter in her voice. "You said your legions would crush Messuwy's. Besides..." the laughter died, replaced by a hard-eyed stare. "...I too have faced the enemy in the field, husband. Or have you forgotten Perire?"

"I have not." Seti grimaced and paced for a few moments, marshalling his thoughts. "It is for this very reason that I must leave you in Men-nefer." He looked around at the few servants carrying on their usual daily tasks and abruptly ordered them from his presence. "My love, I would not ask this of you, but...it is seldom that a king of Kemet is blessed with a warrior wife. When I face Messuwy in the south with two legions, I leave another three in the north to guard a border already inflamed, but few other resources except Medjay. I ask myself if Messuwy's rebellion is only in the south. If his treason has infected others, up here perhaps, then what happens if rebellion breaks out in my rear? That is why I want you to remain in Men-nefer, to guard my back."

"Merysekhmet...?"

"...Is old and not versed in warfare. He can govern the kingdom well enough, but I need a...a general to keep a lid on any unrest in my absence."

"And you shall have it, my husband," Tausret declared. "If anyone dares act against you, I shall lop their head from their shoulders without delay."

Seti laughed and embraced his wife. "I believe you would. I can see I'll be leaving Ta Mehu in safe hands."

The men of the Ptah and Set legions arrived at Men-nefer three days later, exhausted from their rapid march from the northern borders, and Seti immediately ordered an enforced rest. For two days they rested, eating and drinking well, and having any common ailments seen to by the army physicians. Then, on the fifth day, Seti joined his army on the east bank, where he offered up sacrifices to all the gods. Barges were loaded with spare horses and equipment, together with two troops of soldiers, and these embarked ahead of the marching army to set up camp every night. With the aid of the barges, the men could travel light and fast.

It took them all a few days to settle in to the routine. The first day, the barge captains overestimated the distance the men could march and it was not until well after sunset before they straggled into camp, footsore and weary. The second day, they swung the other way, wasting the best part of an afternoon when the soldiers marched up while the sun was still well above the western horizon. Thereafter, they slowly improved, and by the time they drew close to the city of Khent-Min, the army was marching swiftly and decisively between camps.

"The barges go no further," Seti told his legion commanders Besenmut and Ahmes. "We are close enough to Waset that we could be surprised by Messuwy's forces. I want us all together if that happens."

"Messuwy's son Siptah is in Khent-Min," Besenmut said. "He might make a useful hostage."

"I do not war against children," Seti answered, fixing the commander in a stare that soon had him avert his gaze. "Scour the city for supplies, but give the farmers and traders a promissory note for anything you take. These are our people down here as much as in the north and I will not have them suffer for the acts of others."

The army marched south two days later, in battle array. Fast scouting chariots fanned out to look for any sign of the enemy, while Seti guided the legions along the main road that curved away from the eastern river cliffs and into the desert. The Set legion led, the soldiers being the most experienced, though Acting Commander Ahmes was the least experienced in command. The presence of the king would offset that, while Besenmut, with his legion and half-trained auxiliaries brought up the rear.

They met nothing on the long weary days down to Waset. People that normally frequented the road, traders and merchants, melted away in front of the army, leaving them to march alone down the hot dusty road. As they drew close to Waset, Seti pulled his chariots in closer, reluctant to risk them engaging the enemy without being able to strike a decisive blow with his foot soldiers.

"Where will Messuwy meet us?" Seti asked his Commanders.

"There is only one place, Son of Re," Besenmut replied. "Opposite the southeast gate. There is a broad plain there with low hills toward the river and stony desert inland unsuitable for chariots. He'll meet us on the plain."

"My thought exactly."

Seti's army advanced cautiously, circling the walled city to the east and finally approaching Waset from the southeast, where the main gates stood open. Their shadows stood long on the ground before them, the early morning sun warming their backs. The men stopped and waited, catching their breath and leaning on their spears while Seti and his commanders moved out in front in three chariots. They pulled up close together just over an arrow's flight from the city walls and examined the silent city with interest.

"Where is everyone?" Ahmes asked. "Have they all taken fright and fled?"

"What? A whole city?" Besenmut countered. "Perhaps they're just surrendering."

"Then where are they?" Seti demanded. "No, something stinks here."

"I could send some men in to see what's happening," Besenmut suggested. On receiving a nod from the king, he beckoned to his aides and issued his instructions.

A squad trotted toward the open gates with their spears at the ready, and were no more than a spear cast from them when they saw movement in the shadowed streets within the city and stopped. As they stood indecisively, soldiers came pouring out of the gate and the squad hurriedly retreated.

"Ah, now we're seeing something," Besenmut said. "By their banners, they're Amun legion, but not all of them. Either some are loyal to you or the legion is badly understrength."

"And where is the Kushite legion?" Seti asked. "The reports said Messuwy brought them north to Waset, but if that's the case, where are they?"

"Fled when they saw us coming," Ahmes ventured. "They know we'd be too strong for them. Shall I send out scouts to look for them?"

"Later. I would like to know what is happening in Waset first."

"I suppose they are only tribesmen," Ahmes said. "Undisciplined and inexperienced."

"I can't believe Sethi or Khaemter would be so foolish as to venture out of Kush unless they thought they could win," Seti said.

"So where are they?" Besenmut asked. "Still in the city? Afraid to come out?"

"The rebels are either fled or in hiding, Son of Re," Ahmes said. "So what do we do about them?" He pointed at the thousand Amun soldiers standing at the ready in front of the gate.

"Besenmut, call on them to surrender."

The Ptah legion commander saluted and drove his chariot slowly toward the Amun lines, halting when he got within shouting distance. "Where is Commander Merenkhons?" he demanded.

There was a pause, filled only with the shuffling of hundreds of feet in the hot sand. "Merenkhons is no longer Commander, by order of the king in Waset."

"There is but one king," Besenmut replied. "Userkheperure Seti, and he has not ordered the replacement of Merenkhons."

"Not that fornicating boy," the voice from the Amun legion yelled back. "The true king, Menmire Amenmesse. Go back where you came from, Besenmut, or get on your knees to Menmire and beg forgiveness."

"You talk loudly for a coward, whoever you are, hiding behind your men."

The Amun soldiers parted ranks and an officer came stalking through, his face twisted with anger. "I am Commander Menkauhor and I am no coward. Step down from your chariot and I will spill your blood in the sand."

"Surrender, Menkauhor," Besenmut said calmly. "Bend your knee to Userkheperure and maybe he will forgive you."

Menkauhor laughed. "Tell your boy he can surrender to me, now, or I will come over there and spank him." Some of the soldiers around laughed.

"Have you taken leave of your senses?" Besenmut demanded. "You are greatly outnumbered. Surrender now or you and all your men will die."

"Here is my answer," Menkauhor said. He lifted his kilt and urinated on the sand, amid greater mirth from his soldiers. One or two copied his actions.

Besenmut snarled in rage but said nothing, just wheeling his chariot round and driving back to his king. He was too angry to say anything, but Seti just nodded and murmured, "I saw. They will pay for that insult with their lives. Ahmes, take the Set legion and crush those rebels. If possible, keep their commander alive. I will make an example of him."

Ahmes raced back to his legion in his chariot and called out orders to his officers. The men in the various troops sprang forward and the forty chariots of the legion started toward the Amun legion. The chariot squadron soon outdistanced the running men and rapidly crossed the gap of open sand, sweeping around the king and Besenmut in their chariots.

As soon as the chariots had started into motion, the Amun legion fell back, but not toward the gate as Seti had expected, but to a section of the city walls and now stood with their backs to it, their spears grounded in the sand and pointing outward.

"Very clever," Seti said when he saw the manoeuvre. "I wonder who taught them that."

"But they have left themselves no escape, Son of Re," Besenmut said.

"The chariots cannot sweep through them, but must slow and engage them at walking pace, putting the charioteers in danger. Ahmes must call them off and send in the men on foot."

Ahmes was slow to put that plan into action, so Seti whipped his horses into action and drove back quickly to where the legions waited. He shouted out orders to the Troop Commanders, ordering the chariots back and for the Set and Ptah foot soldiers to charge forward. The Set legion and the Ptah regulars obeyed their officers and advanced in relatively good order but the Ptah auxiliaries rapidly devolved into a rabble that streamed forward, interfering with their fellow warriors. As the first of them clashed with the Amun soldiers standing at bay beneath the walls, shouts erupted from behind the king's army in the direction of the river.

Seti heard the clamour and turned in his chariot, striving to see over the heads of his men and through the intervening dust clouds. He could make out little, but something was happening, so he dispatched a chariot to find out. The king reached for his bow and, while a charioteer guided the vehicle through the thinner ranks of men, loosed arrow after arrow into the foe.

The Amun legion was forced back, overwhelmed by the attacking legions, but now the attack was faltering, a tremor running through the packed ranks of men. The chariot returned and the charioteer yelled to the king as soon as he came within earshot.

"The enemy! The Kushite is attacking from the river."

Seti cursed under his breath, knowing he should have sent scouts out as Ahmes had suggested. "Turn," the king ordered his charioteer. He beckoned the bearers of rams' horns to him and told them to turn the Ptah legion immediately, and three troops of Set to join them as soon as possible.

The horns sounded and quickly the chariots of Ptah gathered about their king. Seti murmured instructions to his charioteer and the squadron moved off after him through the dust clouds in the direction of the river and the heavy fighting taking place there. Soon the tall dark bodies of the Kushites could be seen, their ebony skins greyed by the dust, spattered with blood as spears thrust and copper axes chopped and hacked. The Ptah men fought well, but were slowly being pushed back by the men from Kush. Only one thing saved Ptah from utter ruin, the men of Kush liked to single out a man to attack and hurled insults before charging him. If they had attacked as a group, Ptah would have been rolled under the Kushite advance.

Seti signalled to his chariots and they raced up to form a ragged line abreast, charging down on the Kushite foot soldiers. The thunder of hooves and wheels cut through the din of battle and the Kushites turned to look, and then hurried to disengage from the men of Ptah and face the onrushing chariots.

The first line of men went down under hooves and spinning wheels, men thrown aside broken-limbed or crushed in sprays of blood as skulls and ribcages shattered and limbs were sliced open. Seti felt his chariot bounce into the air and land awkwardly, the spokes of one wheel splintering and tipping him to the ground. He rolled as he landed but lost hold of his bow, and came to his feet in a melee of rearing horses, screaming men, and flashing weapons.

Seti straightened the blue leather war bonnet on his head and snatched a copper axe from the ground, turning and slashing as a Kushite warrior confronted him. The Kushite jabbed with his spear and then his eyes opened wide, recognising the royal headdress. He hesitated momentarily, the spear in his hand wavering. Seti stepped inside the arc of the spear and chopped down with the axe, the bright copper blade biting deep into the man's thigh. The Kushite screamed and dropped his spear clutching ineffectually at his mortal wound. Seti wrenched the blade free in a fountain of blood and slashed it sideways across the man's chest. White bone showed through the spurting red wound, and the hot stink of blood filled Seti's nostrils as the man fell back. Another attacked Seti, spear stabbing, keeping the king from closing with him. He hurled the axe. It turned over and over in flight, and despite the Kushite's attempt to evade it, the axe buried itself in the man's face. The Kushite uttered a bubbling scream and fell to the ground.

"Majesty!" came a cry from near at hand, and Seti looked up to see a chariot drawing near. He grabbed another axe from a fallen soldier and ran, grasped the side rail and vaulted aboard the chariot. Seti grinned through a blood-streaked face at the driver.

"Good man." He pointed toward where the banners flew and the Kushite warriors were gathered, and chariots responded, turning toward the enemy leaders. The men of Ptah followed, screaming and slashing at anything that moved, and further off, Seti could see banners of the Set legion start toward his position.

"Messuwy!" Seti yelled. "Surrender and I will let you live."

There was no reply, and moments later the chariots surged into the knot of Kushite warriors, trampling them under hooves and wheels once more. Seti leaned over the chariot rail and chopped with his axe until his arm was covered in blood to the shoulder and the grip grew slippery in his hand. Beside him, men of Ptah and Set slaughtered the enemy, yelling in triumph as the Kushites were pushed back.

A tremor ran through the Kushite line and abruptly they turned and fled, many throwing down their weapons. Seti's men lurched after them, but half-heartedly as exhaustion gripped them. They staggered and the Troop Commanders and lesser officers bullied their men back into some semblance of order, applying their little whips of authority.

Seti caught sight of Besenmut and ordered his chariot through the crowd to the Ptah commander's side. "We have taken the field, Besenmut. The rebellion is crushed."

Besenmut grinned tiredly. "Indeed, Divine One, yet the rebel leaders, Messuwy and Sethi, have not yet been captured."

"They may be among the fallen. Have the men search them out."

"I saw them flee, Divine One, as your chariot charge defeated their legion. They have fled south, no doubt seeking the safety of Kush."

"No haven for them there," Seti said grimly. "I will pursue them until they are dead or captured."

Besenmut nodded. "We must rest the men first, Son of Re."

Seti nodded. "Half a day, no more. What of Waset? The city has surrendered?"

"No, Son of Re. When the Kushites attacked, they relieved the pressure on the Amun legion beneath the walls. They slipped back inside the walls and shut the gates."

"And their commander?"

"Menkauhor? He died. Cut down in the fighting."

"A pity. A clean death was too good for him. Have his body nailed to the gates of Waset. We will have to deal with the rebels inside the city, but not yet. Messuwy and Sethi are my main concern. Leave them alive and rebellion will form around them again."

The Set and Ptah legions camped beside the river a little way above Waset and washed the grime and gore from their bodies, refreshing themselves with a hot meal and having their wounds tended. Physicians went round the more severely wounded and offered them the option of a swift death or the possibility of a lingering one, perhaps at the hands of the city rebels if they should venture out once the army had departed. Several opted to take the quick route to the afterlife.

Losses among the men through death and severe injury were moderate, but by the time the Ptah auxiliaries were distributed among the various Troops, Seti had two legions at almost full strength. He led them south in pursuit of the rebels in the early afternoon, the men eager to get to grips with their enemy. They marched along the east bank of the river, following the plain trail that the retreating Kushites had left, fast scouting chariots spreading out in front of the army to search out units of the rebel army. Close on sunset, they came across a place near the river where the rebels had stopped to rest and cook a meal. Bodies of the wounded who had succumbed to their wounds lay around, and a few were still alive. When questioned, they revealed that the army had moved on not long before, on receiving information from their own scouts that Seti's legions were coming up quickly.

"After them," Seti ordered. "We can deliver the killing blow if we move fast enough."

Besenmut pointed at the setting sun, now low over the western cliffs. "It will be dark soon, Son of Re. We cannot fight in the dark."

"Neither can they." The king would not listen to reason and insisted the men press onward. He sent out scouting chariots again and learned that the rearmost units of the Kushites were no more than a twelfth part of a day ahead, so close that a running man could reach them before the sun dipped below the horizon. The Set legion, with Ahmes in command, was ordered forward and every man, including the following Ptah men, was instructed to divest themselves of everything except their weapons and a single flask of water.

"We are going to catch them and destroy them this day," Seti swore.

A dozen chariots led the way, the king amongst them, and the Set legion followed at a run. The road led away from the river and wound into some low hills, where the shadows of the western cliffs soon overtook them. They raced on through the gathering gloom and, on cresting a low rise, spotted a unit of the Kushites moving slowly through a narrow defile only a few thousand paces ahead of them.

Seti looked to the west and then at the shadows pooling in the narrow valley ahead of them. "Just enough time, I think," he said.

"We should wait," Ahmes muttered. "There is not enough time to be sure of victory. What if the rest of the enemy is close by?"

"Do you see them, Ahmes? I do not. Just a rear unit separated from the rest. We will take them today and follow up on the rest tomorrow." Seti waved his chariots onward and sent his own charging down the road toward the retreating enemy.

A dozen chariots only, yet the noise of their approach echoed off the cliffs and must surely have been heard by the Kushites. They showed no sign that they knew of their pursuer's presence until they were almost upon them. A cry gave warning and the Kushite soldiers dived for the cover of roadside rocks and launched a volley of spears at the chariots without much effect. At the same time, though, a shower of arrows arced overhead from cover further up the hillsides, and men and horses died under the onslaught.

One of Seti's horses was wounded and fell, dragging its partner down. The charioteer leapt to cut the traces and fell dead, struck in the throat. Seti scrambled clear, his own bow in his hand but lacking a target, could only stand impotently in the wreckage of his small chariot squadron. The survivors took shelter behind fallen chariots and dead horses and it was only nightfall that saved them from being annihilated by the rain of arrows from the Kushites in cover. The sound of running feet on the roadway brought fear to their hearts but moments later familiar figures loomed in the darkness from behind them and the men of Set legion rushed over and around. Ahmes barked commands and his men formed a protective cordon around the king.

The Set legion pulled back, leaving the bodies of men and horses, the debris of the chariot squadron, where they lay on the road, and under cover of darkness withdrew to the crest of the slight rise. Here they made camp, though it was a rough and ready affair as they lacked everything except their weapons and the flasks of water they carried. Shortly after moonrise, the Ptah legion found them, and although the men were as lacking in food and water as the men of Set, Besenmut had disobeyed the king and brought with him some food and wine for the king. Seti accepted it without comment and stood in the darkness, sipping on his wine and staring into the mooncast shadows of the southern night that hid his brother Messuwy's rebel forces.

Chapter 24

Menmire Amenmesse speaks:

My brother-in-law Bay spoke truth, but not the complete truth. Yes, Seti was preoccupied with the northern borders, but I was not yet ready to become king. I have an over-strength legion, that of Kush, but it is as yet untried in war and undisciplined. What can one expect of tribesmen? I needed perhaps another year before I was ready, but Bay had whispered of Seti's suspicions of what was happening in Kush, and I knew the opportunity of Seti's attention being elsewhere was too good to miss.

Seti took his army north to counter the foreigners and I struck, forging north out of Kush with two thousand men at my back. More joined me as I marched north, the people of Ta Shemau swarming to my banner, vying with each other to share in my glorious victory. Waset threw open its gates, and the populace thronged the streets as my Kushites marched in and took possession of Amun's City. The traitors were arrested and thrown into prison, and the Amun legion fell under my control. Seti's Prophet of Amun was deposed and Hem-netjer Roma-Rui resumed his rightful place as Voice of the God. Among his first acts was to crown me King Menmire Amenmesse, rightful Lord of the Two Lands, giving legitimacy to all my actions and taking it from those of my misguided younger brother Seti.

Now I am King of Kemet and it will be but a matter of time before my brother Seti is deposed. His actions while pretending to be king are, of course, unlawful, and I have been at pains to correct them. Bakenkhons is gone, though Roma-Rui has, in his mercy, allowed him to stay on as a priest within the temple. Merenkhons has gone, fled with other traitors, and I have appointed a faithful man, Menkauhor, in his place. Neferronpet is gone, and will soon be dead, and Khaemter appointed as Tjaty in his place. The power of Amun dominates the city, and I use the priests of Amun for my own purposes.

I was surprised to find my sister Takhat in the palace. For some reason nobody had thought to tell me that Seti had taken her as wife and got her with child. When Seti came down to Waset he brought his queen, Tausret, and his secondary wife Takhat, but when he went north again he left my sister behind. I did not know whether this is due to some calculation on his part, or at the whim of the gods but my adviser Sethi helped me in this. He said that Seti could scarcely know that I would soon make my move and claim the throne, so how could leaving her behind benefit him. Therefore it must be the gods who have brought this about, and I think I know now what their will is.

A king often marries his sister. This is solely so no other man can marry into the royal family and give him a claim on the throne. No doubt Seti was acting thus when he took my sister as wife, and now the gods have presented her to me just at the time when I am made king and he is deposed. Could their actions be any clearer? I will marry my sister Takhat. Of course, she is already with child, so I shall have to wait a few months. If she has a son, he will have to die, but if she has a daughter I will let the child live. She will marry my son Siptah in time, or failing that, daughters are always useful in cementing alliances.

I knew Seti would contest my seizing control of Waset, but I did not think he would act so swiftly. Scarcely had I made my mark on the southern city than spies arrived bearing news of his advance. My advisers counselled this and that, but I knew I would have to defeat his legions outside Waset. The problem was how. The Set and Ptah legions are well trained and battle hardened, more than a match for the city-soft Amun and my fierce, loyal but undisciplined fighters of Kush. My only hope was to surprise them.

As Seti approached the city, I took the Kushite south, into the low hills close by the river and hid them there. The remnants of the Amun legion waited inside the city with the city gate open, knowing this would attract the attention of Seti. It did, and his army arrayed itself outside the city, facing the gate. Then Menkauhor led the Amun legion out and fixed their attention solely on them. I had hoped that both legions would have engaged the Amun, but only the Set did, leaving the Ptah standing and waiting. I could not wait any longer, so I launched my Kushites at the rear of Seti's formation, taking them completely by surprise. I almost won, but my men were just too undisciplined to fight together, preferring their normal method of fighting, one on one, with much posturing and yelling of insults. Seti's chariots tipped the scales. The terrain of Kush is not suited to chariot warfare, so I had few. I shall have to remedy this.

I withdrew my army, not wanting to lose them all to Seti's rampaging soldiers. As long as I retained a fighting force, I could return to claim what was mine, so I led them south into the low hills, and as I went I devised a means of stopping Seti. The opportunity came as dusk fell, and the forward units of my pursuers made contact with my rearguard. I positioned archers under cover and had a straggling group of Kushite warriors entice Seti's chariots to charge them on the narrow road. They were not expecting the ambush and were slaughtered. Too late I saw that Seti himself was amongst the charioteers tossed onto the hard ground and he managed to withdraw to the safety of his legions.

I hurried my men on, keeping to the road south in the darkness and, as dawn approached, made a stand at a well in the flat land beyond the hills. The road at this point bends eastward away from the river, and finding a well is essential unless you are carrying a good water supply. We had a water supply and a defensible position amidst strewn boulders, so I rested my men while waiting for Seti's army to arrive.

Seti's legions appeared at noon, hot and thirsty, and chagrined to find us in possession of the only water available unless they fancied a long trek to the river. Chariots were useless amidst the boulders, so he mustered his legions and threw them at our position, doubtless anticipating another victory. My warriors were much more organised now though, having their flanks secured by rock and the massive boulders offered protection from his archers. Once, twice, three times, he hurled his men at our position but could not dislodge us. Instead, he withdrew, leaving his men lying on the stony ground like the debris left after the river's yearly inundation.

Seti could not afford such attrition of his forces, and as the day drew on he could see whatever advantage he had held under the walls of Waset disappearing like the water in his men's rapidly emptying flasks. Thirst finally brought an end to his attack and first one, and then the other, of his decimated legions turned and made their way west toward the river.

I sent my scouts out in their wake, and they reported back to me that Seti was heading north, back toward Waset in defeat. I followed, and saw him bypass Amun's city, marching his men back the way they had come. Waset opened its gates to me and I entered the great city, a king returning to the seat of his power, and started making plans for the future. I was determined that I would extend my sovereignty over both Ta Shemau and Ta Mehu, becoming truly Lord of the Two Lands. My brother Seti, who tried to steal the throne from me, will bend his knee to me or die.

Chapter 25
Year 2 of Userkheperure Seti
Year 1 of Menmire Amenmesse

The comings and goings of kings meant little to the men of Set-ma'at, the Place of Truth which was the tomb makers' village on the border of Ta-sekhet-ma'at, the Great Field wherein lay the tombs of kings and nobles. They had their work and if it meant that work stopped on one tomb and started on another, it was all one to them. That was their work life and if they worked from dawn to dusk for nine days out of ten, it was still only part of their overall existence.

Kemetu are very family oriented and every aspect of family life is close to their hearts, children especially. Life was hard for the common man, a daily scrabble for food and shelter with little left over for luxuries. What was not spent on daily needs was put aside for the most important event in any Kemetu life, death. They believed in an afterlife, but this posthumous residence in the 'Field of Reeds' was dependent on the continued existence of the physical body and everything that the physical body needed in life.

The well-off could afford to have experts preserve their bodies after death, to suck the moisture from their corpses and pack it with preservatives and spices so that they could lie in their tombs for eternity. They had tombs built that were furnished with beds and tables and chairs, pots and pans and plates, weapons and toys and the paraphernalia of their work. Servants were provided in the form of little ushabtiu, funerary figurines made of clay or stone or wood, that would, stimulated by magical inscriptions carved upon them, assume the burden of any labour the deceased might be called upon to perform. Food and drink was present too, sometimes real, sometimes represented by detailed wall paintings. The dead person, returning to the tomb, could feast upon these viands and enjoy once more the pleasant occupations they had enjoyed in life.

Not so the poor though. The destitute could hope for little more than a hole dug in the desert sand, a body wrapped in little more than clothing, a few personal items and a loaf of bread and small stoppered bottle of weak beer to sustain them. There was no hope offered of a better existence in the afterlife than they had suffered in life.

The men and women of the Place of Truth were poised somewhere between the two extremes. They worked at labouring jobs for the most part, though Foreman Hay's team was proficient in producing the everyday carvings and paintings on the tomb walls. Specialist sculptors and painters were called in for the really fine work though. Being expert at tunnelling into solid rock, the builders spent some of their spare time constructing their own tombs and those of their families. Whether simple excavations or elaborate chambered tombs awaited them at death, the servants in the Place of Truth could look forward to a reasonably comfortable afterlife.

The scribes of the Great Field carefully recorded everything that entered the village, whether for the use of its inhabitants or for use in the tombs themselves. Oil lamps gave the only light at night and deep inside the rock tunnels and chambers where daylight could not seep. Kenhirkhopeshef and his junior scribes noted the measures of oil drawn each day from the temple stores, and even down to the number of wicks used by each team in every four hour work shift. Every man that worked had his name checked off against the roll and his absence had to be explained by the Foreman, Workman Ahi absent with toothache, Workman Huni absent because of the flux, Sculptor Neferhor absent with a cut hand. Not every absence was down to some illness or accident though. A man might celebrate some festival or other that had a special meaning for him or his family, and might even be absent for a day beforehand to brew beer for the festivities.

The cycle of life passed slowly, season by season. Children were born and many died in the first few years of life. Survivors grew into men who followed their fathers into their profession, or into women who married, usually at an early age, to men their fathers picked for them. After a life of hardship, a man might have amassed sufficient wealth to be able to retire and take his ease in the few years left to him before death brought its release. Scribe Kenhirkhopeshef was one such fortunate man. Already in his seventies in the reign of Baenre Merenptah, he had married a young girl of twelve from the village, an occasion for much celebration. Naunakht came to the marriage if not willingly, at least thankful that the old man would make few demands upon her. She could not refuse, for her father had arranged the match, knowing that Kenhirkhopeshef was a man of great prestige and considerable wealth. More importantly for a young girl barely into puberty, the scribe was noted for his kindness and gentleness. Ten years on, she had voiced no complaints, and managed the scribe's affairs well. She had had no children by the old man but she was content with his company.

Kenhirkhopeshef had a tomb waiting for him, a modest affair cut into the rock face with a small but beautiful chapel and wide carved stairs leading to his burial chamber. Having almost completed his long life, and with his future home assured, Kenhirkhopeshef could afford to relax. On days when he felt some of his old energy pervading his stooped and withered frame, he would accompany the teams to the Great Field and sit in the shade of the cliffs with a flask of water beside him and watch the activity in and around the tombs. His scribes Anupemheb and Paser fussed around and saw to the necessities of his office.

Once when he wandered back at the end of a working day, aching in all his joints and deathly tired, he passed by the village shrines cut into the rock and stopped to examine graffiti scratched into the stone. His fingers traced the common script that semi-literate people who were not trained as scribes used, nothing like the formal hieroglyphs used in temple and tomb, and smiled. Young men had striven for some small measure of immortality by scratching their names near the shrines. Giving in to a whim, he stooped to pick up a rock and, finding a sheltered rock surface free of blemish, scratched his own message to future generations, 'Scribe in the Place of Truth, Kenhirkhopeshef, of his father Panakhte'.

When he felt less energetic, increasingly as the days passed, he sat in the shade with the other old men of the village in the open area near the gate, and talked together. Often, as old men will, they talked of former days and the glorious accomplishments that their younger selves had achieved.

"I remember the old king, Usermaatre, coming to inspect his tomb," Anek mused. He wiped away a thin thread of spittle from his chin. "He spoke to me, you know."

Pait cackled, and slapped his bony hand on a skeletal thigh. "Told you to get out of the way, most like."

"Or chastised you on the botch up you'd made of a carving," added Ramose. "Remember the time you chiselled the nose right off the king's image? I thought the foreman, what was his name? Anhirkawi? I thought he was going to have a fit."

Anek's blood rushed to his face. "You take that back, Ramose. It was not my fault. The rock was rotten."

"And it was Anhirkawi," Nekhen said. "Father of our present Foreman Hay. A good man in his day."

"His son's good too."

"No argument, but Anhirkawi was better."

"I've carved tombs for four kings then," Anek said. "Not many men can say that."

"Everyone here can," Nekhen objected. "Usermaatre, Baenre, Userkheperure, and now Menmire." He laughed. "And with Menmire so new, you haven't actually worked under him."

"Nor Userkheperure," Ramose said. "He's only been on the throne a year or so and you haven't worked for at least that long."

"One of us definitely has," Nekhen said. "Our scribe Kenhirkhopeshef here started back in Usermaatre's day and is still technically working, though he likes to sit on his backside now."

"A scribe's life involves a lot of sitting," Kenhirkhopeshef observed. "And while I'm here with you, my associates are running around making sure everything runs smoothly. They report to me regularly, as you well know, so yes, I have worked through the reigns of four kings."

"Seen some sights too, I'll warrant?"

The old scribe nodded and frowned. Then he slowly eased himself to one side and released a squeak of gas. "I've spoken to three kings, and I daresay if Menmire comes to inspect his tomb I'll talk to him too."

Nekhen stifled a laugh. "I hope you didn't say *that* to them."

"There's not much to inspect at the moment," Anek said. "They've barely started."

"Well, he's only been king for a month," Ramose said.

"I haven't been up there," Nekhen said. "Where is it? Near Userkheperure's?"

Anek shook his head. "As far from him in death as in life, I says. It's in the eastern valley, not far from where Menpehtyre Ramesses is buried."

"What will happen to Userkheperure Seti's tomb then?" Ramose asked. "We were doing so well."

Kenhirkhopeshef shrugged. "Work stops on it. After all, the king pays for everything and the king is Menmire Amenmesse. He's not going to pay for his brother's tomb, seeing as how they don't get on."

"He's still king though, isn't he?" Nekhen asked. "Userkheperure Seti. I mean, he's still alive even if he is in Men-nefer."

"I wouldn't involve yourself in the affairs of kings," Kenhirkhopeshef warned. "A statement like that could prove very dangerous in the wrong ears."

"What did I say?"

"That a certain someone was still king. If the present king in Waset got to hear of it, you could find yourself up on a charge of treason. It could be construed as speaking ill of the king, hinting that he's not really the king."

Ramose nodded sombrely. "Death penalty for sure." Suddenly he grinned, displaying a toothless mouth. "Mind you, they'd only be depriving you of a year of life at best."

"Speak for yourself, you old fool," Nekhen retorted. "I'll see you in your tomb yet."

The old men sat in silence for a time, listening to the life of the village, to the women chattering as they worked and the children playing. Shadows of the western cliffs crept over them and the heat of the day drained away like water in sand.

Nekhen stirred again and muttered, "What about it, though? Userkhe...someone was crowned king and hasn't died. What does that make the other man? Is he really king or not?"

"That's a question for the priests," Kenhirkhopeshef said. "I wouldn't ask them if you value your life though."

"Or for soldiers," Ramose said. "Anyone can be king if he has a large enough army backing him up."

"I was a soldier once," Anek said.

"Nonsense," Nekhen jeered. "You're making up stories."

"I was," Anek declared. "Years ago, when my father Pepi was a sculptor here in the village..."

"I remember Pepi," Kenhirkhopeshef murmured. "He was a good man."

"...I joined up and was in the Re legion with Usermaatre when he went up to Kadesh to sign the peace treaty with the Hatti. That was in the king's...oh, nineteenth or twentieth year, I think.

"Twenty-first."

"Twenty-first it was, thank you Scribe. Well, I didn't see much action, nor earn myself gold of valour, but I seen the power the generals and commanders wielded. One of them could become king if he had a mind to."

191

"May those days never come again," Kenhirkhopeshef said. "Before my time, but I remember my grandfather talking of the times after the fall of the Heretic when a throne was there for the taking by any general with an army at his back." He shook his head slowly. "Bad times."

"Yes, but we're not talking about generals and armies," Nekhen said. "We've got two brothers, both sons of a king and now both crowned as king and hating each other. What's going to happen?"

"What's going to happen is we get on with our work and leave the running of the kingdoms to our betters," Kenhirkhopeshef said. "Let the kings and priests and nobles get on with it. We know how to dig rock, work it, carve stone and keep records. Be satisfied with that."

There was a bit of grumbling and muttering, but the old men shrugged and bowed to the pronouncements of their old scribe. Dusk approached and the work teams from the Great Place returned, tired and dusty. They filed through the gate and separated, each to his own home where wives and daughters brought them fresh water to bathe in, clean garments to change into, and a pot of beer to enjoy while they prepared the evening meal. The old men dispersed too, tottering on bent legs to join their families and seek the solace of the hearth fire, a hot meal and their bed as Nut spread her star-studded body over the Great Field and the village of the Servants of the Place of Truth.

Chapter 26
Year 2 of Userkheperure Seti
Year 1 of Menmire Amenmesse

❝Withdrawn all the way up to Men-nefer, my spies tell me," Sethi said. "He could see how it was here in Ta Shemau, every man's hand against him and only two legions to support him."

"So what now?" Tjaty Khaemter asked.

"Now we consolidate power in Waset, recruit more men and train them up. That'll take the best part of a year, then we march north and oust the pretender from his throne."

"Too long," Amenmesse said from his position by the window, where he stared out at the gardens below. Somewhere in the shrubbery a bird called, its long-drawn-out cry mournful in the gathering dusk. More faintly he could hear the coughing roar of a big cat in the menagerie and the answering screams of the monkeys. It put him in mind of his days as King's Son of Kush, down in Napata, and he felt a twinge of nostalgia for simpler days. He sighed and turned back to face the other two men.

"I can't wait a year. Every day I delay tells people that I accept my brother has a claim to the throne. If it is mine by right, as I claim, then I should wrest it from his grasp immediately."

"We're not ready," Sethi said. He saw a flash of anger in Amenmesse's eyes and added, "Son of Re."

"I can't wait a year," Amenmesse repeated. "Find a way to bring it forward. Three months at the outside, but I want some action taken before that."

"What sort of action, Majesty?" Khaemter said.

Sethi opened his mouth and then glanced at his king. Amenmesse nodded. "Go ahead, Sethi. I'm sure you have ideas."

"Yes, Son of Re," Sethi said. "Show the people that support for your brother is ill advised. Go through the cities, not just Waset, but all the cities and towns of Ta Shemau, and hang a few supporters in each one. Make the people afraid so they don't dare oppose me."

"I'm not sure fear is the best way to rule," Khaemter objected.

"I agree. I'm the rightful king," Amenmesse said. "I should be loved and respected, not feared."

"Time enough to gain their love and respect when you've settled the whole country under your rulership, Son of Re. Let them fear you first and then they'll be so grateful when you offer them crumbs they'll think they're at a feast."

"Some people like Neferronpet deserved to die," Amenmesse said. "But I don't like the wholesale slaughter of others."

"Would you rather forgive them and then find they're plotting to bring back Seti?"

"Of course not, but...I suppose you're right."

"Trust me in this, Son of Re. A swift purge of the main dissidents and we can re-establish Ma'at throughout Kemet."

Amenmesse visibly vacillated and then shrugged. "Do what you must."

"There are other ways to bring the people in line," Khaemter said. "I'm not saying Lord Sethi shouldn't act against dissidents and traitors, just that that need not be all we do to win the hearts of loyal men."

"What are you suggesting?" the king asked.

"Men always need the gods and honouring them has ever been popular. Build shrines, build temples, erect stelae, and make sure the king's name is prominent on them all."

"That's expensive," Amenmesse muttered.

"What is that to you now, Son of Re?" Khaemter asked. "You own the gold mines of Kush and all their output. You can afford anything you desire."

"And there are a large number of inscriptions already in place that honour Seti," Sethi added. "It is a relatively cheap and easy job to have his name chiselled off and your name carved in its place."

"All of which gets your name known to all your subjects without having to kill people," Khaemter finished.

"I like it," Amenmesse said. "I've already given the command to stop work on my brother's tomb and start mine. It will be a simple matter to extend that to monuments and temples."

"I'll have the documents drawn up by the scribes."

"And what of my army? I'm going to need several legions of well-trained men if I am to be victorious."

"That is possible too, with enough gold," Sethi said. "With your permission I'll offer a bounty for every man who joins up. I imagine that'll bring in hundreds, maybe even thousands, from the villages and towns. I can have recruiting officers spin a pretty yarn about the possibilities of loot once we invade Ta Mehu."

Amenmesse frowned. "The northern kingdom is mine too. I don't want to take possession of a ruined land."

"I'll make sure the recruiters don't lay it on too thick," Sethi assured the king. "Besides, once we win we can always deny them the opportunity to loot." He laughed. "It'll be too late for the men to change their minds about fighting then."

"And there are plenty of good men in Kush," Khaemter said. "We had to work within a tight budget before, but now that you have the gold mines and the royal herds at your disposal, we can entice many more tribesmen. They do love their cattle."

"Men alone aren't enough. They have to be trained."

"I have a handful of experienced officers. It will take time but I think we can get three, maybe four legions."

"Within three months?" Amenmesse asked. "I have to invade Ta Mehu and rid myself of my troublesome brother once and for all."

"I'll try, Son of Re."

"Do more than try."

Khaemter and Sethi set off on their separate expeditions within days. Sethi was accompanied by a large squad of Medjay and the dregs of the Amun legion, and cruised slowly upriver. They stopped at every village, town and city, made sure the mayor or local governor swore an oath to Menmire Amenmesse, and then proceeded to round up every person of any note who had openly or covertly supported the previous king known as Seti.

Sethi paraded the captured traitors before the assembled populace, harangued them all concerning the need for everyone to support the only true king of Kemet, and then proceeded to execute the supporters of Seti. Hesitantly at first, and then with increasing enthusiasm, the townsfolk betrayed their neighbours, and if several were motivated by reasons other than loyalty to the new king, Sethi was not going to argue. His terror millstone needed traitors to grind, and the overwhelming message was to be loyal to Menmire Amenmesse or die.

The executed traitors had their wealth confiscated and a fee paid to the accusers, so many rich men died solely because others envied them their wealth. With wealth confiscated, the families of the accused found themselves without the means to bury their dead, and Sethi relieved them of the necessity by having the bodies thrown in the river. So many men floated down the dark green waters that people in Waset were sure some great battle had been fought in the south. As Sethi and his men pursued their bloody course down the length of Ta Shemau to the borders of Kush, they left behind fear and loathing, but also a population cowed and tractable.

Khaemter's mission was more welcome. He toured the towns and villages, seeking out the areas that were the poorest or suffering from localised hunger and offered the men a way out. He cajoled and encouraged, painting a wonderful picture of the riches that were to be had by signing up for one of Menmire's legions. Men made their mark, swearing an oath in front of a priest and receiving a promissory token redeemable for a bag of grain and a copper piece in the capital city. A few would join in every village and more in the towns, and Khaemter and his officers would march on to the next town with the men they had gathered, to find some more. When a hundred men had joined, he sent them off to Waset under the control of officers, for them to start their training.

By the time Khaemter had made his way up the river all the way to Kush, he had sent nearly a full legion of conscripts back to be trained and was feeling very pleased with himself. He left instructions with Commander Tarkahe at the garrison at Abu to scour the countryside for more men, and then took to the road once more with a small cadre of officers to talk to the Kushite tribes.

When Khaemter had marched north with Amenmesse, he had given up the position of King's Son of Kush that Baenre Merenptah had settled on him, leaving the governance of the province in the hands of his deputy, a capable man called Setuy. This Setuy was a commoner, but had risen to become a king's scribe and fan-bearer on the king's right. If he was confirmed in his position, he would become one of the most powerful men in Kemet. This was one of the things Khaemter wanted to see for himself before recommending his protégé to Menmire Amenmesse.

"Welcome, my lord Khaemter," Setuy said, greeting his visitor in the middle of the audience room floor. "The news reached me that you had been made Tjaty of the South."

Setuy was uncertain who held the greater rank between the two of them, so he had decided he would be standing beside the viceregal throne when Khaemter arrived. If he was sitting when Khaemter entered and stood to greet him, he was granting the other man a higher status, and if he remained seated, it might be seen as an insult. Setuy knew he could not afford to make an enemy of the Tjaty.

The next question of protocol was seating. If he sat back down on the throne he was again claiming the higher rank, letting Khaemter sit on it gave him the status, and even sitting on two chairs nearby made him look weak and vacillating. Instead, he had a servant announce that a meal was served on one of the shaded balconies of the palace. The two men walked together through the broad doorway to partake of a light meal.

"I did not think to see you so soon, my lord Khaemter," Setuy said. "I thought your duties in Waset would keep you busy."

"I'm sure your spies gave you ample warning of my arrival." Khaemter helped himself to a selection of fresh fruits he had missed since moving north to Kemet. "And my duties as Tjaty entail more than just the city of Waset."

"Of course...but in Kush? The province is under my control."

"I made you Viceroy when I left," Khaemter said sharply. "I will also be the one to recommend to Menmire whether you be kept on in this position."

"To Menmire? But Userkheperure is king of Kemet. He appointed you and you appointed me."

"And I can dismiss you if I see fit."

Setuy sighed inwardly. Khaemter had at last made their relative positions clear. "Then how may I be of assistance, Tjaty Khaemter?"

"You have heard that Messuwy, son of Baenre, has made himself king in the south? He is now Menmire Amenmesse."

"Yes."

"What then is your understanding of the situation in Kemet? Explain it that I might see if you grasp the nuances."

Setuy busied himself with his food while he considered his answer. He bit into a fig and winced as a seed caught a tender spot in a cracked tooth. "Userkheperure Seti was crowned at Waset last year and rules from Mennefer in Ta Mehu," he said. "Then this year, as you say, Menmire Amenmesse was likewise crowned in Waset and rules from that city." He picked up a fragment of bread and rolled it between finger and thumb. "It is my understanding that neither king desires to rule over just one kingdom but wants to extend his rule over both, ousting the other from power. This is a situation that upsets the Ma'at of the kingdoms as it sets southerner against northerner."

"Is one king more legitimate than the other?"

"My lord Khaemter!" Setuy looked around in some alarm to see if any of the omnipresent servants were within earshot. None were, but he lowered his voice anyway. "If it were anyone but you, my lord, I would arrest them for voicing such a thought."

"Why? It is a reasonable question. Expand on that thought, King's Son of Kush."

Setuy dismissed the servants and walked across to the edge of the balcony, looking over to check if there were any listeners in the shrubbery. He saw Khaemter's sneering smile and flushed. "Menmire Amenmesse is the elder son of King Baenre and under normal circumstances one would expect him to inherit the throne. It is well known there was...uh...friction between father and son, and he was sent to Kush to keep him out of the way. His half-brother Userkheperure Seti is the younger son but managed to secure the position of Crown Prince, perhaps by staying close to his father and insinuating himself into his good graces. Whatever the reason, he became king on the death of Baenre. It was entirely legal and proper."

"You don't know the reason Seti Meryenptah inherited instead of Messuwy?"

The Viceroy shook his head. "You do?"

"Yes. The old king Usermaatre Ramesses had a favourite son called Khaemwaset whom he wanted to inherit. The favourite son died and Merenptah became the Crown Prince. Merenptah had married Khaemwaset's daughter Isetnofret and had a son called Seti, while Merenptah's previous wife Takhat had borne him Messuwy. The old king still wanted Khaemwaset to inherit through his children, so he made Merenptah promise to make Seti Meryenptah his heir, rather than Messuwy. The position of Deputy King's Son of Kush was given to Messuwy as a sop."

Setuy whistled and nodded thoughtfully. "That explains a lot. If Merenptah swore an oath then he had no choice but to make Seti Meryenptah his heir. By any standard he is legitimate."

"Are you saying Menmire Amenmesse is not?" Khaemter asked, his face and voice expressionless.

Sweat beaded on Setuy's brow as he realised the trap he had fallen into. "No, my lord, of course not."

"Then what are you saying? If Seti Meryenptah is a legitimate king, then how can Amenmesse be one too?"

"My lord, I..." Setuy flushed and looked away, visibly distraught.

Khaemter regarded his former deputy with mild amusement, waiting for the man to reach some conclusion. When he saw it was not coming, he prompted, "The priest perhaps?"

"My lord?"

"Who conveys the blessing of the gods onto the king when he is crowned?"

"The Hem-netjer of Amun?" Setuy asked.

"Precisely. And who is the Hem-netjer of Amun?"

"Roma-Rui?"

"Indeed. Roma-Rui crowned Amenmesse in a formal ceremony in Waset this year. What of Seti Meryenptah? Who crowned him?"

Setuy frowned. "Er, Roma-Rui?"

"No, it was Second Prophet Bakenkhons, who Seti raised to the position of Hem-netjer after he dismissed Roma-Rui."

"But..." Setuy thought about what he had been told. "But no man can dismiss the Hem-netjer of Amun, not even a king and...and Seti Meryenptah was not even a king when he did so."

"Therefore?"

"Seti Meryenptah's coronation was illegitimate. Amenmesse is truly king."

"That being so, what will you do?" Khaemter asked.

"Do, my lord? My duty, I suppose."

"Of course, but what is your duty?"

"To obey the king and...and his Tjaty."

"You accept my authority over you as mouthpiece of King Menmire Amenmesse?"

"Yes, my lord. Command me."

"You are ordered to raise and equip an army from among the Kushite tribes. I want three legions within three months."

Setuy went pale. "M...my lord, th...that is im...impossible," he stuttered. "I have neither men nor gold."

"The king has released the production of the royal gold mines into my keeping, and Kush is full of men. Use your imagination, Setuy. I want three legions in three months. Produce them and the king will confirm you as King's Son of Kush."

Chapter 27

Tausret speaks:

We should have killed Messuwy when we had the chance, but now he has had the audacity to crown himself king, as if that farce of a coronation has any true worth. He is a fool if he thinks people will support him. The only reason he has succeeded so far is that he stole the king's gold while down in Kush and has bought the loyalty of venal men. Messuwy has upset the Ma'at of Kemet, and the gods will surely not allow him to continue his destructive course for long.

Perhaps we underestimated the importance of the South to the overall stability of Kemet as a whole. I do not say we made a mistake, for any decision by the king is, almost by definition, the correct one, but equally obviously we have had ill advice. Ta Shemau controls access to Kush, whence derives the gold that runs the kingdoms, and Waset controls access to the Great Field and the royal tombs. I feel like stamping my feet and spitting when I think of Waset in the hands of that man.

I thought my husband would have a fit when the news came to us that Messuwy (I do not like to use the throne name he has taken, for to use it would legitimise his claim) had halted work on his tomb. He raved and swore vengeance, but in truth there is little he can do right now. He has an army, but he also has a responsibility, and he cannot withdraw the legions from the northern borders. So he has sent out the word through Tjaty Hori that men be mustered to strengthen the legions.

Ah yes, Tjaty Merysekhmet died. He was getting on in years and his health often caused him to neglect his duties. Seti asked him if he wanted to step down, but he declined, vowing that he could manage. He did, for about another three days. Then, when he was presiding over the law courts, he clutched his chest and pitched forward onto the stone floor, cracking his head on the step. A physician was sent for but there was nothing he could do except order him be taken off to the embalmers.

The new Tjaty, Hori, comes of an illustrious line and is in fact my cousin. He is the grandson of that Khaemwaset who was most the beloved son of Usermaatre Ramesses and Crown Prince before my adoptive father Baenre Merenptah. Khaemwaset had a son called Hori who is High Priest of Ptah here in Men-nefer, and he also had a son called Hori. This younger Hori is a youthful though serious man of around thirty years, and such is his learning that Seti saw at once that he would make a good Tjaty.

So Hori's first task was to find men for new legions. The existing legions of Re, Ptah, Set and Heru were combed for officers to command the new legions and I was pleased to be able to recommend Ament for one of these positions. I had made him Overseer of Vineyards in Per-Bast, but if I knew him he would be pining for the military life. As it happened, he volunteered for the new legion and, with my influence, became a Troop Commander in the Per-Bast legion, under the command of Setnakhte, who was once Commander of the Amun legion.

The other news we received from the south was of Takhat, my husband's new young wife. When we came north, called by the threat of foreigners on Kemet's northern borders, we left Takhat in Waset. She was heavy with child and did not relish the thought of even a calm river voyage. I was not sorry she stayed behind, for it gave me time with my husband and we found our earlier bonds that had weakened with the deaths of our children were strengthened once more. At the time of leaving Takhat, there was no hint of danger from Messuwy, but while Seti's eyes were fixed on the north, he sallied out of Kush at the head of a small army and crowned himself king.

King. As if that man could ever truly be king. Even being King's Son of Kush was too great an honour for him. Well, the gods will not allow him to dishonour the throne for long, and I have no doubt Seti will be the instrument of their vengeance.

To return to the subject of Takhat, she was with child when we left her in Waset in the care of her women. She has had the child now, and it was a daughter. I have to admit I am happy with that outcome. I know my husband desperately desires a son and heir, but I have to be the one to give it to him. If I do not, he will look elsewhere for the mother of a prince. He thought Takhat was going to be that mother, but he was wrong. The gods still favour me.

And now I have heard that Messuwy means to marry Takhat himself. Not content with stealing a throne, he intends to steal a wife too. Well, I do not begrudge him some small measure of comfort before he is sent wailing down to death. Seti will not take her back after his death, so once more I am the king's only Great Wife. I mean to jealously guard my position, and will, if the gods allow, produce a son.

To this end I have contacted numerous physicians and wise women of Ta Mehu to find out the best methods of ensuring my next child is a boy. The medicines are foul-tasting when taken by mouth, and make me feel unclean when applied elsewhere, but I will do it, such is my determination. Priests have uttered efficacious prayers and scribes have inscribed them on scraps of papyrus which I wear next to my skin or in amulets around my neck. I do not know what else I can do to ensure I bear my husband a son. Every bit of medicine I eat or drink or smear on my private parts, and every magical formula I utter can only enhance the fertility of my belly, but can have no effect on the seed my husband sows there. If he sows male seed, then I must make sure my fertile field is ready for it.

One other thing I must mention. Royal Butler Bay has proved invaluable in these straitened times. His contacts amongst the followers of Messuwy and amongst the common people of Waset have meant that scraps of information are continually flowing to our ears. From such scraps are policies made, and Seti, Tjaty Hori and General Iurudef of the Northern Army have formulated a plan by which we can wrest control of Ta Shemau from Messuwy and send him down into death. When this is all over, and the Ma'at of Kemet is restored, we must think about a suitable reward for our faithful servant Bay.

Chapter 28
Year 3 of Userkheperure Seti
Year 2 of Menmire Amenmesse

Seti's rage was very great when he learned that Messuwy had stopped work on the royal tomb and had executed faithful Neferronpet, the Tjaty of the South. He wanted to rush down there immediately and crush this rebellion, consigning his traitorous half-brother to an ignominious death. Instead, he had to add frustration to the rage that curdled the food in his stomach and robbed him of equanimity when he was told quite forcefully by his Tjaty that he did not have the military resources to impose his will on the south. He ordered Tjaty Hori to set about conscripting more men for new legions and sent fresh orders winging northward to General of the Northern Army Iurudef to settle affairs on the northern border and release all but one legion for duties in the south.

Iurudef swore loudly and colourfully when the order arrived, denouncing the unrealistic expectations of certain people, but retained sufficient control of himself to avoid specifically mentioning the king. There were always people ready to gossip and carry tales to superiors, so it paid to be careful. When his temper had subsided, the general sat down with the legion commanders in the north and worked out a stratagem for bringing the remaining rebels and their Sea Peoples allies to battle. They had prevented the fall of the city of Ghazzat, but the threat remained.

Unfortunately for the plan, the Sea Peoples declined combat and slipped away whenever the Kemetu legions approached, only to return when the soldiers moved on. It was most frustrating, and Iurudef was forced to come up with another idea, as Seti had sent another order demanding the presence of his soldiers immediately.

"Say we sent one of the legions south today," Iurudef asked his commanders. "How long would they be away?"

"You're asking us, sir?" Emsaf said. "The Heru will go where it's ordered, of course."

"It is rather an imponderable, sir," Disebek added. "We've all heard how Messuwy has rebelled and that's why Userkheperure intends to march down there and defeat him, but how long will it take?" The commander of the Re legion shrugged. "If we have to march all the way down to Waset, fight a battle, and then march all the way back, then three or four months at least. If we only have to go as far as Men-nefer to provide support, we could be back in a month."

"Either way, it's too long to leave the border guarded by a single legion," Iurudef said. "A curse on it all, there has to be way to obey the king and safeguard the border at the same time."

"There are the forts too," Emsaf said. "Twelve forts with perhaps a hundred men in each, that's close on another legion."

Iurudef nodded. "They're garrison troops though, not front liners and besides, we can't strip them of their men and leave them defenceless."

"Would the enemy know they're empty though?" Emsaf asked. "If they shut the gates and had a few men on the battlements, they'd still look fully manned."

"For a while anyway," Disebek said. "A pity we can't do the same with the legions."

Iurudef looked thoughtful. "Perhaps we can," he said slowly. "If we put up a permanent camp or two close to Ghazzat and prominently flew the banners of each legion, we could withdraw a legion and the enemy would be none the wiser, for a while, at least."

"It could work, I suppose," Disebek said after a few moments.

"But?" Iurudef asked. "Come on, out with it. What's wrong with it?"

"Well, sir, the enemy will be able to see from the number of men moving around the camp that there's nowhere near a full legion there."

"We could build a stockade, sir," Emsaf said. "Throw up some earthworks high enough that they can't see in."

"It's a lot of work."

"The men won't mind, sir. If you think it will help."

"The enemy would still know something was up," Disebek said. "They expect us on patrol, at least."

"So we would have to keep that up. Say we build two walled camps, big enough to house a legion in each, but in fact divide one legion between the two. If two or three Troops went out on patrol each day, while the ones that stayed behind made plenty of noise, it might still look as if we were all there."

The Heru and Re legions built two large camps just within sight of each other on the flat plains outside the city of Ghazzat. They were far enough away from the walled city that men standing on the walls could not make out the level of activity within the camps, and Iurudef thought that if there was a constant movement of small bodies of men out on patrol and between the camps, it would be impossible to judge how many men there were in each camp. They raised up a rampart of loose rock, securing the edges with larger stones and woven scrub branches, packing the gaps with earth scraped from excavations through the desert sand. Finally, they topped the man-high rampart with large stone blocks commandeered from the Kemetu Governor of the city.

Satisfied that nobody could see inside the camps, Iurudef took his commanders aside and gave them their instructions. He made it clear that each Troop, whether actually on patrol or just making a show of moving between the camps, was to prominently fly the banners of each legion.

"If the Governor of Ghazzat wants to see me or the missing Commander, he is to be told we are on patrol and may be gone some time. Be vague, and make sure the men don't talk to anyone outside the legions. Impress on them that their lives might depend on it."

"So which legion is accompanying you south, sir?" Emsaf asked.

"Heru."

Emsaf grinned, but Disebek scowled. "I'm the senior commander, sir. I should accompany you with Re legion rather than just be left on guard duty."

"This is a very important assignment, Disebek," Iurudef said. "It is imperative that the deception is maintained until we return. If the enemy even suspects the border is almost unguarded, the consequences could be catastrophic. As for the legion that goes, Heru has the fighting edge and so will be the most use to the king, but you are, as you say, the senior commander. I have to leave you the independent command."

Disebek grudgingly accepted his general's decision. "When do you leave?"

"Tonight. It's close to the dark of the moon and it's cloudy. We'll split Heru between the two camps so they can leave without emptying one camp."

"And the chariots?"

"I'll leave you with five. I'm sorry, but that will have to do. If the gods smile we'll be back in a month or so."

Disebek nodded morosely. "Let's hope you still have a legion to come back to."

"Make sure of it, Commander. I'm counting on you."

Iurudef marched the Heru legion south toward Ta Mehu that night, quietly slipping out of the two camps after dark, having sent most of the chariots out previously in several groups. These chariot squadrons headed off in different directions and only turned toward the meeting point with the legion after it was too dark for enemy spies to see their change of course. The Heru legion and chariots were well south by dawn, marching on a course that took them inland rather than along the well-used coast road where anyone might see them. They crossed into Ta Mehu and joined the road once more, making better time through the well-watered lands along the spreading delta of the Great River. Within ten days they were on the marshalling plains opposite Men-nefer where the Per-Bast legion was training.

General Iurudef and Commander Emsaf reported to the king and were pleased to be able to bring a smile to his face by telling him how many chariots they had brought with them.

"A hundred and fifteen chariots, you say. By the gods, that news is like honey in my ears. But you left sufficient behind to guard the north?"

"The Re legion and five chariots under the command of Disebek, Son of Re. It will be sufficient if he is cautious." Iurudef explained the setting up of the camps and the ruse by which the enemy would continue to think there were still two full legions opposing them. "When do we march south, Majesty?"

"Soon. Ptah and Set have already gone and have orders not to give battle but to wait for my arrival. Now you have brought me Heru and Per-Bast is almost ready."

"I saw Per-Bast when I arrived, Son of Re. Who commands it?"

"Setnakhte."

"I don't think I know him. Is he experienced?"

"He commanded the Amun legion in my father's time. When he heard of the plot against him, he was forced to flee."

"What of me, Son of Re? What is my role in this punitive expedition if I do not have a legion to command?"

Seti smiled at his general. "I had thought to offer you a choice. I do not really need a general as I shall be commanding all my troops, but you could come as my aide, or..."

"Or, Son of Re?"

"Queen Tausret and Tjaty Hori are gathering more men from Ta Mehu, to make up another legion. You could stay behind to train them and become their commander."

Iurudef scowled. "And then bring them south to join you?"

"No, you would stay near Men-nefer to guard the northern kingdom."

"I'll come with you as your aide, Son of Re."

"I rather thought you might."

The two legions, Heru experienced and battle hardened and Per-Bast inexperienced and scarcely able to march in their Troops, left for the south two days later. Seti, despite the fact that he was going to war against his own brother, was in high spirits and ranged wide in his chariot, picking off the sparse wildlife of the desert with his bow. The men marched steadily down the road, making good time on the hard-packed stretches, and markedly slower where the winds had blown drifts of soft sand, often obscuring the road. Normally, gangs of labourers would dig and sweep the road clear of debris, but in recent years this practice had fallen into abeyance.

A little south of the crescent scallop that still held the remnants of Akhet-Aten, the capital city of the heretic that had fallen into ruin and disuse, they came across the Set and Ptah legions encamped by a region of huge boulders amidst which was nestled a deep well with sweet water. Some called it the Well of the Scarab, though the reason for that was lost in time.

Seti's eyebrows rose when he saw the camp, and then descended as anger swept over him. He raced his chariot into the camp, scattering soldiers who leapt to escape hooves and wheels and brought his vehicle to a halt in a cloud of dust near the command tent. He was out of the chariot and striding toward the tent as the Commanders, Besenmut and Ahmes, emerged. They saw the face of their king and quailed, prostrating themselves in the hot sand, while the soldiers on guard drew back hurriedly.

"What is the meaning of this?" Seti demanded. "I send my two best legions to confront and contain the enemy, and instead find them skulking many days north of Waset. Must I appoint new commanders?"

Commander Ahmes stuttered, his face in the sand, but Besenmut raised himself to his knees and, with arms outstretched in supplication, spoke to his angry king.

"Son of Re, we have followed your commands, which were to find the enemy and contain him, but not to give battle. The legions of Messuwy are a day's march south of here, and have halted near the Well of Ransut while they scout out our position. Now that your Majesty has arrived, we can give battle whenever you like."

"How many men?"

"Three legions, Son of Re. Or at least, that is how many different banners there are. They are mostly Kushite and undisciplined, swarming rather than marching, and making them difficult to count."

"Get up," Seti told his commanders, and strode into the command tent ahead of them, calling for wine. Besenmut and Ahmes joined him moments later, with Setnakhte, Iurudef and Emsaf at the same time as servants staggered in with a jar of wine, another of river water, and several ornate cups. The king drank and then nodded to Besenmut. "Show me where the enemy is."

Ahmes half-turned toward the entrance before he realised the king did not mean literally. He coughed and hung his head while Besenmut took a staff and scratched a rough map in the scuffed sand of the tent's floor.

"We are here, Son of Re," he said, "and the enemy is, as best we can judge, here, here, and here, straddling the south road, with the Well of Ransut at their backs."

"What are their defences?"

"Almost none. Their left wing is anchored on a field of boulders and their right on a small but steep-sided gully. Nothing ahead of them on or near the road."

"Chariots?"

"A handful, Son of Re. Perhaps twenty at most."

"Who commands?"

"I cannot be certain, Son of Re, but I think it is Lord Sethi."

"Do not ennoble the traitor," Seti snapped. "Is my brother Messuwy there?"

"We have not seen him," Ahmes ventured in support of his brother Commander.

"Nor his banner," Besenmut completed.

Seti stared at the lines in the sand, weighing the strengths of the opposing armies and their dispositions. "We have four legions against their three," he said at last. "And nearly two hundred chariots. Those alone would be able to smash apart Kushite legions, but we need them to be gathered together, rather than strung out on either side of the road. How are we to gather them together for the slaughter?"

Iurudef was the senior officer and the Commanders looked to him. "We must entice them," he said. "Tempt them away from their positions."

"It's a bit obvious, isn't it?" Besenmut murmured. "No commander worthy of the name would let his men break position."

"We're talking about Kushites, though," Setnakhte said. "I know them. Fierce warriors, but undisciplined and troublesome. I think we could offer bait they could not resist."

"Bait?" Besenmut said. "You would not risk the king?"

"No man denies the king an opportunity to strike his enemies," Seti said. "What is your plan, Setnakhte?"

"Just this, Majesty. We strike down the road at the legion sitting on it, and fly the banners of the king. The other legions will not be able to resist the opportunity to win in a single stroke and will leave their positions on the flank and join the battle on the road. When all are gathered in one spot, the chariots charge and shatter the enemy."

"Simple enough," Iurudef commented, "but it puts the king in too much danger. Until the chariot charge, we will be outnumbered three to one."

"I did not say the king had to actually be there," Setnakhte retorted, "only that the royal banners are flown. The king should lead the chariot charge."

"I would dare all," Seti said, "but the chariot squadrons are mine."

"And we stand the best chance of victory with the king leading the charge," Besenmut said.

"I like the plan, Setnakhte," Seti said. "We shall follow it."

"And who commands the 'bait'?" Ahmes asked. "The enemy will surround it and attack furiously."

"It is my plan. I petition you, Son of Re, to grant me the honour of commanding that legion into battle."

"Willingly," Seti responded. "But we must make you appear royal so that every man's eye is upon you and none doubt that I am there in their midst. As well as my banners, you shall wear the blue Khepresh crown."

Besenmut and Ahmes sucked in their breath, while Iurudef raised his eyebrows in shock.

Setnakhte bowed low, his hands outstretched. "I shall die before I bring dishonour on that sacred crown," he said.

The Per-Bast legion advanced down the road toward the Kushite position, the soldiers enthusiastic at the chance to put their training into effect, and looking askance at their Commander, Setnakhte, who was resplendent in kingly raiment and wore the blue war crown. He rode in a chariot above which whipped the banners of Kemetu royalty and of the House of Ramesses, two other chariots behind and to either side. The charioteer reined in the horses that strained, eager for the charge, and Setnakhte turned to his troops and loudly encouraged them to strike a blow against the rebels. Close at hand now, the waiting Kushite warriors raised a jeering cry in reply and hammered on their cowhide shields with their spears.

Setnakhte looked up at the banners flying above his chariot and felt his heart swell with pride. *For this I was born*, he thought. *Userkheperure Seti is a grandson of Usermaatre Ramesses, but I am Usermaatre's son. But for an accident of birth, I would be king now and these would be my men following me into battle.*

The men of Per-Bast raised a cheer and surged forward, losing cohesion as faster-paced men outstripped the slower. Setnakhte's chariot leapt forward too, rapidly closing the gap between them and the Kushite warriors.

Setnakhte drew his bow and loosed an arrow, he was rewarded by an enemy warrior pitching forward onto the road. *Today I am king*, he exulted.

The Per-Bast crashed into the front row of the Kushite, which was already surging forward to meet their northern enemies, and moments later Setnakhte's chariot was in the thick of the fighting, slowed to a walk, and then a stop by the crush of fighting men. More soldiers poured into the wound in the southern army's line, and the Per-Bast, inexperienced in warfare, raised a premature cry of victory.

The two legions had ceased to be fighting units but had disintegrated into hundreds of pairs of men, each struggling to stay alive and to inflict mortal injury on their opponent. Per-Bast men hacked and stabbed with axe and cumbersome long spear while the men of Kush stabbed with short spear and lifted their cowhide shields high, grunting with the effort. Gradually, the impetus of the Per-Bast charge dissipated and the Kushite legion thrust them back, throwing tired men back against their comrades still pressing forward.

Setnakhte shot all his arrows and lifted his ceremonial curved khopesh sword, yelling out encouragement to his men. Over the heads of the men he saw his ruse had worked and the outlying Kushite legions were closing on the battle, reinforcing the central legion. As they did so, the Per-Bast men were borne down by weight of numbers and were forced into a stumbling retreat.

Where are they? Where are the chariots?

As if in answer the ground trembled and a rumbling roar filled the air. Setnakhte looked to the north and lifted his sword high, even as his charioteer tumbled dying to the ground. Now the Kushite warriors were hesitating, drawing back from combat and turning to see what approached. The ones nearest the north road cried out in terror and tried to flee, but there were too many men in the way. The onrushing wave of chariots, King Seti in the forefront, smashed into the chaos of the Kushite legions, trampling broken bodies under hooves and wheels, spraying hot blood to mix with dust in the rippling air.

The rush of chariots slowed as the crush of bodies robbed the horses of their momentum. Kushite warriors trembled as the battle-hardened soldiers of the north, flying the banners of Set, Ptah and Heru carved their way into the milling crowd, men on the edges of the battle already edging away, appalled at the ferocity of the enemy.

Setnakhte saw the enemy army shiver like the reed beds when a fierce northerly wind strikes it, and knew what it meant. "They flee," he yelled, brandishing his khopesh sword. "The enemy flees. Strike them down, men of Per-Bast; kill, O men of Heru; forward, soldiers of Set; victory is in sight, men of Ptah. Hit them hard, for Userkheperure and Kemet!"

A moment later they were in flight. The army came apart around the edges, streaming away from the conflict, down the road toward Waset and out across the desert. Seti's army pursued them, a chaos of running men hacking at the enemy or stopping to rip trinkets from the bodies of the fallen. The Troop Commanders had the rams' horns blown for the recall and junior officers ran after the men, laying about them with their whips until finally the men of the northern legions stopped, and like an ebb tide pulled back to their positions.

Seti called Setnakhte to him and in front of the assembled Commanders and officers, embraced him and praised him. "You shall have the Gold of Valour for your actions this day, Commander Setnakhte."

The bodies of the fallen Kushite were counted and heaped beside the road, while the fallen from the legions were tended by army physicians and then sent back under a small escort. Severely injured soldiers, both friend and foe, were swiftly dispatched and the corpses added to the pile or buried in shallow graves in the hot sun until such time as the families could collect them for proper burial.

The men were fed and water skins were replenished at the well of Ransut before Seti ordered the army to march south. He swore he would rout the remnants of Messuwy's army and hang his brother from the walls of Waset before the month was out, and after the victory earlier in the day, not one officer or soldier who heard him doubted it would happen.

Chapter 29
Year 3 of Userkheperure Seti
Year 2 of Menmire Amenmesse

One consequence of Amenmesse's rebellion and seizing of the throne of Ta Shemau was to upset Ma'at and encourage other dissidents. There were many of these, men who had been refused promotions or positions of importance, and valued themselves more highly than did the king. Few were strong enough to do something about it, but Meryre, son of Meryatum thought himself a rightful claimant of royal privilege, and had large estates with many men.

Meryre marched out of the northwest with a thousand men armed with pitchforks, mattocks and axes, and thought himself a general at the head of his legions. Word of his advance was carried swiftly to Men-nefer, where Tjaty Hori and Queen Tausret stared unbelievingly at the messenger.

"Who is this Meryre?" Tausret demanded.

"One of the swarming grandsons of Usermaatre," Hori replied. "He is the son of Meryatum, Hem-netjer of Re at Iunu."

"Is he mad to think he has some claim on the throne of Kemet?"

"Every son and grandson passed over for riches and position might consider himself injured and seek redress. Why, even I have better claim than this Meryre, being grandson of Khaemwaset who was once Crown Prince." Hori laughed. "I have been honoured and raised up by the rightful king, Userkheperure Seti, so I am content with my lot, but evidently Meryre thinks himself worthy of the royal prerogative."

"What should we do?" Tausret asked. "He has a thousand men."

"Farmers and common labourers for the most part. They will come to their senses and go home."

"We cannot let Meryre's treason go unpunished."

"I would counsel a soft approach, Great Wife. Let me send word to him that he should turn around and go home, and that any complaints he might have will be dealt with in the proper manner once the king returns."

"Is that all? His actions insult the king."

"Then let the king answer him, lady. It is more important to keep the kingdom peaceful than to strike down wrong-doers."

Tausret nodded and they passed on to other business. Hori sent off a messenger to Meryre, bidding him turn around and await the king's pleasure, but he did not, and disaffected peasants from the countryside joined his 'army', swelling its ranks.

Hori brought the news to Queen Tausret this time. "Meryre has had my messenger beaten, and swears he will depose the king and marry his Queen. He is now only two day's march away with a rabble of fifteen hundred men."

Tausret grimaced. "We cannot ignore him any longer."

"You are right, Great Wife, but we lack the resources to meet him in the field. I would counsel shutting the city gates and waiting for the king to return. Let them sit impotently outside the walls."

"I listened to you once before, Tjaty Hori, and we are worse off now than we were before. I will raise an army and go to meet this upstart."

Hori sighed but kept his face impassive. "Whatever you decide is best, Majesty...but where will you find an army? You have only thirty palace guards."

"There is the city Medjay."

"A hundred or so men armed with a staff and a fierce look. You are still outnumbered ten to one."

A small smile crossed Tausret's face. "Perhaps you will join me, Hori?"

"I am a scribe, majesty, not a warrior."

Tausret shook her head gently. "Poor Hori. How many chariots did the king leave us?"

"A few broken ones, some of which have been repaired. Not enough to make a difference against a thousand men." The Tjaty hesitated, seeing the look of determination on the queen's face. "Majesty, it is hopeless. Order the gates shut and we can wait for the king in safety."

"My husband the king left Ta Mehu in my charge, Hori. I will not stand by and see it fall into disorder. Have the Captain of the Guard report to me this afternoon, and the Captain of the Medjay."

"As you wish, Majesty." Hori bowed low and departed.

Later that afternoon, Neferhotep, Captain of the Palace Guard, and Usertem, Captain of the City Medjay bowed low before the Queen. Tausret looked them over carefully and nodded her approval.

"How many men can you release from their normal duties? Assume it is a matter of life or death."

The two men looked at each other. "Forty," Neferhotep said. "Fifty if I must."

"You must. And you, Usertem?"

"I cannot leave the city unpoliced, Majesty, so...one hundred and twenty...maybe thirty."

"Neferhotep, you will be Acting Commander, and Usertem, you are his deputy. Make the palace guards your officers, and the Medjay the enlisted men. I want them equipped for war and ready to march by tomorrow morning."

"Er, who do we...er, we march to join the king, Majesty?" Usertem asked.

"No, there is rebellion in the north. I will lead you and we will quash this rebellion before it gets going. Have your men readied and in place by the north gate at dawn."

The two men bowed and started to the door, but Tausret called them back. "One more thing. I need discipline as firm as hardened bronze. I will explain as we go, but select your most obedient men."

The men were waiting at dawn, just inside the north gate of the city, drawn up in ranks with palace guards as officers and Medjay armed with long spears standing straight behind them. Tausret drove up in a chariot with three others, hastily repaired, behind her. Throwing protocol aside, she took the reins of her chariot herself and invited the two commanders to step aboard. The other chariots followed and the men stepped out at a brisk pace in the cool morning air.

"So," Tausret said, "this is what we face. Fifteen hundred farmers and labourers, maybe more, armed mostly with farming implements and without any military training whatsoever. We have one hundred and eighty men and four chariots, but our men are disciplined and used to the sight of blood. Can we win?"

"Of course, Majesty," Usertem said. "With right on our side, how can we lose?"

Neferhotep nodded slowly. "Man for man, a guard is worth five farmers and a Medjay two. It will be a close run thing."

"Yes, but a hundred and eighty men fighting together, as a unit, can win over ten times that number fighting only for themselves." Tausret looked grim. "Make no mistake, the fate of the kingdom hangs upon our actions today. We fight as one and live, or as individuals or die. Can your men fight together?"

"The guard can," Neferhotep said. "Perhaps they should fight as a unit instead of being divided up amongst the Tens and Fifties of the Medjay."

"They are trained soldiers, and must stiffen the back of the Medjay."

"The Medjay can fight together too, Majesty," Usertem said. "My men are used to relying on each other for support."

Tausret sent her other chariots out to scout the road ahead and they returned quickly, reporting the presence of a swarm of men meandering down the road toward them.

"Draw the men up in units of ninety each on either side of the road, the chariots on the road itself."

The morning sun rose half way to the zenith, hot in a clear blue sky before Meryre's men appeared, sauntering along as if out for a stroll in the countryside. Tausret's men stood at ease and waited for them, and she stood in her chariot along with her two commanders. Insects buzzed and songbirds sang in the grassy fields, while hawks circled lazily above them. Men coughed and murmured, scratching their bodies, and urinating where they stood rather than break ranks.

"There is Meryre's banner," Tausret murmured. "Let us go and see what he has to say for himself."

She drove the chariot out along the road and stopped a hundred paces from her men. The opposing crowd of men slowed and stopped, looking to Meryre to tell them what to do. He emerged from the crowd on foot and, together with a small group of hangers-on and confidants, walked out to meet Tausret.

"Meryre, son of Meryatum," Tausret said. "You are a long way from home. What is your business in Men-nefer and why have you brought these peasants with you rather than letting them work in the fields and farms as they should?"

"You think to oppose me with that handful of men scraped from the streets of Men-nefer?" Meryre asked with a sneer.

"I asked what your business is, Meryre."

"I have come to claim the throne of Kemet. While your husband bickers with his brother, I shall, as grandson of the great Usermaatre, take what is mine and restore Ma'at to the kingdoms."

"I will not argue with you, Meryre. You have no claim to my husband's throne and I bid you return to your home at once or face the consequences."

Meryre laughed. "What consequences? My army will overwhelm your little band and if you are lucky, I will keep you alive as my wife."

Tausret fixed Meryre with a stare but spoke loud enough to be heard by the men closest to them. "Neferhotep, Usertem, mark well these men. There is a deben of gold for each of their heads, but do not seek to impress me by fancy tricks with the sword, axe or spear. Kill quickly and cleanly and slaughter without mercy any man who opposes you."

"Yes, Queen Tausret," they both replied together.

The men who had gathered about Meryre, hoping to share in his success, paled at the threat and drew back, but Meryre called for his men to form up in ranks as Tausret wheeled her chariot and drove back to her waiting men. Neferhotep and Usertem dismounted and joined their units.

Scarcely had they joined their men than Tausret waved her tiny chariot squadron forward. At once, the two divisions of her army leapt forward at a run, though the faster men were careful not to outpace their slower comrades. As a result, the two groups of ninety men hit the loose ranks of farmers and ploughed straight through them even as Tausret's four chariots burst upon Meryre and shattered his little group. Meryre himself went down under the hooves of her horses, the chariot bouncing and lurching over the fallen bodies. Screams arose all around and within moments, Meryre's army of farmers turned tail and ran, streaming across the fields, throwing away their makeshift weapons. Neferhotep and Usertem let them go, their men contenting themselves with a jeering bellow of laughter and self-congratulatory cheers.

They collected the heads of Meryre and his cronies and mounted them on spears. Then the little army marched back to Men-nefer in triumph, voices lifted in songs of praise for General Tausret, Warrior Queen of Kemet.

When Hori added his song of praise back at Men-nefer, Tausret told him to be quiet. "You should know better than any common soldier or Medjay that it is hardly a feat of arms to have conquered peasants armed with sticks. The gods smiled on us, but it could so easily have gone the other way."

"That may be true, Great Wife, but if the king had returned to find Meryre occupying his capital city, it may have been a bloody battle to oust him. You have done the king and Kemet a great service today."

"Well, enough said. Now, have Ramose the Treasurer open the treasury, Hori. I promised Neferhotep and Usertem ten gold deben each, and I want a kite of silver awarded to every man in my little army."

The men cheered their queen once more when the silver was distributed, and promptly spent it all on drink and women. Two died that night as a result of drunken brawls, and one fell in the river and drowned, which was three more than had died in the brief battle that ended Meryre's revolt. Guard and Medjay alike swore eternal allegiance to Queen Tausret and vowed they were her men whenever she needed them.

Chapter 30

Userkheperure Seti speaks:

In this the third year of my reign, the gods of Kemet continue to smile upon me and the House of Ramesses. I have gathered the Two Kingdoms together and spread the peace of Ma'at to all men, dispensing justice and keeping the land safe from enemies external and internal. I build shrines and temples to all the gods, and where I do not build I cause the shrines and temples to be repaired, repainted and refurbished. All men are content and they praise me to my face.

One thing remains undone and for this I din the ears of the gods, offering up the finest of the king's flocks and herds, unblemished animals and the fruit of the fields. I need a son and heir, for though I am still a young man, I would have a son beside me before I become an old man and can no longer guide him in the art of war, teach him of law and kingship, and instruct him in the ways of the gods. My beloved Queen Tausret has not given me a living son, and every child her field produces is weak, without the strength needed for a future king of Kemet. I love her, but she is unable to give me what I desire most. I took my sister Takhat to wife, hoping that my seed in a different field might give me the son I need, but alas, she could only give me a daughter.

And now Takhat has fallen into the hands of Messuwy, my half-brother. Well, he will do her no harm, I suppose, though my pride suffers. A king should be able to prevent such things happening, and the fact that they do only shows me the gulf that exists between the Kemet that should exist and the one that does. Ma'at has been shattered, and the only way it can be restored is for Messuwy to perish.

I just had an errant thought, would Ma'at be restored if I perished and Messuwy lived? I have no son, so Messuwy would likely inherit as son of a king. It is a terrible thought, for surely a man who grasps the throne, seizes the *heka* and *nekhakha* of kingly authority without the permission of the gods, cannot fail to bring down destruction upon the land. For the sake of

Kemet, if not for the sake of my unborn son and heir, I must strike the usurper down and consign him to oblivion.

My initial foray to Waset was ill-considered, I can see that now. My rage conquered my good sense and I hurried to impose my will on the unruly south, thinking that my mere presence would be enough to set matters right. I should have seen that the rot was too deep to be brushed aside, and that I would need to excise the stink and decay of rebellion. For that I needed men, and I had not brought sufficient for the job. I was forced to withdraw to the north, leaving Messuwy alive, and he came back stronger than ever.

This time I came south with battle-hardened legions and struck his Kushite soldiers a mighty blow at the well of Ransut, routing them and driving them before me like the desert sand when the strong west wind blows. They fled south, at first in terror, but then their commander Sethi took them in hand and set up ambushes, assaulting my brave men by a series of cowardly attacks. Proceeding more cautiously than before, my legion commanders lost touch with the enemy and the southerners were able to pull back as far as Waset without being brought to battle once more.

Here the enemy rallied and turned to face us, less than three Kushite legions against my four. They could not hope to win and I exulted, knowing that the end of this civil war was at hand. Before the day was out, I would hang my brother Messuwy from the walls of Waset, along with his jackals Sethi, Khaemter and Roma-Rui. Thus I celebrated my victory in my mind's eye and confidently sent my legions forward, mighty Heru, steadfast Ptah, brave Set, and young but fierce Per-Bast.

As before, my disciplined legions and swift chariots carved their bloody way into the swarming Kushites, but this time they did not flee in panic. Sethi had stiffened their backs and put fire in their bellies. They brought sharp copper knives and darted in upon the chariots, dying in windrows beneath hooves and wheels, but ever more threw themselves forward and the sharp copper blades sliced into the legs of my beautiful horses and cut them down. How those horses screamed, and my brave charioteers added their fear-filled cries as they too joined them in death. My chariot squadrons came to nothing and my legions pressing forward were halted and then slowly forced back.

I marvelled at this and upbraided General Iurudef from where we stood together in my chariot on a low rise overlooking the plain of battle. I had waited with twenty chariots to sweep down on Messuwy when I saw whence he fled. Now, as I saw my men turned back, I asked Iurudef for an explanation.

"How is it that my fine legions cannot prevail against the Kushites here in the shadow of the walls of Waset, when they so easily put them to flight at the Well of Ransut?"

He pointed, his arm shaking slightly. "See, Son of Re, how the Kushites are joined by others who were hiding in the city."

I looked, and indeed saw that men, dark and tall, were streaming from the city to join the Kushite army. As their strength grew, so their bravery waxed and that of my men waned. Kushite warriors, naked save for furred and feathered arm bands and anklets, leapt into open spaces between the fighting men, dancing and cavorting, hurling insults at their foes. Then, uttering cries that chilled the hearts of our men, they plunged forward, copper blades rising and falling. Our men fell back before their ferocity, and still the Kushite army grew in size.

"We must pull back, Son of Re," Iurudef said in a low voice. "If we do not, our legions will be slaughtered."

"The king does not run," I said coldly. "I am the grandson of Usermaatre."

I could hear Iurudef grinding his teeth, and thought that anger or fear would shake his voice, or that he would be injudicious in his speech, but when he spoke he was calm and considered. "A tactical withdrawal, Son of Re." He ventured a small smile. "The movement of men upon a battlefield. Nothing more."

Against my will, I could see the sense in his words, for my legions were crumbling in front of me. My heart ached within me as I thought of Messuwy claiming a victory when I had sworn to hang him on the walls of Waset, but if I did not act soon, I would lose all chance of that ever happening. I gave the order and the rams' horns blared out, cutting through the dust and din of battle.

My legions withdrew in an orderly fashion, each protecting the other, while the army of Sethi continued to press forward, uttering cries of triumph. Back we went, until the high walls of Waset were lost in the dust and haze, and there the Kushites halted, allowing us to break off the battle. The defeat galled me, and sat like sour wine in my stomach and throat. I called my commanders to me and demanded their counsel.

"A temporary setback, Son of Re," Iurudef said.

"Fall back further and gather our men for another assault," Emsaf opined.

"Attack at once, before they can gather themselves," Besenmut said.

"I think we could defend this position," Ahmes offered. "Let us retreat no further but instead gather ourselves and attack once more tomorrow."

"I agree," I said. "It rankles that I must withdraw in the face of my brother's army, for he is a usurper, one who dishonours the throne of Kemet."

"Then, Son of Re, let us put our legions in order and attack the rebels before they can regroup," Besenmut said.

I looked around at my commanders, weighing their words, and then at the one who had not yet said anything. "And what do you say, Setnakhte?"

"Son of Re, my fellow commanders are all northerners, born of Ta Mehu families, whereas my mother, who was a concubine of the great Usermaatre, came from Waset. I have spent many years in Ta Shemau, and am familiar with Kushites and the way they think."

"Yes, yes, we all know you are a son of Usermaatre's later years," Iurudef said. "And I have Kushites in the northern legions. I know how they think and it is not too different from other Kemetu. A soldier is a soldier..."

"But these are not soldiers," Setnakhte cut in. "They are tribesmen pulled out of the wilderness and do not know how to be soldiers. You saw them leaping and dancing before plunging into battle. Are those the actions of a soldier of Kemet?"

"So what is your point, Commander Setnakhte?" I demanded.

"Forgive me, Son of Re, I will get to the point. The Kushite tribesman wants to sit in his own village drinking barley beer and eating beef from his own herds, surrounded by his women and children. He has been enticed to fight by the promise of plunder or some such reward, but if the war drags on he will look more and more fondly at what he has left behind, and one night he will just slip away and go home. My advice, Son of Re, is to withdraw as far as needful, even up as far as Ta Mehu, drawing Messuwy's army after you. We know they have something like five thousand tribesmen and the Amun legion, but in a month, if Messuwy has not brought them a decisive victory, they will start deserting him. Wait another month and you can destroy his depleted army."

My commanders counselled immediate attack or fearful retreat, but only Setnakhte gave me a reason for his considered advice. I hated to appear cowardly in the face of the enemy, but I hated indecision even more. I looked at the faces of my commanders, all of them waiting like sheep to see which way I would move, except for Setnakhte. He looked much as I imagine his father and my grandfather, Usermaatre Ramesses, must have looked as a young man, eager for glory and to get to grips with the enemy, but on his terms. *I will have to watch this man carefully*, I thought.

"We move north," I said. "Let us draw this rabble all the way up to Ta Mehu, and there destroy them."

We retreated north, three legions in good order with one hanging behind in seeming disarray, and drawing the huge Kushite army after us. Whenever they drew too close, the legion hurried its pace and whenever they fell behind, the legion slowed its march, encouraging them onward. In this way, we drew the Kushites north and then held them a little north of the ruined city of Akhet-aten. We sat in a defensive position and waited but now, instead of immediately attacking, Sethi halted his army and camped, as if waiting for something.

"Now you will see, Son of Re," Setnakhte said. "The Kushite flood has reached high water and must soon recede."

Chapter 31
Year 3 of Userkheperure Seti
Year 2 of Menmire Amenmesse

Sethi's temper had been gradually fraying as his army moved further away from Waset. Under the walls of Amun's city, as he held the huge army of Kushites in his hands, he could almost believe himself King of Ta Shemau. Menmire Amenmesse and his Tjaty Khaemter remained within the city, attending to such kingly matters as the governance of the local populace and making sure that sufficient shrines were erected and inscriptions carved that would enhance the king's reputation. Amenmesse even made trips over to the Great Field to check on how his tomb was progressing and to make sure that his brother's inscriptions were being defaced.

While Amenmesse played at being king, pretending that all men accepted him as God-on-Earth, it was left to Sethi to face the disciplined army of the north with his mob of unruly tribesmen. He knew that the Kushites were redoubtable warriors, but they really only liked obeying their own tribal chiefs and exhibited more reluctance to do as they were told than a pride of lions. He had had to use extraordinary means to get them to fight the northern legions at all, and he found that command was a balancing act between threat and reward.

When Khaemter had recruited the Kushites, he had made extravagant promises of gold and cattle and women for every man, and now that Sethi had inherited them, he found himself having to make good on these promises. Gold was easy enough now that they had the gold mines of Kush in their hand, and there were large herds of cattle that had been confiscated from land owners slow to donate their wealth to the new king. The trouble was, as soon as cattle were handed over to the tribes, they wanted to take them south immediately, deserting their duties. Sethi countered this by making an example of a hundred or so men, flaying them alive for desertion, and then persuading the tribal chiefs to graze their new acquisitions on sweet grass and only send them south in the charge of boys brought up from Kush specifically for that purpose.

The other problem was the promised women, and although the whores of Waset ably played their part, the number of virile young Kushite men seeking solace quite overwhelmed them. Disappointed men sought their pleasure elsewhere, mostly among the free women of Waset and the Amun legion spent much of its time keeping the peace within the city. Sethi was relieved when he could drive his cumbersome army north in pursuit of the retreating legions. Not only did it give the men something to occupy their time, but it also relieved the pressure on the women of Waset. Now it was the villages and towns along the road north who suffered.

At first, Sethi did what he could to limit the depredations of the Kushites, but after a while gave up and let them seek their pleasure where they might. As he explained to the mayors of the towns and deputations of village elders, "What would you have me do? They are many and I am one."

"A good general can control his men," one mayor pointed out. "This never happened when Userkheperure marched past."

"Such things are expected of foreign invaders," complained another mayor, "not soldiers of Kemet."

"Technically, I suppose you could argue that these men are not Kemetu, but rather are Kushite tribesmen," Sethi said. "They have a different view on life."

"It is not right. I must take my complaint to the king."

"As you wish, but Menmire is too busy to see you."

There was a long pause, and then the complaining mayor said, "I mean the king in Men-nefer."

Sethi smiled. "That would be a dangerous journey, and ultimately an unsatisfactory one. It would be better to just ignore it. The army will be moving north in a few days and your troubles will be at an end."

"Men in the town have died defending their wives and daughters..."

"Buildings have been burned, crops taken..."

"Women have been raped and some abducted..."

"We demand justice."

Sethi stared at the last speaker, and then at the others in his command tent. "Demand? You demand justice? Really?"

The mayor swallowed hard. "Ev...every man can petition the king."

"Ah, petition. Yes, you can ask the king for justice. For a moment there I thought you were demanding something from the king. Perhaps I misheard you?"

"Y...yes, my lord. I meant we must ask the king for justice."

"An excellent idea. Tell my scribe how many men have died, how many women have been raped, how many abducted, and also any damage done to your towns and crops and I will see to it that you are paid compensation. Will that satisfy you?"

"H...how much compensation, my lord? The damage and injury is extensive."

"I will leave the exact amount awarded up to the court officials, but I am minded to make a gift of gold to every mayor and headman of every town and village we pass." Sethi smiled at the avarice blossoming in every face. "Let me think, a deben of gold apiece? For you personally, you understand? Any award made to you for damage is entirely separate."

"My lord is generous."

"And...and very fair."

"Yes, I am, aren't I? The deben of gold is to make you go away. I have more important things to do than listen to the whining of every self-important official in every squalid hamlet in Kemet. Put your complaints in writing to my scribe if you must, but for now...get out."

The mayors and elders filed out, and Sethi galvanised his cumbersome army into motion once more, sending out Troops to harass the rearguard of the retreating army, and others to forage along the rich river pastures. But the further he pushed into the north, the more discontented his Kushites became. By the time he reached the ruins of the Heretic's city, reports of desertion were filtering in from his officers, and within another month, his army was visibly shrinking from day to day. Sethi cajoled, he threatened, and he made horrific examples of some recaptured deserters, but still they slipped away by night, taking with them everything they could carry.

Five days south of Men-nefer, he suffered his first battle loss. A Troop had been harrying the rearguard as usual and pressed a little too close in their eagerness to snatch spoils from fallen soldiers. An officer of the Per-Bast legion rallied his men and struck back, inflicting significant losses on the Kushite horde. They withdrew, leaving the northern army in possession of the field.

Sethi launched a full scale attack and drove the foe northward again, but a day later they stood their ground once more and faced him. Attrition had weakened the southern army and the northern one was once more heartened by the presence of its king. The two armies clashed and shattered into a melee of fighting men, individuals fighting rather than groups. Back and forth swayed the ant's nest of struggling men, but gradually the Kushites were forced backward.

Sunset saved the southern army, and under cover of darkness they withdrew, leaving the northerners to regroup and ready themselves for the next day. When Sethi drove his army northward the next day, he found the legions blocking his way, arrayed for battle, and he hesitated, allowing his men to slow and halt within sight of the enemy. The armies stared at each other across an intervening stretch of sand and loose rock as the sun rose high and then dipped toward the west. One of Sethi's Troop Commanders, Qenna, a tall and muscular man bedecked with animal skins and feathers, approached his general with a troubled frown creasing his dark scarred skin.

"My lord Sethi," he rumbled. "Do we not attack? My men grow restless."

Sethi turned from his regard of the enemy dispositions, his face bleak. "You have men left? I thought they had all deserted, fled south like the swallows."

Qenna's troubled frown vanished as anger washed across his face. "My men do not run."

"Then I commend you, Commander Qenna," Sethi said. "So many have that I am no longer certain of victory should I attack. The only thing that gives me cheer is that the enemy stands as idle as us. They also do not feel confident of victory."

"We gain nothing sitting here like old women," declared Qenna. "Let us attack and clear these would-be soldiers from our path and then march on to Men-nefer."

"No. They outnumber us. We must build fortifications and defend them until reinforcements can arrive from the south."

Qenna openly sneered at what he plainly considered a cowardly and dishonourable approach to war, but did as he was ordered. The Kushite army of Menmire Amenmesse dug sand and shifted rock, bringing in wood from the river valley to construct forts strung across the road. The fortifications effectively blocked the northern army from advancing as the flanks of the cordon of forts were protected by the river cliffs to the west and rocky desert to the east. What it also accomplished though, as Sethi found to his cost, was that the forts robbed his own men of the will to move further north. It was too easy to sit safe and secure behind the palisades.

For a time, the King in the North attempted to bypass the blockade by sending troops in barges upriver, but Menmire sent boats also and harassed any vessels that dared the southern waters. Soon, the river too was effectively blocked by small fleets of boats.

Months passed in stalemate. Sethi alleviated his desertions by cycling his men between the security of the forts in the north and the pleasures of Waset in the south. He scoured the river valley for food and women to keep his men content, and kept them on their collective toes by instituting raids against the legions dug in to the north. It was after one of these raids that the situation changed.

Qenna had led the raid himself, plunging deep into the camp of the Ptah legion, killing and looting, before withdrawing rapidly in the face of stiffening resistance. He took with him a Leader of Fifty they had captured, and when they got back to the forts, put him to the question. Qenna and his men were not really interested in what a junior officer might reveal, but it was an opportunity to enjoy a bit of entertainment at the man's expense. His screams filled the night and the men sat around enjoying pots of beer and roasted beef while making bets as to when he would next lose consciousness.

The man gabbled, screamed and pleaded, blood sheeting his body, and saying anything he thought might bring the pain to an end. Just before he died, he said something that made Qenna take notice. He immediately got up and strode across to the command tent in one of the other forts and sought audience with Lord Sethi.

"My lord, General Iurudef and the Heru legion have left for the northern border."

Sethi looked up from his meal and pushed the plate to one side. "How do you know?" he asked.

Qenna told him.

"A man will say anything to stop the pain."

"Perhaps, my lord, but I'm inclined to believe it."

"Why?"

"When we raided the Ptah camp, the tents were not full. It might be that they no longer sleep five to a tent, or that some were out on patrol, but it could also be that the Ptah men are spread out, trying to give us the impression that all parts of their line are still occupied."

"Hmm." Sethi considered it, idly pushing a scrap of bread around on the plate with his finger. "You suspect, but you don't know?"

"I think it likely, my lord," Qenna replied. "And if it is true it would give us a great advantage. We could attack and end this war once and for all."

"Do not fill your cup with more wine than is in the jug, Commander. We need to..."

"What do you mean, my lord?" Qenna interrupted.

Sethi sighed. "We only have the unsubstantiated word of a dead prisoner. I think it would be unwise to base strategy on this. Lead another raid, Qenna, and catch some more men. If they all tell the same story then I might believe it."

Qenna did so the following night and captured another four men. Under torture they all offered up essentially the same story, which the Kushite Commander duly reported to Sethi.

"There's one other thing, my lord," Qenna said. "Two of them said that King Userkheperure is also absent. He has gone back to Men-nefer with units of the Per-Bast legion."

"Has he, by the gods?" Sethi exclaimed, rising to his feet. He paced, filled with nervous excitement. "They've never been weaker than they are at the moment then. Now is our time. Have the men ready themselves, Qenna, and send for the other commanders. I will talk to them..." he grinned despite himself. "Five days and we could be knocking on the gates of Men-nefer. Once Seti is dead, we can unite Kemet again."

Qenna nodded solemnly and saluted, before hurrying off to find the other Troop Commanders. They ran to Sethi's tent, eager at the thought of action after so long. Sethi talked to them at length, debating plans and organising the men. With both the king and General Iurudef absent, and over a legion under strength, for the first time in months, Sethi's Southern Army had a numerical ascendancy. Coupled with an imaginative plan and complete surprise, Sethi was confident of complete victory.

In the darkness before the dawn, a large force of Kushites crept through the broken land to the east of the legions, evading or silently killing any guards they found, and at first light rushed silently out of the rising sun, stabbing and slashing at the unprepared Set legion. The northern soldiers were disciplined and rallied swiftly under the guidance of their officers, with reinforcements pouring in from the centre of the line, men of Per-Bast and Ptah, and it was then that Sethi struck with his main force.

Screaming loudly, Kushites swarmed through the gaps in the line, overwhelming the thinly spread Ptah legion and rolling the Per-Basts ahead of them. They caught the Set soldiers from behind, and caught between two attacking forces, hundreds died. Surviving units fled north in disarray and the Kushites pursued them, killing many more. Many of the Ptah legion broke for the river, and were hunted down in the reed beds or picked off by archers in the fleet of boats patrolling the sluggish waters.

Commander Setnakhte drew the fleeing Per-Bast legion together even as he retreated and waves of yelling black men from the south broke on his steady ranks before washing impotently back, unable to break the disciplined formations. All through that long day, the legion withdrew toward the north, sacrificing men to defend each cubit and stadium, but remaining steadfast and secure. Other fugitives gravitated toward perceived safety and swelled their ranks, countering the attrition of warfare. By the time the sun set, the Per-Bast legion was a lot closer to Men-nefer and larger than when they had fled their position. Units of Set and Ptah were present, and these men were pressed into the service of Per-Bast Troop Commanders.

Sethi was elated that night, and indulged in some premature celebration with his commanders, certain that the next day would see the annihilation of the Northern Army and days later their triumphant arrival at a defenceless capital city. The men celebrated too, passing round jugs of beer and roasting whole oxen over the cooking fires while physicians treated as many of the wounded as they could, mercifully dispatching others.

The next day at dawn, Sethi arrayed his Kushites, ready to destroy his enemies, but found that they had withdrawn many stadia during the night and were ensconced in a natural rock formation just to the east of the road. He was tempted to just march past them toward Men-nefer, but realised if he did so he would be leaving a battle hardened legion in his rear. They would have to be winkled out of their rocky fort first.

He attacked, throwing wave after wave of yelling men at the holed-up legion, only to see them retreat leaving the defenders almost unscathed. Night fell, and his own men licked their wounds and recuperated beside campfires, while the Per-Bast men kept watch from their cold and cheerless rock bastions. Sethi was troubled by his inability to dislodge the enemy, but took heart from their self-evident discomfort and straitened circumstances. They were without food, water and fire. *Tomorrow will witness their destruction*, he told himself.

By noon the next day, the Kushites were no nearer victory and Sethi's anger and frustration was growing. If he concentrated his forces on a few places in the defensive circle, he had the advantage of numbers but only a few men at a time could fight in the narrow gaps between boulders. On the other hand, if he spread his forces out, he lacked the strength to push through before the enemy could rally men from another part of their circle. Not for the first time, Sethi regretted a skill that his Kushites lacked, that of the bow and arrow. Few tribesmen made war with the bow, much preferring the short stabbing spear, but that was a distinct disadvantage in the cramped conditions of the rocky redoubt. *If only I had archers*, he thought. *I could stand back and pick them off one by one.* He consoled himself with the fact that the Per-Bast legion had no chariots, few archers, and even fewer arrows. It might take time, but the Per-Bast legion would eventually be worn down.

The next day, the war of attrition was having a visible effect. More and more, Kushites pushed into the defensive circle, stabbing the enemy before being driven back, and toward midday, the attackers gained a foothold in the rocky fort and redoubled their efforts. Then a man came running to report to Sethi of movement on the road north.

"Soldiers, my lord."

"How many? Under what banner?" Sethi tensed, waiting for the news that would spell his failure to take Ta Mehu.

"Per-Bast. No more than a Troop."

Sethi relaxed. Calling for Qenna, he issued terse orders. "It is just the men who escorted Seti returning to their legion. Detach two hundred men and wipe them out. Show the defenders there is no hope."

Qenna grinned and ran to his men, calling them from the battle and together they raced to intercept the Troop of Per-Bast men. The northern men were waiting for them in a tight knot, and as the Kushites drew close, the front ranks knelt revealing archers and behind them young boys clutching baskets of arrows. Qenna yelled to his men to increase their speed, knowing their only hope lay in close-quarters fighting where the stabbing spear came into its own. Instead, a flickering shadow crossed the sun and then his men were toppling into the dust amid groans and screams. Again and again, the thrum of bowstrings sounded and sheaves of young men died, littering the ground, and throwing their comrades into confusion.

The officer in charge shouted a command and the kneeling men leapt up and forward, bronze swords and axes lifted high as they raced forward, slaughtering the wounded and confused Kushite warriors and leaving only a remnant, twenty or so, to escape back to Sethi. Qenna saluted his general, his face grey with pain from the arrow in his arm and an axe wound in his hip.

"Archers, my lord, with many arrows. I lost two hundred men within the space of twenty breaths."

"Withdraw the army from the assault," Sethi spoke, his face twisted with anger. "Overwhelm them. Destroy them before they can do any more damage."

Qenna saluted and limped away, shouting orders. The Kushite army withdrew from their assault on the fortified position and swarmed toward the tiny force of archers and axemen. The flood of men sweeping across the sand looked unstoppable, vastly outnumbering the troop of Per-Bast men, but clouds of arrows slew tens and then hundreds.

Sethi joined his men in the attack on the Per-Bast troop, desiring greatly to destroy them before they slaughtered his army. Despite his fury and the bravery of his bodyguard, he could not close with them, but could only stare across heaps of dead and wounded to where the enemy commander, a mere Troop Commander, directed the defence of his small command.

"I see you!" Sethi screamed above the din, "and if I ever reach you, you will die."

The Kushite attack faltered and then, under the goading of their officers, swept forward again, but now Setnakhte and his legion poured out from their rocky bastion and caught the Kushites in the rear, throwing them into confusion. Though still possessing numerical superiority, the Kushites broke and fled south, running to escape the arrows and axes that had slain so many of their comrades.

Sethi cursed, but could not halt his men's' retreat. He could only follow, trying to retain some semblance of command, but it was many stadia and two days later before he managed to reform the remnants of his once-great army. Qenna still limped from his axe wound, but his desire for revenge was great. He harangued his men, assuming overall command of the units and reported to Sethi.

"Give us the word, Lord Sethi, and we will teach those northerners a lesson. My men are ready to advance on Men-nefer again."

Sethi scowled and shook his head. "Not yet. We have suffered too many losses to be certain of victory. We must withdraw and build up the army again."

By the end of the month, Sethi's Kushite army had retreated almost as far as Waset once more, and he had sent word to Menmire Amenmesse and Khaemter that he needed more men.

Chapter 32
Year 4 of Userkheperure Seti
Year 3 of Menmire Amenmesse

Setnakhte guarded the North Road for a month, until General Iurudef returned from the northern border with a revitalised Re legion and several hundred auxiliaries garnered from the towns and villages of Ta Mehu. At this time, Setnakhte marched his Per-Bast legion back to Men-nefer and sought audience with the king.

Userkheperure Seti and Queen Tausret received the Legion Commander and his Troop Commanders in the main throne room of the palace, and arranged for the hall to be crowded with courtiers and nobles. Setnakhte led his officers in and they all bowed low before the King and Queen, extending their arms in ritual supplication.

"Arise, my good and faithful servant," Seti murmured. "Arise, you and your officers and accept the rewards a grateful king bestows on his brave commanders."

Seti beckoned and servants hurried forward, bearing a heavy chain of gold and several golden bracelets.

"Legion Commander Setnakhte, for your many acts of bravery in defeating the Kushite horde, I bestow the Gold Chain of Valour upon you and grant you a setat of rich farmland in the sepat of Abdju."

Setnakhte bowed once more and then stood while Tjaty Hori hung the gold chain around his neck.

Hori embraced the commander and whispered in his ear. "An incentive to keep fighting, Setnakhte. The land is currently in the possession of the southern usurper."

Setnakhte grunted, and when Hori had withdrawn, addressed the king. "My thanks, Userkheperure. I look forward to taking possession of my land."

Seti nodded and smiled. "Let the Troop Commanders of the Per-Bast legion step forward." The five men advanced and bowed low again. "Your bravery has been noted and is hereby rewarded. Let every Commander accept a gold bracelet of one deben weight."

Each commander received the gift of a grateful king from the hands of Tjaty Hori, bowed once more and stepped back.

Seti waited and then said, "It is with sorrow that I hear that Acting Legion Commander Ahmes of the Set legion fell during the battle against the Kushite horde. Commander Iurudef of the Set legion is confirmed as General of the Northern Armies, leaving the position of Legion Commander vacant." The king paused and glanced at Queen Tausret before smiling and continuing. "It is my will that Troop Commander Ament of the Per-Bast legion be raised to the position of Commander of the Set legion. May he continue to defend Kemet and the House of Ramesses all the days of his existence."

Ament prostrated himself, tears of gratitude in his eyes, and Tausret bade him take his place with pride, as he had earned the honour shown him.

Hori then announced one further action. "Let Royal Butler Bay stand forth."

The Amorite stepped forward, his face impassive, though those nearest him noted a slight tremor in his limbs. Nobody knew whether he was to be honoured or castigated, and some remembered that he was related by marriage to the southern usurper. These people drew back lest they be contaminated by the proximity of a man who must surely now be accounted a traitor.

"Royal Butler Bay," Seti said. "You have served me faithfully these past several years and I am minded to reward you. Some have cautioned me in this regard, reminding me that your sister was married to my usurping brother, and that your loyalty is divided. I reject that view as I have seen no evidence of anything but your devoted service. Alas, Ramose the Treasurer, my faithful servant is on his deathbed, so I must make provision for his absence. I can think of no better man to take up his burden and his privilege. Accordingly, I am making you, Bay, Overseer of the Sealed Things, Treasurer and Chancellor of the Two Kingdoms, second only to Ramose in that regard while he lives."

Bay looked dazed at this sudden fortune, but collected his wits rapidly and bowed low before the king. "May I prove worthy of your trust, Userkheperure."

Hori dismissed the gathering, but told Ament to stay behind. "At the express wish of Queen Tausret," he murmured. He ushered Ament and Bay aside and into a smaller chamber where food and drink had been set out on tables and servants stood ready to minister to their needs.

Ament wandered over to the tables to view the fare but he did not take anything. He looked across at the new Chancellor who was standing by the door with a bemused expression on his face. "Took you by surprise, I'll warrant," Ament said.

Bay nodded slowly. "It appears we have both risen in the world. I think..." He was unable to complete his thought as the door opened once more and the king and queen entered.

Bay and Ament at once bowed, but Seti smiled. "Get up, get up. I will stand for no formality today. I have honoured you both because you have done me a great service. Now is the time to eat and drink and forget our cares." The king beckoned to a servant who immediately poured rich dark wine into a beautiful blue glass cup and handed it to him. Another poured wine for the Queen, and others for the two honoured commoners.

They drank, and Bay commented on the wine, praising it. Seti nodded. "From the Royal Vineyards. Now tell me, Chancellor Bay, how is your nephew Siptah? Have you word of him?"

Bay hesitated. "No, Son of Re. He is in Khent-Min, under the protection of Menm...of your brother...and I have not heard anything for nearly a year."

"How was he then, a strong lad? He'll have been...what? Six years old?"

"Seven, Son of Re. Eight by now, but not strong, my lord. He was born with a withered leg and though he can walk, he limps badly. I fear he will never be a soldier."

"Well, we'll see. He can always ride in a chariot providing his arms are strong. He is my nephew, you know, as well as yours."

"Yes, my lord."

"I will not see him suffer for who his father is. I will find him duties suitable to his station and abilities."

"Y...you are most generous, my lord."

"Nonsense," Seti cried. "What sort of a king would I be if I waged war on children? Is that not right, my beloved?"

"Indeed, husband," Tausret confirmed with a gentle smile. "And speaking of children, I am hopeful that my lord will soon have a son of his own to provide for."

Seti stared at his queen. "You are with child? How long have you known?"

"Not long, my beloved. The physicians declare I am healthy and carrying a boy."

"Let us pray to all the gods that is so," Ament said.

"I shall offer up a sacrifice of thanksgiving at the altars of Min and Mut myself," Bay added.

They drank again in celebration, and then the servants offered food, goose and beef, fine-ground bread, lettuce, radishes and onions, dates, cucumbers and melons. The king ate heartily, engaging Bay in talk while Tausret drew Ament to one side.

"You are well, my friend?"

"I am indeed, my lady." He fingered the gold bracelet on his left arm. "Do I have you to thank for my reward and appointment?"

"Not in the slightest. Setnakhte commented on your bravery and how you saved the day with your archers. As soon as the king heard, he knew what he should do."

"Well, I thank you anyway, my lady."

"I was sorry to pull you away from your duties as Overseer of Vineyards in Per-Bast," Tausret went on. "Your boys are well? The slaves from Timna? What were their names...Jer something, I think, was one of them. Outlandish Retenu names."

"Jerem and Ephrim, my lady. They are well, and help me in my work."

"And your sister Ti-ament? How is she getting on with that Kaftor husband of hers?"

Ament grinned. "She and Zeben have three children now, a boy and two girls."

"And yourself? Have you found some nice girl to warm your bed?"

"None worth more than a tumble, my lady." Ament saw the look on the queen's face and hurried on. "I'm not the type to settle down, my lady. All I need is my duty, my food and drink, and an occasional girl when the need strikes me. I'm a soldier, plain and simple."

"Never plain and simple, Ament." Tausret looked pensive, and chewed on a piece of bread in silence for a few moments. "I have need of a loyal soldier."

"I am yours to command, my lady. As always."

"It might be dangerous."

Ament shrugged. "More dangerous than war?"

"And it would take you from your duties as legion commander."

"That is more difficult. Userkheperure appointed me; I cannot cease my duties without his permission."

"I will arrange that."

"Then tell me what I must do, my lady."

"What is the biggest threat to Kemet and the Ma'at of my husband's reign?"

"Menmire...your pardon, my lady. The southern usurper."

"Do not be afraid to call him by his throne name...except perhaps in front of my husband," she added with a smile. "I once refused to think of him by that name, but Messuwy was anointed king by the Hem-netjer of Amun and I suppose has a right to be called Menmire, even though Roma-Rui was deposed as Hem-netjer and there was already a king of Kemet. But you are right; his presence disturbs Ma'at. He must be removed."

"That is what we are all trying to do, my lady. Unfortunately, he sits in Waset while Sethi ventures out with his Kushite army. Perhaps if we can carry the war down into Ta Shemau, we may be able to tempt him out."

"Meanwhile, the common people of Kemet suffer."

"That is always the way of war, my lady."

"We must bring it to an end, for everyone's sake."

"Of course, but how? We are already doing what we can, legion against legion."

"Sometimes a single man can achieve what an army cannot."

Ament frowned. "I am not sure I discern your meaning, my lady."

"A single man with a pot of poisoned cream struck down Baenre. Perhaps another man can strike down Menmire and put an end to the war."

Ament stared. "You would have me become an assassin? I have no knowledge of poisons."

"There are other methods, but can you think of a better way to swiftly end this war? Our armies are evenly matched after three years. Must Kemet suffer for another three...or even thirty?"

"But...I am known to many people."

Tausret smiled. "Take off your jewellery, your badges of office, and put on an ordinary workman's kilt and you would blend into any crowd of men. You once sailed upriver with a boy and girl, so I know you can do it. The question is...will you?"

Ament hesitated. "If you ask it of me, my lady, but as I said before, the king has commanded me to take up the Set legion. I cannot disobey him."

"I will ask him to let you return to your home for a month before taking up your command. He will grant it, and that will give you time to sail south and kill Menmire."

"But to kill an anointed king..."

"Anointed by a false Hem-netjer. The gods will look kindly on the restoration of Ma'at."

Ament did not look convinced. "If you say so, my lady, but...well, let me take the Set legion upriver in barges and we can strike at the heart of the rebellion in an honourable way."

"No. We have tried the army way. It is time we tried something subtler. A single man silently walking the streets of Waset, moving through the rooms of the palace like a servant, may strike the usurper dead where legions have failed."

Ament considered the notion for some little while as he chewed on fatty goose meat and bit into a crisp onion. "Very well, my lady, I will try it," he said at last.

Tausret clapped her hands in delight, attracting the attention of several servants who hurried toward her. She waved them away. "Excellent. I shall issue instructions that everyone is to assist you in whatever you need."

"Please say nothing to anyone, my lady...except the king, of course. I will slip away quietly in a day or two, after making a show of going home. The fewer people who guess my destination, the less chance there is of betrayal."

Chapter 33
Year 4 of Userkheperure Seti
Year 3 of Menmire Amenmesse

A few days after the ceremony where Setnakhte was awarded his gold chain, news came to Men-nefer of such importance that Tjaty Hori felt the need to interrupt the king as he took his leisure in the palace gardens. He hurried along the paths; his sandaled feet crunching in the fine gravel, one hand holding his long robe aloft so he would not trip on it and the other making sure his ornate wig of state did not slip on his shaved head. The king sat under a tamarind tree near a reed-lined pool with his queen, talking and holding hands, and Hori hesitated to disturb their peace. Then he took a deep breath and plunged forward. At once, guards who had been previously unseen in the shadows, leapt out with spears levelled and challenged him.

"It is all right, Re-It, Paner, you may let my Tjaty through," Seti called, turning and rising to his feet. "Come, Hori, what is the matter? I can't remember when I saw you so flustered."

Tausret rose too and cocked her head on one side as Hori bowed. "Is it the rebels?" she asked. "Have they broken through?"

"No, my lady," Hori said. "Iurudef has them bottled up south of Khent-Min."

"Then what?" Seti asked.

"Grandsons of Usermaatre again, Son of Re. They think to take advantage of the unrest and seize the throne of Ta Mehu."

"Like Meryre," Tausret said with a laugh. "And look what happened to him. Head on a spike for a month and then fed to the crocodiles."

Seti joined in the laughter. "Yes, my Queen is veritably a lion of Kemet...or should I say lioness? Perhaps I should have that title appended to your others in the temples."

"Forgive me, Son of Re...my lady...," Hori said. "The present threat is nothing like that of Meryre. Without wishing to detract from your victory, my lady, Meryre led a thousand peasants. These two, Ramses and Meryma'at are both grandsons of Pareherwenemef, actually command trained men. Their armies are small, but you will need to recall a legion to answer them."

"Pareherwenemef?" Seti asked. "He died even before Khaemwaset, and I thought without issue."

"He had a daughter called Nefertari, and she had sons by a nonentity. One of them, Ratep I think, gave birth to these two brothers who have estates on opposite sides of Ta Mehu."

"No claim at all then. Leave them alone and they'll lose interest."

Hori bared his teeth in a semblance of a smile. "They both like to say they are sons of Usermaatre, but Pareherwenemef was never in the line of succession and the blood is well diluted now. They have no support outside their own men, and hope to take advantage of unrest in the kingdoms." Hori hesitated and then continued, picking his words with care. "Forgive me, Son of Re, but you should take this threat seriously. If you leave them alone, others will take heart from your inaction. Show any sign of weakness, and other nobles could join their rebellion. You must crush them completely, and at once, and for that you will need at least one legion drawn either from the south or the northern borders."

"Two brothers, you say?" Seti asked. "How do they plan to rule? Who is to be king?"

Hori shrugged. "Meryma'at is the elder and has the larger army. I imagine he intends to make his brother Tjaty under him."

"You say they have trained men," Tausret said. "How trained and how many?"

"Ramses has about two hundred veterans settled in the northwest, north of Perire, and can command another five hundred peasants. So far he has not moved from his lands, but I expect he will march southeast soon and try to meet up with his brother. Meryma'at has somewhat more men, maybe as many as a thousand, and is on the move south from Djanet. Most of his force is military men with a number of mercenaries of the Sea Peoples."

"Chariots?" Seti asked.

"None."

"And what forces have we around Men-nefer?"

"Not enough, Son of Re. A few hundred men recovering from wounds..."

"How many able to fight?"

Hori shrugged. "Two hundred? Three?"

"Plus the Medjay," Tausret said. "They served me well before."

"Against peasants," Seti observed.

"I would be prepared to take them out against these pretenders," Tausret said.

"I was not here then, wife of my heart, or I would not have permitted it. What's more, you are with child. No, I will take what men we have and march to meet Meryma'at, he seems the more immediate threat. If I can get to him before his brother joins him, I can smash the rebels individually."

"You will still be much outnumbered," Hori said.

"I shall send a messenger north to the border, ordering a legion down. I shall catch Meryma'at between two armies and crush him."

Seti started striding off, caught up in the excitement of a new war, but Tausret ran to catch him up. "Let me take a small force of Medjay and at least delay Ramses. If he reaches his brother before you, their army will be too strong."

"Obey me in this, my love. I will not risk you and our child. Stay safe here in Men-nefer until I return."

Tausret heard the harshness in her husband's voice and lowered her head, saying no more. She knew that if she pushed, he would extract a promise from her or institute a direct command for Hori to keep her back. Without such a promise or command, the possibilities were more numerous.

As soon as the king got back inside the palace with Hori at his heels, he was barking orders, sending servants scurrying to find army officers and stores, stirring up the ants' nest that was the palace and the city. He sent messengers north to the border, both by river and road, exhorting Commander Disebek to bring the Heru legion south, leaving only the forts between the northern enemy and the rich lands of Ta Mehu. It was a gamble, but one that Seti felt he had to make. If the gods were on his side, all would be well.

Priests ran to berate the ears of the gods, and within a day, Seti had taken himself across the river to where the wounded soldiers were recuperating. Physicians examined every man, and if he was capable of holding a spear and walking, he was pressed into service. Army officers scoured the city and towns for other men, even conscripting artisans and farmers, in an effort to swell the ranks, and three days after the news had reached his ears, Userkheperure Seti marched north along the Great Military Road toward the elder of the two rebelling brothers.

The dust kicked up by Seti's army still hung in the air, when Tausret started issuing her own orders. Neferhotep marshalled the palace guards, and Usertem's Medjay volunteered to a man to join the Queen's army. Everyone remembered the previous expedition and wanted to share in the spoils of another campaign.

"Strip the palace and city of every man," Tausret instructed. "There are so few men left that there will be no crime while we are away."

Each commander calculated the forces at his disposal. "Eighty guards, fully armed and ready," Neferhotep reported.

"Two hundred Medjay, but only half armed with spears," Usertem added. "The others have their staff of office."

"It will have to do. Go now and prepare your men. We leave at daybreak."

As expected, Hori objected to the Queen's plan, but there was little he could do. The king had not instructed him to prevent the queen from leaving, nor from hindering her in any way. Furthermore, the palace guard had already enlisted in her army, so nobody would be obeying a mere Tjaty. He capitulated with as much grace as he could muster, and looked the other way as the tiny force marched out the next day, heading north on the western side of the river as they strove to intercept the men of the younger rebel.

Tausret rode in one of the two chariots the king had left behind, sending the other one ahead to scout the land and find the rebels. A day after they left Men-nefer, not long before sunset, the scout reported back that the rebels had been sighted preparing to cross the river branch. Tausret picked up the pace of her little army, determined to reach Ramses before he took his army out of reach. She made it while his army was split, some on the western bank, some on the eastern, and as they came in sight, Ramses' men shouted an alarm and formed up in a semicircle to protect their comrades embarking in dozens of tiny boats.

Guard Commander Neferhotep frowned as he scanned the ranks of soldiers facing them. "I don't like it, my lady," he said quietly. "They look experienced, though there are several grey heads among them."

Usertem pointed toward the river. "Whatever we do, we'd best do now," he said. "They're starting to bring some men back."

Neferhotep nodded. "I think we could just take this lot now, but not if they get reinforcements."

"Sound the horns for attack, my lady? We have not got long before nightfall."

Tausret had also been scrutinising the soldiers facing her and knew Ramses was a far more formidable foe than had been Meryre. She doubted her little army could defeat even these few rebels on the near side of the river, let alone the others if they recrossed the water.

"No," she said. "Let's try something else first. Send a man forward under a flag of truce and say that Queen Tausret desires to talk with Ramses son of Ratep."

"Forgive me, my lady," Neferhotep said, "but I think that's a mistake. You're only giving them time to ship more men back. A quick throw of the dice now and we could win this."

"At the cost of how many good Kemetu lives? We only have to delay them long enough to prevent them joining with Meryma'at before the king can destroy him."

Neferhotep sent a herald forward under a flag of truce and both armies watched as he spoke with an officer of the forces of Ramses. The officer turned and walked back into his own lines but returned shortly to give his commander's answer. Neferhotep's herald reported that Ramses had agreed to meet Tausret, and had offered the hospitality of his command tent, provided she came alone. If not, then he would fight her here on the banks of the river.

"We have waited too long," Usertem said morosely. "He's brought most of his fighting men back over to our side."

"Then my plan is already working," Tausret said. "We have delayed him for a fifth part of a day. Let's see if I can make it longer by talking with him."

"You're not seriously thinking of accepting his invitation, are you my lady? You'll be putting yourself completely in his power."

"I'll be safe enough...I think. I doubt he'll risk the goodwill of common men by waging war on a woman."

Neferhotep turned away, muttering something about the gullibility of women, but Tausret chose to not hear. She called for her chariot and took the reins herself, guiding it through her own men and across the narrow strip of pasture toward Ramses' men. They drew aside as she approached and closed ranks behind her, preventing her from escaping if she changed her mind. She approached the shore and an officer stepped forward to grasp the horses' bridles and halt the chariot.

Tausret stayed in the vehicle, looking around her until she spotted a man standing by the only tent that had been erected near the river. He approached and inclined his head toward her.

"Lady Tausret, you are welcome in my tent."

"I do not know you. Who addresses me?"

"I am Ramses, son of Ratep, descended from Pareherwenemef, third son of the great Usermaatre himself. You are welcome, cousin. Will you not alight and have a cup of wine with me?"

Tausret said nothing but got down and allowed herself to be shown into the command tent, where stools had been hastily set out and wine poured into cups. She sat without being invited and arranged her skirts while Ramses sat down opposite her.

"Why are you here, Lady?" Ramses asked after they had both sipped on their wine. "What can you hope to achieve with your tiny force?"

"I would ask the same, Ramses son of Ratep. You have left your estates with many armed men, more than you need to ensure your safety. Some might wonder why you have done so, and ascribe motives that are less than flattering to your loyalty."

Ramses' nostrils tightened and he glared at the queen sitting across from him. "My loyalty is to Kemet, and always has been."

"Did you not once take an oath of loyalty to Userkheperure Seti? Has he sent for you and your men? Does he know you are marching across Ta Mehu?"

"Lady, you should go back to your palace and concern yourself with womanly matters. Leave the governance of the Two Lands to those who know."

"I am Queen Tausret Setepenmut, Great Wife of King Userkheperure Seti. My counsels are listened to by the king, I have governed the kingdoms in his absence, and I have taken the field against the enemies of Kemet. I, like you, am descended from Usermaatre and from his son Sethi and my adoptive father Baenre Merenptah. You will pay me the respect due to my position, Ramses son of Ratep, or this discussion is at an end. We can face each other in battle instead, and we will let the gods of Kemet decide who will be the victor, an anointed Queen or a man with ideas above his station."

Ramses glared at Tausret, his lips a thin line in his flushed face and his knuckles white around his wine cup. Then his eyes dropped and he said,

"Your pardon, Lady. I misspoke." Every word was ripped reluctantly out of his mouth.

Tausret inclined her head graciously. "You are forgiven, Lord Ramses. Now, pour us some more wine and tell me why you are here. Perhaps you have some legitimate reason for taking armed soldiers across Ta Mehu."

Ramses poured more wine and they sat in silence for a time, sipping from their cups. At length, he put his cup aside and addressed the issue that lay between them. "Lady Tausret, you know as well as I that the Ma'at of Kemet is disturbed, brother wars against brother, no man is safe in city or country, and only the enemies of Kemet can benefit."

"And you would restore Ma'at by leading armed men against the king?"

Ramses nodded slowly. "You are aware that our ancestor Menpehtyre wrested the throne from the Heretic and his brothers, setting his son Menmaatre on the throne after him?"

"I know the history of our family. What is your point?"

"Menpehtyre laid the foundation, Menmaatre strengthened it and the great Usermaatre Ramesses, built the great temple that is Kemet. Plainly our house has the favour of the gods, as for nearly a hundred years we have had a stable and strong government. Even after Usermaatre ascended to Re, Kemet remained strong under Merenptah, but what has happened since?" Tausret remained silent, so Ramses continued. "The peace of the Two Kingdoms has been shattered, with Userkheperure Seti setting up as king in the north and Menmire Amenmesse in the south. After time out of mind, the Two Kingdoms are sundered and brother fights brother. Can you imagine that the gods want this?"

"Obviously not," Tausret said. "On this we are agreed. But is more fighting the answer?"

"When a physician encounters a suppurating wound he cuts it out, does he not? That is all I intend, to strike swiftly and cleanly, and excise the rottenness that infects the body of Kemet."

"When a physician wields his copper knife, all too often the patient dies. Would you kill Kemet by excising its life?"

"Not its life, Lady; only its false king."

"Then why are you marching east to join your brother against my husband? You should be marching south to join your forces with ours and defeat the usurper in Waset."

"Ah, my Lady, your husband is the false king."

Tausret frowned. "You cannot mean that."

"Lady, the hour is late. Whatever we decide, our men cannot fight at night. Let us end our discussions for now and resume in the morning after we are rested and fed. I would like to convince you that my cause, my brother's and mine, is just."

"Very well, Lord Ramses. A truce then, for tonight. We camp close by and in the morning you may try to convince me that you are in the right and I will do the same. Agreed?"

"Agreed, my Lady."

Neferhotep and Usertem were relieved to see their queen returning unharmed, and questioned her about what had transpired, but she would say nothing except issue some odd commands.

"Have the men fed and then stand to arms all night. I want them to make a lot of noise, clashing of swords and axes, uttering of war cries, shouting of orders, they must believe they could be attacked at any moment. In fact, do anything that will ensure the rebels have no sleep."

"If our men remain awake all night it will affect their fighting ability tomorrow," Neferhotep objected.

"We're not going to fight them, they outnumber us. All that fighting would achieve is our death."

"Then why, my lady?"

Tausret smiled. "Wait and see, and pray to the gods."

Chapter 34
Year 4 of Userkheperure Seti
Year 3 of Menmire Amenmesse

Ament returned to Per-Bast and spoke to his young companions Jerem and Ephrim. He told them of his incipient journey to Waset and what he hoped to accomplish for the sake of the Queen. Jerem insisted on going too, and the younger boy Ephrim was only a heartbeat behind him. Ament had mixed feelings about their desire to join him on his perilous mission, not wanting to take the boys into danger, but would be glad of their company.

"How will we kill the false king?" Jerem wanted to know. "By stealth or face to face?"

"I'll plunge a dagger into his heart," Ephrim volunteered.

Ament found himself smiling at their enthusiasm, but sat the boys down and spoke firmly to them. "You will not be involved in the death of the king. That is my job. The only reason I am considering taking you to Waset is as a disguise. They may be looking for an assassin, but not for a father with two small sons in tow."

Jerem made a face and nodded, but Ephrim's face lit up with joy.

"You are going to be our father?" he cried.

Ament opened his mouth to tell him they were only acting the part of being a family, but seeing the expression on the younger boy's face, just nodded. "Yes," he murmured. He ruffled Ephrim's hair.

They left the next day, from the docks of Per-Bast, in a small fishing boat. The boys looked with interest at the battered but river-worthy craft, at the patched sail and fishing nets bundled in the prow. Jerem dug a fingernail into the wood and prised up a small piece, flicking it into the slowly flowing water.

"Couldn't you have bought a better boat, master? A new one, even. This one will sink before we get half way to Waset."

"A new boat would be noticed, and we don't want to attract the attention of anyone. Besides, you should be thankful we're using a wooden boat. Poor people use ones made out of rushes. This tells people I'm a moderately successful fisherman, but nobody will look twice at a man with his young sons."

"They'll see soon enough that we're not real fishermen."

"That's where you are wrong, young Jerem," Ament said. "My father was a fisherman and though I've become a soldier and an Overseer, I know how to fish."

"Will you teach us, fath...master?" Ephrim asked.

"Count on it. By the time we get to Waset, you'll know how to catch and clean fish like a boy born to the trade. And call me 'father', both of you. I want that to be natural."

Jerem nodded. "Very well...father. But aren't fish already clean? They live in water, after all."

Ament laughed. "Wait and see."

He spent the first few days showing the boys how to handle a boat in the slow current of the easterly branch of the river; how to raise and lower the sail; how to steer, to tie knots, and how to bale out the bottom when water leaked in through gaps between the boards. They had brought enough supplies from home to take them through those first days, but by the time they drew level with and then passed Men-nefer, Ament started their instruction on the art of fishing.

They spent a day in the shallows near a reed bed, getting to grips with the techniques of throwing a weighted net into the water and pulling it in without capsizing the boat, or else pulling a net behind the boat and hauling it over the stern. Ament kept a watchful eye out for crocodiles as a small boy would make a tasty snack for one of the armoured beasts. He showed them the muddy trails on the riverbanks where a crocodile had slipped into the water as they approached, and pointed out the tiny disturbances on the rippled surface of the river where the nostrils and eyes of the predator followed them.

"They'll leave you alone for the most part," Ament said, "though you have to be careful. They like fish as well as small boys, and they've been known to hit a boat and tip people into the water."

Stores ran low by the time they were a few days south of Men-nefer, so they started fishing in earnest, at first just cooking their catch every evening when they put into shore, and later selling the excess to farmers along their way.

"Anyone can catch fish for themselves," Ament told them, "but farmers are working in the fields from dawn to dusk, so they're happy for someone to trade some fish."

Ament showed the boys how to gut and clean the fish, saving the bloody remnants to attract more fish. "The guts will also attract crocodiles, so be careful." If he judged that crocodiles were in the area, they took their catch onto the riverbank and cleaned them there. They ate well, and both boys became proficient in all aspects of fishing by the time they reached the stretch of the river near Waset.

Here they came across the first signs of warfare, burnt out villages, plundered fields, and few people working the land. The people were unfriendly too, less inclined to trade their meagre crops for fish, and viewing their visitors with open suspicion. Ament took to camping on the western shore, and they survived largely on a diet of fish from then on.

They tied up at one of the lesser docks at Waset, the boys waiting by the boat while Ament went in search of the Overseer of Wharves, paying him a small sum in copper for the right to tie up there.

The overseer stared at him suspiciously. "You're not from around here, are you?"

Ament shook his head, mentioning a village several days north of there. "Thought I'd show my boys the big city. It's coming up for the Opet festival and who knows; maybe we'll get to see the king. That'd be a great treat."

The overseer shrugged. "Maybe, but Menmire doesn't like crowds. Stays in the palace most of the time." He yawned and scratched his ample belly. "Anything else?"

"Do you know of a place that might rent me and my sons a room for a while? Nothing too expensive."

"There's any number of places if you're not too fussy. You could try the Heru tavern near the market, though they might be too costly for a mere fisherman. Some of the brothels might rent you a room..." the overseer winked and grimaced "...though you might have to take a woman with it. I take it your wife's not with you?"

"She died," Ament said. "The tavern sounds fine; I'll try there."

Ament collected the boys from the boat and attached the little docket from the Overseer of Wharves that gave him permission to tie up his boat there for ten days. Then he wandered through the streets of the city, asking directions for the Heru tavern. He found it without much trouble, but they had no rooms for hire, instead recommending a house near the Great Temple of Amun. A room there cost him a little bit more than he hoped he would have to pay, but the owner just shrugged when Ament protested.

"Prices are rising. Blame it on this war. If one or other of the kings would win or agree to divide the kingdoms, we could get back to normal."

Ament was a little taken aback that such a thing would be openly discussed with a stranger, but merely nodded, offering no opinion. Later, as he walked the streets with the boys, listening in on street-corner gossip or chatting idly with merchants and common folk, he found that the room owner's comment was by no means isolated. A low hubbub of discontent roiled the city, comments only dying away when squads of Kushite warriors trotted past.

"Who are they?" Ephrim asked, pointing at a squad. "Why are they black?"

Ament pushed the boy's hand down and waited until the soldiers had passed out of earshot. "They are men from Kush, in the south, and they are all dark-skinned. Fierce warriors too. You must have seen them before, there are a few in the northern legions, though they make up most of the southern legions."

"We've seen a few," Jerem confirmed. "But none of them were wearing plumes and skins like these ones."

The markets fascinated the boys who had only seen smaller affairs in the Retenu villages or in Per-Bast more recently. They stood and stared at the colourful crowds of people, letting the cacophony of a thousand voices wash over them, and the odours of a city assault their nostrils. Boys of their own age and younger ran and played in the streets, darting and weaving between the legs of the adults, snatching food from a stall, throwing dung at a stall holder who objected. Dogs barked, donkeys brayed, geese honked and pigs squealed, from a distance came the lowing of cattle and bleating of goats in their pens, and over it all was laid the resonating bellows of rams' horns from the temples. Unwashed bodies, sweat-stained dresses and kilts, animal dung trodden underfoot by sandaled feet, all raised a strong stench which mingled with the aromas of spices, cooking meats, baking bread and freshly brewed beer, drifting in the hot dusty air of Kemet's largest city.

Ament guided his boys through the throng, buying a loaf of bread and a pot of weak beer. He led them away from the market and they sat on the wide steps of a temple dedicated to Min and ate their meal. They ate the bread hungrily, washing it down with weak beer and spitting aside a few stone chips caught up in the bread.

"What do we do now?" Jerem asked. He looked around carefully to make sure they were not overheard. "About Menmire, I mean. How do we kill him and when?"

Ament shook his head. "I don't know. From what I've overheard, he stays in the palace, rarely venturing out."

"Can we get into the palace then?"

"Possibly, though I'll go alone if that happens. You and Ephrim will stay safe in our room."

"I can help," Jerem protested.

"Me too," Ephrim added.

"Absolutely not. If I get the chance, I'll strike the usurper down and make my escape. If I'm caught or killed, I don't want you anywhere near me. You two will stay in the room and if I don't return...well, you'll have to make the best of it. I'll leave you a little copper, all I've got, and you can sail the boat back downriver. I've shown you how and you're good enough, Jerem."

The boys were unhappy but agreed to obey Ament. "Perhaps it won't come to that, mast...father," Jerem said. "I think I know how you can get into the palace. You're a fisherman, so you turn up with a basket of fish and..."

"It doesn't work quite like that," Ament said gently. "If the Waset palace is anything like the Men-nefer one, of which I was Captain of the Guard, if you remember, food is seldom bought straight from the farmer or fisherman. I'd have to take my catch to a seller, and then someone from the palace would come with a list..."

"What's a list?" Ephrim asked.

"All the things he needs written down so he doesn't forget. As I was saying, the palace official would buy my fish from the seller and use his own servants or slaves to carry them into the palace."

"Can everybody write?" Ephrim asked.

"Very few can. Maybe one in a hundred and most of those are scribes or officials. Of course, it depends what you mean by writing. If you mean the hieroglyphics in the temples, then only the priests and senior scribes, but if you mean the little twists and squiggles of the common script, then a lot more. If you're a shopkeeper or even a farmer, you still need to keep track of what you've sold or bought, so a lot of people can write a few symbols that remind them of what's happened."

"Can you write, father?" Jerem asked.

Ament nodded. "Only the common script though. I don't have much use for anything more."

"Then could you write something that says you are taking a basket of fish to the palace? If they thought you had been sent by the person who buys food, they'd let you in."

Ament thought about this, and then nodded slowly. "It might work, providing the buyer was still out in the city. If he was in the palace, they might ask him if he had sent me."

"So we just need to watch until he leaves."

They put their plan into operation the next day, waiting outside the palace for kitchen staff to emerge and asking who they should talk to about providing fish for the palace.

"That'll be Ramose," one of the kitchen helpers said. "I don't like your chances though. He has a good deal with Pentamut in the fish market. You might be able to bribe him though, if you have gold."

"Can you point Ramose out to me?"

"You can't mistake him, he's fat and is blind in one eye."

"We'll have to think of something else," Jerem said as they wandered down to the fish market. "We don't have any gold."

"We don't need it," Ament said cheerfully. "We know the name of the buyer and seller. Now we just need to know if this Pentamut employs anyone special."

They found Pentamut's stall in the fish market, and under the pretence of examining the fish on display, found out that he employed men off the street to carry his wares rather than using his own staff. Ament offered his services as a carrier, but was quickly seen off by a pair of well-muscled men.

"Don't you get no ideas, stranger," said one of them. "We is the men what carries for Pentamut. Come round here again and we'll break your legs."

"Or worse," added the other man.

Ament smiled and nodded and said he would not dream of encroaching on their territory. He led the boys away.

"How did that help?" Jerem asked.

"It's all coming together," Ament assured him. "We wait until Ramose is out, then I turn up at the kitchen with a basket of fish, saying they come from Pentamut. Street men deliver his fish, so they won't expect anyone special. Once I'm inside the palace, I can slip away and find the king."

"Won't somebody ask you what you're doing? You'll be a stranger."

"If this palace is anything like the Men-nefer one, everyone knows what their own duties are and ignores everyone else. I'll pick something up and carry it about looking as if I belong there until I find him."

"Then what?"

"Then I'll have to see. If he's alone, I'll kill him. If not, I'll have to wait until he is."

"And what do we do?"

"Once I'm inside, you go back to our room and wait. If I'm not back in a day, go down to the boat and sail it home. It will mean I've failed."

The next morning at dawn, Jerem and Ephrim hung around outside the kitchen entrance, tossing stones, and waited for Ramose to make an appearance. When he did, waddling down to the markets with a small retinue of servants. The boys ran to the river, where Ament waited with a basket of freshly caught fish. He had prepared the scrap of paper which he would show the kitchen staff the night before, and all it said was 'a basket of fresh fish from Pentamut, for the palace' and had Ramose's name appended. It was all that was needed, and a busy servant impatiently waved him through to the kitchens and pointed out where to leave his burden.

Although the day was still cool, the brick ovens outside the kitchen were already churning out heat, rippling the air and wafting waves of hot air mingled with the aromas of baking bread and roasting meats into the palace. Ament heard his belly signal its hunger, but decided against trying to filch a little food. The risk was too great, and he did not want to draw attention to himself, so he casually wiped his hands on a cloth and, picking up a wooden platter with four empty cups on it, slipped out of the kitchen and into a corridor. Servants hurried back and forth, intent on their own errands and, as Ament had expected, paid him little attention. Anyone who saw him assumed he was carrying out some duty assigned him by an overseer and did not think to question it.

As he neared the residential areas of the palace he noted that the kilts and tunics of the servants were of better quality, and he glanced down at his own stained kilt. He realised he would soon stand out if he did not somehow smarten himself up. Turning aside from the inner chambers, he walked back toward the storage rooms and after a bit of searching, saw maidservants coming out of a room bearing clean linens. Inside, he found stacks of bed linens, but also bundles of fresh kilts. Quickly, he swapped his own for a clean one, tucking the soiled one behind a stack of sheets. Then he resumed his journey toward the inner rooms of the palace, knowing he now blended with the other servants.

Whenever Ament was out of sight of other servants, he ducked his head into rooms, but as the morning wore on he still had not found any trace of the king. He was turned away from one section of the palace by two huge Kushite soldiers armed with spears, and he suspected the royal rooms lay beyond. There seemed to be no way past the guards, so he wandered away, wondering whether he should try approaching the royal suite via the gardens. Then an overseer stepped out of a room, stared at him and beckoned.

"You. Come here."

Ament quailed, wondering if he should turn tail and run.

"Are you deaf? Come here. I need those cups."

Ament approached the overseer, casting his eyes downward.

"Bring them in and put them on the table," the overseer snapped. "Quickly now, and don't look at anyone. There's no need to bow or abase yourself. Just put the tray down and go and stand by the wall."

The overseer gave Ament a slight push in the small of his back and he tottered into the room, recovered his balance, and set the tray and cups down on a table where jugs of wine were set out, together with plates of fruit. Keeping his head lowered, he walked to the edge of the room and stood with his back to the wall. Only then did he raise his head and look at the people with him.

Sethi, the Southern General, was staring across the room at him, while only a pace or two away, their faces half-turned away, were Tjaty Khaemter and King Menmire Amenmesse.

Chapter 35
Year 4 of Userkheperure Seti
Year 3 of Menmire Amenmesse

The next morning, Tausret rode back to Ramses' camp once more, past her own tired troops and through ranks of nervous rebels fully armed and prepared for battle. She smiled and waved to the men, asking after their families. Ramses came out of his tent yawning and red-eyed, and scowled at Tausret as she dismounted from her chariot.

"Why the noise all night, Lady? Several times I thought you were going to attack us."

"You must forgive my men, Lord Ramses. They are city born and bred and jump at every little noise out here in the countryside. An owl flies over and they see a ghost, a jackal howls and they hear a demon. A superstitious lot."

"Well, what now?"

"I suggest we carry on with our discussion. I believe you were going to tell me why you believe my husband Userkheperure Seti is a false king."

Ramses nodded and ordered a servant to bring beer and bread to his tent. "Unless you have already eaten, Lady?"

Tausret smiled. "I will willingly eat with you, Lord Ramses."

Despite her avowed intention of discussing Ramses' reasons for rebellion, Tausret turned the conversation aside as they ate, recounting anecdotes and amusing trivia of court life, and asking questions about Ramses' home life. She discovered he had a grown son from a previous marriage and an infant one from his present one.

"Sons are a blessing," she murmured.

"Yes, I will have someone to succeed me," Ramses said.

"How is that going to work, Lord Ramses? You are the younger son, I understand, so if you were to succeed in your rebellion, your brother Meryma'at would be king. Where does that leave you?"

"I would be Tjaty of the combined Kingdoms."

"That would be enough for you? I'd have thought someone of your ability and ambition would want more."

"It is enough for me, Lady. The gods made me the younger son, so I am ready to take up the position they made me for."

"What if the gods made you for greater things, Lord Ramses? By settling for less you could be going against the will of the gods."

"I see what you are doing, Lady Tausret, and it is not going to work. You will not turn me against my brother."

"I did not think so, but..." Tausret smiled and spread her hands in a deprecating shrug. "I had to see if it was a possibility."

"As long as we understand I am loyal to my brother, we can continue this discussion."

Tausret glanced outside the tent at the position of the sun. "Perhaps it is late enough we could enjoy a cup of wine together."

"An excellent idea. You know, Lady Tausret, I enjoy talking to you. I had no idea women could be so intelligent. Perhaps when this is all over you would consider retiring and becoming the wife of the Tjaty?"

"An intriguing idea," Tausret murmured. "There is something I must ask, Lord Ramses, of a delicate nature." She cleared her throat and lowered her eyes. "Campaigning is so much more convenient for men, whereas women have...ah, needs for privacy."

Ramses frowned. "I'm not sure I understand, Lady. Unless...ah, you need somewhere private to...yes, we have no women with us, but I shall have my men erect some screens for your use."

A little later, Tausret had used the screened area to relieve herself and was back in the tent enjoying a cup of wine and some dried dates and figs on a platter. "I really can't fault your hospitality, Lord Ramses."

Ramses smiled and said, "Have you thought about my proposal, Lady Tausret?"

"Please allow me a little more time, Lord Ramses. It is a big decision to make, and we don't even know if the circumstances will make such a union possible."

"I feel confident they will."

"Then again, I am Queen at the moment. Will I be content to be just a Tjaty's wife?"

Ramses tutted. "You are trying to turn me against my brother again."

"Not at all, but if everything is as you say, perhaps I should look to your brother for my future well-being."

"My brother has already promised his wife that she will be queen."

Tausret sighed. "Well, in that case, tell me why you think that my husband, King Userkheperure, is a false king."

"Nothing simpler, Lady. The first-born son has always inherited the throne of his father."

"Baenre Merenptah was thirteenth son of Usermaatre."

"Now Lady, you know that before he could inherit, his twelve elder brothers had to have died. The eldest surviving son always inherits. And Baenre was the cause of all Kemet's problems. His eldest son was Messuwy, and he should have inherited his throne. Instead the younger son Seti claimed it, contrary to all custom, and now wars brother against brother, Kingdom against Kingdom to prevent Messuwy, Menmire Amenmesse, from claiming his rightful place."

"So you believe Menmire is the rightful king? Your brother is not claiming the throne after all?"

Ramses frowned. "No, that is not what I am saying at all. Neither brother is supported by the gods and must be removed."

Tausret thought for a few minutes. "I can see why you claim Userkheperure should not be king as he is the younger brother, but why do you say Menmire as elder brother should not be either?"

"Because he rebelled against the anointed king."

"But you say Userkheperure was not the legitimate king?"

"That's right."

"But if he wasn't the legitimate king, then how is Menmire doing wrong by rebelling against him?"

Ramses stared at Tausret.

"But if Userkheperure is not really the king, then Menmire must be; or if Menmire is just a rebel, then Userkheperure must be king."

Ramses shook his head, frowning. "You are a woman and don't understand these things."

"If one or other of the present kings of Kemet are legitimate, then what of you and your brother, Lord Ramses? By rebelling, you are putting yourselves in the wrong. The gods will not support you."

"You don't understand, Lady Tausret."

"Lord Ramses, you said earlier that Baenre Merenptah was the cause of all Kemet's troubles. Does that mean that the great Usermaatre Ramesses is our guide in what is right? After all, he was so loved by the gods that he reigned for sixty-seven years."

"Yes, yes you have it," Ramses said, relief evident in his voice. "Usermaatre was right to leave the throne to his eldest surviving son, but Baenre was not. The choice he made was a bad one."

"Let me be sure I understand you, Lord Ramses. Usermaatre's decisions as regards the succession were correct, but Baenre's were wrong?"

"Yes. There you have it, Lady Tausret. Those wrong decisions have led to Kemet's present troubles and what Meryma'at and I seek to do is restore Ma'at by putting the descendants of Pareherwenemef, Usermaatre's third son and the eldest son to have living descendants, on the throne. It is as if it was a return to the days of the great Usermaatre."

Tausret nodded, and a small smile crossed her face. "Then would it surprise you to learn, Lord Ramses, that it was the great Usermaatre himself who put my husband on the throne?"

Ramses stared. "How can that be when he was no more than a child at the time of Usermaatre's death and Baenre his named successor?"

"Khaemwaset was Usermaatre's favourite son, agreed?" Ramses nodded and Tausret continued. "When Khaemwaset lay dying, Usermaatre extracted a promise from Baenre that Khaemwaset's line would continue on the throne."

Ramses frowned again. "He had two sons, Ramesses and Hori. Ramesses died during Baenre's reign, and Hori became Hen-netjer of Ptah at Men-nefer. The present Tjaty is his son. Did he mean that Tjaty Hori must become king?"

"You forget he had a daughter called Isetnofret."

"A daughter cannot become king."

Tausret smiled. "Not often, but she married a king. She was the wife of Baenre and their son is Userkheperure Seti, our present king in the north. Menmire Amenmesse in the south is an older son, but by Takhat, Baenre's other wife."

Ramses nodded slowly, his brow furrowed in thought. "I think I see the path of your argument. You are saying that Userkheperure is descended from Khaemwaset, where Menmire is not."

"Exactly. Baenre was a legitimate king, inheriting as eldest surviving son and by Usermaatre's orders, and my husband Userkheperure is also legitimate, inheriting by Usermaatre's direct order. That is why Baenre named him Heir, despite being the younger son."

"Y...yes, I see this now," Ramses muttered.

"So, if you seek to depose my husband, the legitimate king, you array yourself against the gods and Ma'at."

"I see this now, but what can I do except hurry to meet my brother Meryma'at and apprise him of this knowledge."

"It is too late for that, Ramses son of Ratep. By now, the king will have met your brother with two battle-hardened legions and either captured or killed him. This rebellion is over."

Ramses paled and started to his feet. "You have kept me here talking when I should have been marching to help my brother. You shall die for this."

"And destroy your family?" Tausret asked, though her heart beat faster at the threat of death. "Why do you think I marched to meet you with a tiny force that could not hope to win any battle? I was confident that I could show you the folly of your rebellion, and by your own admission, I have. Go home, Ramses son of Ratep, and tend to your estates. I will tell the king you were misled, and he will leave you alive. Harm me, though, and you know that the anger of the king will wipe your family from the face of Kemet, and your name will be a curse on the lips of strangers for a thousand years."

Chapter 36
Year 4 of Userkheperure Seti
Year 3 of Menmire Amenmesse

Ament felt as if his heart had stopped within his chest and his breath caught in his throat. His glance darted to the table, hoping to see a weapon he could use, for at any moment Sethi would recognise him as one of the enemy commanders and raise the alarm. Then all hope would be gone of his completing his mission. He saw nothing on the table save a pottery jar of wine and imagined bringing it down hard on Amenmesse's head. *It might be enough*, he thought. He tensed his muscles, working out how many steps he needed to get to the table, and then on, jug in hand, before anyone could stop him.

Sethi turned away, back to answer a question the king put to him, and Ament sagged against the wall, feeling sweat break out on his trembling body. He heard a low hiss of disapproval from the overseer and stood up straight again, turning his attention to the three men drinking wine from the cups he had brought in.

"There's nothing I can do without more men," Sethi stated. "I need at least another five thousand to be sure of conquering the northern legions."

"Khaemter," Amenmesse said. "That is your responsibility. Find my general the men he needs."

"Easier said than done, my lord. I've scraped the oil jar of the last dregs for his present army." The Tjaty sketched a mock bow toward General Sethi. "Perhaps if you hung onto your men, we wouldn't have this problem. From what I hear, two men in every five have deserted within three months, and another is dead from wounds or starvation."

"Don't tell me how to manage my men," Sethi said, glaring at the other man. "I don't see you managing an army in the field. You just sit back here in Waset eating and drinking and enjoying the palace women."

Khaemter laughed, though bitterness crept into his voice. "I could scarcely do worse than you. You had the northern army on the brink of defeat and you let them slip out of your grasp. As for managing an army in the field, have you forgotten I was military commander in Kush before I was appointed King's Son?"

"With able officers to do your bidding, anyone could succeed there against tribesmen. Try using those same tribesmen to beat trained legions."

"But that is what you are asking Khaemter for, isn't it?" Amenmesse asked. "Another army of Kushite tribesmen?"

"I'd rather they were Kemetu farmers than tribesmen, but if they must be, at least turn them over half-trained. The last lot wouldn't listen to orders and ran at the first sign of trouble."

"I heard about that," Khaemter said. "You impaled a hundred and flogged five times that number." He turned to the king and shook his head. "And he wonders why he has so many desertions."

"I have to maintain discipline," Sethi grumbled. "All I ask is some properly trained soldiers and I'll deliver Ta Mehu to you, Majesty."

"It doesn't sound like too much to ask," Amenmesse said. "Find the men, Khaemter, and make sure at least some of them are Kemetu. Perhaps you could strip the city of its Medjay. They'd make passable soldiers."

"If I take the Medjay, crime will go up."

"You think I care about that?" Amenmesse asked. "If the choice is between having no crime in Waset and no kingdom either, or lots of crime but gaining a kingdom, which one do you think I will choose? I have no interest in commoners unless they can be turned into soldiers. Find me those men, Khaemter. That's an order."

Khaemter accepted the inevitable. "Yes, Majesty."

Sethi smirked and turned the conversation onto other matters, demanding more equipment, armaments, and women for his men's enjoyment. The arguments followed a similar path, with Khaemter protesting that the southern kingdom could not afford any more, and Amenmesse ordering him to find what Sethi needed.

"You cannot order free women of Kemet to open their legs for tribesmen," Khaemter stated. "It's bad enough you've forced the city prostitutes to work for half pay, but there are decent women out there, wives and daughters of loyal Kemetu, who have suffered rape by our army."

"I'd have thought they were grateful for a lusty man," Sethi said with a grin. "Some of those tribesmen are remarkably well endowed."

"You really have no idea, do you?" Khaemter asked. "Your attitudes are turning the common people against us. Women don't enjoy being raped, and their men are angry. Sooner or later they're going to do something about it."

"All the more reason to have a strong army then."

Ament listened to the discussion with ill-contained excitement. It seemed as if the southern kingdom was on the brink of falling apart, and all it needed was a good strong push. Killing Amenmesse would be that good strong push, for while the common people might still support the king, it was evident they hated his ministers for the hardships they visited upon men and women.

But how do I kill him? he thought. *If I had a blade I could do it now, but I couldn't bring one in with me, the guards would look askance at a servant with a sword.*

Sethi was staring at Ament again; his forehead creased in a frown, and Ament hurriedly composed himself, acting out the part of a lowly servant.

"I know that man," Sethi said.

"Eh, what man?" Amenmesse said. "The servant? I doubt it."

"You've probably just seen him around the palace," Khaemter said. "Now, we were talking about the gold production from..."

"Never mind that." Sethi strode across to Ament and stared into his face from close range. "Who are you? Where have I seen you before?"

Ament lowered his eyes and said nothing.

"Answer Lord Sethi," hissed the overseer.

"Well?"

"I don't know...Lord Sethi."

"I've seen you somewhere just recently," Sethi said. "But where? Doing what?"

"I don't know, my lord."

Sethi stared a little longer, then shook his head. "It will come to me." He snapped his fingers at the overseer. "How long has this man been a palace servant?"

"I...I don't know, Lord Sethi. I don't know all the palace servants...but he was just another servant in the hallway when I called him in. He was carrying cups..."

"Enough. Bring him along to my quarters when I leave. I will question him further."

"Is that really necessary?" Khaemter asked. "I would have thought you had more important things to do."

"Do you suspect him of something?" Amenmesse asked. "We can rid ourselves of him easily enough."

"No, Majesty. I'd like to know where I've seen him though."

"Very well." Amenmesse yawned. "This discussion has become boring. Do with him as you wish. I'm going to lie down for a bit."

The king left, and all the guards but one left with him. Sethi and Khaemter took the remaining guard, the overseer and Ament and started back through the palace toward the guest suites where Sethi was staying. Ament tried to look innocuous and servile as he walked behind the Tjaty and Sethi, but his mind was racing, seeking some way out of his present troubles.

I've missed my opportunity to kill the king, and now Sethi means to get to the truth so I won't get close to him again. But perhaps I can salvage something. Sethi is their general, and surely their army would be less without him. Could I kill him somehow?

Khaemter and Sethi continued to talk as they walked, but Ament paid little attention. He was looking for a way to escape or strike back at his enemies. There were too many people around though, too many people to stop him, no matter what he attempted. He glanced back at the guard, wondering if he could wrest his short curved sword from his waist or his spear from his hand. The man was watching him though, so he turned his attention to the overseer. Overweight, and soft from palace living, the man posed no danger to Ament, but also offered no opportunity that he could see. Glumly, he turned his attention back to the Tjaty and the General.

They came to Sethi's rooms and the five of them passed inside. It was a large room with a broad window along one wall that admitted cool breezes and the pleasant aromas of plants from the palace gardens. The overseer told Ament to wait against the wall near the door upon the General's pleasure, so he did, positioning the overseer between himself and the guard. Sethi and Khaemter were now talking about the training of new conscripts and in particular, the use of archers.

"There are tribes in the western desert that are proficient with the bow and arrow," Khaemter said. "They are fiercely independent though."

"Send emissaries to them. Archers would be invaluable in our..." Sethi broke off and frowned.

"What? Sethi?"

Sethi swung round and stared at Ament. "That's where I saw you."

"What are you talking about, Sethi?" Khaemter demanded. "Who did you see?"

"That man...or one who looked just like him."

"Where? When?"

"The Troop that employed archers against us. The Per-Bast archers that broke the back of my army. He was commanding them."

"Him? He's just a servant. You must be mistaken."

"Who are you?" Sethi demanded, stepping a pace closer to Ament.

Ament licked his lips, feeling vulnerable and unable to do anything. "Ament," he whispered.

"Address Lord Sethi properly, you fool," the overseer said. The man reached out and grabbed Ament's arm.

Ament shook free and then, as the overseer tried to grab him again, pushed him back violently. The overseer reeled back and collided with the guard, making the man drop his spear with a clatter. Ament leapt toward the unbalanced men and grasped the guard's sword from his belt, swinging it and connecting with the soldier's belly and the thigh of the overseer. The two men went down but the guard kicked out at Ament and he staggered back toward the wall, dropping the sword.

Sethi retreated a few paces and yelled for guards, Khaemter adding his urgent voice. Already Ament could hear shouts in the hallway and knew if he was to act it would have to be swiftly. Bending, he scooped up the fallen spear, hefted it to test its balance, and looked at the two men across the room. Shouts and the sound of running feet snatched at his attention, so in a fluid motion he threw the spear, sending it whiffling across the room toward Sethi. While the spear was still in flight he turned and raced toward the window, vaulting over the sill even as the spear struck and armed men burst into the General's room. He heard a cry of agony from his victim as he crashed through shrubbery and rolled onto a gravel path, and then he was onto his feet and running. Men poured after him, some following him through the window, others coming out through doors, scattering servants and gardeners. It was these same servants that enabled Ament to reach the street though, as the pursuing soldiers could not easily decide who the man they were after was.

Ament burst out onto the street, and pushed his way through a small crowd gathering to see what the commotion was. He felt a hand pluck at his kilt and lifted his arm to strike at his assailant before he saw the scared face of Jerem looking up at him.

"I told you to go to our room," he gasped. "Where's Ephrim?"

"He's waiting by the boat, father."

Ament grabbed the boy and hurried off down the street in the direction of the waterfront with a clamour rising behind them. People in the street were now shouting and men and women were surging away from the palace as soldiers poured out into the streets. Before they were halfway to the docks, rumour had overtaken them and there were stories of murder and mayhem being shouted from street corners.

"The king is dead."

"General Sethi's dead."

"The Tjaty has been foully murdered."

"General Sethi has rebelled."

"The king from the north has invaded."

Down through the crowded streets they ran, the populace swarming like a kicked ants' nest, and ran clear of the last buildings and out onto the city wharves where their boat was tied up. Ephrim was waiting in the boat, sitting white-faced and anxious as Jerem and Ament ran across. He saw them and burst into tears.

"W...where were you? What...what's happened?"

"Cast off the ropes, Jerem," Ament ordered. "Ephrim, it's all right, steer us out into the current while I get the sail up."

Soldiers ran onto the dock as Ament pushed the little boat away. The current gripped the craft and, with Ephrim's hand on the rudder, swung it away from the wharf.

"Stop!" somebody yelled.

"There, that boat. Stop it."

"That man, stop him. He killed the Tjaty. Gold for the man who stops him."

Men eager for the reward ran for other boats tied up nearby, soldiers joining them, and several put off in pursuit. They were heavily loaded though, and cumbersome, wallowing into the current where Ament's boat sped before them, sail upraised and angled to catch the light breeze. Soldiers stood in the pursuing boats, balancing as the boats rocked, and threw their spears, but none came close. Others ran along the shore, for a time keeping pace with the boat, but Ament and the boys were well out into the current now, being snatched downriver and away from their pursuers.

Chapter 37

Menmire Amenmesse speaks:

How can this happen? Am I not safe in my own palace, in Amun's City, surrounded by my own loyal men? How can an assassin gain entry to my private rooms? The man was there; no more than ten paces from my royal person, listening to me speak to my ministers. The gods were surely with me today, afflicting me with tiredness so that I would cut short my meeting with Khaemter and Sethi. If they had not, the assassin may have aimed his weapon at me, and I would now be lying dead in the Place of Purification rather than Tjaty Khaemter.

The man took a spear from a guard and threw it, striking down Khaemter, though it was Sethi he aimed at. I have this from the mouth of the Overseer of the Royal Wine, who was present at the time. He says that Sethi pulled Khaemter toward him as the spear flew, so the sharp copper blade bit deep into the Tjaty's chest rather than into Sethi's. I can understand his action, and indeed I forgive it, for I can more easily replace Khaemter than I can my General of Armies. The assassin escaped downriver, and I have no doubt he was in the pay of my vile brother in the north. Failing to find an opportunity to kill me, he struck at the man he thought next most important in the kingdom. In that he failed too, for though Khaemter was competent enough, and loyal, there are others that can take his place.

I raised up Amenmose to become Tjaty of Ta Shemau. A grandson of the Hem-netjer of Heru, I thought he would be a person I could rely on, but I was mistaken. He was loyal enough, I suppose, but incompetent. Given the task of raising troops for my army, he failed, and even at home, in the administration of Waset and the southern kingdom, he proved less than useful. A Tjaty is there to lessen the load placed upon a king's shoulders, not add to it. Amenmose could not even deal with the trivial affair of a quarrel between the Servants in the Place of Truth. I know what happened, for I was the one who had to deal with it when Amenmose failed.

The Scribe of the Place of Truth, Kenhirkhopeshef, was old and his faculties were fading, leading to a lack of control over the men under his hand. Neferhotep led one of the teams of builders, and Hay the other, but a man called Paneb caused the trouble. He was hot-headed and indulged in beer often and wine when he could get it, and fiercely resented the fact that his foster-father Neferhotep passed him over for honour in favour of one Hesysenebef, another foster-son. Paneb was married to Wa'bet, a daughter of Foreman Hay, but still hoped to inherit the place of Foreman of the other team when his foster-father died. When it became apparent that Hesysenebef had secured favour in Neferhotep's eyes, Paneb drank heavily and assaulted Neferhotep, chasing the old man down the street of the village and threatening to kill him.

Neferhotep, instead of taking this to the elders of the village as he should have, appealed to Tjaty Amenmose, and astoundingly, Amenmose heard the case. He found for the old man and Paneb was punished with a beating, but that was not the end of the case. Paneb felt he had been unfairly punished and appealed to the priests of Amun who brought it to my attention. The case they made on Paneb's behalf was persuasive and I countermanded the decision of my Tjaty, ruling in the man's favour.

I have little doubt that professional jealousy on the part of the priests of Amun was involved, in that Amenmose was a grandson of a priest of Heru, and I am certain that there was an exchange of gold to ensure first the conviction of Paneb, and then his appeal. Well, such things are not uncommon, but Amenmose was at fault for not containing the quarrel. Paneb brought forth evidence that pointed toward Neferhotep having appropriated goods destined for the tombs, and even claimed that this was the reason for losing his temper. Neferhotep brought counter-accusations, saying that Paneb had stolen stone from my brother Seti's tomb to construct his own. I could not ignore such an accusation, for such men rob the dead of their afterlife, but Paneb's was the lesser crime as my brother Seti is not truly king. So I found in favour of Paneb, restoring him to his position in the Place of Truth. There was insufficient evidence to convict Neferhotep of tomb robbing, so I left him as Foreman with a caution. I dismissed Amenmose for incompetence, for what I have raised up I can cast down again. Roma-Rui, the Hem-netjer of Amun, immediately put forward his own candidate for the position of Tjaty, but I refused to immediately appoint a replacement.

You may wonder why I concern myself with such a minor affair as the squabbles between workers in the Great Field, but in truth this is what it means to be king. I have been king in Waset for three years now, and though I have extended my suzerainty over Ta Shemau, I am no nearer ousting my brother from Ta Mehu and becoming Lord of the Two Lands. I am mindful of the discontent within my kingdom, for nobody benefits from war and continued lawlessness, so I must govern my people with as much justice as I can muster. In the main, they are peasants and beneath my consideration, but lawlessness undermines my rule and disturbs Ma'at.

This state of affairs cannot continue. I can see that I will have to take the field at the head of my army and face my brother in battle. I must end this stalemate one way or another, and either my brother falls or I do.

Chapter 38
Year 4 of Userkheperure Seti
Year 3 of Menmire Amenmesse

▌▌You would have taken this upon yourself, Commander Ament?' Seti asked, incredulity colouring his voice. "To strike down an anointed king?"

Userkheperure Seti shifted on his throne, frowning at Ament as he stood before the king in the audience room with a selection of courtiers and army commanders bearing witness to his interrogation. Queen Tausret sat beside her husband on a slightly lower throne and looked intently at Ament. She opened her mouth to say something but evidently thought better of it, sitting back on her seat.

Ament said nothing but cast a reproachful look at Tausret.

"Whatever your intent, you failed," Seti went on. "Messuwy still lives, as does his General of Armies. You only struck down Tjaty Khaemter, who was the voice of honour and moderation in my brother's court."

Seti continued to stare at Ament, and nobody in the room said anything. Ament looked toward Tausret again, the appeal in his eyes bringing a flush to her cheeks.

"I made you Legion Commander," Seti said. "It seems you knew better though, deciding to strike on your own, without telling anyone. I value innovation in my legion commanders, but not stupidity, and am minded to reduce you to the ranks."

"My lord," Tausret murmured. "Do not be too harsh on him. It was my idea."

Seti turned and stared at his wife. "I should have guessed. You put him up to this?"

"I commanded him, my lord. The fault is mine...though I commanded him to strike down Menmire."

"You do know what my brother looks like, I take it?" Seti asked Ament.

"Yes, Son of Re," Ament murmured. "I had no means to strike when in his presence, but later, when with Khaemter and Sethi, I had the means and did so, reasoning that any death would be better than none."

"You should have waited until you had another opportunity."

"Son of Re, Sethi had recognised me and had I waited, I would have been the one to die."

"So instead of the death of a disobedient legion commander whom I doubt I would miss, Tjaty Khaemter, who is...was...a good man, dies instead. Khaemter was perhaps the one decent man in my brother's court. So tell me, Commander Ament, where is the benefit in this turn of events?"

"My lord, that is not fair," Tausret murmured.

"You are telling me I should blame you instead?" Seti asked. "Must I command you to stay out of politics and war? Confine yourself to womanly pursuits?"

"You could, my lord, but would I listen?" Tausret smiled and placed her hand on her husband's arm. "Who can resist when King Userkheperure and Queen Tausret ride to battle? As the brothers Meryma'at and Ramses found out."

Seti laughed despite his annoyance at the news of the debacle in Waset. "I fought and destroyed Meryma'at's army, whereas you just talked until Ramses gave up. I should send you as my ambassador to Hatti. After a day of talking, they would surrender all claims to Amurru."

Tausret's eyes flashed with anger but she restrained herself. "Perhaps Commander Ament's efforts had a less than desirable outcome, but it was a good idea. We should not upbraid him for this, my lord."

"Perhaps not, but what has it benefitted us?" Seti asked.

"Son of Re," Tjaty Hori said. "The news is not all bad. Reports from spies in Waset indicate that the assassination has had an unsettling effect on the southern kingdom. Your brother never ventures outside the palace except with a squad of soldiers to guard him and never allows any weapon to be brought into his presence."

"Aye, Majesty," Setnakhte said boldly. "The effect on the southern army has been considerable too. Your brother may be king in Waset, and Sethi may be his General, but it was Khaemter that bound the kingdom together. He was the one who recruited men from the Kushite tribes, the one that persuaded ordinary farmers to lay aside their mattocks and pick up a spear, the one that cajoled merchants, fishermen and whores into giving their all for the army. They will miss his efforts."

"You really think it will make a difference?" Seti asked.

"Yes, Majesty. We should gather every man at our disposal and hurl them at the throat of the enemy before he can recover."

Seti considered the words of his Tjaty and of his Commander. "We have waged war against my brother for three years now, without winning a decisive victory. Every time we win a battle, he retreats and then returns and throws my army back. We find more men and attack again, and again he throws us back. The sand from Men-nefer to Waset is soaked with the blood of Kemetu and Kushite, and I am loath to spill more."

Courtiers and commanders openly stared at their king, aghast at the tones of defeat present in his voice, but nobody was prepared to argue with him. They cast surreptitious glances at each other, waiting for somebody else to brave the king's wrath. In the end, Tausret spoke for them all.

"You are the legitimate Lord of the Two Lands, my husband, while your half-brother is the usurper. The gods of Kemet demand that you stand by the oaths you swore on your coronation day to rule your people with justice and mercy, and to establish Ma'at in all the land. If the only way you can do this is to spill the blood of both your enemies and those loyal to you, then that is the will of the gods." Tausret arose from her throne and stepped down onto the floor before kneeling in front of the king and holding out her hands to him. "The war has dragged on for three years because you have sought to save your kingdoms from bloodshed and misery, but it has not worked. Your brother has no such desire for peace but will spill the blood of every man in Kemet if it will bring him to the throne. You must overthrow him by overwhelming force, my lord, or else step aside and let another be consecrated in your place, someone who will not flinch at what must be done."

Tjaty Hori cried out in horror at this idea, as did many of the courtiers, but the army commanders regarded the king keenly to see how he would react.

Seti stared at his wife. "You dare to suggest I step down from the throne?" he whispered. Suddenly he leapt to his feet and strode across to where Tausret knelt, staring down at her with his fists clenched by his sides. "You dare call me a coward?"

"Not a coward, husband, never a coward." Tausret looked up at the king, her face open and smiling. "Rather a king too concerned for the welfare of his people."

"What? Explain yourself."

"You want to spare your people the horror of war, and that is a commendable virtue on the face of it, but a worse fate for the people of Kemet would be for Menmire Amenmesse to be king over both kingdoms."

"Don't use that name," Seti growled.

"Then expunge it from the living world, King of Kemet. For the sake of your kingdom, for the sake of the people, gather your armies and stamp Waset flat if that is what it takes." Tausret rose to her feet and took her husband gently by the shoulders. "And if not for your kingdom and for your people, King of Kemet, then for the son that moves within my belly. If Menmire Amenmesse wins, he will kill your son and cast his body into the river so that his spirit must wander unhomed throughout eternity. Is that what you truly want?"

Now Seti took his wife by the shoulders and searched her face earnestly. "It is true? You know you will have a son? You have my son inside you?"

Tausret nodded, trembling with the emotion of having confronted her husband the king. "The physicians have watered wheat and barley with my urine and assure me it is so. Will you protect him, husband?" she whispered.

Seti stroked her face gently, oblivious to the courtiers and commanders around them. "With my life," he replied.

"Not with that, for you are very precious to me. Just say that you will have a throne to pass on to our son many years from now."

Seti smiled, but the good humour in his eyes faded and became a fierce desire. He turned to the audience and roared, "By the gods, I will. Mobilise every legion. We march south to crush my brother and end this war."

The king dismissed everyone save for the Tjaty and his military officers and got down to planning the war. Tausret excused herself, but Seti's attention was already elsewhere and he spared no more than a glance and a nod for his wife and unborn son.

"Every legion," he declared. "Even the ones on the northern borders. I want so many men that even the hordes of Kush cannot stand against me."

"It would be fool...dangerous to strip the frontier, Son of Re," Hori said. "The Hatti, the Amorites or the Sea Peoples...even the Retenu are just waiting for the chance..."

"More foolish to play it safe," Setnakhte growled. "Protect the north from foreigners and lose the lot to the southern bastards. If it is handled well, the foreigners will be cautious about invading. By the time they do, we will return and throw them back."

"Setnakhte speaks truth," Ament commented. "For three years we have played safe and are no nearer winning."

"Exactly," Seti said. "If we strip the frontier, how many legions have I?"

"Heru, Ptah, Set, Re, Per-Bast..." Hori shrugged. "Five trained legions and we could probably scrape up two more if we hire men from the sepats."

"Find me five more," Seti demanded. "Take every man who can hold a spear or an axe. I don't care if the cities hold nothing more than chattering women, old men and children, if the vineyards stand untended and the flocks wander unhindered. I want every man, Hori, even you."

The Tjaty went pale. "Son of Re, I am yours to command, of course, but we cannot leave the land untended, the fields unploughed for...for...it may be months."

"Let women run things. I'm sure my wife would agree they are capable."

"Majesty, please." Hori gulped. "You cannot be serious...to let women rule..."

"I shall leave Queen Tausret as ruler over Ta Mehu while I am in the south, for I know her worth. As for peasant women, if she can rule her household, she is capable of more. Let the women of Kemet take up the reins of power and guide the Kingdom while the men are away."

Chapter 39
Year 4 of Userkheperure Seti
Year 3 of Menmire Amenmesse

Khaemter's skills were sorely missed; his subtle blend of reward and threat that brought men flocking to the banners of Menmire's southern legions. General Sethi's demands were blunter and lacking finesse, but after the first hundred or so men who refused to join up were publicly hanged, he expressed satisfaction at the numbers that resigned themselves to their fate. Viceroy Setuy of Kush, having already fulfilled his promise to supply men, scoured the wilderness again and sent another three thousand Kushite tribesmen north. Though they were unruly and undisciplined, they swelled the ranks of the army quite satisfactorily.

Sethi paraded his army on the wide plains outside the walled city of Waset and invited Menmire to inspect them. The king drove through the gate in his war chariot, his blue leather war-crown on his head and adorned with gold, driving up and down the ranks of his army, cheered by thousands of voices. When he reached the most recently recruited Kushites, they broke ranks and swarmed around the royal chariot, beating their short spears on cow-hide shields and uttering fierce cries of approbation. Taken aback at first, Menmire went pale, thinking he was about to be attacked, but General Sethi fought his way through the crowd and stood in the chariot with his king, inciting the warriors to even more enthusiastic cries.

"With an army like this," Menmire said, "how can I lose?"

The army moved north almost immediately, leaving a depleted land in its wake. Every scrap of food found in the fields and storehouses was consumed, every item of any use plundered from villages and towns as if they were a conquering army moving through enemy territory, rather than through the southern Kingdom of Ta Shemau. Nobody dared to complain, for the men were pressed into service, the women raped, and the children left to cry themselves to sleep or huddle clutching their empty bellies until they died of starvation. Menmire came across one such village while he was out hunting, quartering the desert after his army had passed through. Standing in his chariot, he looked at crying women and dead children. He called Sethi to him after he returned to camp and told him what he had found.

"I am concerned for my people," Menmire told his general. "They have suffered enough. They should not have to put up with further travails."

Sethi shrugged. "It is the nature of war. If you are to secure your throne, sacrifices must be made." He seldom now offered his king any honorific.

Menmire frowned at his general's off-hand manner. "I gain a throne and they make the sacrifice."

"If it gives you comfort, you can be generous with what we capture in the rich lands and cities of Ta Mehu."

"And the dead children?"

"Many children die, even in times of peace."

"And the raped and battered women?"

Sethi stared at his king and shook his head slowly. "It is in a good cause. Your army's needs come first."

Menmire sighed. "I suppose you are right."

"Of course I am right. They are peasants and deserve no better. Their only purpose is to serve you in whatever capacity they can. Besides, the fewer mouths there are to feed, the easier it will be for the survivors."

The Kushite army swept northward like a cloud of voracious locusts. All thoughts of discipline were forgotten as troops broke down into roving bands, legions into hungry hordes. Hours before they camped for the night, the men would spread out, scouring the thin ribbon of farmland adjoining the life-giving river, denuding the fields of produce, killing any animal that moved or man who disputed their right. When the army moved on, women and children descended on the trampled fields and ripped up the grass, stuffing it into their mouths to quell their hunger. Few of the Kushite warriors knew how to fish, so nets in the fishing boats or by the ramshackle huts were passed over and the wealth of food beneath the waters of the Great River was ignored. Women in many villages were forced to learn new skills to provide food for their depleted families, but mastered the art of fishing quickly enough to stave off starvation.

Spies from the north reported that Seti's army was on the move, ten legions strong and were no more than two day's march away. When he heard, Sethi uttered a great oath and struck the spy chief, telling him to speak the truth without exaggeration.

"It is the truth, General," the spy chief quavered, lifting his head from the dirt floor of the command tent. "I recognised the banners of Ptah, Set, Heru, Re and Per-Bast."

"That's only five legions, and I don't believe even that. Seti would not leave the northern borders unprotected."

"General, there were other legions but I did not recognise the banners."

"They sought to deceive you by flying banners without meaning. Five legions would be over seven thousand men and I do not believe Ta Mehu can find that number."

"Are you certain of that?" Menmire asked. "We have close on nine thousand men, but not as disciplined as the northern legions. If they have seven to our nine it will be a close-run thing."

"Son of Re," the spy chief murmured. "Believe it. Over ten thousand men face us."

"That is nonsense," Sethi declared. "You have been deceived, now go back and count the enemy again."

"Yes, General."

"And you will not breathe a word of your lies to the men. If I hear any rumour circulating among the men, I will tear your throat out. Is that understood?"

When the spy had left, Menmire begged Sethi for the truth. "He is right though, isn't he? My brother has ten thousand men?"

Sethi regarded his king thoughtfully before answering. "Probably."

"Then we cannot win."

"That depends on many things. What will lose us the fight before it has even begun is if the men get an inkling of what awaits us."

"Then it's hopeless, for the spies must already have talked. Rumours will be spreading even as we talk."

"Then we must move fast and engage the enemy before their superiority becomes apparent."

"To what end if we are outnumbered?"

Sethi sneered openly. "To the end of securing your throne, of course. War is not exact. You cannot measure man against man, so many chariots, so many archers, and determine an outcome. Everything depends on the determination of the Commanding General, on the lay of the land, the element of surprise, and above all, the will of the gods. We have Amun-Re on our side, so we shall make it work."

Sethi drove his unwieldy army north, his officers encouraging the tired men with the use of whips and threats of dire punishment. Despite his best efforts to keep the enemy strength secret, rumours abounded, and the nearer they got to Seti's legions, the more reluctant the Kushites became.

The vanguards of the two armies came in sight of each other a little east of the abandoned city of Akhet-aten, where the eastern cliffs receded from the river in a great scallop. A few thousand paces further north was a flat plain suitable for chariots and Sethi knew that to engage the enemy there would be death. He had very few chariots and the northern legions would employ their superiority in that regard and cut his army to pieces. Instead, he halted his men and ordered that they cook a meal and consume all their stores. Then, he ordered a thousand of his men to turn east, into the desert and make a show of turning the flank of the northern army. As he had expected, Seti countered this move by sending two of his legions to intercept them. Sethi mounted a low rise of land and shaded his eyes, searching the enemy ranks for clues as to who opposed him. He saw many banners, but only three he recognised, those of Ptah, Set, and Heru.

"Mount your chariot, Menmire," Sethi said. "Show yourself to your army."

"I thought we weren't going to use chariots," Amenmesse said. "You said we were badly outnumbered."

"We would be fools to lay ourselves open to a chariot charge, but the men still need to see you. They need to be reminded of who they are fighting for. Show yourself; wave to them; encourage them to victory."

The king rode through the ranks in his chariot and the men, driven on by the whips of the officers, cheered him and drummed their spears against their hide shields. While they were thus occupied, Sethi turned to his deputy, Qenna, to discuss the coming battle.

"Three legions oppose us, in addition to some loose aggregations of men gathered under banners of their own. I have no doubt that Seti has recruited every man he can, calling them legions, but they will be untrained. It is only Ptah, Set, and Heru we have to worry about. The other two, Re and Per-Bast, have moved to intercept the group I sent east."

"Two legions will cut that group to pieces, sir," Qenna said.

"A necessary sacrifice. We split the enemy forces and can attack each separately."

Qenna nodded. "We attack frontally?"

"I'd rather they attacked us, but I cannot make them. I have no desire to fight on the plain, where chariots would win the battle for them."

"Perhaps we could send men down into Akhet-aten and then north along the narrow riverbank? The ground will be too soft for chariots, but we could hit them hard in the western flank and then, as they turn to meet us, assault them from the front?"

"Show me."

Qenna took a spear from a guard and drew in the sand, outlining the river, the crescent of the city and the relative positions of the two armies.

"I will lead the river group myself, sir. Give me two thousand men and I will turn the heads of the enemy."

"You shall have them, Qenna. May the gods go with you."

Qenna selected his men and led them off, running westward until they came to the cliffs above the ruined city, and then down the narrow defiles, dried stream beds, that led to the lower levels. They passed the dark entrances of many roughly carved tombs, some with the emblem of the Heretic still carved into the walls, an Aten with outstretched rays ending in little hand clutching ankhs. Qenna made a Kushite sign to ward off evil as they passed the tombs and then thrust them from his mind.

The level ground beneath the cliffs was strewn with mounds of crumbling mud brick, and it took him a few moments to recognise the uneven topography as the ruined remains of the city. Here and there, he saw small buildings still standing, and as his Kushite horde streamed across the broad crescent, Qenna saw men and women amongst the ruins. None were armed or made the least threatening gesture, so he ignored their presence and ran to the north end of the city where the cliffs crowded the river once more.

The cliffs faltered and dipped a stone's throw from the water and a narrow road followed the river's edge before ending in a strip of scrubby vegetation. Once upon a time these had been fields and pastures farmed by the city dwellers, but a hundred years of neglect had returned them to a state where only goats could scratch a living. The strip of scrub was bordered by the river on one side and by a steep slope on the other, the vegetation there giving way to stone and sand.

Qenna led his men along the strip, estimating the distance they had come and how far north of them was the enemy position. He called a halt and ordered his men to rest and drink before the next phase. While this was happening, he took two men and climbed the slope to see what lay just out of sight. The slope was steeper than it looked from the bottom, and Qenna found his feet slipping in the sand and loose rock, but managed to clamber to the top, breathing hard by the time he got there.

The plain he had seen by his General's side in the south stretched before him and the northern legions were everywhere. He and his companions crouched, hoping they had not been seen, and he tried to estimate what part of the horde would be most advantageous to attack. Qenna had to remember that his purpose was not to win the battle, but rather to provide a sufficient distraction so as to allow the main army a killing blow. He pointed to a group of standards and told his men to go back down to the river, march the men another five hundred paces upriver and then ascend the slope.

Time passed, and Qenna sat back in the sand while he waited, watching a hawk wheeling slowly in the pale blue dome of the sky above him and wishing he was back in Kush, sitting outside his hut while one of his wives brought him a pot of millet beer. He heard rams' horns sound behind him and scrambled back to where he could see Seti's army. The soldiers were moving, but without haste and did not look as if they were bracing for an attack. Then stones moved to his left and he saw his own men creeping into position. He moved across to them and started giving orders.

"The enemy are perhaps three hundred paces away. When I give the signal, run for them silently until you are seen and then yell loudly. Press home your attack with the short spear and hold for as long as you can. When I say, we fall back to the river, drawing them after us. This will leave their flank open for our army to crush them."

Qenna gave the signal and climbed upward, his companions alongside. They came over the lip of the slope and rushed toward the enemy as a long black line. Shouts erupted from the northern army when they were spotted, and men turned toward them, raising their weapons. Qenna screamed his tribe's war cry and others around him joined in, and seconds later they were upon the enemy, short spears stabbing, shields blocking return blows. There was little order to the attack, scarcely more in defence, as men singled out an opponent and tried to kill him. Spears thrust, axes rose and fell, and men on both sides fell to the hot sand, spilling their blood and their life.

The Kushites were too spread out to achieve much, failing to pierce the northern line, and gradually the northerners achieved the ascendancy, piercing the black line of attackers and driving the rest back. Qenna dispatched another man, scarcely more than a boy, and drew back a few paces, panting as he sought to make sense of the battle. Around him his blood-spattered companions fought on, though many now littered the sand, and he knew they had achieved all they could hope for. He gave the second signal, and his men streamed back toward the slope, drawing the undisciplined elements of the northern army after them.

Qenna looked to the south, hoping that General Sethi was making the most of the opportunity, but could see nothing. Only a low swell as of thunder came to his ears and he hoped it was the sound of thousands of feet stamping the ground as they charged the enemy. The supposed attack of the main Kushite army did not lessen the pressure on his own men though, and as they retreated to the lip of the slope, the treacherous nature of the ground betrayed them. Losing their balance, their guard dropped, allowing the enemy spears and axes to find their mark. Many Kushite warriors died as their feet slipped in the loose rock and their deaths caused their companions to lose heart. Suddenly, his whole force was in precipitate retreat, pouring down the slope into the low scrub beneath.

With cries of triumph, the northern soldiers threw spears after the fleeing Kushites, killing many more and then archers ran up and picked off stragglers as they ran and hid amongst the scrub or took to the water to escape. Blood brought crocodiles and before long the river was threshed into bloody foam as the scaly beasts exacted a terrible toll.

Qenna and a few hundred survivors fled back south through ruined Akhet-aten, pursued by units of the Heru legion. They could hear the sounds of fighting as it drifted down the high cliffs and knew that somewhere to the east the main Kushite army was attacking. Qenna hoped that the sacrifice of his men had provided enough of an advantage to turn the tide of the battle.

The men of the Heru legion closed with Qenna's men in the rubble-strewn streets of the Heretic's City, cutting down some and engaging others in hand-to-hand combat. Fewer now reached the steep paths past the tombs and made it to the tops of the cliffs, where they found the whole desert plain swarming with a mass of soldiers fighting individual battles with an opponent. There was little order to the fighting, and as one man dispatched another, one more took his place. Dying men lay groaning or screaming in the hot rock and sand, while dead men impeded the movement of the living. Back and forth the mass of men swayed, first heaving their way north and then driven south again before recovering and falling back once more.

Qenna made his way through the throng to where Menmire Amenmesse fought alongside General Sethi, their personal banners flying proudly above them. Whole units of the northern army pressed them hard and swarms of warriors defended their king. The deputy fought his way to Sethi's side.

"My lord General, we were driven back."

"So it seems," Sethi retorted, stabbing a man with his short spear. He was spattered with blood and panted with the effort. "I saw you pull back and flee the enemy."

Qenna wrested an axe from a soldier and split the man's skull open before answering. "There were too many, sir. Did we draw enough men away from the main body?"

"Nowhere near enough."

"Then the attack has failed?"

"Not yet." Sethi waved his men forward and Amenmesse in his chariot urged his horses forward, the Kushites gathering their strength to forge forward again. On the uneven ground of the battle plain, the southern warriors, used to fighting individual battles, gained the upper hand and pushed the northern legions back despite their numerical superiority. The forward movement gained pace as the legions retreated, unable to fight as effectively in retreat as when they were advancing.

"Keep together," Sethi yelled to the men. "Keep your men in their units," he shouted at his Kushite commanders.

Amenmesse and the handful of chariots he possessed smashed their way through scattered units of Set, Ptah and Heru, but were unable to break troops under determined leaders when they kept their men under control. Still the northern army retreated, and the Kushites raised a great shout of victory, pouring out of the broken ground onto the great flat plain that lay beyond. The king exulted, and waved his men onward.

"We have beaten them," Amenmesse cried. "Kill them all, and bring me my brother. Gold and land, riches beyond counting for the man who brings me my brother's head."

Sethi grimaced as he saw the Kushite army obey their king and spread out like a flood, chasing legions that had now clumped together again. The enemy no longer retreated but stood and waited for the mob of southerners to lose all cohesion. He pointed to the north and yelled to signallers to sound the rams' horns.

"It's a trap," he shouted. "Pull back; form into your units."

The rams' horns sounded, but were drowned by the nearby victory cries of the Kushites and by a gathering thunder that shook the ground. Sethi fell silent and stared across the plain, beyond the seething mob that his army had become, and saw the massed chariot formations of the legions racing toward them. A hundred chariots...two...as many as five hundred chariots, plumes on the horses' heads dancing, charioteers urging their beasts onward and archers standing poised in each one.

The chariots slashed across the open ground and smashed into the Kushites who had seen the danger and turned to flee, stumbling and impeding their companions close behind. The plain became a jumble of plunging horses, flashing metal and black bodies, volleys of arrows dealing death, wheels crushing, stained clubs and bright blades throwing sprays of blood into the air. Shouts turned to screams as the Kushite army disintegrated, hurling themselves away, and running, streaming back past Sethi who vainly exhorted them to stand and fight. Amenmesse stood ashen-faced in his chariot nearby, watching as his hopes of victory soaked away like water on sand. Then he turned his chariot to the south and whipped it into motion, fleeing along with his men.

Sethi cursed his king and, gathering a handful of faithful men about him, set off across the tide of men toward the fastness of the eastern desert. Here, in the jumble of rocks and drifts of sand, they could outpace the enemy chariots and fight their way through the enemy soldiers that followed in their wake. They made it to a maze of intersecting gullies and hid until the day ended, nursing their wounds. As the sun set beneath the western desert, Sethi climbed to the highest point and looked to the east and south in the fading light. Dust rose to the dusky heavens and he could just make out the mass of men that comprised his army, still running and hear, faint in the distance, the clash of metal and cries of anguish as his men died. He raised his fists to the sky.

"May the gods curse you, Menmire Amenmesse. You have lost me my army."

Chapter 40

U serkheperure Seti speaks:

Once more I am Lord of the Two Lands, King of Ta Mehu and Ta Shemau, Master of all the lands between Amurru and the southern wildernesses of Kush.

All right, perhaps that is a slight exaggeration because my half-brother Messuwy, he who called himself Menmire Amenmesse, is still alive. He has taken refuge within the walled city of Waset and has closed the gates against my victorious army, but he has nothing left except surrender. I shall enjoy seeing him grovel before me in chains before I pass sentence on him and remove him entirely from the memory and knowledge of the Land of Kemet.

I have called for the rulers of Waset, the lords and the principal citizens to appear before me to hear my words and I believe they will come, for I have promised them safe passage. They will come for no other reason than to see if there is any way out of the disaster that has befallen them. Their choices are limited, they must appease me or suffer utter destruction. While I wait for them to come, I will tell you how I arrived at this position of power, though it is hardly surprising that the rightful king should prevail. The gods of Kemet were on my side after all.

I amassed a huge army, drawing off even the legion that guarded the northern borders, and drove them southward, the five legions of Set, Ptah, Heru, Re and Per-Bast. To these I added men conscripted from the towns and villages of Ta Mehu, men who counted it an honour to fight for their king, and formed five more temporary legions. They were named for Sopdu, Shu, Wadjet, Sobek and Sekhmet, and bravely did their banners fly beside those of my battle-toughened soldiers. I did not have enough weapons with which to arm them, so many of them wielded simple mattocks or fire-hardened sticks. It was enough, for they bolstered the proper legions and gave the impression that our strength was greater than it was.

One thing we had a lot of was chariots. Horses grazed in the pastures of Ta Mehu, and the weapons shops of the north fashioned many chariots in the month it took to assemble the army. I marched south with nearly five hundred chariots and three thousand horses, stripping the countryside of fodder as we went. We met the enemy a little north of Akhet-aten and when I first saw the southern horde, even I had my doubts. The armies were of equal size but the way they swarmed over the ground made them look as if a sandstorm was rushing toward us; a host of locusts stripping the land bare of sustenance.

Then my spies reported and I felt better. We outnumbered them, but the coming battle would not be straightforward. Our strengths were our chariots and our discipline, while theirs was the ferocity of their warriors. To be sure of victory, I would have to force them to fight on our terms. There was a perfect chariot plain, but the Kushites halted before they got there and camped. They refused to be drawn out, so we went to meet them on broken ground where the fighting would be man to man.

Messuwy, or his dog Sethi, I could not be sure who commanded the horde, feinted to the east. I countered by sending two of the untrained legions, Wadjet and Shu, to mark them, but gave them the banners of the Re and Per-Bast legions so the enemy would think I was dividing my trained army. Then the Kushites feinted to the west, along the river, assaulting the Heru legion from the side, and as they did so, charged my army as they advanced over the broken ground.

Here the Kushites displayed their strength and many men died beneath the stabbing spears and clubs of those fierce southern warriors. For a time, they must have thought they could win, but I had not yet displayed our own strengths. First, my wonderful trained legions showed their discipline, streaming back as if the battle was lost, enticing the mob of Kushites to follow them onto the hard flat plain. When most had followed, the legions turned to fight once more and between the serried ranks thundered the massed chariots of our other strength. We broke the back of Messuwy's army that day and harried them for ten days as they fled south. Some reached Waset and hid within its walls, and some surrendered, throwing themselves on my mercy, but most of those who lived threw away their spears and clubs and continued running south, disappearing at last into the wildernesses of Kush.

I gave those who surrendered a choice, die loyal to Messuwy or swear allegiance to my throne. Most changed sides and I dispersed them through my existing legions, instructing that they be trained up as proper soldiers. I gave a private warning to my commanders that at the slightest sign of treason they should instantly be put to death.

And so I came to ancient Waset, Amun's City, and encamped outside its walls. The army ringed the city and boats packed with soldiers invaded the dock areas. The defenders broke down houses and piled timbers and rocks as a bulwark against my men, so they could go no further. My commanders asked for permission to force the issue, but I did not want to turn the streets into a slaughterhouse. I meant to bring the city under my just rule and to that end I wanted to first give them the choice of acceding to my demands.

The gates opened and a procession wound its way out toward my tent, men of the city, elders, nobles, officials. The fear on their faces was apparent as they walked between the silent ranks of my legions, despite the assurances of safe conduct I had given, and when at last they entered into my presence, their limbs trembled and they knelt before me, arms outstretched in supplication. I stared at them for a time, letting their fear sweat trickle down their bodies and stain their clothing. Then I bade them rise and state their desires. One of them, a Fan-bearer and Troop Commander of the Amun legion, bowed respectfully and spoke up, offering all the titles due to me.

"Divine Father, Great One, Lord of the Two Lands, Lord of Appearances, Mighty Bull, Son of Re, Userkheperure Seti, we, the people of Waset greet you and humbly ask your intentions as regards the city and its people."

"Who are you to ask this of me?" I demanded. "I am King of Kemet, Lord of the Two Lands, and Waset is mine to do with as I wish. I am not accountable to you or any man."

"Majesty," he said, bowing once more. "No man can question you or your actions, but rather we ask what you would have us do."

"That is simple," I replied. "Let my brother Messuwy, who styles himself Menmire Amenmesse, come out of the city and kneel before me, begging my mercy. Also, let the man who styles himself the General of Armies, Sethi, do likewise, and with him the man who purports to be the Hem-netjer of Amun, Roma-Rui. Let them both abase themselves before me. Then you shall throw open the gates of Waset and let my army clean out the dross and refuse that pollutes Amun's Holy City, namely, the misguided and traitorous supporters of my brother's regime."

287

"Son of Re, we can ask these men to kneel before you, but it is not in our power to force them."

"Then why are you here?"

"Son of Re, we seek only to know your mind so we may obey you in all things that are within our power."

"Then carry my words to the city and tell them that they have three days to accede to my wishes. If the men I have named are not kneeling before me by sunset on the third day, I will unleash my army and destroy every man, woman and child in the city. I have spoken. Let it be so recorded."

They left my presence and entered Waset once more, the gates closing behind them. For three days there was no sign, and then a herald came out, fear written large on his face, and he was led trembling into my presence. He abased himself and spoke, his voice shaking with fear.

"My lord Userkheperure Seti, I bring you the word of my royal master Menmire Amenmesse, Lord of Waset and Protector of Ta Shemau. He bids you take your men and depart from his lands, returning to your northern kingdom. My lord Menmire bids me tell you that his General Sethi is even now gathering an even larger army and if you are still here when he comes, he will exact bloody retribution for your crimes."

My commanders and advisers cried out in horror at the insult to me in this message and called on me to impale the herald before razing the city to the ground, but I told them that I would honour the man's office and send him back unharmed.

"As for your master," I told the herald, "tell him that I will wait here eagerly for Sethi's arrival and publicly impale him when he arrives. As for the city, I shall not spill the loyal blood of my men in taking it, but will wrap the city up so tight that no scrap of food or drop of water shall enter it. When the people are so afflicted with hunger that they remember who is truly Lord of the Two Lands, they may deliver Messuwy into my hands and beg my forgiveness. Then I will let them live once more."

And so it was. My men surrounded the city and allowed not so much as a dove or a rat to enter, and killed every man who tried to leave. Within days, the lack of food started to have an effect and though they dug wells to obtain water, their strength started to give out. It will only be a matter of time before the desperate citizens of Waset rise up and oust my brother from his pretend throne.

Chapter 41
Year 5 of Userkheperure Seti
Year 4 of Menmire Amenmesse

The flood came and the level of the water rose until it lapped at the fallen stone and timber that blocked the entry of Seti's soldiers above the docks. Water seeped into the lower city, and people drank from the stagnant pools and fell sick, adding to their woes. Then the water receded and thirst took hold again as the water in the wells fell away too. Hunger was ever-present, but the city had never looked so clean, or so empty. The streets were often deserted as people stayed home rather than waste energy searching for food or fuel, and only gangs of children still roamed, looking for rats, small birds or insects. Cattle, horses, donkeys and goats had long disappeared, dogs following shortly after. Cats lasted a little longer as they had a religious aspect that protected them until hunger pains grew too insistent.

People lived...and died, and now rumours swept the city that the embalmers were no longer preparing whole corpses for burial. Stories spread of cannibalism. Young children were abducted from their homes, and several times a man would be beaten to death for being seen in the company of a boy or girl. Medjay would intervene, but half-heartedly, and were often content just to look the other way as every death meant one less mouth to feed.

The palace suffered too, but to a lesser extent as Amenmesse and his adherents still possessed wealth. In the early days of the blockade, food could still be bought for gold or jewels, or given up in return for future favours. As famine bit deep, however, prices rose beyond the means of the common people and rioting broke out. Mobs would storm a warehouse, or the silo of a grain factor, and once even the royal stables, and the populace would be beaten back by men of the Amun legion. Amenmesse took control of the remaining food supplies and had it doled out to his remaining friends and to the men who still guarded him, though there were few of those left. In the absence of Sethi and Khaemter, his main supporters were the Hem-netjer of Amun, Roma-Rui and the most recent commander of the Amun legion, Samut.

"Son of Re," Samut said, apprehension written plainly on his face. "We cannot continue much longer. My men are weakening and soon we will not be able to keep the peace in the city."

"Is that what you call it?" Roma-Rui asked. "My priests are jostled in the streets and men mutter against the king with impunity."

"I have a depleted legion and they cannot be everywhere."

Amenmesse stirred on his throne. "What about the Medjay?"

"The Medjay are next to useless, Majesty. They prefer to sit at home and drink weak beer rather than patrolling the streets."

"Really? Where do they get the beer from? Even my priests can't get more than the occasional jug."

Samut shrugged. "There is still grain to be had if you're willing to pay for it, or steal it. Some people would rather brew beer with it than bake bread."

"They should be giving it to the temple," Roma-Rui complained. "Even the god needs to eat."

A half smile crossed Amenmesse's face. "The god or his priests?"

"It is the same thing," Roma-Rui said stiffly.

"Well, either way, we need food quickly or...or there is no hope."

"General Sethi will come and defeat my brother's legions."

"You cannot seriously believe that, Son of Re," Roma-Rui said. "It has been five months since any man saw him alive. He is dead."

"If he was dead, my brother would have paraded his body outside the walls. No, I tell you he is alive and raising men for my relief."

"Raising men from where? You have seen the throngs of Kushite warriors that are now part of your brother's legions? Those are the ones who surrendered. The others have run off back to their villages and now milk their herds and pleasure their wives."

"They were gathered once; they can be gathered again," Amenmesse said obstinately.

"There might be another possibility, Son of Re," Samut said. "If General Sethi has raised men, he might find it hard to get close to Waset without provoking a battle."

"But that is precisely what he must do. How else will he break the blockade on the city?"

"Perhaps he has insufficient men to be certain of the outcome. If that is the case he will rely on the presence of your royal self, Son of Re, to hearten his men and turn their hearts into lions."

"Well, if that's the case I don't see what can be done," Amenmesse said. "I am here and he is there, so he must come to me."

"Or you could go to him."

Amenmesse stared. "What are you talking about?"

Samut licked his lips and cleared his throat. "I...I think we could smuggle your Majesty out of the city."

Amenmesse continued staring at his legion commander, but now his fingers tapped a staccato rhythm on the arm of his throne. "My brother has this city locked up tighter than a virgin's passage. There is no way out."

"Forgive me, Son of Re, but there is."

"Do you know what he is talking about, Roma-Rui?"

"No, Majesty, but I think if there truly was a way out it would either have been used to invade the city already, or else it has been blocked."

"It exists," Samut declared. "Few people are aware of it and none dare use it for the way is dangerous. I would not suggest it were your Majesty not imprisoned in the city."

"Go on then. Where is this magical way out?"

"In a small House of Embalming set into the wall of the city. There is a lower room which acts as a storehouse for unguents and resins and behind a cracked stone sarcophagus in it is a passage which leads to the riverbank some two hundred paces north of the wall."

"I have never heard of such a thing," Roma-Rui said. "How do you know this?"

"I was not always a soldier. Before I joined the legion I was an apprentice embalmer in that self-same House. As a youth I investigated the tunnel and walked it far enough to see daylight at the other end."

"But you did not walk it to its end?" Amenmesse asked. "How then do you know it ends at the river?"

"The tunnel is flooded at the far end, the water waist deep and...and there was a crocodile. I did not dare go further, but the presence of a crocodile means it must be connected with the river."

"Under water perhaps," Roma-Rui commented.

Samut shook his head. "I saw daylight. It is open to the sky."

Amenmesse considered this tale for a while. "Why then has the enemy not made use of it? I cannot believe they would ignore the presence of a way into the city."

Again Samut shrugged. "I do not know, Son of Re, but perhaps the entrance is hidden by reeds, or the ground has fallen in on it, or perhaps a crocodile lives within it still."

"It would be a small matter to kill the crocodile."

"Indeed, Son of Re, but why would they bother killing a beast in its lair if they did not suspect there was a tunnel or that it led anywhere?"

"Let us assume this tunnel exists and that I can use it to go out of the city," Amenmesse said. "I find myself on the riverbank...but what then? I am in the midst of my enemies. I would do better to remain here. We can hold the city for as long as there are men left alive. Why take the risk when Sethi can be no more than a few days away?"

"I think Commander Samut is right, Majesty," Roma-Rui said. "You are effectively imprisoned in Waset. If we can get you away from the city you will be able to rally all your supporters, particularly those who think you are shut up in the city, and deal a mighty blow to your brother's army with or without the help of General Sethi."

"And we can steal a fishing boat easily enough," Samut added.

Amenmesse thought a while longer, chewing his lower lip and frowning. "I will need men with me I can trust."

"Not too many," Samut cautioned. "The arrival of a body of men on the riverbank will attract notice. Two men perhaps, one to steal a boat and another to guard your Majesty while he does so."

"You?"

"I would be honoured, Son of Re, but I have men better suited for the task. I intend to lead a break out in the south to divert attention there."

Amenmesse nodded. "Go then, Commander Samut, and arrange matters, but in the greatest secrecy. No man beyond us three must know I have left Waset."

Two days later, Samut welcomed his king into the silent and deserted House of Embalming and ushered him and the two guards who accompanied him down a flight of stone steps and into the storeroom. He had already moved the stone sarcophagus aside, revealing a black hole in the wall whence moist air gusted, stinking of rotten mud and crocodile excrement.

"In there?" Amenmesse asked. "It stinks."

"I have trodden the passage as far as the water, Son of Re, and can find no trace of a crocodile. It may be that there is one closer to the river, but you have two armed guards. As for the mud, well...the river is clean and will soon wash off the noisome residue."

"It is dark too."

Samut showed the king a bundle of resin-soaked torches. "More than enough to light the way," he said.

Amenmesse contemplated the opening for a time and then nodded. "You said you would create a diversion."

"Yes, Son of Re. As soon as you enter the tunnel I will run to the southern gate and create a disturbance such as will draw the enemy's attention from the north. It will take you a twelfth part of a day to negotiate the tunnel, so I will time the disturbance accordingly."

"And the fishing boat? What if we can't find one?"

"I have seen from the walls that there are many fishing boats drawn up along that stretch of the river. It will be a simple matter to steal one and sail across the river to the western shore. The priests in the House of Eternity of Nebmaatre are loyal to your cause. They will aid you."

Amenmesse motioned for his guards to precede him into the tunnel. They lit torches from an oil lamp illuminating the storeroom and, after handing one to the king and clasping the others with their spears, ducked into the low tunnel. Amenmesse made as if to follow and then stopped. He turned to Samut and looked at him gravely.

"I will not forget this, Samut."

"May the gods speed you on your way, Son of Re."

Samut watched as King Amenmesse made his way along the narrow passage, his figure lit fitfully by the flickering light of the torch, and then hurried up the steps and through the deserted House of Embalming with its odours that evoked nostalgic memories of youth. The daylight dazzled him as he emerged onto the streets of the city and he made his way through them to the southern end where the main gate pierced the wall near the Great Temple of Amun. Here he found Bakenkhons, Fourth Prophet of Amun, waiting for him.

"It is done?" Bakenkhons asked.

Samut nodded. "Menmire Amenmesse is on his way out of the city."

"Then we must act at once."

"You have men on the gates?"

"Of course. How many men will you take with you?"

"None."

"Is that wise?"

"I must have men with me I can trust absolutely, and you are the only man I would have with me."

Bakenkhons smiled briefly. "I must stay in the temple and open the gates when all is accomplished."

Samut nodded. "We are doing the right thing, aren't we?"

"It will bring the war to an end. Now come, let us do this thing before we are discovered."

Samut and Bakenkhons walked to the south-eastern gate where a small group of men waited, fidgeting with nervousness. Relief showed on their faces when the Fourth Prophet turned up and two of the men greeted him effusively.

"Open the gate," Bakenkhons ordered. "Quickly, before anyone else arrives."

The men leapt to obey, and wrestled the huge timber gates, easing them apart enough for Samut to slip through the gap.

"May Amun bless you," the priest murmured.

"Halt! You there, what are you doing?"

Bakenkhons turned to see a squad of temple guards approaching at a run. He stepped to meet them, holding up his arms. "Who are you to question me? I am Fourth Prophet Bakenkhons and I..."

"I know who you are," said the officer in charge, "and I answer directly to the Hem-netjer himself. I ask you once more, what are you doing and why is the gate open?"

One of the guards ran past and, shouldering Bakenkhons' men aside, peered through the gap between the timbers.

"Sir, there is a man out here...it is Commander Samut and he is...he is walking toward the enemy."

The officer ordered his men to hold Bakenkhons and strode toward the gate, staring out at the figure of Samut some fifty paces away.

"Commander Samut, what are you doing out here? Come back at once."

Samut said nothing, just hunched his shoulders and continued walking.

"Commander Samut, the Hem-netjer of Amun, Roma-Rui, orders you to return."

Samut ignored him.

"Return or I will order my men to kill you."

Samut looked back over his shoulder and saw two archers standing by the officer just outside the gate. He hesitated a moment and then kept walking.

An arrow hissed past him and buried itself in the sand. Samut took to his heels, jinking and swerving as other arrows slashed through the air. One ripped through his kilt, grazing his thigh and he stumbled before running on.

Now the commotion had attracted the attention of the enemy soldiers and a number of them ran out to intercept him, spears or axes in hand. Others drew their bows and showered the Waset archers with arrows, driving them and their officer back inside the city. Samut was surrounded and he held his arms out while blood trickled down his leg and his chest heaved with his exertion.

"I am Commander Samut of the Amun legion," he said. "Take me to the king."

"What king is that?" jeered one of the soldiers. "Your cowardly king is hiding in Waset."

"There is only one king of Kemet," Samut replied. "Userkheperure Seti. Now take me to him, for I have news that he needs to hear."

Chapter 42
Year 5 of Userkheperure Seti
Year 4 of Menmire Amenmesse

The day-to-day business of a kingdom does not stop when the king is at war, it only becomes more complex. Almost every day that Seti was on campaign, and every day now that he was encamped outside Waset, he held court as if he was in his throne room in Men-nefer. A stream of messengers raced north and south on the Royal Way, connecting the king with his Tjaty and through him, every part of Ta Mehu. Other messengers visited every city in Ta Shemau, apprising the governors and officials of the changed status of the sons of Baenre Merenptah and bringing back carefully phrased assurances of loyalty.

A town grew up around Seti's command tent and the basic living quarters behind it. Every aspect of life in a royal palace was duplicated there on the dusty plain outside Waset, and after several months of stalemate, the issue of the war against his brother was assuming an unreal air. His troops had scoured the countryside for any sign of General Sethi, for Seti meant to execute him publicly outside the city so that the inhabitants should lose heart, but he was nowhere to be found. None of the bodies of the fallen resembled him and aside for a few vague tales of his appearance between Waset and Kush, he seemed to have been swallowed up by the desert.

There were other matters to divert the king. Of consuming importance was the pregnancy of Queen Tausret. The physicians had assured her the child would be the longed-for and much needed heir to his father's throne. At present, the only person with some claim to the Double Throne was Menmire Amenmesse and after him his son Siptah. Seti quite liked the young boy, eight years old now, but he was not of his own blood, of his own loins, and Seti thirsted to have his own son succeed him.

The other matter that was becoming of pressing importance was the northern frontier. Whether the Kanaanites, Hatti, and Sea Peoples were unaware that no legions guarded the entrance to Ta Mehu or whether they were just unready to pluck the ripe fruit that were the rich lands of the river country, they would not be forever. As soon as his army had invested the rebel stronghold, Seti had sent two legions north. Two legions would have been enough ordinarily, but while Sethi remained unaccounted for, he dared not send his experienced legions away. Instead, the legions of Wadjet and Sobek had gone north to face the Nine Bows, and they would have to suffice.

Seti held court in his tented throne room and listened to his scribes reading out messages and petitions. Some people even brought their requests before him in person and these tended to receive a quicker and often more favourable response. He missed the presence of his Tjaty, but relied instead on the advice of his army commanders, particularly General Iurudef and Commander Setnakhte.

Seti yawned and stretched as he dismissed the latest petitioner, instructing the scribe to take down a note for Chancellor Bay to release a deben of gold to the bearer. "I think I will stop here," he said. "What other business remains?"

"Three more petitions, Son of Re," said the head scribe, "Nothing that cannot wait upon my lord's pleasure...and a letter that purports to come from Queen Tausret, though it is not easy to decipher the script. If it is indeed from the Queen, then her scribe needs a reprimand, if not a beating."

Seti took the letter, looked at it and laughed. "It is written in Tausret's own hand. She prides herself on being able to write but she has an atrocious style."

The head scribe flushed and bowed to hide his embarrassment. "My apologies, Son of Re. I had no idea."

Seti waved the scribe away and looked at his army commanders. "You will join me for refreshment?"

"Delighted, Great One," Iurudef said. Setnakhte said nothing but bowed briefly.

The king led his two commanders into his personal tent where servants had laid out a simple meal, fresh-baked bread, a variety of braised vegetables and slices of fatty beef. There was also a choice of wine and barley beer.

While his commanders ate and drank, Seti broke open the seal on his wife's letter and scanned the contents. It was short and to the point and his face lit up as he read the words.

"Listen to this. Queen Tausret has given birth to a boy. He is lusty and cries incessantly but with a strong voice. The physicians agree he is healthy."

"Wonderful news, Son of Re," Setnakhte exclaimed.

"Indeed, Great One," Iurudef agreed. "May your son be the first of many."

"I have no doubt that he will be," Seti said. "I must give the news to the army; it will hearten them to know that the dynasty of the great Usermaatre lives on."

"It will gladden them for your own sake, Great One," Iurudef said. "Have you chosen a birth name?"

Seti cogitated for a few moments. "I think his name should reflect his inheritance. Seti-Merenptah, I think."

"Perfect," Iurudef said. "Named for two strong kings."

"And a legitimate heir to continue your line," Setnakhte agreed.

Seti accepted a cup of strong rich wine from a servant and drank deeply, wincing as the river-cooled drink sparked a pang of pain in a worn tooth. He called the head scribe in and gave orders that the news of his son's birth be proclaimed and that an extra beer ration was to be issued to the army that evening as a celebration.

"Yes, Son of Re. The captain of the guard requests an audience. He says he has captured a man who claims to be Commander of the Amun legion. I told him he must wait."

"Amun legion, you say? Where did they capture him?"

"I do not know, Son of Re."

"What do you think, Iurudef? I thought the Amun was locked up in the city."

"So did I, Great One. If they are indeed outside, then my scouts have failed and will pay for it."

"Send the captain of the guard in."

The scribe hurried off and a few moments later Huni the captain entered the royal tent and dropped to his knees. "Son of Re, I have captured a man who says he is Commander of the Amun legion."

"The Amun legion is out? Why was I not told?"

"Son of Re, only this man came out of the city...though archers also came out and shot at him as he ran."

"Doesn't sound like any proper commander," Iurudef commented. "More likely some common soldier who has lost his nerve and seeks to exaggerate his importance."

"That was my thought," Seti said.

"Son of Re, he wears a commander's armband," Huni said.

"Not impossible to come by," Iurudef said. "I still think it likely he is a common soldier."

"It should be easy enough to tell," Setnakhte murmured. "Send for him, Son of Re."

"Ah yes, I was forgetting," Seti said. "You were in the Amun legion once."

"I did so have that honour, Divine One."

Seti nodded. "Very well. Bring him in and we shall see."

Captain of the guard Huni left the tent and returned a few minutes later, pushing a scrawny young man ahead of him. "On your knees," he growled.

The prisoner shook off Huni's grasp and bowed deeply before Seti. "Greetings, Son of Re," he said. "I am Samut, Commander of the Amun legion and I come before you today, bearing news that I am sure you will welcome."

"That remains to be seen," Seti said. He pointed at the armband and asked, "Yours?"

"Yes, Son of Re."

Seti looked to Setnakhte. "Is he who he says he is?"

Setnakhte nodded slowly. "His name is Samut, and he used to be Leader of a Hundred. He could well have been promoted."

"So you are who you say you are," Seti said. "What is this news that you say I will welcome?"

"Your brother Menmire Amenmesse seeks to flee the city and join up with General Sethi."

"By the gods, that would be a disaster," Setnakhte exclaimed.

"But a very unlikely event," Iurudef said. "The city is locked up tightly and we would see anyone who left. As you found out yourself, Samut."

"There is a tunnel, and as we speak, the king treads its muddy floor and will soon be out of Waset."

"There is only one king, Samut," Setnakhte said. "Be careful what you say."

"My apologies, Son of Re, I meant no disrespect, only that ...er, the man who calls himself king within Waset, is about to escape."

"Where is this tunnel?"

"It runs under the wall to the bank of the river."

"I have never heard of such a tunnel, though I lived in Waset many years," Setnakhte said. "How is it that you know of it?"

"I was an embalmer before I became a soldier, and the tunnel runs from the House of Embalming where I used to work."

"And where does it end?"

"On the riverbank, north of the city."

"Can you be more precise?"

Samut shook his head. "I only saw it once, when I was a youth. I think I could find it though."

"How many men are with him?"

"Just two guards. He hopes to take a fishing boat and cross the river."

"How long before my brother exits the tunnel?" Seti asked.

"Not long. You should hurry."

"I can have a squad ready very quickly," Setnakhte said.

"Wait," Seti ordered. "Why are you doing this? Has my brother wronged you that you should seek vengeance?"

"No, Son of Re, I..."

"And do not tell me it is because you suddenly realised I am the true Lord of the Two Lands."

"No, Son of Re. I am only a humble soldier and the rights and wrongs of the succession are beyond the compass of my poor mind. As far as I can tell, you are both anointed kings and worthy of the throne..."

"Then why? Do you hope for a reward? A reward for betraying your master?"

"Only, Son of Re, that you will let me serve you. You are both kings, but this war is tearing the entrails from our beloved Kemet. One of you must win, and win quickly. That winner would seem to be you, Userkheperure Seti. Your brother will not willingly surrender until every man, woman and child in Waset are dead, so I seek to take the choice out of his hands and deliver it into yours."

Seti stared at the kneeling man and then nodded, reaching a decision. "Setnakhte, take a squad and this man and apprehend my brother. I want him unharmed. As for this one, if he is telling the truth then I shall reward him; if he lies, I shall punish him."

Setnakhte saluted and left the king's tent, dragging Samut with him. Within minutes, a squad of men was running across the plain toward the northern end of the city. As they neared the river, Samut slowed and looked around him. He pointed.

"There, I think. In that reed bed."

Setnakhte set his men to search the swampy ground in and around the reed bed and a few moments later one of them hissed and pointed to where a man in a fishing boat was sculling the tiny craft toward them.

The man in the boat caught sight of the soldiers and stood up to get a better view. Setnakhte pointed again. "Kill him."

Three archers immediately let fly and the man collapsed overboard, his cry of warning cutting off abruptly. The reeds swirled, and soldiers ran forward, their spears at the ready. A man erupted from a thicket, sword slashing at the soldiers closing on him, and quickly died as spears plunged into his body. Another man appeared, also holding a curved sword, and attacked the soldiers.

"Don't hurt him," Samut yelled. "It is Menmire."

"Stand back!" Setnakhte ordered, and as the men withdrew, he called on Amenmesse to surrender. "Lay down your weapon, Menmire Amenmesse. We have come to take you before you brother, in honour if you will have it so; in chains if you will not."

"I see you have the traitor with you," Amenmesse replied. "How much gold has he earned from this deed?"

"Not for gold, master," Samut said, starting to weep. "Only that the killing should stop. Forgive me, Menmire."

"A fine soldier you turned out to be, Samut. Afraid of blood spilled in defence of your king. Well, I will not forgive you your treachery, and if my brother is fool enough to trust you then he deserves to die too." Amenmesse threw down his weapon and stared at the man beside Samut. "Setnakhte, isn't it? Another traitor."

"I follow the true king. Come now, Menmire, and face your brother's judgement."

Setnakhte dispatched a messenger to the king and then escorted Amenmesse and Samut back to the royal tent where he found Seti seated upon a throne, dressed in full regalia. Setnakhte bowed and presented Amenmesse, and then he retired to the edge of the tent with Samut. Iurudef and a handful of guards stood behind the throne, watchful as Amenmesse strode up to Seti.

"Well, little brother, you are still playing the king, I see."

Iurudef started forward, his hand on his dagger. "You will address the king properly, brother or not."

Seti extended a hand as if to restrain his general. "Stay, Iurudef."

"At least you have a firm hand with your dog," Amenmesse sneered. "Go back to your kennel and bark, Iurudef, and leave your betters to converse."

"Enough, brother," Seti said quietly. "It is at an end. The gods have decided the fate of Kemet."

Amenmesse shrugged. "So it would seem. What happens now? I must die, of course."

"I have no such intention. You are my father's eldest son and I honour you as such...but no more than that."

"You are a fool, little brother. In your place I would not hesitate."

"Perhaps not, but I choose to be merciful. I have it in mind that I can find you a court position somewhere. Until this day, your son Siptah was my heir..."

"But no more?"

"Rejoice with me brother, for I have a healthy son. I have named him Seti-Merenptah and he shall succeed me on the throne."

Amenmesse scowled. "You are to be congratulated then."

"Ah, I know what troubles you. Do not think that I shall put Siptah aside completely. He is my nephew after all. I shall create a place for him too."

"You are very generous."

Seti smiled. "You will drink with me, brother? Have some food perhaps?"

Hunger warred with pride in Amenmesse's face. "There have been food shortages in Waset lately."

"Of course, but that ends today, as soon as they open up the gates. I will take no reprisals against anyone, why should I? They are all my people."

"You said there was food?"

"Over there." Seti pointed to the table on which were spread the remains of the earlier meal. "Take what you will."

Amenmesse crossed to the table and stared at the food, with an effort restraining himself from cramming meat and bread into his mouth. He ate quickly, without tasting, until the hunger pains in his belly had eased. Then he became more selective, choosing the soft bread inside the loaves, dipping morsels in goose grease, or slicing off slivers of fatty beef with a short-bladed bronze knife.

Seti came to stand beside his brother and looked sideways at him, almost shyly. "It has been many years since we were together," he said. "You have aged. One could almost think you an old man, though I still remember the man you were."

Amenmesse chewed and swallowed, and then drained a cup of wine. "You no longer have the form of the boy you were, but whether you are a man, I cannot say."

"Do you have no kind word for me, brother?"

"Why should I? You stole my inheritance."

Seti sighed. "That old tale again? You know the truth of it. The throne came to me by the will of Usermaatre and Baenre. You tried to take the throne but you failed. Accept it Messuwy."

"I am Menmire Amenmesse."

"You were once, but now you are plain Messuwy again and your fate depends on my goodwill. You would do well to remember that."

Amenmesse cut a fig in two and bit into half. He tapped the knife blade gently on a wooden platter in front of him, staring down at the bowl of fruit.

"You have an infant son, whereas I have a child already grown."

"What of it?"

"Only that in a choice between our two lines, most reasonable men would choose mine."

Seti laughed. "The choice is no longer there. My line has been chosen."

"Let the gods decide."

As Amenmesse spoke, he gripped the short knife firmly and whirled, striking out at his brother. Iurudef shouted and lurched forward, Setnakhte and the guards a heartbeat behind him, but they were too late. The sharp bronze blade slashed through the fabric of Seti's tunic, scoring a path across his arm and plunging at an angle into the flesh of his chest.

Seti staggered back with blood blooming on the linen of his tunic and Amenmesse followed, blade stabbing forward. Iurudef threw himself between the two brothers, while Setnakhte collided with Amenmesse, hurling him to the floor and the spears of the guards stabbed down.

"Hold!" Seti bellowed, wrestling his General aside. "Do not harm him."

The guards arrested the downward motion of their spears, though their bright blades hovered near the fallen man's throat and chest. Setnakhte scrambled to his feet and plucked the knife from Amenmesse's grasp.

"He deserves to die," Setnakhte said. "He raised his hand to the king."

"He is still my brother, and I do not want his death." Seti looked down at Amenmesse, the blood dripping from his arm and chest. "Why would you do that when I had granted you your life?"

"Life as what?" Amenmesse asked. "As nobody? I am a king." He shrugged and tried to push aside the spears. "Either let me up or kill me. The gods have spoken."

"Indeed they have, Messuwy my brother." Seti signed to the guards. "Let him up and guard him well. Put him in chains until I decide his fate."

Iurudef pulled aside Seti's tunic as Messuwy, who was once Amenmesse, was led away. He grimaced when he saw the wound.

"Call a physician," he said to Setnakhte. "It looks to be a clean wound, but it bleeds freely and needs seeing to."

"Enough of that," Seti replied. "It is a scratch, no more."

Chapter 43

Chancellor Bay speaks:

My life and my future hang in the balance. Userkheperure Seti has triumphed and Menmire Amenmesse has fallen. If that was not enough, Queen Tausret has given birth to a healthy son who will likely succeed his father on the throne, and my own precious nephew, Siptah, will be relegated to obscurity. If he survives, that is. It is almost certain that my sister's husband Menmire will be executed and so often the family of the fallen follow them into death. Perhaps the arm of death will extend even to me, though I have ever sought to openly be of service to Userkheperure and Tausret.

The king has sent for me and I must obey his summons, travelling on the royal barge upriver to Waset. A soldier handed me the summons in the presence of Tjaty Hori and stood watching me, his hand on his sword. My first thought was of flight, but where would I run except back to my native Amurru? Even if I could give this soldier the slip I would be hunted down and handed to the king in chains. Ignominy would only cheapen my death.

Does Hori know my fate? Has he been told? He gave no sign of it, smiling pleasantly as if I had been favoured by the king. Hori knows I am related to Menmire by marriage, and the more I consider my position, the more certain I am that Menmire has let slip my subtle connivance in the death of Baenre and my support of Menmire himself. I cannot blame Menmire if he has spoken of my complicity, for few men have the strength to withstand the questions put to them by the king's executioners. I know I will crumble quickly under their tender ministrations. Userkheperure will not easily forgive what he must see as treachery so my death will not be a pleasant one.

The question before me is this. Do I assume the king demands my presence so he can execute me, or am I worrying too much? If the former, then I either escape or die by my own hand. It would not be hard to kill myself for I have access to poisons and to weapons. A short draught of a bitter potion or a swift thrust of a sharp dagger into my throat and all my worries will be behind me. Even a noose in the privacy of my own chambers. I am not a Kemetu such that I would fear the judgement of the gods, but an Amorite who knows that the gods do not frown on a death by one's own hand. Doubt stayed my hand though, and I embarked on the royal barge. There would be time enough when we get to Waset, for my dagger remained undiscovered...

I remember little of my voyage upriver though I expected it to be my last. I cannot remember my thoughts at all, only scenes that passed before my eyes. I sat in the prow and watched the dark green waters cleave into white foam, the sunlight dancing and shaking on the expanse, reed beds and lilies sliding past, pehe-mau snorting and blowing in the shallows, crocodiles disturbing the water with only their snouts showing and a ripple behind where their powerful tails sweep. Birds wheeled above me in the bright blue firmament with the sun-god Re baking my body despite the sunshade of an awning spread for my enjoyment and the cool following breeze. I saw men fishing from the banks or from small boats, casting nets and hauling them aboard filled with silvery fish. Men tended herds of cattle or farmed the verdant pastures where the life-giving waters sustained the crops. Villages slipped past, the smoke of their cooking fires tainting the crystal air and awakening hungers in my belly and in my heart. Truly the land of Kemet, the black-soiled land along the valley of Iteru, was blessed by the gods. Visions of burgeoning life, the sounds of the peasants carried across the water to my ears and the odours of farming all fanned in my heart a desire to live.

What would I not give to wander this land without thought of position or power, without wealth or even where my next meal was coming from, if only I could look upon such beauty forever? I took out my dagger and looked at it. The blade shone in the sunlight, but the fruit of that blade was darkness and dust, a whispering of my spirit in the underworld far from the light of day. It could spare me pain and ignominy, but was the price worth it if I wandered forever in the land of shadows? Better to live a little longer and die knowing that every day I staved off death brought me a little more joy. And who knows? Maybe the king would let me live and I could see the day when my nephew Siptah became a man and took up whatever task the king allowed him.

Without further thought, I drew back my hand and flung my sharp dagger into the river. It tumbled over and over, the blade reflecting back the sunlight as if it was ablaze with fire and then plunging into the cool depths of the water with a splash. A nearby flock of ducks took to the air in an explosion of wings and the captain of the barge looked round, startled. He saw nothing amiss, and greeted me warmly, deferring to my position and offering wine and honey cakes. My melancholy had disappeared with my dagger and I accepted his invitation gladly, sitting on the foredeck and drinking wine, eating honey cakes and dates, and conversing on recent events.

We arrived in Waset, a city that still bore the scars of war. The people were silent, gaunt, with haunted eyes, and the children begged with outstretched hands rather than playing in the streets. I marched with my guard up to the palace, holding my fear in check, determined that I would face the king proudly.

Userkheperure Seti awaited me in the formal throne room and I advanced with downcast eyes before first bowing, and then lowering myself to the ground. I lay on the cool tiles and uttered the usual phrases of praise, and more begging forgiveness for my supposed transgressions.

"What is this, Chancellor Bay?" the king said, and I thought I detected surprise in his voice. "Arise and greet me, faithful servant."

My breath caught in my throat and warmth flooded my body as I realised I had worried without cause. I rose to my knees and then to my feet, whereupon Userkheperure came down from the throne and embraced me.

"I have looked for you these many days, my friend," Userkheperure said. "As you see, I have conquered at last, but I need help in ministering to the southern kingdom. Will you help me bring Waset and Ta Shemau back into the fold?"

What could I do except offer my assent? I was high in the king's esteem and could perhaps use my position to secure the future of Siptah. A look of pain crossed the king's face and I saw that he favoured his left arm,

Chapter 44
Year 6 of Userkheperure Seti

The population of Waset hurried to distance itself from the former King of the South and the many nobles and officials of the city abased themselves and pointed fingers at their fellows, accusing them of being traitors while only they had remained loyal. Seti listened and held his own counsel, while a scribe made a note of all their names.

"What will be their punishment?" Bay asked.

"I will take no action against them, but neither will I show favour. How can I trust any of them?"

"There must be some you can trust, Son of Re. You will need good men to restore the city to its former prosperity."

Seti smiled at his Chancellor. "I have good men."

"I shall be returning to Men-nefer with you, Son of Re, and your other good men are army officers who will also lead their legions back to their proper stations. You need at least a Tjaty who can govern Waset and the Ta Shemau in your absence."

"I wish they had not killed Neferronpet. He was a loyal Tjaty."

"He has a grown nephew, I hear," Bay said. "Paraemheb."

"Send for him. I will talk to him and if he is suitable, make him Tjaty for his uncle's sake. Who else do I need?"

"A loyal Hem-netjer of Amun."

Seti grimaced. "I tried to rid myself of Roma-Rui once before. He is the chosen one of Amun, so I cannot lightly rid myself of him despite his disloyalty."

"Then reward him with estates in the north and make him Hem-netjer in Men-nefer. You can keep an eye on him there and you can limit his contact with the south. The present high priest in Men-nefer, Amenhirkashef, is old and should be retired."

"You see why I value your advice, Bay? Should I bring back Bakenkhons as Hem-netjer in Waset?"

"He is languishing as Fourth Prophet, but the very fact that Roma-Rui let him remain even in that position indicates he did not think him much of a threat. He was not effective before; don't give him another chance."

"Who then? The Second or Third prophets?"

Bay shrugged. "They are competent, I have no doubt, but the fact that Roma-Rui kept them on is suspicious. I think they are tainted."

"Who then?"

"Your Royal Secretary Mahuhy. He is the son of Nedjam, Overseer of the Royal Bedchamber by his wife Ta-nekhenemhab. Both are of good family, and loyal."

"Is he qualified?"

"Yes, Son of Re."

"Mahuhy it shall be then. Send for him as well."

"He will need to be elected by Amun."

"That can be arranged. I will suggest to Roma-Rui that it would be in his interests to comply with my wishes."

"So let it be done, Son of Re. Next there is the matter of the Amun legion and the Commander in the South."

"Samut is already Legion Commander," Seti pointed out.

"You would trust him, Son of Re? He betrayed your brother quickly enough."

"One could argue that he was being loyal to me."

Bay nodded. "He had many opportunities to be loyal, yet he waited until your brother could not possibly win before changing sides. Remember that he rose through the ranks by promotions coming from Sethi and the commanders he appointed."

"He did me a service though, and saved many lives, so I feel I should reward him."

"You are the king, Son of Re, and we are all guided by your will."

"Counsel me."

Bay thought for a few moments, seeking the right phrases. "Samut could remain as Legion Commander, but perhaps given an estate as reward for his service, an estate that calls him away from Waset from time to time. His deputy could be an officer promoted from one of your loyal legions, to act as Commander when Samut is away, and to watch upon his loyalty at all times."

"Good, good. I can think of several worthy officers for the position of deputy. And what of the Commander in the South? Who is worthy to be made General?"

"I would have said Iurudef were he not already General in the North. Second only to him is Setnakhte, who is a loyal officer and a talented Legion Commander."

"I had considered him," Seti agreed. "He comes from the best family," he said with a smile, "a son of Usermaatre yet is not overly ambitious. A decent wife and a grown son by the name of Ramesses, I believe. A daughter too, though I cannot remember her name. Yes, I think Setnakhte will do. Send him to me."

"As you command, Son of Re," Bay said. He made a notation on a papyrus scroll, and then consulted a list he had made earlier. "There are a number of lesser posts to be considered, positions like mayor, Medjay Commander, the overseers of grain, fisheries, wharves, temples, for instance, and several more in the palace itself. The present incumbents are compromised and should be replaced. I have a number of names for your consideration..."

"It is too much for me," Seti said. "When I have appointed Paraemheb as Tjaty, you and he can work through the list, raising up those you think are worthy."

"As you wish, Son of Re. There is one other matter, two perhaps, though they are tied together. Your brother did not do much building while he was er...king in the south, but he did some. Do you want those buildings destroyed, or just have his name obliterated?"

"What buildings did he erect?"

"Shrines to various gods, for the most part. Here in Waset and throughout the south. Also a number in Kush when he acted as King's Son there."

"I think we can just cause his name to be erased and mine inscribed in its place."

Bay looked uncomfortable. "He er...made a few statues too, Son of Re. Notably showing him seated with his son Siptah on his lap."

"Be easy on this score, Bay, for I know the boy is your nephew. I have sworn no harm will come to him," Seti said. "He is blameless in this and already suffers enough under the affliction visited upon him by the gods." The king pondered for a few moments. "Cause the head and torso of those

311

statues to be changed to my own, or if it is not possible then to be destroyed, but leave the person of Siptah intact."

"Thank you, my lord."

"You said there was a second part attached to this issue?"

"Yes, Son of Re. It is the matter of the royal tombs in Ta-sekhet-ma'at. Your brother stopped work on your own tomb, of course, and has gone a good way toward building his own. I hear it has particularly fine carvings."

"Well, we can't have that, can we? Work is to stop on my brother's tomb and all the carvings of his name are to be chiselled out. Start work on my own again...and that of Queen Tausret."

"What of Queen Takhat?"

Seti sighed. "I cannot show her undue favour if I am to keep good relations with Tausret for our son will be our heir. Takhat, on the other hand, was taken in marriage by my brother to cast doubt on the paternity of any children by her, so I can scarcely take her back. Her child by me was a daughter anyway, so does not enter into the succession." The king thought some more. "Takhat can have my brother's tomb, after it has been suitably cleansed of his inscriptions."

"I shall arrange for all your wishes to be carried out, Son of Re."

"I will inspect the tombs in Ta-sekhet-ma'at. Arrange it."

Two days later, Seti took his new Tjaty Paraemheb and Chancellor Bay over the river to visit the Great Field. A squad of soldiers from the Ptah legion accompanied them as security, while Setnakhte, newly appointed as General of the South, ripped through the military forces at his disposal like a sharp bronze sword, both in the Amun legion and within the auxiliaries that were to be left behind as a new legion. Samut, the Amun Commander, scurried to do the General's bidding while Ament, his new deputy, watched him with the eyes of a hawk.

There were chariots waiting on the western shore. Seti rode with Bay in one of them, and Paraemheb took the other, while the squad of soldiers ran behind. The day was hot, and the sun beat down fiercely with waves of heated air making them sweat, especially the soldiers who also had to put up with the acrid dust churned up by the chariot wheels and horses' hooves. Seti called a halt at the Mortuary Temple to Nebmaatre and insisted the men refresh themselves with cool water before carrying on. Past the temple, the road split, one branch leading toward the dry hills and the great gap in the cliffs that hid Ta-sekhet-ma'at. As the road rose slowly to the workers' village, the residence of the Servants of the Place of Truth,

Seti slowed their pace to a walk, allowing the soldiers the opportunity to catch their breath.

"It has been years since I was up here," Seti remarked to Bay. "There was an old man called Kenhirkhopeshef, who was the Scribe of the Great Place. He had been Scribe most of his life, his fingers in everything, managing every detail of the village life and the tombs despite the fact he looked like he'd be needing his own tomb before the day was out. I was amazed to learn he is still in charge."

"Such men are a lesson to us all, Son of Re," Bay replied. "He must have lived a life of exemplary virtue for the gods to reward him so."

Seti nodded. "Both my grandfather and father lived to be old men."

"Exactly, Son of Re. A life spent in service to Kemet and the gods. May your life be extended also, my lord, so that Kemet may once more know the peace of Usermaatre."

"Oh, I intend to live for a long time, Bay, and hand over to my son Seti-Merenptah when he is an old man. Ah...see...we come to the village."

There were a number of people gathered outside the village waiting for the royal party. Seti stepped off the chariot, wincing as he jarred his left arm, and was quickly joined by Bay and Paraemheb. The villagers bent low, their outstretched hands parallel with the dusty ground as they made their obeisance. Seti told them to rise and the Scribe of the Great Field tottered forward, supported by a stick and a young man that Seti took to be his grandson Remaktef.

"Son of Re," Kenhirkhopeshef quavered in a thin voice. "Greetings. Forgive me, but I am unable to accompany you today. If it is your will, my grandson Remaktef shall speak for me."

"Take your ease, Scribe Kenhirkhopeshef," Seti replied. "You have given good service these many years. Sit in the shade with a pot of beer and let younger men act for you. Scribe Remaktef, perform your duty."

"Son of Re," Remaktef said. "This is the village of Set-ma'at and these are the Servants of the Place of Truth, dedicated from generation to generation with excavating and decorating the tombs of kings and exalted persons within Ta-sekhet-ma'at." He spoke fast, almost gabbling his words, and Seti smiled, for he recognised phrases that Kenhirkhopeshef had used when last he visited the village. Evidently, this was a speech learned by heart.

"Great One, there have been changes since the last time you were here. Neferhotep, Foreman of the First Team has passed into the West and his place has been taken by Paneb, son of Nefersenet..."

Paneb the Foreman bowed to the king as Remaktef spoke, but Seti saw an arrogant look in his eye.

Seti frowned, and motioned the scribe to silence. "Your elevation is recent, Paneb. In fact, it was one of Paraemheb's first actions. His predecessor absolved you of blame for the death of your adoptive father, Neferhotep."

"That is so, Son of Re," Paneb said. "I showed that Neferhotep stole building stones and used them for his own tomb. Thus was I justified in my actions."

Seti nodded. "So said Tjaty Amenmose, who was appointed by my brother. One could argue that as my brother's reign was not legitimate, nor was any decision made by those he appointed."

Paneb scowled, but hid his displeasure by bowing deeply.

"Paraemheb, you will reopen this case and examine the evidence. I will not have my Servants of the Place of Truth steal or kill with impunity."

"It shall be done, Son of Re," the Tjaty said.

Remaktef made as if to continue, but Seti silenced him again. "I will go up to the tombs. Remaktef, you will accompany me."

Paraemheb took Remaktef with him in his chariot, and the royal party continued on into the dry and sun-baked valleys where the tombs of the kings and queens of Kemet lay. The day grew hotter as the sun reflected off the cliffs and valley floor, dazzling their eyes and bringing out prickles of sweat that dried in an instant. At length, they came to the side valley that housed the unfinished tombs of Userkheperure Seti and Tausret his queen. They dismounted and stood near the black hole in the rubble beneath the cliff face that was the king's tomb, looking into the silent darkness.

"Son of Re," Remaktef said. "It grieves me that nothing has been done on your tomb for four years, but what could we do? The king...your brother ordered the work to stop on your tomb, so we...we could only obey. On the Queen's...well, he did not give us specific directions, so work continued. It is nearly finished."

"I understand," Seti replied, "but you will resume work on mine immediately. You still have the plans?"

"Yes, Son of Re."

"Good, then there should be no delay. My brother has a tomb?"

"Yes, Son of Re. It is in the main valley. Do you want to see it?"

"No, but work on it is to cease from this day. Paraemheb will give you instructions of its future modifications, but those are of low priority." Seti looked around at the towering cliffs and the bone-dry dust and rubble that made this place seem even more desolate than the open desert.

"Remaktef, if you were to start a new tomb, where would you place it?"

"A...a new one, Son of Re?" Remaktef licked his dry lips and looked at his king in some consternation. "I...I thought you would have the old tomb refurbished, my lord. There is nothing wrong with it that a month or so cannot put right. It would take much longer to dig out a new one."

"Just answer my question, Remaktef. Where would you situate a new tomb?"

The scribe stared around him, shading his eyes from the glare, striving to remember everything he had learned about these dry valleys. "There are suitable places in the main valley..."

"No. It must be close by."

"Then...forgive me, Great One, but I cannot be certain of the structure of the underlying rock and whether it is suitable for excavating a long passage..."

"I understand. Choose a place, Remaktef. The best place in this valley."

The scribe pointed down the valley, past Tausret's tomb. "I would look there first, Son of Re. In the rock face a little past the Queen's tomb."

Seti walked down to the indicated place, his sandaled feet crunching and slipping on the loose surface. He glanced at the entrance to Tausret's tomb, and then at the place near it.

"There?"

"Yes, Son of Re."

"What do you think, Paraemheb?"

"Much like any other place, my lord," the Tjaty said. "If the scribe says it is a good place, then he should know."

"And what do you say, Bay?"

"I think that anyone buried here would count it a great honour to face eternity alongside you and Queen Tausret."

"Well said, Bay," Seti said with a laugh. "Do you feel honoured?"

"Son of Re?"

"You are looking at the site of your own tomb, Chancellor Bay. You have served me well, and I would reward you suitably."

Bay gaped for a moment and then fell to his knees in the sharp rubble. "You do me too much honour, Great One."

"You accept my gift?"

"Oh yes, Son of Re. Thank you."

"So, Remaktef. You will record this place as the site of the tomb of Chancellor Bay. Hire as many men as you need, and send the requests for supplies to Paraemheb. I want work on this tomb to start immediately, and I want mine and the Queen's to be finished inside of five years."

Chapter 45

Menmire Amenmesse speaks:

I am still housed within the Royal Palace in Waset, but my accommodation is scarcely worthy of a king. I have a suite of rooms but the cedar doors are barred and guards stand at every door and window. They have been drawn from my brother's loyal legions, Set, Ptah, Re, and Heru, and I have no friends there. I am allowed servants to tend to my needs, but they too are drawn from the legions, and are not as servants should be. A proper servant is one who supplies my needs, is self-effacing and discreet, but these are insolent and openly sneer at my plight. In truth, it is hard to squat above a pot and empty my bowels with a man standing watching me, a look of hatred on his face.

I have complained, sending messages to my brother and his new Tjaty, but to no effect. I must make the best of my captivity, spending my days sitting at a window and thinking. If only I had someone to discuss matters of importance with me. What am I saying? What matters of importance? My world has shrunk down upon me so it now encompasses three small rooms, where once I called the whole of Kemet mine, from Abu almost to Men-nefer, and the province of Kush besides. Now I am alone, uncertain of my fate. I have asked after my son Siptah, but no one will tell me anything. I do not even know if my brother has taken his revenge upon my poor, innocent child.

What could I have done differently? I go over every action from the day I sailed south from Men-nefer all those years ago to take up my position of Deputy King's Son of Kush. Sethi was only one of my companions then. Did I allow him too much freedom? Should I have maintained a tighter control over his actions? The common people hated him and through him, me. A king should be feared, but should he also be loved by his subjects? That is a novel thought and after a few moments' consideration, I tentatively reject it. Love is good, but fear is enough providing one has the armed might to back it. My greatest failing, if failing it is, was to leave the army in Sethi's care and attend to matters of state. I should have left those matters to Khaemter and concentrated on defeating my brother's legions. I know I am a better general than Sethi, though I have never had the opportunity to prove it. After all, I am descended from the great Usermaatre, whereas he is but a short step or two above a commoner.

From time to time, people come to see me, or rather, to look at me, for they merely stand in the doorway, peering past the crossed spears of the guards, and will not answer when I implore them for news. They are high-ranking army officers for the most part, but also include court officials, and even the new Tjaty Paraemheb came once. I must hope that one of my...

My heart beats faster and I must turn away from the guards lest they see the awakening hope in my eyes. If ever there was proof that the gods have not forgotten me, it was this. I was entertaining the hope that one day one of my trusted servants would have occasion to visit me, when in walked Hemaka, a junior scribe that I had praised once for his work. He was dressed as a common servant, carrying some cleaning implements. Taking them into the inner room, he casually signed for me to remain silent. I followed him into the room and saw that we were alone.

"Greetings, Menmire Amenmesse," he said in a low voice. "Forgive me if I do not bow before you, but if I am recognised, all our work is undone."

I nodded my acceptance of this lack of protocol. "Who sent you, Hemaka?"

He looked around quickly, and then took a pace closer. "General Sethi, my lord. He plans an attack on the palace."

"Then you should tell him that Waset is crawling with the enemy. He would need an army to retake the city. Does he have an army?" I added hopefully.

"No, my lord. He recognises he cannot retake the city, but believes that a few brave men can rescue their king and spirit him out of the city."

"I am scarcely alone here. You see how I am guarded."

"I do not know the details, my lord, but General Sethi has made good use of the gold at his disposal and has made a number of bribes, buying the loyalty of men in responsible positions. He is confident that on the day, the right men will be in place and you will be able to leave the palace."

I felt like shouting aloud my joy, but I restrained myself. "When?" I asked.

"Soon, my lord. You must hold yourself in readiness."

Hemaka paused and appeared to be struggling with some inner turmoil. I pressed him to speak and with a show of reluctance, he continued.

"Menmire, please know that these are not my words, but come from General Sethi. He asks what your purpose will be if you are freed. He says, 'Of what use is one more free man if he wishes to live in obscurity? I need a man prepared to take up the heka and nekhakha of kingly authority once more and wield power in the land. Ask of Menmire if he forgives his brother Seti and wishes to live in peace with him and his heirs, or will he destroy him with the army I will raise for him'?"

I felt anger rise within me, anger that anyone would doubt I was a king. I stared at Hemaka until he quite forgot his earlier resolution and dropped to his knees in front of me, arms outstretched.

"Forgive me, Son of Re," he murmured. "They are not my words. I am but the messenger."

"Get up," I said, "before you are seen."

He rose to his feet and gathered his cleaning implements. "What message shall I take back to General Sethi, my lord?"

"Tell him that Menmire Amenmesse is still King of Kemet, and that if I have an army behind me I will crush my usurper brother and kill him and his son and his bitch wife. Tell him that I am King of all Kemet and my son Siptah will be king after me."

Hemaka bowed and smiled. "I will tell him, Son of Re. Be ready."

He left my presence and I returned to my bedchamber and composed my thoughts. It would not do to let any of the guards see my mood had changed. It only took one man to see that Amenmesse now had something to smile about, to carry word of this odd occurrence to his superiors, and my last hope would dry up like spilled water on a hot day. No, I must watch my every move, my every expression, the timbre of my voice. And

Chapter 46
Year 6 of Userkheperure Seti

" **How** can you know this?" Seti demanded. "He would never admit something like that to someone he did not trust fully." The king stared suspiciously at his Tjaty. "Why should my brother trust you?"

"Not me, Son of Re, but rather one of his former servants, a scribe called Hemaka. He admitted everything to him, believing he was still loyal."

"So my brother spoke injudiciously to this Hemaka, who then came bearing tales to you? Is that what you are saying?"

"Yes, my lord; that is indeed what I am saying."

"I don't believe it."

Paraemheb frowned. "What is it you do not believe, my lord?"

"Is it not obvious? My brother is locked in his suite, unable to talk to anyone but hand-picked soldiers and a handful of trusted servants. How then is he going to hatch a plot to break out and assassinate me? He would have to bribe or suborn several men at least. Do you have the names of these traitors?"

"No, my lord; that is not what happened. Hemaka took a message to your brother purporting to come from General Sethi. He was to lead a band of men to rescue your brother from captivity. Your brother sent a message back to Sethi..."

"So this Hemaka is one of Sethi's men, after all? From what you were saying, I thought perhaps he was in your employ."

"He is, my lord."

"Oh, speak plainly, Paraemheb. Who exactly is this Hemaka?"

"A man in my employ. Formerly, he was a scribe in your brother's court."

"So who was he working for when he took this tale of rescue and death to my brother? Sethi or you?"

"He was working for me, my lord."

"So the message he carried from Sethi...?"

"Did not exist, my lord."

"So what was the point? There is no plot to break my brother out and reinstate him. Sethi does not have an army. My brother is no threat at all."

"Perhaps not this time, my lord," Paraemheb said. "But while your brother remains a prisoner, while he remains alive, there is always the possibility of a plot."

Seti turned to General Setnakhte who had remained silent to this point. "And what do you think, Setnakhte?"

"I think your brother Amenmesse desires your death, Son of Re."

"Don't use that name," Seti snapped. "He is not King of Kemet, and never was."

"Forgive my outspokenness, Son of Re, but he was, in the eyes of Ta Shemau and Kush at least. The south supported him and I have no doubt he still has many supporters in Waset. Give him the chance and he will be king again."

"He is a focus for discontent, my lord," Paraemheb added.

"What would you have me do?"

Paraemheb glanced at Setnakhte, who shrugged and turned away. The Tjaty cleared his throat. "You must rid yourself of this threat, my lord."

"Kill him, you mean? No, I will not do that. He is a son of my father, my elder brother, and..." Seti shook his head. "I will not kill him."

Without turning, Setnakhte said. "Yet you would have Sethi killed in an instant, if he was in your hand."

"That is different," Seti protested. "He is a scion of the nobility, and dangerous besides."

"Dangerous?" Setnakhte whirled to face his king, anger on his face. "Yes, Sethi is dangerous, while Menmire Amenmesse is alive..."

"Don't use that name," Seti shouted. "How many times must I tell you? I don't recognise his claim. He is nothing but my brother Messuwy."

"Then you may call him Messuwy if you wish, Son of Re, but I call him Menmire Amenmesse so you may recognise the fact that many people still think of him that way and always will. Sethi is dangerous while your brother is alive, but he would be no more than just another bandit chief if your brother was dead. Menmire Amenmesse is a danger to your life and your throne, to the life of your Queen and your infant son. If Sethi dropped dead today, Amenmesse would still be a danger. He will be a danger as long as one person wants to see him on your throne in your place. Nobody can achieve that today...or tomorrow...but what of a year from now? Two? When you have returned to Men-nefer or your attention is elsewhere, fighting against Kemet's foes? What if discipline grows lax and somebody breaks him out? Will you wait until he stands at the head of another army before you recognise he is dangerous?"

Seti stared at his General, appalled at the anger directed at him.

"He is right, my lord," Paraemheb said.

"Son of Re, I am completely loyal to you, for you are grandson of Usermaatre and son of Baenre who was his heir, just as you were Baenre's heir. The gods themselves placed you on the throne of Kemet, and I will defend your right to be there to the death. I can never recognise your brother's claim and it is only because I can see the dangers that arise from letting him live that I speak out now." Setnakhte advanced on his king and bowed, holding out his arms in supplication. "Give the command, Son of Re, and I will rid you of this menace to your family."

"He is my brother," Seti whispered.

"When he first rebelled, you swore you would have his liver," Setnakhte said. "I was not there, but your words were carried to my ears. Was this report false, Son of Re?"

"No, but I was angry..."

"Then what has changed, Son of Re? Is it that now he has spilled the blood of thousands of your people? That he has shaken the pillars of the southern kingdom and turned many people from their loyalty to you? Tell me, Son of Re, that I may understand how these things make him less worthy of death."

Seti turned away, shaking his head. "He is deserving of death, I know, and if I was to meet him on the field of battle, I would kill him without regret."

"But?"

"But he is a helpless prisoner in my household, without his son who is also my prisoner, without friends, without even a sycophant to praise his name to his face."

"He has friends still, my lord," Paraemheb said. "They are in hiding now, but they exist."

"And wait only the opportunity to raise your brother up again," Setnakhte added. "They cannot make just anybody a king in your place, so they need your brother alive. You cannot make a dead man king."

"I will not kill him. He can do no harm by himself."

"And if Sethi appears with an army? What then, Son of Re?"

"Then I will re-examine my decision. Until then, I do not want to hear more of this. Do you understand?"

"As my lord commands," Paraemheb said.

"I hear and obey, Son of Re," Setnakhte said.

Setnakhte accompanied Paraemheb back to the Tjaty's quarters, pacing in silence alongside him until they were alone once more. The General threw himself down on a couch and stared at his companion.

"If he was somebody other than the king, I would call him a fool," he muttered.

"Hold your tongue, by the gods," Paraemheb said. "Such talk will serve no purpose except to get you arrested for treason."

"You know what I'm talking about. He's no fool, but sometimes he acts like one."

"He still feels for his brother," Paraemheb said simply.

"And such blindness could still unravel the fabric of Ma'at. Why can he not see that to leave the man alive is to invite disaster?"

Paraemheb shrugged. "There is nothing we can do while the king feels this way."

"I disagree. I think we must act in the king's best interests, whether he approves or not."

"You would sacrifice yourself for the good of the kingdoms? The king could not countenance leaving you unpunished if you openly flout his will."

"I did not say it would be done openly," Setnakhte said. "Only that it must be done."

"How?"

"Better you do not know."

"You swore an oath to obey the king, just now," Paraemheb protested. "As did I. We cannot break our oaths."

"I don't know what you swore to, but evidently I heard the king say something different." Setnakhte smiled and leaned back on the couch. "The king said he wanted to hear no more of this until Sethi turned up with an army, that is what I promised."

"You chop at words, General. You understood the meaning of his words as well as I."

"Perhaps, but it makes no difference. I will act in the best interests of the king and Kemet and once he gets over his initial anger, he will see the sense in it."

"You may be dead by then."

"That is in the hands of the gods."

Paraemheb contemplated Setnakhte's words. "Why are you telling me all this? Do you seek my help?"

"I don't need it, Paraemheb, but it would help."

"I could go to the king with this."

"You could," Setnakhte admitted. "But you won't. You can see the sense in my words though you make a show of reluctance. I do not contemplate this action for my own benefit, but only to preserve the Ma'at of Kemet. You see that, don't you?"

Paraemheb nodded slowly, reluctantly. "When? And how, for that matter. The men guarding him are drawn from the loyal legions and I doubt they'll obey even General Setnakhte."

"No, but they won't be here much longer. The king must soon return to his capital, he has already sent Chancellor Bay north. He will want to see his son, for one thing; and show himself on the northern borders. When he does that, he'll take the northern legions and leave me with Amun and the auxiliaries that I will form into a new legion, Mut perhaps, as consort of Amun. I'll replace Samut and raise up Ament. Then Amenmesse will try to escape and unfortunately be cut down in the attempt by the loyal men guarding him."

"But when the king finds out..."

"When the king finds out, it will be too late. Too late even to make much sense of the events. The men concerned will have been transferred, the reports written in such a way as to make the killing wholly necessary." Setnakhte smiled. "Who knows, maybe Sethi will have been seen approaching Waset and this news made the prisoner try to escape."

"And if Sethi does not put in an appearance?"

"Use your wits, Paraemheb. It does not matter if he comes or not, I only need the idea that he comes. Amenmesse tries to escape and my men kill him. With his death ends the last danger to the true House of Ramesses."

Chapter 47
Year 6 of Userkheperure Seti

Scarcely a month passed before news came to the court of Userkheperure Seti in Waset that there was trouble on the northern borders. The Retenu tribes were restless and the Sea Peoples were once more stirring from their cities on the Great Sea and raiding along the coast and into the several mouths of the Great River. At once, the king ordered his legions north by land, meaning to follow within days by barge to Men-nefer. He left General Setnakhte in charge of the southern army, with a refurbished Amun legion and the newly constituted Mut legion as the backbone of the south.

"You have a great responsibility, Setnakhte," Seti said. "You must keep the peace not only in Waset and Ta Shemau, but also in Kush. I realise you will be stretched thin with only two legions, especially if there is any trouble, but you have permission to raise auxiliaries as needed."

"I will not let you down, Son of Re."

Seti smiled and nodded. "I know you won't. You have good men under you and I recommend you rely on Ament as your second."

"I will use him as he deserves, Son of Re."

The king looked sharply at his general and opened his mouth as if to ask what he meant, but instead nodded. "Kush will be a thorn in your side, as Messuwy and Sethi made their mark down there. You will need to rule them with a rod of hardened bronze."

"I thought Setuy was still King's Son of Kush."

"Yes, but I do not fully trust him. He has bent his knee to me and sworn his loyalty, but he served Messuwy and Khaemter rather too well. He continues to rule Kush in civil matters, but I give you charge of all matters military. You will have a document from my scribe to this effect."

"My thanks, Son of Re." Setnakhte hesitated, then, "If I am to hold supreme military power in the south, may I also appoint my deputy to rule in Kush when I am in Waset?"

"You have someone in mind?"

"Hori, son of Kama. He is First Charioteer of His Majesty, and King's Messenger to Every Land."

"A good man," Seti agreed. "I had thought to take him north with me, but if he would serve you well down here, I will assign him to you."

"Thank you, Son of Re."

"One other thing, Setnakhte. You know my thoughts on this already but I will repeat them so there is no misunderstanding. My brother Messuwy is to remain under guard at all times. He is not to converse with anyone alone, nor is he permitted to receive letters or send them. His person is sacred, being of the royal family, and he is to remain safe and unharmed. Do you understand me, Setnakhte?"

"I hear, Son of Re, but what if there is a rescue attempt by Sethi or...or anyone? If there is a danger they might succeed, should I then..."

"No, not even then. Faced with the choice of killing him or letting him go free, you will let him go free. I would rather be tasked with hunting him down again than let him be slaughtered in a cage." Seti stared at his General as if trying to read his thoughts. "You are not to kill my brother Messuwy...under any circumstances."

"As you wish, Son of Re."

"You swear it? On the gods? Or must I put it in writing?"

"I swear it."

Userkheperure Seti set out the next day, his barge tugged northward by the river's flood current. The king stood at the stern, between the two men on the twin rudders, staring back at the city as its walls slowly slipped out of sight. He had battled the south too long to be untroubled at leaving, and he knew that he would have to make some decision concerning his brother before long. In the meantime, there was a voyage of several days to face, and very little to occupy his time.

"Time," he muttered under his breath. "That is indeed the question. How much time?" His right hand crept to the stained bandage on his left bicep where his wound still wept pus. The flesh felt hot and swollen beneath his fingers, and he cried out involuntarily as one finger probed too deep. The two men on the rudders stared at their king but swiftly lowered their concerned gaze when Seti glared angrily at them.

The voyage north was swift as the river in early flood bore the king quickly to Men-nefer, and a mere six days later the barge nosed in toward the docks where a huge crowd had turned out to welcome their victorious king home.

Tjaty Hori led the official delegation of priests, court officials and nobles, together with Chancellor Bay, while the prominent businessmen of the city waited to greet their king. The businessmen had outlaid a substantial amount of gold to deck the city in banners of rejoicing, and the provision of meat, bread and beer for the common citizens, served on trestle tables at every street corner. All a man or woman was required to do to earn this largesse was to shout their praises of the king as he made his way through the streets to the palace. This was no hardship for the people because the civil war between the Two Brothers was over and the kingdoms could now look forward to a time of peace and prosperity. Some men were already likening it to the reign of the king's grandfather Usermaatre Ramesses.

Queen Tausret waited for her husband in the shade of a large linen umbrella, a nurse standing beside her with the young prince Seti-Merenptah in her arms. She smiled at the crowd gathered on the docks as the royal barge eased toward the wharf, warmed by the love the common people had for their king.

The river lapped high against the upper flood docks, the strong current gripping the hull of the barge and threatening to pluck it away despite the efforts of the oarsmen. Sailors leapt for the wharf as the barge nosed in and gently bumped against thick reed mats hung over the edge, ropes being quickly wound around bollards and tied off. A painted gangplank was put into place and held in place by slaves, while everyone's attention turned to the barge, awaiting the appearance of the king.

He appeared on the deck, under the awning, in company with the barge captain, and a great shout of joy went up, startling wildfowl in the nearby reed beds. The thunder of their wings and their honks of alarm swelled the uproar as Seti moved slowly toward the gangplank, but the noise died away to a muttered rumble. For some reason, the barge captain remained close to the king, almost too close to be proper, given his station. In fact, he almost appeared to be supporting the king.

Seti lifted his right arm as a salute to the people of Men-nefer and the cheering swelled again, but then he stumbled and a gasp of horror erupted as the barge captain openly laid hands on the king, holding him up. The captain spoke to a sailor nearby and the man leapt ashore and raced to the waiting Tjaty, dropping to his knees and talking rapidly.

Tjaty Hori whirled and beckoned to the court physician, who looked startled and then moved toward the barge, his assistants in his wake. Hori, Chancellor Bay and two royal butlers followed. They boarded the barge and clustered around the king.

The court physician, Re-Usey, gasped in dismay when he saw the king's swollen, fevered arm. "Son of Re, we must treat that immediately. Lie down that I might minister to you."

"What, and appear weak before the people? I will walk to the palace and then you may apply your remedies." Seti swayed where he stood, and sweat broke out on his brow. "Perhaps...perhaps a chair," he muttered.

Chancellor Bay immediately ordered one of the royal butlers to find a chair to convey the king, and sent the other to tell Queen Tausret about the king's condition. "Make sure she realises that there is nothing she can do down here. She must appear strong and unconcerned, and have the palace ready for the king."

Hori called for the guards and started them clearing a path through the streets for the passage of the king's chair, and when that conveyance arrived, made sure Seti was ensconced in it securely before ordering it up to the palace as fast as the bearers could carry it. The people still cheered as the king passed by, but their cries were now of joy alloyed with concern, and rumours multiplied in his wake.

Seti collapsed in his seat as his bearers approached the palace and they hurriedly set the chair down to prevent him toppling from it. Re-Usey supervised his assistants carrying the king into the shaded palace and along deserted corridors to the king's inner chamber. Bay had ordered the palace staff away, and Tausret waited in the bedchamber, her face pale with dismay and taut with worry.

"Will he be all right?" she demanded of Re-Usey as his assistants laid him gently on the bed.

"With respect, Great Lady, I cannot tell until I have examined him."

"Then do so, physician, and tell me what you need and it shall be sent for."

"I have what I need, but have the room cleared."

"I have sent for the priests of Heka, Serket, Sekhmet and Ta-Bitjet," Bay said. He started ushering people from the room and uttered a string of commands to the guards by the door. "Admit no one save by my permission," he told them.

Re-Usey leaned over Seti and cut back the sleeve of his tunic with a sharp knife. The king moaned as the knife slid between the fabric and his tightly swollen arm, and cried out as it was freed of its constraints. One of the assistants murmured and pointed, and the physician leaned closer, wrinkling his nostrils at the stench that arose from the suppurating wound.

"There is a demon in the king's arm," Re-Usey declared.

"Can you get rid of it?" Bay asked.

"That is a matter for the priests," the physician replied. "They will have to say prayers and if they write the prayers on papyrus, I can bind them to the arm."

"His arm has been wounded," Tausret pointed out. "How did that happen?"

"Does it matter?" Hori asked. "The demon gained access to the wound, but why should it matter how?"

"His brother stabbed him with a knife he had been using to cut meat," Bay said. "The knife slashed his arm and also wounded his chest. That injury healed, but his arm has not."

"Is it not strange that the demon would enter the arm wound instead of the chest wound?" Tausret asked. "If it had entered the chest, the king would probably have died by now."

Hori shrugged. "Who can understand the ways of a demon?"

The priests arrived and immediately ranged themselves around the king's bed and started their prayers, intoning incantations while their acolytes erected small shrines and burned incense. Other acolytes started inscribing prayers onto papyrus. Meanwhile, Tausret knelt beside her husband and closely examined the wound on Seti's arm. She wrinkled her nose at the stink and delicately touched the hot and swollen flesh with a fingertip, probing around the ugly gash that wept pus.

"Re-Usey, what is pus? Why is it here?"

The court physician pursed his lips and frowned. If anyone else had asked he would have given a sharp answer, but that was not advisable with the queen.

"It is thought that the body produces it, Great Lady. We know the brain produces mucus to wash away dust from the nose and throat, and it would seem that it also produces pus in wounds, though exactly why, we cannot tell."

"To wash something away?" Hori hazarded.

"But what?" Re-Usey countered. "And why only some wounds?"

"Could it be that the demon brings it?" Tausret asked. "If there is no pus in the chest wound where the demon did not enter, but there is in the arm wound where the demon did enter, then it seems likely the pus is a result of the demon's presence."

"It is hard to argue with your logic," Bay commented.

"It is possible," Re-Usey allowed. "And it is likely that when we expel the demon, the pus will leave also."

"What if we removed the pus ourselves?" Tausret asked. She picked up a cloth and gently wiped the wound, drawing blood-tinged pus away. "Could we remove the pus and thereby drive the demon out?"

"That is back to front," the physician said. "It would disturb ma'at to go contrary to accepted wisdom."

"On the other hand, the demon is killing the king," Bay said. "How would it hurt to try such a procedure?"

"I...I cannot recommend it," Re-Usey said.

"I will take responsibility," Tausret said. She wiped the wound again and Seti moaned at the touch. "Look. His arm is especially swollen just here above the wound, with the hot skin drawn tight as a drum. It is as if the demon or its pus sits right underneath." Tausret stopped her wiping and stared at her husband's arm for several minutes while the droning incantations of the priests continued, and the clouds on incense grew thicker.

"Hand me a sharp knife, Re-Usey."

The physician looked at Hori and Bay, making no move to obey the queen.

"Why do you want a knife, Great Lady?" Bay asked.

"Is it not obvious? The demon must be excised."

"That...that is a very dangerous action, Great Lady," Re-Usey protested. "We should allow the gods to act through the prayers of the priests."

"Will that work?" Tausret demanded. When the physician did not reply, she asked again, adding, "Have you known it to work?"

"On occasion, Great Lady." Re-Usey hesitated and then admitted, "Seldom when the wound is this bad."

"Then we must take the risk, I must take the risk. Give me the knife."

Re-Usey looked at Hori and Bay again, but this time they just shrugged. He took a sharp copper knife from his bag of instruments and handed it to Tausret. She examined the blade and tested it with her thumb.

"This is going to hurt the king," she said. "You must hold him down."

"Lay hands on the king?" Hori gasped in dismay. "I cannot."

"You must." Tausret waited until the two officials and the physician's assistants had overcome their scruples and grasped the king's limbs firmly and then touched the swollen arm gently, the knife poised above the inflamed flesh.

"Forgive me, husband," Tausret murmured, and drew the sharp copper blade across the taut skin, piercing deep into the arm. Blood and pus fountained up, spattering Tausret's face and arms, as Seti surged up, fighting the grip of the men holding him and uttering a great inchoate cry. The men forced him down again and he struggled weakly before collapsing.

"Is...is he dead?" one of the assistant's asked.

"No, but while he is unconscious, let us clean away this filth of the demon's presence." Tausret wiped down the king's arm, using cloth after cloth as the blood-streaked pus flowed and then slowed, bright blood alone taking its place. The flesh of the arm remained hot and red, but was not as swollen as before, and when the queen pressed her fingers into the wound, it was mostly blood that issued forth.

The physician called for water and drew the queen aside gently, motioning his assistants forward. "Leave him, Great Lady, and we will clean him and bandage his wounds."

Tausret allowed herself to be drawn away. "Wash every trace of pus from his wounds, Re-Usey," she said. "For I believe the demon resides in such filth. You saw how it leapt out of his arm when the knife pierced it. When the wounds are clean, then bind them with clean cloths and apply the prayers as the priests desire. We have done what we can, and it is now in the hands of the gods."

Userkheperure Seti lay as if dead for three days, while the city and an ever-expanding circle of the country wailed the loss of their young king, uttering lamentations and offering sacrifices to the healing gods. Tausret stayed by her husband's side, wiping away his sweat with river-cooled water and washing the wounds afresh twice a day. After the second day, there was no sign of pus and the priests ventured the hope that their prayers had driven the demon from the king's flesh.

On the fourth day, Seti stirred and groaned, his eyelids fluttering open, and he stared at the face of his wife. He whispered through dry, cracked lips and Tausret bent close to listen, but could make no sense of the words.

"Bring watered wine mixed with honey," she ordered, and when it was brought, spooned tiny amounts into Seti's mouth, massaging his throat gently until he swallowed.

Life returned to the king's eyes, and he managed a weak smile. "I saw the gods," he whispered. "While I lay here, my Ba journeyed to the Land of the Dead and spoke with the gods."

"Rest now, my love," Tausret said.

"They said it was not my time and I saw myself old on the throne and my son reigning after me..."

"Hush," Tausret admonished. "Sleep now and gather your strength."

Seti slept, and when he awoke he said he could remember nothing of what he had said. Tausret remembered, and in the days ahead it gave her comfort to believe the gods still looked favourably on the House of Ramesses.

The second wound, the one Tausret had inflicted with the sharp copper knife, healed quickly, the flood of released blood apparently having washed the cut flesh clean of all traces of the demon. Red fragments of flesh still clung to the original wound though, and gave the king considerable pain. He set such ills aside and insisted on standing at the Window of Appearance in the palace where he could be seen by the gathered multitudes.

He dressed with care in the finest raiments, adorned with an inlaid pectoral and golden arm bands. The double crown, coupled with this gaunt face, gave him the appearance of aged wisdom and many older men whose memory stretched back that far, said he resembled the old king, Usermaatre. Seti was careful not to move his left arm, keeping it hanging by his side and covered with a loose-fitting tunic, but he waved with his right hand and made signs of blessing with it, smiling as the cheering of his people washed over him.

When Queen Tausret appeared beside the king, holding the infant Prince Seti-Merenptah in her arms, the noise of the population of Men-nefer rose until the royal couple could hardly hear themselves speak. Tausret waved and smiled, and held up the Prince, until Seti leaned against her, pain showing in his face.

He leaned close and whispered, "I am sick, my love."

Tausret beckoned to Chancellor Bay and had him make an announcement from the Window, telling him what to say as she drew the king back into the room.

Bay held his hands up for quiet, and when the sound had fallen away sufficiently, spoke. "People of Men-nefer, rejoice that your King Userkheperure and Queen Tausret are here, and that the young Prince Seti-Merenptah is healthy. The king bids you finish your tasks and duties of the day without complaint, and he will order prime cattle slaughtered so that you may feast and celebrate tonight. May Userkheperure Seti, Son of Re, Lord of the Two Lands and High Priest of Every God rule us all for a thousand years."

The physicians were called again, and the priests. They discussed treatments, this amulet or that prayer, such-and-such a dung or plant juice or packing in honey, and in the end the Hem-netjer of Set offered a treatment that appealed to their sense of rightness.

"Our land of Kemet is a land in balance, red land and black land, as we all know. Kemet however is angered by the war waged between brothers that disturbs such a natural balance," the priest of Set said. "If the red wound inflicted on the younger brother by the older is ever to heal, it must draw strength and healing from the rich black soil of the land. The blackness of the soil will balance the redness of the angry flesh and bring healing Ma'at to the king's body. I say let the king's wound be packed with the good black earth of Kemet and bound tightly, while prayers are once more offered up to the gods."

And for a time, the treatment seemed to work.

Chapter 48

U serkheperure Seti speaks:

It is no use complaining. The gods have spoken and though I do not like what they have to say, I must bend to their will. My brother Messuwy's hand has reached out over months and across the length of the Iteru to strike me down. The knife he wielded has let in a poison which works its way ever deeper into my body despite the efforts of my wife, the court physician and a whole bevy of priests. They tell me what they want to believe, that I am a young king with many years still ahead of me, but I know differently, for the gods spoke to me as I lay sleeping in my fever.

It was the strangest thing.

I have never fully understood the many components that make up a man, but as I understand it, the Ib is my heart and is where my will and emotions lie, my Sheut or shadow is that part of me cast by the light of Re, the Ren is my name bound about by the rope-like protective Shenu, the Ba is the part of me that makes me who I am, the Ka is the spirit that energises my body. Now the Khat is my physical body and when I die the Ba and Ka unite to reanimate my Akh, which I suppose is the magical non-physical counterpart of my Khat. At least, that is what the priests tell us.

Anyway, my Khat lay on the bed, administered by my beloved wife, by the priests and court physician, while I hovered above, near the ceiling of the bedchamber, looking down on them. I remember thinking that the priest of Sekhmet had had his scalp cut while it was being shaved, for I could see a tiny trickle of dried blood where others could not see. What part of me hovered there I do not know, but I think it was my Ba, for the Ka supposedly only leaves when the ceremony of the opening of the mouth is performed. That did not happen, so it must have been my Ba alone that rose up.

I drifted through the ceiling as if through wide portals, or as if I was no more than smoke, and nobody remarked on my passing. I saw the palace and the city pass beneath me, and then suddenly I was walking on springy green turf and the air was cool and moist upon my skin though the face of Re still smote my head and shoulders. I walked for a time alone, and then others were with me, though I did not see them arrive.

"Welcome Userkheperure Seti," spoke a voice beside me.

I turned to look at the speaker and saw a tall man clad in rich raiments and gold, and his beautiful face shone with holiness, by which I understood him to be Ptah of the Beautiful Face. Around him were arrayed other beings, noble of bearing, and I recognised Re and Heru, and Amun and Tefnut. I would have fallen to my knees in worship, but Ptah shook his head.

"That is not why you are here, Userkheperure," he said.

"Why then am I here, Lord of Truth?" I asked. "Am I truly dead?"

"Not yet." He pointed to where a thin silver cord trailed behind me. "While the cord remains, your Khat remains alive."

"Then I am soon to die?"

Ptah nodded, and then added. "But not yet. Return to your body and to your wife and son. Enjoy them while you may, for your time is short, Userkheperure."

"What will happen, Lord of Truth? What does the future hold?"

"That is not for man to know. Kemet will endure."

"What of my son, Seti-Merenptah?"

"Kemet will endure."

With that, I felt myself falling and within moments felt my eyelids open and the lovely face of my Tausret swam into view.

"I saw the gods," I whispered. "I journeyed to the Land of the Dead and spoke with the gods."

"Rest now, my love," Tausret said.

I opened my mouth to tell her what Ptah had said, that I was to die shortly, but decided I could not visit that upon her. Besides, it might all have been a dream, for what man can truly know the future? So I lied.

"They said it was not my time and I saw myself old on the throne and my son reigning after me..."

"Hush," Tausret admonished. "Sleep now and gather your strength."

I slept, and when I woke I feigned ignorance of what I had said before. For a time, I lay in my bed thinking, and then I decided the word 'soon' meant different things for gods and men. Like Kemet, the gods endure while men live their brief lives and pass away, so to the gods the fact that I would die soon could mean a day, a year, or fifty years. However long it was, it was wasted if I lay in bed waiting for death, so I got up.

Perhaps I arose too quickly. My Ka was willing but my Khat was still weak and my arm still pained me. Sweat beaded my brow and the pulse raced in my temples, but I willed myself to stand as if nothing was wrong. I managed to show myself at the Window of Appearances so that the people would know they still had a king, but afterward, I was quite exhausted. Still, I was determined to continue my life. I sent for my Tjaty and General Iurudef, and learned of the depredations the Sea Peoples were making on our northern borders.

No matter what span of life was still allotted to me, no king of Kemet could stand idly by and allow these foreign incursions, so I bundled Iurudef off with instructions to gather the legions in preparation of a major offensive. I would drive the Sea Peoples back inside their cities at the very least.

Then I went to where my beloved Tausret played with my infant son and sat with her, greedy for her company, and enjoying the sights and sounds, the remembered feel and familiar aromas of her lovely body. Seti-Merenptah is a strong and lively little boy, already making attempts to stand upon his own two feet and the firmness of his grasp on my extended finger is amazing for one so young. I can see the strength of the king he will one day become, and know that Kemet is in good hands. If the gods call me home soon, I know my queen will guard him and set him upon the Double Throne in due course. She has good counsellors, Tjaty Hori and Chancellor Bay, to call upon, and strong well-trained legions to guard against unrest. Truly, now that the threat of my brother has been put to rest, the security of my kingdom is assured.

Chapter 49
Year 6 of Userkheperure Seti

L ate in the final month of Akhet, the inundation, when the water was receding from the flooded fields, leaving rich black silt spread over the land, Userkheperure Seti took a ferry over the still swollen river to the eastern bank. There, at the head of a small squadron of chariots, he drove north and east along the royal road to join his legions for the coming war.

Seti chose not to drive his own chariot as his arm was hurting him again. The arm throbbed and felt hot and, despite being packed with fresh, cool black silt from the heart of Ta Mehu, showed livid red streaks ascending up to the shoulder. He hung on to the wicker frame of the war chariot with his right hand and tried not to sway against the body of the charioteer with his left. His head was hot, he sweated profusely despite the coolness of the day, and his pulse hammered in his temples.

He broke his journey regularly, despite the need to join up with his legions, as he just felt too unwell to put in a full day's travel. As camp was set up each day, Seti took himself down to the muddy edge of the river, stripped off his bandages and bathed the swollen blistered flesh of his left arm. For two or three days, nobody dared comment on the king's condition, despite the obvious pain he was in, but eventually his charioteer ventured an opinion.

"Forgive my presumption, Son of Re, but your wound needs the attention of a physician...or a priest," he added.

Seti grimaced and swayed where he stood. "We will stop at Iunu. There are physicians and priests aplenty there."

The king's charioteer took it upon himself to dispatch a chariot ahead of the squadron to alert the authorities in Iunu of the king's arrival and of his condition. After a few moments' consideration, he also sent one back to Men-nefer to carry the word to the queen.

The priests of the numerous temples in Iunu were waiting for the king and ushered him into the temple of Atum, the creator god, where the most experienced physicians were on hand. They almost had to carry the king from the chariot to the temple, and laid him on a bed covered with clean linen for the examination. Normally circumspect in their speech, especially in front of an exalted patient, the physicians and priests discussed the course of the king's affliction.

"The flesh rots. You can smell it from ten paces."

"You can hear it too. The flesh crackles like a fire through dry reeds when you press the swollen flesh."

"Indeed, a fire burns within him..."

"...and it will consume him unless it is doused."

"What can be done?"

"The black earth cure has not worked."

"Or rather, the blackness has passed into his flesh and wars with the redness within, threatening to carry life away before it like the inundation."

"The time for such remedies has passed."

"Could the arm, containing the blackness and redness within, be cut off?"

"He would never survive the operation."

"And if he did, he would be a crippled king."

"What say the Nine of Iunu? Will you speak for them, Hem-netjer of Atum?"

The high priest of Atum, clad in all his ceremonial regalia, stood over the supine king and looked down, compassion in his eyes. "All things pass," he said. "The gods set out a span of life for every man and it avails nothing to fight against what the gods have ordained."

"The king is scarce of middle age," protested one of the younger physicians. "Can nothing be done?"

"Prayers will be offered up for the life and health of the king," the Hem-netjer of Atum said. "But prayers are only the words of men and though they beat about the heads of the gods like bats on a summer night, the gods answer only to their will."

Seti's eyelids fluttered open and he looked up at the gathered physicians and priests. He licked his lips and attempted a smile. "Am I dying?" he asked.

None of the physicians could meet the king's gaze, or any priest save that of Atum. He smiled down on the fevered man on the bed and said, "It is likely, Son of Re."

"How long?"

"Who can say? That is with the gods."

"Is my beloved...is the Queen here?"

The king's charioteer stepped forward and cleared his throat. "Queen Tausret has been sent for, Son of Re."

A pained smile crossed the king's face. "Really?" he whispered. "I did not think I would ever meet a man who could 'send for' the queen and live."

The charioteer flushed deeply and stammered. "M...my apol...apologies, Son of Re. I meant to say she has been...been notified."

Seti lay in silence for a time. The rays of sunlight cast golden patches on the floor and walls of the chamber and slowly moved as the face of Re ascended and then began its slow descent to the west. The senior physicians drifted away, telling each other that nothing could be done. A junior apprentice bathed the king's face with a cool, damp cloth, and the Hem-netjer of Atum sent the other priests away, but stayed himself.

"Pray she comes soon," Seti muttered, "for I feel the wings of death beating me about my face."

"Is there a message I should give her if she does not?" the priest asked. "It is a long way to Men-nefer and back."

"Tell her I love her...and my infant son..."

"All of Kemet knows that," the priest said with a smile.

Seti shook his head weakly. "It is as the gods said, but I wish I could have lived to see my son ready to sit upon the throne."

"Be strong, Son of Re. The queen will come swiftly when she hears the news. You may yet gaze upon her once more."

Shadow fell upon the chamber as the sun sank and passed below the western horizon. The king's breathing became hoarse as he struggled against the rotting blackness that now claimed his whole left arm and was starting to invade his chest. Torches were sent for and flickering light and shadow replaced the warmth of the day. As the night chill crept into the chamber, a fleece was brought for the king and tucked around his shivering form. Seti moaned as it was set about him and pushed it away with his good arm.

The torches burned low and were replaced. Another young physician took the place of an exhausted one and kept the king comfortable, but the priest remained standing beside the bed through the long night, counting the seconds between each ragged indrawn breath and watching the king's life soak away like water in sand.

At cockcrow the king rallied, opening his eyes and making a weak movement with the fingers of his right hand. The priest brought him water in a simple wooden cup and held his arm beneath the king's burning head as he sipped cool river water. As the dawn lit the room with a faint rosy glow, the priest saw that the blackness had spread onto the king's chest and neck. The bed linen was soaked with watery blood and stank of rottenness.

"Tausret..." Seti breathed. "Is she...?"

"She is coming, Son of Re, but I think not quickly enough. If you have words for her, you must tell me."

The queen came with the noonday heat, windblown and covered in dust, the horses that drew her chariot soaked with sweat and staggering in their traces. Far behind her, the two-man chariots of her escort laboured toward the city and the outlying spiral of temples dedicated to the Nine of Iunu.

Tausret leapt from the chariot and strode to the tall figure of the Hem-netjer of Atum where he stood in the inky shade of the great temple.

"Where is he? Take me to him. Quickly."

"There is no hurry, Great Lady. The king has passed beyond the cognisance of men."

A soft moan escaped Tausret's lips and for a moment she clutched at the priest's arm for support. Then she straightened and her eyes no more than glistened with tears held rigidly in check.

"Take me to him," she commanded.

The priest led her to the inner chamber where the king's body now lay on pristine linen sheets. Incense burned in braziers, filling the room with a sweet smell that could not quite cover the stench of rotting flesh. Tausret's lips thinned when she entered the room and her eyes now glittered with anger.

"How long has the king lain in death? Why have the embalmers not taken him, for already the stink of death is upon him."

"Not so, Great Lady, for what you smell is the stink of his last illness. He died but a sun's finger width before you arrived, calling upon you with his last breath. The embalmers are on their way here even as we speak."

Tausret wept at the news, her slim body shaking with grief, but then she brushed her tears away with her hands, and with a visible effort composed herself. "Send the embalmers back then, priest of Atum, and have a swift boat prepared. I will carry the body of my husband the king back to Men-nefer where he shall lie in dignity in the Place of Purification."

"He would be treated with respect here in Iunu, Great Lady. There is no need..."

"I will take him to Men-nefer where he belongs, priest. Now find me that boat."

Swiftly a boat was found, a fishing boat rather than a barge, because Tausret could not wait for one to be brought from Men-nefer. Instead, she oversaw the loading of the king's body upon the deck. She allowed the embalmers to pack the body about with spices and incense, for already the corpse was bloating and the rotting flesh of the arm and chest gave off a stench that appalled any who came too close. Tausret sailed not long after the sun's zenith, with two companion guards and the owner of the boat who had been paid in fine gold to sail his vessel.

Tausret sat beside the body of her husband all the way to Men-nefer, and paid no heed to the stench that surrounded her and blew with them on the light northerly wind that sped the boat up the river. From time to time, the guards and the boat owner surreptitiously vomited over the side, seeking to hide the disrespect to the king's person implicit in their actions.

And so they came to white-walled Men-nefer as the dawn broke the next day, having sailed by moon and starlight through the night. The city was in mourning, with every colourful banner removed and black banners mixed with red in honour of the god Set and Seti the king named for him. The boat pulled up to the royal wharf and willing hands conveyed the king's body onto a bier. Faces smeared with river mud turned to follow the passage of their king and a great wailing arose from the population as the procession wound its way through the streets to the Place of Purification and the waiting embalmers.

Tausret spoke with the Head Embalmer as Seti's body was hurried off to be packed in natron. She gave simple instructions that he was to be treated as a king.

"Of course, Great Lady, that goes without saying, but..." The embalmer's voice trailed off and he licked his lips.

"But?"

"Great Lady, the body stinks already. Was nothing done to preserve it?"

"The stink is of the king's last illness, though it has been nearly a day since he died. Do your best, your very best. Spare no expense."

"I shall work on the body myself, Great Lady."

Tausret nodded and left the man to his task in the Place of Purification. She returned to the palace and started through to her rooms, waving away her companions. Tjaty Hori bustled up, as did Chancellor Bay, their faces carefully set in expressions of horror and grief.

"Great Lady," Hori said. "Even in these grievous times, we must make provision for proper governance. Shall I take charge?"

Anger flitted across the queen's face, swiftly extinguished. "Thank you, Hori. Take care of the day-to-day business of Men-nefer and Ta Mehu, as is your purview. Chancellor Bay, I want you to send out fast messengers to General Iurudef in the north and General Setnakhte in the south. I want them here in Men-nefer just as soon as they can manage."

"Yes, Great Lady," Bay said. "With how many legions?"

"No legions; just them. I want them here quickly and without fuss. There are decisions to be made."

"My Lady," Hori said hesitantly. "Only the king can order the generals away from their stations."

"The king is dead..."

"Yes, Lady, but..."

"...and I act in his name. Until my son Seti-Merenptah is crowned king over Kemet, I am the Regent. Do you dispute it?"

Hori glanced at Bay and saw his non-committal expression. He swallowed and bowed. "No, Great Lady."

"Then do as I command, both of you."

Tausret turned on her heel and strode quickly for her suite of rooms, dismissing her servants and shutting herself in her bedchamber. There, out of sight of all eyes but those of the gods, she gave vent to her grief, crying aloud and tearing at her dust-stained and grimy clothing.

Chapter 50

Tausret speaks:

For ten days I gave in to grief. Tjaty Hori governed the north and Tjaty Paraemheb the south while I mourned the loss of my beloved. We are taught that all things happen by the will of the gods, but I asked them loudly and with many tears how Kemet was served by snatching my Seti away at such a young age. He was a good king and would have achieved more than the records of the temples attest had not his brother absorbed most of his energy. His death was down to his brother too, and for that I would not forgive him.

So grief occupied my days as I wept within my rooms, my only companions being my women and my dear son, my husband's only living legacy. Tjaty Hori called upon me several times, but each time I sent him away, saying I could not yet face the world. The city mourned with me, the usual bustle and noise of commerce and daily life being muted, but gradually the exigencies of life intruded on the common people and by degrees invaded my privacy. One day, I knew that my period of grief had come to an end. I would have to face the world again and rule Kemet in my husband's place. Decisions had to be made, and I would have to be the one to make them.

Five days had passed from my commands being sent out to the arrival of General Iurudef from the northern borders and five more before a boat arrived from Waset. Hori came to my chambers again on the eleventh day to tell me that my presence was needed and I was ready for him, bathed and dressed in my queenly finery.

General Iurudef bowed low when I entered the throne room and I bade him rise before turning to the man standing beside him. I was taken aback to find it was not General Setnakhte but rather Deputy Commander of the Amun Legion, Ament.

"I had not thought to see you here, Ament, though you are welcome," I said as he came forward and bowed in his turn. "Where is Setnakhte?"

"He is indisposed, Great Lady," Ament replied. "He bade me come in his stead."

"Does he not realise how important this meeting is?"

"I think he knows only too well," Chancellor Bay said quietly. "And that is the reason he sends another in his place."

"What do you mean?"

"Only that the succession must be decided, and Setnakhte is a son of Usermaatre, though with a lowly concubine."

"He has designs on the throne?" Iurudef asked, shock showing in his face. "How dare he?"

Bay shrugged. "His claim is weak while Userkheperure's son lives, but if his direct line was to die out, some would support him. I do not call him disloyal, but he would not favour the only other contender for the throne, Userkheperure's nephew Siptah, and so he absents himself lest he be forced to declare himself against Siptah."

"Siptah?" I said. "He is a good boy but crippled and sickly; hardly kingly material. Besides, he is son of that traitor Messuwy, and I will not countenance that man's offspring on the throne."

"I do not put him forward, Great Lady, for that would be presumptuous. It is not my place to argue for him, but I remind you all that Userkheperure Seti specifically absolved the boy from any of the blame of his father's actions," Bay said.

"And the fact that he is the son of your sister Suterere has nothing to do with it," Iurudef said.

"I would not put my family's interests ahead of Kemet's."

"How selfless," Iurudef said dryly. "And I don't believe it for a second."

"Enough of this senseless bickering," I exclaimed. "My son by the king, Seti-Merenptah, is the heir, and that is the only consideration."

"Your son is only a baby, Great Lady," Hori said. "He cannot possibly rule."

"Obviously not," I replied. "That is why I shall rule in his stead, as regent, until he comes of age."

The two military men nodded their assent, and Bay kept his face expressionless at my words, which surprised me, for I thought I knew his heart. What surprised me more was Hori's objection.

"Great Lady, undoubtedly Seti-Merenptah is his father's son, and by law should ascend the throne of Kemet, but there are other considerations.

The kingdoms have just gone through a time of great unrest, where brother fought brother and everyone suffered the loss of Ma'at. What Kemet needs more than anything else is a time of healing. The people need to see that the times of unrest are behind us, and what better way to do that than to bring the brothers together in Kemet's future?"

"I hope you are not talking of raising the traitor Messuwy to the throne," Ament said. "The army would oppose you and the country would be plunged back into civil war."

"No, not Messuwy, but rather his son," Hori said. "Seti-Merenptah is plainly the heir, let no man dispute that, but Kemet needs someone on the throne that can unite the Lands. Someone that people know to be of royal descent. I say, let Siptah rule as king until Seti-Merenptah comes of age."

"Never," I said. "That would be to allow Messuwy the victory."

"He would be king only until Seti-Merenptah is old enough," Hori said.

"And when Siptah has a son and wishes to make him heir?"

"It could be a condition of his enthronement, that Seti-Merenptah is his heir."

I looked at Bay. "You remain silent, Chancellor, while another speaks to your family's benefit."

"I am your servant, Great Lady," he replied. "I hesitate to put my nephew forward lest it seems self-serving, but really, Siptah is a grandson of Baenre Merenptah, as is Seti-Merenptah, and who better to hold the throne of Kemet until your son comes of age?"

"Only hold? You do not seek to make him king permanently?"

"We know the gods are fickle," Hori said. "Anything could happen in the twelve or fourteen years of Seti-Merenptah's minority, either to him or to Siptah."

"I have already said I would act as regent during that time," I replied. "What need of Siptah?"

"Except you are a woman, Great Lady, and Kemet is traditionally ruled by men."

"There are exceptions."

"Indeed, Great Lady, but none particularly successful. If there is a war..."

"I have led legions in battle."

"Even so, Great Lady, a man, even a boy, would unite both sides of Kemet's recent War of Brothers. And if you think a boy is not up to the task, then think of Nebkheperure Tutankhamen. A boy when he was made king, but he ruled successfully for ten years..."

"Or rather his uncle Ay ruled for him," Ament said.

"And he had a strong general in Horemheb to guard Kemet's borders," added Iurudef.

"We have strong generals now," Hori pointed out. "You and Setnakhte, with strong legions under them. Also, in place of Ay, we have the superlative skills of Queen Tausret and Chancellor Bay to guide him politically, and a strong Tjaty to govern each of the kingdoms."

And so I was persuaded. Kemet needed healing after the civil war that had so thoroughly disrupted Ma'at and I knew in my heart that our son Seti-Merenptah was too young to reign, even with me as regent. I had nothing against Siptah except that he was the son of Messuwy, so why should he not reign until Seti-Merenptah was of age? I did not want the throne for myself; I would be content as regent. I had advisers in Hori and Bay, and strong generals to guard the frontiers. Best of all I had a good friend in Ament, and I resolved to bring him back to Men-nefer to resume the command of the Set Legion or even a local legion that would guard Seti-Merenptah until he came of age. Siptah would have to be shunted aside when that time came, but if it came to a choice between a crippled king and a strong prince and heir of the former king, I had no doubt whom the gods would choose.

Ah, my beloved husband Seti, I grieve that you have passed the portals of death, but I shall ensure that our son rules after you and to that end I will rule Kemet no matter who actually sits on the Double Throne. I make that my vow.

The story of the
Fall of the House of Ramesses
will conclude in
Book 3: Tausret

Places, People, Gods & Things in Fall of the House of Ramesses

Abdju
city of Abydos, near modern day el-'Araba el Madfuna

Abu
(1)   city of Elephantine, near modern day Aswan
(2)   elephant

Ahmes
(1) neru pehut, Shepherd of the Royal Anus
(2) Commander of the Set Legion after Iurudef is promoted to General of the North

Akh
magical non-physical counterpart of the physical body or Khat

Akhet-aten
the city built by the Heretic, Akhenaten

Amenhirkashef
High Priest of Amun in Men-nefer

Amenhotep
(1) Third Prophet of Amun in Waset
(2) Troop Commander elevated to Commander of the Amun Legion by Messuwy

Amenmesse
born Messuwy, eldest son of Merenptah, later king Menmire Amenmesse

Amenmose
Tjaty of the South after Khaemter; grandson of the Hem-netjer of Heru

Ament
Leader of Five, later Leader of Fifty, Guardian of Tausret and Seti, then demoted. Later made Captain of Palace Guard, Troop Commander of Per-Bast Legion, Commander of Set Legion, deputy Commander of the Amun Legion; Adviser to the Queen.

Amun
creator deity, local god of Thebes (Waset), often worshipped as Amun-Re (Amun-Ra)

Amunherkhepershef
eldest son of Ramesses II

Amurru
roughly equivalent to modern day Syria

Anapa
the god Anubis

Anapepy
Chief Scribe of Merenptah and Seti II

Aniba
administrative capital of Wawat (Northern Kush)

Anupemheb
(1) a scribe in the Place of Truth
(2) court physician under Seti II

Asar
Osiris, god of the underworld and resurrection

Ashkelon
a Philistine city

Atum
the Creator god

Auset
the goddess Isis. Sometimes called Aset or Iset

Ba
the self

Baenre
throne name of Merenptah

Bakenkhons
Second Prophet of Amun in Waset, later Hem-netjer

Bay
an Amorite servant, Scribe, later Royal Butler, then Chancellor, also brother of Suterere and uncle of Siptah

Behdet
city south of Waset, modern day Edfu

Ben-ben
the sacred mound of creation; also the capstone on a pyramids and by extension the whole pyramid

Bennu
a bandit leader in Kush

Bes
god worshipped as protector of mothers, children, childbirth

Besenmut
Commander of the Ptah legion under Merenptah and Seti II

Deben
a unit of weight that in the New Kingdom was about 91 grams. Divided into ten kite.

Disebek
Commander of the Re legion

Djanet
city in the north-east of Ta Mehu, Tanis

Djau
Troop Commander of the Amun Legion; Acting Commander in the absence of Merenkhons

Djehuti
the god Thoth

Duamutef
a protection god of the Canopic jars, son of Heru

Eilah
a coastal town on the east side of the Land of Sin; modern day Eilat

Emsaf
Commander of the Heru Legion

Ephrim
a Canaanite slave boy at Timna, rescued by Ament

Geb
god of the earth

Gebti
or Gebtu, Coptos, modern day town of Qift

Gezer
a Philistine city

Ghazzat
modern day Gaza

Great Field

Ta-sekhet-ma'at, Valley of the Kings
Hapi
a protection god of the Canopic jars, son of Heru. The river god

Hatti
the Hittites
Hay
a Foreman of the Great Field

Heka
the Crook, a symbol of kingly authority

Hemaka
a junior scribe in the service of Amenmesse

Hem-netjer
High Priest

Henen-nesut
Herakleopolis, city near modern day Beni Suef

Henty
hedgehog

Henuttaneb
mother of Tausret

Heru
the god Horus

House of Purification
The House of Embalming

Hori
(1) son of Khaemwaset, later Hem-netjer of Ptah and Governor of Men-nefer
(2) son of Hori (1), Tjaty of the North
(3) son of Kama; First Charioteer and King's Messenger

Huni
Captain of the Guard in Seti IIs court outside Waset

Hut-hor
the goddess Hathor

Hut-Repyt
city in Ta Shemau, near modern day village of Wannina

Hut-waret
city of Avaris in Ta Mehu that was absorbed into the city of Per-Ramesses; centre of worship of the god Set

Ib
the heart

Intef
embalmer in Men-nefer

Iteru
the Great River; the River Nile

Iunu
a northern city, Heliopolis, now north-east edge of Cairo

Iurudef
Commander of the Set Legion; later General of the North

Jerem
a Canaanite slave boy at Timna, rescued by Ament

Jochim
Chief of the Shechite tribe in the Land of Sin

Ka
the vital essence, the soul

Kadesh
town in southern Amurru or Syria, site of a battle between the Hittites and Egyptians under Ramesses II

Kaftor
one of the Sea Peoples, the Philistines

Kament-Huy
Governor of the Ahment nome (administrative district)

Kemet
the land of Egypt

Kemetu
Egyptian, the people of Egypt

Kenhirkhopeshef
Scribe of the Great Field

Khaemter
Troop Commander in Napata, elevated to Viceroy after Messuwy is deposed, Tjaty of the South under Amenmesse

Khaemwaset
fourth son of Ramesses II, Sem-priest of Ptah

Khat
the physical body

Khent-Min
city north of Waset, modern day Akhmim

Khepresh Crown
the Blue Crown commonly worn in battle; it was made of cloth or leather

Khepre
Khepri, an aspect of the sun god Re

Khmun
Hermopolis, city in Ta Shemau near modern day El Ashmunein

Khonsu
god of the moon; son of Amun and Mut

Khopesh Sword
curved sword evolved from a battle axe; later had more of a ceremonial function

Khufu's Horizon
the Great Pyramid of Giza built by Khufu c.2560 BCE

King's Son of Kush
Viceroy of Nubia

Kush
Nubia

Kushite
people of Kush

Ma'at
Goddess of Truth and Justice; also the concept of truth, order, law and balance

Mahuhy
Royal Secretary under Seti II

Medjay
an elite paramilitary police force

Menkauhor
Troop Commander of the Amun Legion; later made Legion Commander by Menmire Amenmesse

Menmaatre
throne name of Seti I

Men-nefer
ancient capital of Lower Egypt, Memphis

Menpehtyre
throne name of Ramesses I

Mentmose
Chief Palace Physician under Merenptah

Mentopher
Mine Overseer at Timna

Merenkhons
commander of Amun Legion under Seti II after Setnakhte demoted

Merenptah
thirteenth son of Ramesses II, King of Egypt, father of Seti and Messuwy

Meres
Garrison Commander at Eilah

Meryma'at
a grandson of Pareherwenemef, a rebel

Meryre
son of Meryatum, priest of Iunu; a rebel

Merysekhmet
Tjaty of the North under Merenptah and Seti II

Messuwy
eldest son of Merenptah, later King Menmire Amenmesse

Min
god of fertility

Mose
estate owner near Ta-senet who supported Messuwy

Mut
the mother goddess; consort of Amun

Nakhtu-aa
close-combat troops

Napata
capital of Kush

Nebamen
Military Commander at Timna

Nebmaatre
throne name of Amenhotep III

Neferhotep
(1) a Foreman of the Great Field
(2) Captain of the Palace Guard after Ament

Neferronpet
Tjaty of the South (Ta Shemau)

Neith
goddess of war and hunting

Nekhakha
the Flail, a symbol of kingly authority

Nekhen
Hierakonpolis, city of Hawks, south of Waset, opposite modern day El
Kab

Nine of Iunu
The Ennead of Iunu; the nine gods associated with creation, Atum, Shu,
Tefnut, Geb, Nut, Asar, Auset, Set, Heru & Nebt-Het

Nubt
city in Ta Shemau, modern day town of Kom Ombo

Nut
goddess of the night

Opet Festival
A celebration held annually in Waset in the second month of the Inundation

Paneb
adopted son of Neferhotep; a troublemaker

Panhesy
a Leader of One Hundred in the Ptah Legion

Paraemheb
Tjaty of the South under Seti II after the fall of Amenmesse

Pareherwenemef
third son of Ramesses II

Paser
a scribe in the Place of Truth

Pehe-mau
hippopotamus

Per-Asar
a city in Ta Mehu

Per-Bast
Bubastis, a city in Ta Mehu

Perire
a city on the western border of Ta Mehu

Per-Ramesses
the capital city of Ramesses II

Per-Wadjet
city in Ta Mehu near modern day Desouk

Pesheskef
a spooned blade used in the ceremony of the Opening of the Mouth

Place of Purification
the House of Embalming

Place of Truth
the village where the workers in the Valley of the Kings resided

Ptah
god of craftsmen and architects, associated with the city of Men-nefer (Memphis)

Qebehsenuef
a protection god of the Canopic jars, son of Heru

Qenna
a Troop Commander in the Kushite army

Ramesses
(1) King of Egypt (Ramesses II)
(2) second son of Ramesses II
(3) son of Khaemwaset
(4) son of Setnakhte, later Ramesses III

Ramose
(1) Treasurer under Seti II, succeeded by Bay
(2) Overseer of Fish in Waset

Ramses
a grandson of Pareherwenemef, a rebel

Re
(Ra) sun god, often worshipped as Amun-Re or Atum-Re

Rekhmire
embalmer in Men-nefer

Remaktef
a scribe, grandson of Kenhirkhopeshef

Ren
a man's Name

Rephidim
a tribe of the Land of Sin, named for a place of the same name

Retenu
Canaan, present-day Israel, Jordan, and Lebanon

Re-Usey
Physician of the King's Mouth under Merenptah and Seti II

Ribu
a tribe in eastern Libya

Roma-Rui
Hem-netjer of Amun in Waset

Royal Butler
a high-ranking official in the Royal Court

Samut
Commander of the Amun Legion under Amenmesse

Sea Peoples
a loose amalgamation of sea-faring tribes from around the Mediterranean. Included the Phoenicians, Greeks, and Philistines. Other tribes include the Ekwesh, Denyen, teresh, Peleset, Shekelesh and Sherden.

Seb-Ur
an instrument used in the ceremony of the Opening of the Mouth

Sekhmet
warrior goddess and goddess of healing

Senet
a popular game involving a board and pieces

Sepat
a nome, or administrative district

Serket
goddess of healing venomous stings and bites

Set
Seth, god of desert, storms, disorder and violence, Lord of the Red Land (desert)

Setat
a unit of area, 10,000 square cubits or 0.276 hectares

Setau
Viceroy of Kush before Messuwy

Sethi
(1) ninth son of Ramesses II
(2) son of Horire, military adviser to Messuwy, later General under Menmire Amenmesse

Seti
(1) Seti I, father of Ramesses II
(2) son of Merenptah, later Seti II

Set-ma'at
the Place of Truth; the workmen's village near the Valley of the Kings

Setnakhte
a younger son of Ramesses II by one of his concubines, commander of the Amun legion, and later General of the South

Setuy
King's scribe, fan-bearer on the king's right hand, deputy Viceroy under Khaemter; later King's Son of Kush

Shenu
the rope-like protective surround of the Royal Name; the cartouche

Sheut
the shadow self

Shu
god of the air

Sin
Land of Sin; Sinai Peninsula

Siptah
son of Messuwy by Suterere (also called Ramesses-Siptah)

Sobek
a god associated with the Nile crocodile

Sopdu
god of the sky and eastern borders

Stela
(plural: stelae) a stone commemorative slab, often with an inscription

Suterere
sister of Bay, wife of Messuwy, mother of Siptah

Ta-Bitjet
a scorpion goddess

Takhat
(1) daughter of Ramesses II, wife of Merenptah, mother of Amenmesse and Takhat (2) daughter of Merenptah by Takhat (1), wife of Seti II

Ta Mehu
Lower Egypt (in the north)

Taremu
Leontopolis, city in Ta Mehu, modern day Tell al Muqdam

Tarkahe
Governor of Abu

Tarqa
an officer of the Amun Legion

Ta-sekhet-ma'at
The Great Field, Valley of the Kings

Ta-senet
a city south of Waset, modern day Esna

Ta Shemau
Upper Egypt (in the south)

Tausret
daughter of Sethi (1), adopted daughter of Merenptah, wife of Seti (1)

Tawaret
goddess of childbirth and fertility

Ta-ynt-netert
Dendera, a city north of Waset, near modern day Qena

Ti-ament
sister of Ament

Timna
a valley north of Eilah in the east of the Land of Sin; a site of ancient copper mining

Tiy-merenese
wife of Setnakhte

Tjaty
Vizier, the highest official to serve the king

Tjenu
Thinis, a city north of Waset, possibly near modern day Girga

Ur Hekau
an instrument used in the ceremony of the Opening of the Mouth

Userkheperure
throne name of Seti II

Usermaatre
throne name of Ramesses II

Usertem
Captain of the Men-nefer Medjay

Ushabti
(plural: ushabtiu) a funerary figurine placed within a tomb that is intended
to act as a servant for the deceased in the afterlife

Wadjet
goddess, patron and protector of Ta Mehu, protector of kings and women
in childbirth

Waset
capital city of Ta Shemau, Amun's holy city, Thebes

Wawat
province of Northern Kush

Wenefer
Governor of Iunu

Zawty
a city north of Waset, modern day Asyut

Zeben
husband of Ti-ament

Zephan
local tribesman at Timna

You can find ALL our books up at Amazon at:
https://www.amazon.com/shop/writers_exchange

or on our website at:
http://www.writers-exchange.com

All our Historical Novels
http://www.writers-exchange.com/category/genres/historical/

About the Author

Max Overton has travelled extensively and lived in many places around the world-- including Malaysia, India, Germany, England, Jamaica, New Zealand, USA and Australia. Trained in the biological sciences in New Zealand and Australia, he has worked within the scientific field for many years, but now concentrates on writing. While predominantly a writer of historical fiction (Scarab: Books 1 - 6 of the Amarnan Kings; the Scythian Trilogy; the Demon Series; Ascension), he also writes in other genres (A Cry of Shadows, the Glass Trilogy, Haunted Trail, Sequestered) and draws on true life (Adventures of a Small Game Hunter in Jamaica, We Came From Königsberg). Max also maintains an interest in butterflies, photography, the paranormal and other aspects of Fortean Studies.

Most of his other published books are available at Writers Exchange Ebooks, http://www.writers-exchange.com/Max-Overton.html and all his books may be viewed on his website: http://www.maxovertonauthor.com/

Max's book covers are all designed and created by Julie Napier, and other examples of her art and photography may be viewed at www.julienapier.com

If you want to read more about other books by this author, they are listed on the following pages...

A Cry of Shadows
{Paranormal Murder Mystery}

Australian Professor Ian Delaney is single-minded in his determination to prove his theory that one can discover the moment that the life force leaves the body. After succumbing to the temptation to kill a girl under scientifically controlled conditions, he takes an offer of work in St Louis, hoping to leave the undiscovered crime behind him.

In America, Wayne Richardson seeks revenge by killing his ex-girlfriend, believing it will give him the upper hand, a means to seize control following their breakup. Wayne quickly discovers that he enjoys killing and begins to seek out young women who resemble his dead ex-girlfriend.

Ian and Wayne meet and, when Ian recognizes the symptoms of violent delusion, he employs Wayne to help him further his research. Despite the police closing in, the two killers manage to evade identification time and time again as the death toll rises in their wake.

The detective in charge of the case, John Barnes, is frantic, willing to try anything to catch his killer. With time running out, he searches desperately for answers before another body is found...or the culprit slips into the woodwork for good.

Publisher: http://www.writers-exchange.com/A-Cry-of-Shadows/
Amazon: http://mybook.to/ACryOfShadows

Adventures of a Small Game Hunter in Jamaica
{Biography}

An eleven-year-old boy is plucked from boarding school in England and transported to the tropical paradise of Jamaica where he's free to study his one great love--butterflies. He discovers that Jamaica has a wealth of these wonderful insects and sets about making a collection of as many as he can find. Along the way, he has adventures with other creatures, from hummingbirds to vultures, from iguanas to black widow spiders. Through it all runs the promise of the legendary Homerus swallowtail, Jamaica's national butterfly.

Other activities intrude, like school, boxing and swimming lessons, but he manages to inveigle his parents into taking him to strange and sometimes dangerous places, all in the name of butterfly collecting. He meets scientists and Rastafarians, teachers, small boys and the ordinary people living on the tropical isle, and even discovers butterflies that shouldn't exist in Jamaica.

Author Max Overton was that young boy. He counted himself fortunate to have lived in Jamaica in an age very different from the present one. Max still has some of the butterflies he collected half a century or more ago, and each one releases a flood of memories whenever he opens the box and gazes at their tattered and fading wings. These memories have become stories--stories of the Adventures of a Small Game Hunter in Jamaica.

Publisher: http://www.writers-exchange.com/Adventures-of-a-Small-Game-Hunter/
Amazon: http://myBook.to/AdventuresGameHunter

Ascension Series, A Novel of Nazi Germany
{Historical: Holocaust}

Before he fully realized the diabolical cruelties of the National Socialist German Worker's Party, Konrad Wengler had committed atrocities against his own people, the Jews, out of fear of both his faith and his heritage. But after he witnesses firsthand the concentration camps, the corruption, the inhuman malevolence of the Nazi war machine and the propaganda aimed at annihilating an entire race, he knows he must find a way to turn the tide and become the savior his people desperately need.

Book 1: Ascension
Being a Jew in Germany can be a dangerous thing...

Fear prompts Konrad Wengler to put his faith aside and try desperately to forget his heritage. After fighting in the Great War, he's wounded and turns instead to law enforcement in his tiny Bavarian hometown. There, he falls under the spell of the fledgling Nazi Party. He joins the Party in patriotic fervour and becomes a Lieutenant of Police and Schutzstaffel (SS).

In the course of his duties as policeman, Konrad offends a powerful Nazi official who starts an SS investigation. War breaks out. When he joins the Police Battalions, he's sent to Poland and witnesses there firsthand the atrocities being committed upon his fellow Jews.

Unknown to Konrad, the SS investigators have discovered his origins and follow him into Poland. Arrested and sent to Mauthausen Concentration Camp, Konrad is forced to face what it means to be a Jew and fight for survival. Will his friends on the outside, his wife and lawyer, be enough to counter the might of the Nazi machine?
Publisher: http://www.writers-exchange.com/Ascension/
Amazon: http://mybook.to/Ascension1

Book 2: Maelstrom
Never underestimate the enemy...

Konrad Wengler survived his brush with the death camps of Nazi Germany. Now, reinstated as a police officer in his Bavarian hometown despite being a Jew, he throws himself back into his work, seeking to uncover evidence that will remove a corrupt Nazi party official.

The Gestapo have their own agenda and, despite orders from above to eliminate this troublesome Jewish policeman, they hide Konrad in the Totenkopf (Death's Head) Division of the Waffen-SS. In a fight to survive in the snowy wastes of Russia while the tide of war turns against Germany, Konrad experiences tank battles, ghetto clearances, partisans, and death camps (this time as a guard), as well as the fierce battles where his Division is badly outnumbered and on the defence.

Through it all, Konrad strives to live by his conscience and resist taking part in the atrocities happening all around him. He still thinks of himself as a policeman, but his desire to bring the corrupt Nazi official to justice seems far removed from his present reality. If he is to find the necessary evidence against his enemy, he must first *survive...*

Publisher: http://www.writers-exchange.com/Maelstrom/

Amazon: http://mybook.to/Ascension2

Book 3: Dämmerung

Konrad Wengler is captured and sent from one Soviet prison camp to another. Even hearing the war has come to an end makes no difference until he's arrested as a Nazi Party member. In jail, Konrad refuses to defend himself for things he's guilty and should be punished for. Will his be an eye-for-an-eye life sentence, or leniency in regard of the good he tried to do once he learned the truth?

Publisher: http://www.writers-exchange.com/dammerung/

Amazon: http://mybook.to/Ascension3

Fall of the House of Ramesses Series, A Novel of Ancient Egypt
{Historical: Ancient Egypt}

Egypt was at the height of its powers in the days of Ramesses the Great, a young king who confidently predicted his House would last for a Thousand Years. Sixty years later, he was still on the throne. One by one, his heirs had died and the survivors had become old men. When Ramesses at last died, he left a stagnant kingdom and his throne to an old man--Merenptah. What followed laid the groundwork for a nation ripped apart by civil war.

Book 1: Merenptah

The House of Ramesses is in the hands of an old man. King Merenptah wants to leave the kingdom to his younger son, Seti, but northern tribes in Egypt rebel and join forces with the Sea Peoples, invading from the north. In the south, the king's eldest son Messuwy is angered at being passed over in favour of the younger son...and plots to rid himself of his father and brother.

Publisher: http://www.writers-exchange.com/Merenptah/
Amazon: http://mybook.to/FOTHR1

Book 2: Seti

After only nine years on the throne, Merenptah is dead and his son Seti is king in his place. He rules from the northern city of Men-nefer, while his elder brother Messuwy, convinced the throne is his by right, plots rebellion in the south.

The kingdoms are tipped into bloody civil war, with brother fighting against brother for the throne of a united Egypt. On one side is Messuwy, now crowned as King Amenmesse and his ruthless General Sethi; on the other, young King Seti and his wife Tausret. But other men are weighing up the chances of wresting the throne from both brothers and becoming king in their place. Under the onslaught of conflict, the House of Ramesses begins to crumble...

Publisher: http://www.writers-exchange.com/Seti/
Amazon: http://mybook.to/FOTHR2

Book 3: Tausret

The House of Ramesses falters as Tausret relinquishes the throne upon the death of her husband, King Seti. Amenmesse's young son Siptah will become king until her infant son is old enough to rule. Tausret, as Regent, and the king's uncle, Chancellor Bay, hold tight to the reins of power and vie for complete control of the kingdoms. Assassination changes the balance of power, and, seeing his chance, Chancellor Bay attempts a coup...

Tausret's troubles mount as she also faces a challenge from Setnakhte, an aging son of the Great Ramesses who believes Seti was the last legitimate king. If Setnakhte gets his way, he will destroy the House of Ramesses and set up his own dynasty of kings.

Publisher: http://www.writers-exchange.com/Tausret/
Amazon: http://mybook.to/FOTHR3

Haunted Trail A Tale of Wickedness & Moral Turpitude
{Western: Paranormal}

Ned Abernathy is a hot-tempered young cowboy in the small town of Hammond's Bluff in 1876. In a drunken argument with his best friend Billy over a girl, he guns him down. Ned flees and wanders the plains, forests and hills of the Dakota Territories, certain that every man's hand is against him.

Horse rustlers, marauding Indians, killers, gold prospectors and French trappers cross his path and lead to complications, as do persistent apparitions of what Ned believes is the ghost of his friend Billy, come to accuse him of murder. He finds love and loses it. Determined not to do the same when he discovers gold in the Black Hills, he ruthlessly defends his newfound wealth against greedy men. In the process, he comes to terms with who he is and what he's done. But there are other ghosts in his past that he needs to confront. Returning to Hammond's Bluff, Ned stumbles into a shocking surprise awaiting him at the end of his haunted trail.

Publisher: http://www.writers-exchange.com/Haunted-Trail/
Amazon: http://mybook.to/HauntedTrail

Glass Trilogy
{Paranormal Thriller}

Delve deep into the mysteries of Aboriginal mythology, present day UFO activity and pure science that surround the continent of Australia, from its barren deserts to the depths of its rainforest and even deeper into its mysterious mountains. Along the way, love, greed, murder, and mystery abound while the secrets of mankind and the ultimate answer to 'what happens now?' just might be answered.

GLASS HOUSE, Book 1: The mysteries of Australia may just hold the answers mankind has been searching for millennium to find. When Doctor James Hay, a university scientist who studies the paranormal mysteries in Australia, finds an obelisk of carved volcanic rock on sacred Aboriginal land in northern Queensland, he realizes it may hold the answers he's been seeking. A respected elder of the Aboriginal people instructs James to take up the gauntlet and follow his heart. Along with his old friend and award-winning writer Spencer, Samantha Louis, her cameraman, and two of James' Aboriginal students, James embarks on a life-changing quest for the truth.
Publisher: http://www.writers-exchange.com/Glass-House/
Amazon: http://mybook.to/Glass1

A GLASS DARKLY, Book 2: A dead volcano called Glass Mountain in Northern California seems harmless...but is it really?
Andromeda Jones, a physicist, knows her missing sister Samantha is somehow tied up with the new job Andromeda herself has been offered to work with a team in constructing Vox Dei, a machine that's been ostensibly built to eliminate wars. But what is its true nature, and who's pulling the strings?
When the experiment spins out of control, dark powers are unleashed and the danger to mankind unfolds relentlessly. Strange, evil shadows are using the Vox Dei and Andromeda's sister Samantha to get through to our world, knowing the time is near when Earth's final destiny will be decided.
Federal forces are aware of something amiss, so, to rescue her sibling, Andromeda agrees to go on a dangerous mission and soon finds herself entangled in a web of professional jealousy, political betrayal, and flat-out greed.

Publisher: http://www.writers-exchange.com/A-Glass-Darkly/
Amazon: http://mybook.to/Glass2

LOOKING GLASS, Book 3: Samantha and James Hay have been advised that their missing daughter Gaia have been located in ancient Australia. Dr. Xanatuo, an alien scientist who, along with a lost tribe of Neanderthals and other beings working to help mankind, has discovered a way to send them back in time to be reunited with Gaia. Ernie, the old Aboriginal tracker and leader of the Neanderthals, along with friends Ratana and Nathan and characters from the first two books of the trilogy, will accompany them. This team of intrepid adventurers have another mission for the journey, along with aiding the Hayes' quest, which is paramount to changing a terrible wrong which exists in the present time.
Publisher: http://www.writers-exchange.com/Looking-Glass/
Amazon: http://mybook.to/Glass3

Kadesh, A Novel of Ancient Egypt

Holding the key to strategic military advantage, Kadesh is a jewel city that distant lands covet. Ramesses II of Egypt and Muwatalli II of Hatti believe they're chosen by the gods to claim ascendancy to Kadesh. When the two meet in the largest chariot battle ever fought, not just the fate of empires will be decided but also the lives of citizens helplessly caught up in the greedy ambition of kings.
Publisher: http://www.writers-exchange.com/Kadesh/
Amazon: http://mybook.to/Kadesh

Hyksos Series, A Novel of Ancient Egypt

The power of the kings of the Middle Kingdom have been failing for some time, having lost control of the Nile Delta to a series of Canaanite kings who ruled from the northern city of Avaris.
Into this mix came the Kings of Amurri, Lebanon and Syria bent on subduing the whole of Egypt. These kings were known as the Hyksos, and they dealt a devastating blow to the peoples of the Nile Delta and Valley.

Book 1: Avaris

When Arimawat and his son Harrubaal fled from Urubek, the king of Hattush, to the court of the King of Avaris, King Sheshi welcomed the refugees. One of Arimawat's first tasks for King Shesi is to sail south to the Land of Kush and fetch Princess Tati, who will become Sheshi's queen. Arimawat and Harrubaal perform creditably, but their actions have far-reaching consequences.

On the return journey, Harrubaal falls in love with Kemi, the daughter of the Southern Egyptian king. As a reward for Harrubaal's work, Sheshi secures the hand of the princess for the young Canaanite prince. Unfortunately for the peace of the realm, Sheshi lusts after Princess Kemi too, and his actions threaten the stability of his kingdom...
Publisher: http://www.writers-exchange.com/Avaris/
Amazon: http://mybook.to/avaris

Book 2: Conquest

The Hyksos invade the Delta using the new weapons of bronze and chariots, things of which the Egyptians have no knowledge. They rout the Delta forces, and in the south, the unconquered kings ready their armies to defend their lands. Meanwhile in Avaris, Merybaal, the son of Harrubaal and Kemi, strives to defend his family in a city conquered by the Hyksos.

Elements of the Delta army that refuse to surrender continue the fight for their homeland, and new kings proclaim themselves as the inheritors of the failed kings of Avaris. One of these is Amenre, grandson of Merybaal, but he is forced into hiding as the Hyksos sweep all before them, bringing their terror to the kingdom of the Nile valley. Driven south in disarray, the survivors of the Egyptian army seek leaders who can resist the enemy...
Publisher: http://www.writers-exchange.com/conquest/

Amazon: http://mybook.to/conquest

Book 3: Two Cities

The Hyksos drive south into the Nile Valley, sweeping all resistance aside. Bebi and Sobekhotep, grandsons of Harrubaal, assume command of the loyal Egyptian army and strive to stem the flood of Hyksos conquest. But even the cities of the south are divided against themselves.

Abdju, an old capital city of Egypt reasserts itself, putting forward a line of kings of its own, and soon the city is at war with Waset, the southern capital of the Nile Valley, as the two cities fight for supremacy in the face of the advancing northern enemy. Caught up in the turmoil of warring nations, the ordinary people of Egypt must fight for their own survival as well as that of their kingdom.

Publisher: http://www.writers-exchange.com/Two-Cities/
Amazon: http://mybook.to/TwoCities

Book 4: Possessor of All

The Hyksos, themselves beset by intrigue and division, push down into southern Egypt. The short-lived kingdom of Abdju collapses, leaving Nebiryraw the undisputed king of the south ruling from the city of Waset. An uneasy truce between north and south enables both sides to strengthen their positions.

Khayan seizes power over the Hyksos kingdom and turns his gaze toward Waset, determined to conquer Egypt finally. Meanwhile, the family of King Nebiryraw looks to the future and starts securing their own advantage, weakening the southern kingdom. In the face of renewed tensions, the delicate peace cannot last...

Publisher: http://www.writers-exchange.com/Possessor-of-All/
Amazon: http://mybook.to/Possessor-of-All

Book 5: War in the South

Intrigue and rebellion rule in Egypt's southern kingdom as the house of King Nebiryraw tears itself apart. King succeeds king, but none of them look capable of defending the south, let alone reclaiming the north. Taking advantage of this, King Khayan of the Hyksos launches his assault on Waset, but rebellions in the north delay his victory.

The fall of Waset brings about a change of leadership. Apophis takes command of the Hyksos forces, and Rahotep brings together a small army to challenge the might of the Hyksos, knowing that the fate of Egypt hangs on the coming battle.

Publisher: http://www.writers-exchange.com/War-in-the-South/
Amazon: http://mybook.to/WarInTheSouth

Book 6: Between the Wars

Rahotep leads his Egyptian army to victory, and Apophis withdraws the Hyksos army northward. An uneasy peace settles over the Nile valley. Rebellions in the north keep the Hyksos king from striking back at Rahotep, while internal strife between the Hyksos nobility and generals threatens to rip their empire apart.

War is coming to Egypt once more, and the successors of Rahotep start preparing for it, using the very weapons that the Hyksos introduced-- bronze weapons and the war chariot. King Ahmose repudiates the peace treaty, and Apophis of the Hyksos prepares to destroy his enemies at last. Bloody warfare returns to Egypt...

Publisher: http://www.writers-exchange.com/Between-the-Wars/
Amazon: http://mybook.to/BetweenTheWars

Book 7: Sons of Tao

War breaks out between the Hyksos invaders and native Egyptians determined to rid themselves of their presence. King Seqenenre Tao launches an attack on King Apophis but the Hyksos strike back savagely. It is only when his sons Kamose and Ahmose carry the war to the Hyksos that the Egyptians really start to hope they can succeed.

Kamose battles fiercely, but only when his younger brother Ahmose assumes the throne is there real success. Faced with an ignominious defeat, a Hyksos general overthrows Apophis and becomes king, but then he faces a resurgent Egyptian king determined to rid his land of the Hyksos invader...

Publisher: http://www.writers-exchange.com/sons-of-tao/
Amazon: http://mybook.to/SonsOfTao

TULPA
{Paranormal Thriller}

From the rainforests of tropical Australia to the cane fields and communities of the North Queensland coastal strip, a horror is unleashed by those foolishly playing with unknown forces...

A fairy story to amuse small children leads four bored teenagers and a young university student in a North Queensland town to becoming interested in an ancient Tibetan technique for creating a life form. When their seemingly harmless experiment sets free terror and death, the teenagers are soon fighting to contain a menace that reproduces exponentially.

The police are helpless to end the horror. Aided by two old game hunters, a student of the paranormal and a few small children, the teenagers must find a way of destroying what they unintentionally released. But how can they stop beings that can escape into an alternate reality when threatened?

Publisher: http://www.writers-exchange.com/TULPA/
Amazon: http://mybook.to/TULPA

Scythian Trilogy
{Historical}

Captured by the warlike, tribal Scythians who bicker amongst themselves and bitterly resent outside interference, a fiercely loyal captain in Alexander the Great's Companion Cavalry Nikometros and his men are to be sacrificed to the Mother Goddess. Lucky chance--and the timely intervention of Tomyra, priestess and daughter of the Massegetae chieftain--allows him to defeat the Champion. With their immediate survival secured, acceptance into the tribe...and escape...is complicated by the captain's growing feelings for Tomyra--death to any who touch her--and the chief's son Areipithes who not only detests Nikometros and wants to have him killed or banished but intends to murder his own father and take over the tribe.

LION OF SCYTHIA, Book 1: Alexander the Great has conquered the Persian Empire and is marching eastward to India. In his wake he leaves small groups of soldiers to govern great tracts of land and diverse peoples. Nikometros is one young cavalry captain left behind in the lands of the fierce, nomadic Scythian horsemen. Captured after an ambush, Nikometros must fight for his life and the lives of his surviving men. Even as he seeks an opportunity to escape, he finds himself bound by a debt of loyalty to the chief...and his own developing love for the young priestess.
Publisher: http://www.writers-exchange.com/Lion-of-Scythia/
Amazon: http://mybook.to/Scythian1

THE GOLDEN KING, Book 2: The chief of the tribe of nomadic Scythian horsemen is dead, killed by his son's treachery. The priestess, lover of the young cavalry officer, Nikometros, is carried off into the mountains. Nikometros and his friends set off in hard pursuit.

Death rides with them. By the time they return, the tribes are at war. Nikometros must choose between attempting to become chief himself or leaving the people he's come to love and respect to return to his duty as an army officer in the Empire of Alexander.
Winner of the 2005 EPIC Ebook Awards.
Publisher: http://www.writers-exchange.com/The-Golden-King/
Amazon: http://mybook.to/Scythian2

FUNERAL IN BABYLON, Book 3: Alexander the Great has returned from India and set up his court in Babylon. Nikometros and a band of loyal Scythians journey deep into the heart of Persia to join the Royal court. Nikometros finds himself embroiled in the intrigues and wars of kings, generals, and merchant adventurers as he strives to provide a safe haven for his lover and friends. With the fate of an Empire hanging in the balance, Death walks beside Nikometros as events precipitate a Funeral in Babylon...

Winner of the 2006 EPIC Ebook Awards.

Publisher: http://www.writers-exchange.com/Funeral-in-Babylon/
Amazon: http://mybook.to/Scythian3

We Came From Konigsberg
{Historical: Holocaust}

Based on a true story gleaned from the memories of family members sixty years after the events, from photographs and documents, and from published works of nonfiction describing the times and events described in the narrative, *We Came From Konigsberg* is set in January 1945.

The Soviet Army is poised for the final push through East Prussia and Poland to Berlin. Elisabet Daeker and her five young sons are in Königsberg, East Prussia and have heard the shocking stories of Russian atrocities. They're desperate to escape to the perceived safety of Germany. To survive, Elisabet faces hardships endured at the hands of Nazi hardliners, of Soviet troops bent on rape, pillage and murder, and of Allied cruelty in the Occupied Zones of post-war Germany.

Winner of the 2014 EPIC Ebook Awards.

Publisher: http://www.writers-exchange.com/We-Came-From-Konigsberg/
Amazon: http://mybook.to/Konigsberg

Sequestered
By Max Overton and Jim Darley
{Action/Thriller}

Storing carbon dioxide underground as a means of removing a greenhouse gas responsible for global warming has made James Matternicht a fabulously wealthy man. For 15 years, the Carbon Capture and Sequestration Facility at Rushing River in Oregon's hinterland has been operating without a problem...or has it?

When mysterious documents arrive on her desk that purport to show the Facility is leaking, reporter Annaliese Winton investigates. Together with a government geologist, Matt Morrison, she uncovers a morass of corruption and deceit that now threatens the safety of her community and the entire northwest coast of America.

Liquid carbon dioxide, stored at the critical point under great pressure, is a tremendously dangerous substance, and millions of tonnes of it are sequestered in the rock strata below Rushing River. All it would take is a crack in the overlying rock and the whole pressurized mass could erupt with disastrous consequences. And that crack has always existed there...

Recipient of the Life Award (Literature for the Environment):

 "There are only two kinds of people: conservationists and suicides. To qualify for this Award, your book needs to value the wonderful world of nature, to recognize that we are merely one species out of millions, and that we have a responsibility to cherish and maintain our small planet."

Awarded from http://bobswriting.com/life/

Publisher: http://www.writers-exchange.com/Sequestered/
Amazon: http://mybook.to/Sequestered

Strong is the Ma'at of Re, A Novel of Ancient Egypt
{Historical: Ancient Egypt}

In Ancient Egypt, C1200 BCE, bitter contention and resentment, secret coups and assassination attempts may decide the fate of those who would become legends...by any means necessary.

Book 1: The King

That *he* is descended from Ramesses the Great fills Ramesses III with obscene pride. Elevated to the throne following a coup led by his father Setnakhte during the troubled days of Queen Tausret, Ramesses III sets about creating an Egypt that reflects the glory days of Ramesses the Great. He takes on his predecessor's throne name, names his sons after the sons of Ramesses and pushes them toward similar duties. Most of all, he thirsts after conquests like those of his hero grandfather.

Ramesses III assumes the throne name of Usermaatre, translated as "Strong is the Ma'at of Re" and endeavours to live up to the sentiment. He fights foreign foes, as had Ramesses the Great; he builds temples throughout the Two Lands, as had Ramesses the Great, and he looks forward to a long, illustrious life on the throne of Egypt, as had Ramesses the Great.

Alas, his reign is not meant to be. Ramesses III faces troubles at home--troubles that threaten the stability of Egypt and his own throne. The struggles for power between his wives, his sons, and even the priests of Amun, together with a treasury drained of its wealth, all force Ramesses III to question his success as the scion of a legend.

Publisher: http://www.writers-exchange.com/The-King/
Amazon: http://mybook.to/StrongIsTheMaatOfRe1

Book 2: The Heirs

Tiye, the first wife of Ramesses III, has grown so used to being the mother of the Heir she can no longer bear to see that prized title pass to the son of a rival wife. Her eldest sons have died and the one left wants to step down and devote his life to the priesthood. Then the son of the king's sister/wife, also named Ramesses, will become Crown Prince and all Tiye's ambitions will lie in ruins.

Ramesses III struggles to enrich Egypt by seeking the wealth of the Land of Punt. He dispatches an expedition to the fabled southern land but years pass before the expedition returns. In the meantime, Tiye has a new hope: A last son she dotes on. Plague sweeps through Egypt, killing princes and princesses alike and lessening her options, and now Tiye must undergo the added indignity of having her daughter married off to the hated Crown Prince.

All Tiye's hopes are pinned on this last son of hers, but Ramesses III refuses to consider him as a potential successor, despite the Crown Prince's failing health. Unless Tiye can change the king's mind through charm or coercion, her sons will forever be excluded from the throne of Egypt.
Publisher: http://www.writers-exchange.com/The-Heirs/
Amazon: http://mybook.to/StrongIsTheMaatOfRe1

Book 3: Taweret

The reign of Ramesses III is failing and even the gods seem to be turning their eyes away from Egypt. When the sun hides its face, crops suffer, throwing the country into famine. Tomb workers go on strike. To avert further disaster, Crown Prince Ramesses acts on his father's behalf.

The rivalry between Ramesses III's wives--commoner Tiye and sister/wife Queen Tyti--also comes to a head. Tiye resents not being made queen and can't abide that her sons have been passed over. She plots to put her own spoiled son Pentaweret on the throne.

The eventual strength of the Ma'at of Re hangs in the balance. Will the rule of Egypt be decided by fate, gods...or treason?
Publisher: http://www.writers-exchange.com/The-One-of-Taweret/
Amazon: http://mybook.to/SITMOR3

The Amarnan Kings Series, A Novel of Ancient Egypt
{Historical: Ancient Egypt}

Set in Egypt of the 14th century B.C.E. and piecing together a mosaic of the reigns of the five Amarnan kings, threaded through by the memories of princess Beketaten-Scarab, a tapestry unfolds of the royal figures lost in the mists of antiquity.

SCARAB - AKHENATEN, Book 1: A chance discovery in Syria reveals answers to the mystery of the ancient Egyptian sun-king, the heretic Akhenaten and his beautiful wife Nefertiti. Inscriptions in the tomb of his sister Beketaten, otherwise known as Scarab, tell a story of life and death, intrigue and warfare, in and around the golden court of the kings of the glorious 18th dynasty.

The narrative of a young girl growing up at the centre of momentous events--the abolition of the gods, foreign invasion, and the fall of a once-great family--reveals who Tutankhamen's parents really were, what happened to Nefertiti, and other events lost to history in the great destruction that followed the fall of the Aten heresy.
Publisher: http://www.writers-exchange.com/Scarab/
Amazon: http://mybook.to/ScarabBook1

SCARAB- SMENKHKARE, Book 2: King Akhenaten, distraught at the rebellion and exile of his beloved wife Nefertiti, withdraws from public life, content to leave the affairs of Egypt in the hands of his younger half-brother Smenkhkare. When Smenkhkare disappears on a hunting expedition, his sister Beketaten, known as Scarab, is forced to flee for her life.

Finding refuge among her mother's people, the Khabiru, Scarab has resigned herself to a life in exile...until she hears that her brother Smenkhkare is still alive. He is raising an army in Nubia to overthrow Ay and reclaim his throne. Scarab hurries south to join him as he confronts Ay and General Horemheb outside the gates of Thebes.
Publisher: http://www.writers-exchange.com/Scarab2/
Amazon: http://mybook.to/ScarabBook2

SCARAB - TUTANKHAMEN, Book 3: Scarab and her brother Smenkhkare are in exile in Nubia but are gathering an army to wrest control of Egypt from the boy king Tutankhamen and his controlling uncle, Ay. Meanwhile, the kingdoms are beset by internal troubles while the Amorites are pressing hard against the northern borders. Generals Horemheb and Paramessu must fight a war on two fronts while deciding where their loyalties lie--with the former king Smenkhkare or with the new young king in Thebes.

Smenkhkare and Scarab march on Thebes with their native army to meet the legions of Tutankhamen on the plains outside the city gates. As two brothers battle for supremacy and the throne of the Two Kingdoms, the fate of Egypt and the 18th dynasty hangs in the balance.
Finalist in 2013's Eppie Awards.
Publisher: http://www.writers-exchange.com/Scarab3/
Amazon: http://mybook.to/ScarabBook3

SCARAB - AY, Book 4: Tutankhamen is dead and his grieving widow tries to rule alone, but her grandfather Ay has not destroyed the former kings just so he can be pushed aside. Presenting the Queen and General Horemheb with a fait accompli, the old Vizier assumes the throne of Egypt and rules with a hand of hardened bronze. His adopted son, Nakhtmin, will rule after him and stamp out the last remnants of loyalty to the former kings.

Scarab was sister to three kings and will not give in to the usurper and his son. She battles against Ay and his legions under the command of General Horemheb and aided by desert tribesmen and the gods of Egypt themselves. The final confrontation will come in the rich lands of the Nile delta where the future of Egypt will at last be decided.
Publisher: http://www.writers-exchange.com/Scarab4/
Amazon: http://mybook.to/ScarabBook4

SCARAB - HOREMHEB, Book 5: General Horemheb has taken control after the death of Ay and Nakhtmin. Forcing Scarab to marry him, he ascends the throne of Egypt. The Two Kingdoms settle into an uneasy peace as Horemheb proceeds to stamp out all traces of the former kings. He also persecutes the Khabiru tribesmen who were reluctant to help him seize power. Scarab escapes into the desert, where she is content to wait until Egypt needs her.

A holy man emerges from the desert and demands that Horemheb release the Khabiru so they may worship his god. Scarab recognises the holy man and supports him in his efforts to free his people. The gods of Egypt and of the Khabiru are invoked and disaster sweeps down on the Two Kingdoms as the Khabiru flee with Scarab and the holy man. Horemheb and his army pursue them to the shores of the Great Sea, where a natural event...or the very hand of God...alters the course of Egyptian history.

Publisher: http://www.writers-exchange.com/Scarab5/
Amazon: http://mybook.to/ScarabBook5

SCARAB - DESCENDANT, Book 6: Three thousand years after the reigns of the Amarnan Kings, the archaeologists who discovered the inscriptions in Syria journey to Egypt to find the tomb of Smenkhkare and his sister Scarab and the fabulous treasure they believe is there. Unscrupulous men and religious fanatics also seek the tomb, either to plunder it or to destroy it. Can the gods of Egypt protect their own, or will the ancients rely on modern day men and women of science?

Publisher: http://www.writers-exchange.com/Scarab6/
Amazon: http://mybook.to/ScarabBook6

Made in the USA
Monee, IL
02 September 2022

13122139R00223